D1211927

The Fourth Shore

The Fourth Shore

The Confines *of the* Shadow
Volume II

Alessandro Spina

Translated by
André Naffis-Sahely

Arcade Publishing • New York

First English translation printed in 2018 by Darf Publishers, UK.
Originally published by Morcelliana in 2006 as *I confini dell'ombra*.

Arcade Publishing books may be purchased in bulk at special discounts for sales promotion, corporate gifts, fund-raising, or educational purposes. Special editions can also be created to specifications. For details, contact the Special Sales Department, Arcade Publishing, 307 West 36th Street, 11th Floor, New York, NY 10018 or arcade@skyhorsepublishing.com.

Arcade Publishing® is a registered trademark of Skyhorse Publishing, Inc.®, a Delaware corporation.

Visit our website at www.arcadepub.com.

10 9 8 7 6 5 4 3 2 1

Library of Congress Cataloging-in-Publication Data is available on file.

Cover design by Erin Seaward-Hiatt

Print ISBN: 978-1-628-72836-1
Ebook ISBN: 978-1-628-72839-2

Printed in the United States of America

CONTENTS

Translator's Note

This middle section of Alessandro Spina's *The Confines of the Shadow: In Lands Overseas*, is set in the nervously restless years prior to the outbreak of World War II, a time when the Italian colonists in Libya's cities of Tripoli and Benghazi felt more confident than ever in their courageous industriousness as they attempted to refashion the inhospitable African land beneath their feet into a replica of their beloved motherland. A few exceptions aside, all the stories in Colonial Tales are set in Benghazi during the 1930s and early 1940s and – unlike in the other instalments of Spina's eleven-volume epic – all of the characters are Italian. Not a single Libyan makes an appearance here and that is the point: it is part of Spina's pointed critique at colonial Italy's refusal to even acknowledge its native subjects. Indeed, the Italians grew so confident in their unchallenged hold over the *quarta sponda* – or 'fourth shore,' squaring the Italian boot's three other shores – over these years, that they officially annexed the province to Italy in 1939, by which time Italian settlers made up over a third of Libya's urban population and owned extensive land holdings in the interior of the country. Those familiar with narratives of the British presence during the Raj will recognise the intimately theatrical scenes Spina sets for his readers as he chronicles an episode in Italian history that has been nearly obliterated from the country's collective memory. Time stands perfectly still in Spina's Benghazi while the ladies chatter and their husbands talk of war. The city's wide avenues are dotted with cafés where people gossip and orchestras play, yet Spina's narrators often take the reader on a tour of the surrounding area's Greek ruins – the remnants of the once-powerful city-states of the Libyan Pentapolis. Spina's tableau is vast: his stories feature haughty grande dames, industrialists, aristocrats, politicians, revolutionaries, servants, functionaries, prostitutes, dressmakers, policemen, school teachers, poets, musicians and knaves – whether in uniform or not. Nevertheless, this section of Spina's epic rightfully retains a militaristic feel: after all, the military was in charge in Italian Libya, and as such, many of the stories are set in the Officers' Club, where the soldiers sleep with one another's wives, scheme against one another, stage one-man shows, eat, drink, philosophise and discuss Italy's chances in the coming war, blissfully unaware that their artificial presence in that conquered land is soon to vanish entirely. As I mentioned in my introduction to Volume One of *The Confines of the Shadow*, Spina's officers perfectly typify his concept of the 'shadow': their minds are haunted by the maddening darkness – or hollowness – of the colonial enterprise, and yet they are simultaneously unable to extricate themselves from it, bound to serve their masters – in this case the Fascist bureaucracy and its Supreme Leader, Benito Mussolini – until the bitter end. And bitter it was.

Author's Note

This sequence of novels and short stories takes as its subject the Italian experience in Cyrenaica. *The Young Maronite* (1971) discusses the 1911 war prompted by Giolitti, *The Marriage of Omar* (1973) narrates the ensuing truce and the attempt by the two peoples to strike a compromise before the rise of Fascism. *The Nocturnal Visitor* (1979) chronicles the end of the twenty-year Libyan resistance; *Officers' Tales* (1967) focuses on the triumph of colonialism – albeit this having been achieved when the end of Italian hegemony already loomed in sight and the Second World War appeared inevitable – and *The Psychological Comedy* (1992), which ends with Italy's retreat from Libya and the fleeing of settlers. *Entry into Babylon* (1976) concentrates on Libyan independence in 1951, *Cairo Nights* (1986) illustrates the early years of the Sanussi Monarchy and the looming spectre of Pan-Arab nationalism, while *The Shore of the Lesser Life* (1997) examines the profound social and political changes that occurred when large oil and gas deposits were discovered in the mid-1960s. Each text can be read independently or as part of the sequence. Either mode of reading will produce different – but equally legitimate – impressions.[i]

---

i The dates indicate the original publication dates of each of the novels in the original Italian.

Officers' Tales

THE COUNT OF LUNA

'You must learn how to behave in respectable circles,' Mrs Macchi said. 'The whole town frequents Mrs Boratti's house. You're eleven years old, and five or six years from now, you'll be a lady. If you keep getting invited to that house, it'll certainly come in handy...'

...when you want to get married, Emma finished her thought.

Mrs Boratti had studied vocal pedagogy and could sing a fairly decent soprano, which she kept fine-tuned by practicing while Emma's father accompanied her on the piano. 'Mrs Boratti is so very kind; needless to say, we're not up to her usual standards. But you see, she behaves as though we weren't so different at all.' On more than one occasion, Emma had tried to explain that she didn't want to go to Mrs Boratti's house any more, that those little pastries always made her feel nauseous – but her mother didn't want to hear any of it, and she insisted on dragging her daughter along with her anyway.

'Mrs Boratti always humiliates us!'

'It's not true: she's a very kind lady, and she's always so sweet with you. Besides,' she peevishly added, 'if what you say is true and she does humiliate us, then it's best you get used to it.'

Emma had even tried to repay Mrs Boratti's kindness by being unkind, but the latter pretended not to notice. Instead, as soon as they'd returned home, Emma's mother would smack her daughter and say: 'You better not do that again for your own sake, and remember that Mrs Boratti is paying for those hours we spend with her.' Emma eventually resigned herself to the situation. She would turn the pages of the music scores, drink tea and eat pastries. She simply couldn't understand why there had to be so much drama in order to secure that cheque at the end of every month.

'Look!' her mother exclaimed in cheerful satisfaction. 'There are a lot of people today. Emma, make sure you help the lady when the tea is brought out.'

Standing in the vestibule, Mrs Macchi tried to see who was in the main hall. 'Important people, very important people. Make sure you curtsy.'

Resigning herself, Emma curtsied before all the ladies. 'Such a pretty girl, such a pretty girl…' Captain Mosca's wife said. Mrs Macchi was introduced to people she didn't know: they were so courteous, almost thoughtfully so. Mrs Macchi's cheerful self-contentedness grew apace: the ritual of introductions felt like an initiation rite, and had the rhythm and meaningfulness of a sacred dance. 'You see?' Mrs Macchi whispered into Emma's ear, as though she'd just stepped backstage for a brief moment, 'even the Prefect is here.' Emma even curtsied before a gentleman who'd been awkwardly standing next to the window. Captain Mosca's wife laughed, but given that Mrs Macchi was absorbed by all the introductions, she didn't notice anything at all. The gentleman looked as though he were saturated with water and was as flaccid as an octopus. Emma confusedly realised that she had humiliated him. Yet remedying the situation was out of the question: the gentleman was already standing in front of Mrs Russo. She curtsied, leaving the greenish gentleman to stew in the bitterness of that humiliation.

Standing next to the piano, an officer leafed through the music scores. The complicated ritual of bows and introductions didn't interest him in the slightest. Emma noticed him as soon as she'd sat down. He stood apart from everyone else, but his presence featured heavily in people's conversations. The ladies talked, laughed, sipped their tea and munched pastries: and yet they observed the officer's silence as though it were part of the evening's entertainment.

Once the merry-go-round of tea had come to an end, Mrs Boratti stood up, and although it wasn't exactly clear whom she was addressing, she asked: 'May we begin?' Having been instructed, Emma's mother also jumped to her feet, while the paunchy guest courageously struggled to stand. Emma devotedly followed her mother, and went to sit next to her beside the Bechstein baby grand piano, which was black and shiny. Mrs Boratti and the paunchy man, a bank employee, lingered close to one another in the cove created by the piano, while the officer, who had just paced in a circle around the instrument, came to a stop right behind Emma and leaned his hands against her chair. Emma felt his presence as though he were a cloud hovering above her head. Yet what really frightened her were his hands, whose strength seemed to have turned her chair into stone. The ladies followed the five characters' movements with cheerful amazement as their comments interwove into a dense, delicate tapestry.

As soon as Mrs Macchi began to play – just a few introductory notes – the ladies fell silent. The Prefect put down her cup, left the remains of a little pastry next to it on the saucer, and gracefully thrust her chest forward in an effort to better hear the performance. Her behaviour, which seemed unduly dramatic, if not alarmed, conferred her with an aura of extraordinary importance. She was sat on the right side of the sofa. Yet her presence and attitude transformed that sofa into a royal dais. Mrs Boratti smiled at her, as though she were an interpreter asking her regal guest for permission before going ahead. The Prefect gave her consent with a gracious smile.

In a small voice, Mrs Macchi read out the few lines assigned to the character of Ines. She stood apart from all the others, almost exaggeratedly so. Mrs Boratti could claim for herself almost all of the stage, which had been carved out of the living room starting from the piano's side. The paunchy man looked very ill at ease. He trembled, incapable of standing up on his own two feet: he'd lost his center of gravity. He had gone to stand next to Mrs Boratti, who having hurried through Ines's lines, proceeded to launch into the beautiful aria: *Tacea la notte placida* (*Silent was the night*)… The aria was long, and the tenor's awkwardness grew apace in a crescendo: it was as though his body, a bladder full of water, might explode at any moment, leaving no trace of that bulky man except a tiny puddle on the floor. Yet he completely lacked the courage to move. The bank employee exuded a confused sense of modesty, as though he'd been forced to bare his naked frame to the ladies' prying eyes.

During the final and most difficult part of the aria, Mrs Boratti regained her confidence and she hit every single note with a ballerina's agility: '*Per esso io morirò/per esso io morirò!/ Ah, si, per esso io morirò/per esso io morirò, morirò*' (*I will die for him/I will die for him!/Oh, yes, I will die for him/die for him!*)…

Thus, when the Prefect raised her hands (which were as light as powder puffs) as soon as her friend the soprano concluded the final notes, and clapped them twice, one against the other – the applause seemed well deserved to everyone assembled, and the ladies nodded their heads. Relaxed, Mrs Boratti smiled, and this smile remained stretched out for the rest of the night, laying like a red carpet at the Prefect's feet.

The officer hadn't removed his hands from the back of Emma's chair for a single instant. He occasionally leaned over to better hear the notes being played, but his hands remained where they were. Emma had often stood up to turn the pages of the score, but the chair, which the officer's hands had turned to stone, didn't reflect any of her movements. Those hands were as strong as a chain. Mrs Boratti's aria, to which Emma had paid scant attention, and which had risen out of the depths of the monster-prince's prison stood out like a patch of blue sky, and felt as fresh as a slice of the sea. Emma was well aware of the fact that those sounds and images – now that she found great delight in the intricate rituals of the Prefect's court, the conversations revolving around the rim of the tea cups, the secrets concealed in a smile, even in the slightest curl of the lips, as intricate a process as bowing and curtsying – were dictated by her status. Like all forms of slavery, even the one experienced by the monster-prince had made all things appear inordinately more valuable. Emma named those things with the anxiety of one who would be forced to leave them behind: as though she'd finally seen things in all their splendour just before they vanished forever.

If the officer had lifted his hands, Emma would have been freed on the spot, but the world would have lost all shape and solidity. The monster-prince's chains were life itself. Emma was very distressed: for the first time in her life she had a secret, and this relationship – a mixture of attraction and fear – produced in her the strongest sentiments she'd ever felt. It was simply incredible how the officer could make his presence known through the sheer force of his immovable hands.

For the first time in Emma's life, she had met a character with all the hallmarks of a fairy tale hero. She felt as though their entire relationship hinged on that secretiveness. Had she spoken, had she revealed her secret, the monster-prince's kingdom would have fallen apart and all her new feelings would have vanished with it. Emma felt that keeping that secret would be an incredibly difficult task, if not an outright ordeal. If she managed to overcome that challenge, she would win the keys to the prince's kingdom. But if she failed, she would be doomed to dwell in the Prefect's greyish, silent realm, its stagnant pond.

Having learned to abide by the court's expectations, which were regulated by murky, yet binding laws – a reality which, having spurned adventure, refined itself through the art of repetition – Emma had detected a mysterious presence in the officer: the strength of his hands, and before that his deep-seated silence, had left no doubt as to that.

When the officer finally mouthed his first words – tragic, gloomy notes: like a horse's hooves tearing the night's silence asunder – the living room's precious harmony was irrevocably shattered, and everything was turned on its head. Emma held her breath. The strength of those hands had been transmuted into sound. The Prefect's world seemed to shrink until it was small enough to fit inside a pencil case.

Fear messed up the order of those notes: Emma had trouble following the song on her score. She moved only hesitantly and was late in turning a page. Yet the officer's hand preceded hers, and having swelled disproportionately to its actual size, it took the entirety of Emma's field of vision. The monster displayed an agility that was simultaneously graceful and persecutory. With his trembling voice, the paunchy man intoned Manrico's fiery chant: '*Deserto sulla terra…*' (*Earth is a desert…*). That song was so undignified that the ladies, stuffed inside that pencil case, couldn't help but burst out in amused laughter. The poor man strained his voice, which nevertheless had much trouble leaving his mouth: a vague, lukewarm trickle of sound issued from his lips, just a few slimy, greenish notes. The Count of Luna's brief interjections exploded like thunder and lightning: the fearful, trembling living room stood before him like a landscape. And in a tiny corner of that landscape, the unhappy bank employee played out his solitary agony.

Emma's head sank into her shoulders. Keeping his hands firmly fixed, the officer bent over and straightened himself back up, like a bear's ferocious, tender dance. Yet his voice gave them no respite. Emma felt as though she was being chased by a hound. The Prefect had picked up her cup of tea again and was sipping from it as though she were praying. One of the Count's more brutal 'No!'s left Emma on the edge of her seat. Everyone was screaming and her mother's fingers ran along the keyboard as though possessed. The Count's lines were full of difficult, stressed syllables: '*Di geloso amor sprezzato*'… (*My spurned and jealous love*). Emma couldn't even understand what that meant. That voice made her feel like her head was being repeatedly hit by a sledgehammer: '*Ei più vivere non può/no, ei più vivere non può, no, no, no, no/ei più vivere non può, ei più vivere non può…*' (*He can live no longer/no, he can live no longer, no, no, no, no/he can live no longer, he can live no longer*).

The Prefect and the social order she represented, like multiple rows on a dais, reemerged from the shadows at the end of the first act. The pencil case once again resumed the living room's former dimensions.

Mrs Boratti smiled, instructed the servant to serve everyone a second cup of tea, and both graciously accepted and gave thanks. Even Mrs Macchi stood up. Running her fingers up and down the keyboard trying to keep up with that delirious trio had completely worn her out. She dried her hands with her handkerchief. The paunchy gentleman headed back towards his seat, and despite his heaviness, he sank into it. Emma didn't budge. She contented herself with leaning back against her chair, now that the officer had finally moved his hands.

'I even got a little frightened myself,' the Prefect daintily said.

'As for me,' Major Russo's wife said, 'I really like this particular opera by Verdi. His *Othello* and *Falstaff* ring as pathetically false as an oaf's attempt at good manners…'

It sounded like the cheerful banter of people who'd just fled a storm's furies. 'It's so rare to be able to hear a little music out here in this colony. My dear Mrs Boratti…'

Mrs Boratti scoffed: 'But no, what are you saying? It was Mrs…' all the while smiling gratefully at the Prefect, 'we just improvised a tune for you, that's all…'

Yet all were interrupted by the officer's song: '*Il balen del suo sorriso…*' (*The flash of her smile*). The officer's presence amidst a gathering of ladies was most unusual. Alongside her normal education, Emma had learnt all the conventional replies dictated by conversation. Through the sheer weight of his presence, the officer had run roughshod over that education and its brittle rules – as though a gust of wind had just swept a cobweb away. His melancholic song didn't seem to want to persuade anyone: in fact it appeared perfectly situated in solitude. Those notes swallowed up that landscape piece by piece, like the night's approaching shadows. The ladies fell silent again immediately. Mrs Boratti sat on the sofa's armrest. Emma's ear was sufficiently trained to notice that the aria was being sung too slowly. The notes had trouble leaving the officer's throat. Emma felt an unspeakable sadness. She was distracted by the Count's song that she was no longer keeping an eye on the score: her mother nudged her with her elbow, but Emma failed to even notice it. Her heart had swelled inside her chest. That song was unbearably melancholic.

'Very good, very good…' the Prefect murmured. The officer replied with a very slight nod of the head. The other ladies kept quiet and instead headed towards the pile of pastries like an army of ants. Emma felt she'd been privileged to hear that song. Henceforth, she would learn to appreciate tenderness in a man.

When Mrs Macchi launched into the Soldiers' Chorus on her piano, the ladies, having grown mused, began to sing along: '*Squilli, echeggi la tromba guerriera,/chiami all'armi, alla pugna, all'assalto;/fia domani la nostra bandiera/di quei merli piantata sull'alto…*(*Let the warlike trumpet sound and echo,/call to arms, to the fray, the attack;/may our flag be planted tomorrow/on the highest of those towers.*)

Captain Mosca's wife had been the first to intone those words, and the others had followed suit. At which point even the Prefect bravely lent her voice to a few lines: '*No, giammai non sorrise vittoria…*' (*No, victory has never smiled*). Even Mrs Boratti, who had been taken by surprise by the unexpected song, lent her confident voice to it. By that point, the ladies were singing their hearts out: Emma observed them and was struck by the sweetness of their warlike grace. As for her, Emma experienced a new, delicate sensation: regret. The ladies' bellicose chorus functioned like a fan, while the Count's love song shocked her and filled her soul with fear. As far as Emma was concerned, teatime at Mrs Boratti's had taken on the specificity of a geography lesson: on one end lay the Prefect's little realm, while the Count's gloomy kingdom had swallowed up everything else. Such a smooth relationship, which had been publicly articulated, could only exist within the confines of a court and the cardboard cutout people that populated it. Yet all real relationships are secret and inexplicable – and just like any other form of knowledge – they're harrowing too.

Mrs Boratti was visibly pleased: that afternoon tea's success had exceeded all expectations. The Prefect was careful to protect the importance of her presence there, but she consented to keeping track of all the changes that had occurred within her court. As a matter of fact, by cheerfully joining in with the chorus of conversation, she tried to embody those very changes.

While the ladies, having finished their chorus, returned to their seats while exchanging self-congratulatory looks and compliments (the room was still saturated with their tender squeals, after a round of passionate attacks and amorous victories) Mrs Macchi read a few pages while sitting in front of the piano and then launched full-swing into the role she'd been assigned, Azucena's: '*Aita! mi lasciate*!…' (*Help! Let me go!*)

Her yell broke the ladies' tender hearts, and they suddenly fell silent.

'*S'appressi. A me rispondi, e trema dal mentir*!' (*Approach. Answer me, and don't dare lie to me*!) Azucena wasn't trembling, but the ladies – frightened out of their wits – certainly were. The Count's voice loosened them from gravity's grip, leaving them to float like algae swept about by the waves. Mrs Macchi crisply enunciated her words: '*D'una zingara è costume/mover senza disegno…*' (*It's the gypsy's custom/to wander without aim*).

Her clarity was clearly an attempt to resist the violent, gloomy waves being emitted by the Count. The gypsy's arioso – '*Giorni poveri vivea/I lived days of poverty*' – was very well received: the Count's arrogance and brutality seemed to stop short at the perfect blue sky evoked by the gypsy's song. The ladies were pleasantly surprised to discover their inner penchant for popular veins.

The lack of an actor able to take on Ferrando's bass-baritone meant the ladies were denied the chance to hear more of the gypsy's songs. 'What's going to happen now?' Mimi Russo asked Captain Mosca's wife. 'Terrible things!' the latter gracefully replied. The excitement emanating from the piano certainly presaged what was to come. Their excitement knew no bounds when Azucena quickly launched into her brief chant: '*Deh! rallentate, o barbari,/le acerbe mie ritorte./Questo crudel martirio/è prolungata morte!…*' (*Pray, loosen, barbarians,/the chains that bite me so./This cruel torture/is like a drawn-out death!*).

A murmur of pity ran through the assembled crowd.

Emma was paying close attention. Meanwhile, the strain of keeping up with all the accompanying parts, as well as playing the role of Azucena, had clearly taken a toll on her mother. Her arms would spread out and quickly come together again, part of her efforts to keep her fingers attached to her hands despite the score's demands that they remain impossibly scattered along the keyboard. Her right foot worked the pedal. Her mother's voice streamed in torrents out of her distorted mouth. Emma experienced a deep emotion, she'd understood that favour had been bestowed upon them: her mother had escaped the cardboard tableau she'd typically been confined to and had sprung to actual life. Emma's eyes darted back and forth between her mother's hands and her mother's face. It was a completely different face, fresh and re-energised: '*Trema! V'è Dio pei miseri/e Dio ti punirà!*' (*Beware! God protects the helpless,/and God will punish you!*)

It was ravishing. But the Count's sudden appearance: '*Tua prole, o turpe zingara,/Your brood, foul gypsy*,' that tangle of words which Emma couldn't make any sense of, fell upon that girl with such force that she failed to suppress an upsurge of fear within her. The score she'd been turning was now crumpled in her hand. Her mother could no longer see all the notes she was supposed to hit. Implacable, the Count continued – '*Potrò col tuo supplizio/ferirlo in mezzo al cor!*' (*With your torture then/I can wound his heart!*) – seemingly unbothered as to the fact the piano wasn't sounding all the proper accompanying notes. Those missing notes emphasised the stressed syllables: three or four ladies got up, looking visibly agitated. Without the musical buffer produced by those notes, and with the Count violently invading her mind with his voice,

Emma couldn't take it any longer: she betrayed the Count with a cry and threw herself weeping into her mother's arms.

As all the lamps had been switched back on, Mrs Boratti's sitting room shone with light. Behind Emma's shoulders, Professor Boratti bestowed kindly smiles upon his guests. Another gentleman, Dr Finigara, was chatting to the paunchy man. 'She got a four in Latin yesterday,' the mother awkwardly said, 'and she can't stop crying about it.' Dr Finigara, the head physician at the Civic Hospital, listened attentively, as he'd been expressly requested to help put a stop to that crying.

Having grown suddenly irritated, Emma loosened her hand out of the Prefect's grip. She had indeed gotten a four in Latin, but that had happened a month earlier (she'd stumbled on the third conjugation and the possessive of *ium*). Her mother had reverted back to her usual lies, having certainly been ashamed by her daughter's weeping, and for which she would surely be scathingly criticised eventually. In a considerate tone, Mrs Boratti asked: 'All better now?' Emma knew she was beside herself with fury: she had spoiled a highly successful afternoon of tea and music. 'Would you like some orange soda?' she asked Emma.

'Answer her!' her mother ordered her in a loud voice, as though they'd been alone. Emma dried her eyes and stood up. 'No, thank you, Mrs Boratti.'

'Tell the Prefect that you're sorry you got so frightened,' her mother said.

'There's no need for that, no need,' the Prefect retorted, growing irked.

The incident had to be brushed aside as soon as possible. The ladies were getting bored. The little girl's cry had been amusing enough a distraction, but now it was time for it to be over. 'Could the little girl go home on her own?' Mrs Boratti asked. It was an order. 'Of course, of course,' Mrs Macchi replied in haste, 'say goodbye to the ladies, Emma.'

The officer was completely unperturbed. The tender scene prompted by the girl's cry had played out in front of his eyes and failed to elicit any interest in him, just like the ritual of bows and introductions before it. Bringing others to tears was simply a singer's duty (and honour), but as far as consolation was concerned, that was a servile task best left to the chorus. Even the girl wasn't comforted by it.

Emma attempted to etch his portrait into her memory: the precious raw material for that task had nothing to do with what the ladies most admired about him: his reserved, almost hostile appearance. Instead it was composed of the strength of his hands, the impetus behind his anger, his melancholy feelings.

Violence, melancholy and solitude – the little girl repeated to herself, as though she'd just stumbled upon a talisman – *are a prince's true clothes, his uniform.*

Emma said goodbye to the ladies one by one, as well as Professor Boratti and his assistant. But not the officer. She had unknowingly failed to greet him at first, and she wasn't about to knowingly say goodbye to him now. This too was a secret relationship.

She crossed the room, walking the tightrope of that secret.

THE LIEUTENANT WITH AGATE EYES

'And I'm telling you we're not going to that dance,' the Commendatore said, irritated: 'I haven't slaved for thirty years just to give my daughter away to some dandy.'

'His father's a lawyer.'

'My daughter's not going to marry a soldier, she's going to marry a man who works for a living. When I die, her husband will take over my business.'

'We can't run roughshod over Emilia's feelings like that, Giacomo!'

'Don't start talking nonsense, and don't be so melodramatic. My daughter's feelings are subject to my will, and I only want what's best for her.'

'If we don't go to the club it'll cause a scandal.'

'You can only answer scandal with another scandal' the Commendatore retorted, vexed.

'You should at least remember that it was General Desiderius Occhipinti himself who invited us. Giacomo – come tomorrow we'll have the whole army against us!'

'I'll take them on.'

'I promise you – and I promise you on Emilia's behalf too – that it will all be finished tonight. But… I beg you… let her say goodbye to that man.'

'That *man*?' the Commendatore interjected, losing his patience, 'he's just a magazine cutout, he's not a man! Have you seen his legs?! They look more like wings than legs: They're great when it comes to dancing a waltz, but they won't do him any good while standing in a factory.'

'You don't mean to suggest we should want to fall in love with our own son-in-law and judge whether his legs are good enough or not?'

'I can judge a man just by looking at him. And that little lieutenant's got agate eyes, have you noticed that? They lack any depth, they're gorgeous to look at, and they've cast a spell on Emilia, but they don't see anything, like gemstones refracting light. When you shake his hand, you can't feel the nerves, or the muscles of his fingers. I won't argue that it might well be perfectly shaped, but it lacks any strength whatsoever. His uniform is just like his skin: clean and fresh, like he'd never even put it on, it's like it was his natural plumage, it bears no sign of any physical strain; and by the end of the night, there's still not a crease in sight. He can't even warm up that uniform, or fill it enough to make it look tailored, he's got the absent-minded grace of a mannequin. That little lieutenant looks good in a shop window, but put him out on the street and he'll fall down and die.'

'He doesn't necessarily have to take over your business, you know.'

'So who have I been working so hard for?' the Commendatore exclaimed, 'so I could see the business taken over by whom exactly?'

His wife looked at him, hesitantly. She could still force a few admissions out of him – 'Look at that little lieutenant dancing with Emilia' he'd said the first time he'd laid eyes on him, 'look at how he moves, he's so quick on his feet.' But there was no hope. The ordeal of the office desk – the inexorable requirement for anyone to be granted his daughter's hand, an enigma which had to be solved in order to marry the heiress of that great factory – would only humiliate that young paper soldier.

The Commendatore stood up. 'I'm going to inform Emilia that we won't be going to the club tonight. My daughter won't ever forgive me for this.'

'Don't be dramatic, that's enough now, don't be so dramatic. The lieutenant is like a string of pearls, and right now we're telling her that she can't have it: she'll cry a little and then it'll all be over. It's just like if you'd missed out on a big business opportunity at the office, you'd feel bad too.'

When the mother stepped inside the girl's room, she found her sitting next to the window with a book in her hand.

'Are you reading, my dear?'

Emilia half turned to face her.

'You know, your father can really be odd at times. This little lieutenant has certainly got him all scared up.'

'What about the dance?' Emilia softly asked.

'The dance? Sure, there'll be a dance tonight,' her mother stammered, 'but we won't be going.'

Emilia rose and the book slammed shut in her hand.

The mother's eyes filled with tears.

'Calm down, my daughter, calm down, I swear I fought for you. But you know how strong-willed he is.'

The daughter entered the sitting room where the father was reading the newspaper.

The father raised his eyes. They looked at one another for a long time.

'I swear I won't marry that man, daddy, not if you don't want me to. But tonight we're going to the dance.'

'Why aren't you a man, Emilia? The strength of your willpower offers some consolation: Whenever you speak I cheer up because I can feel the presence of a proper heir. Now it doesn't really matter whether we go to the dance or not. We can go, if you like… but only for an hour. Your mother says you need to say goodbye to that officer. Fine. If it's so important so be it.'

'Thank you, darling.' the mother said, with tears in her eyes.

'I really don't understand what all these tears are for!' the Commendatore exclaimed. 'What time are we going?'

'Eleven.'

'Eleven it is.'

Come eleven o'clock they made their entrance into the Officers Club, on Corso Italia. The Commendatore was a solidly built man, with authoritarian features. He never enjoyed himself at parties: but he had gratefully accepted the general's invitation as though it had been a medal. After the day's tension, the mother got dressed in a hurry, without taking much care.

The general extended Commendatore Curzi a warm welcome. An army corps general still outranked an industrialist, at least in the colonies – even though this particular industrialist was the Chairman of the local chamber of commerce and a trustee of a few charities – but the government had made the region's industrial development a top priority, for both economic reasons as well as, more importantly, for propagandistic purposes. And that man was a formidable go-getter. The soldier held him in high regard and didn't leave him waiting in the reception room.

'Emilia grows more beautiful by the day, Commendatore.' the general said, joyfully making it known he remembered the girl's name.

The dance had begun. The orchestra played a tango. On entering the room, Emilia immediately spotted the agate eyes on the other side of the orchestra. She also noticed the Commendatore – while his wife looked around herself – looking very frightened. They sat down at Colonel Lanza's table. The latter's wife, a sweet-natured blonde with withered features, complimented Emilia. 'You're really very pretty, very pretty.' Emilia had been sitting there for over a half hour and nobody had paid her any mind. 'You know, Emilia,' the colonel's wife began, keeping her voice down so that the Commendatore and her husband wouldn't overhear her, 'springtime and life are brief and go by quickly, just like a waltz. You whirl about and then the music ends, and then life gives you leave to go.'

A captain came to ask Emilia to dance. He was a melancholy man, very courteous, and he even confided in her a little, what seemed like snippets of a conversation he was secretly carrying on with himself.

'Everybody's here,' he said, 'but the dance feels a little stiff – doesn't it?'

'It's eleven thirty.'

'Does Emilia have a clock inside her head tonight?'

The mother kept scanning her surroundings. *Maybe he didn't show up?* she asked herself, frightened. *Maybe it's for the best, maybe it's for the best*… and she folded her black lace shawl again.

Every time the Commendatore's eyes scanned the room, he would find those agate eyes: they were hiding behind the orchestra's red festoons as though peering through a thick wood. Yet the unerring Commendatore would always find them again right away, like the fine hunter he was. He had fixed his gaze upon him as though he were his prey.

Emilia returned to her table. The colonel asked her if she was having a good time. After Emilia's measured response, and drawn by the brilliant notes being played, he stood up. He would step in and ask the girl to dance. He was shorter than Emilia, whose head hovered just above his. Meaning that every time she turned, Emilia's eyes could run along the length of the room and admire those agate eyes beyond the orchestra's festoons.

'We watched you grow up, little Emilia,' the colonel said, affectionately.

Emilia clasped his hand.

'A little melancholic tonight?'

'Tell me,' the colonel's wife asked her, drawing Emilia close to her as soon as they got back to their table, 'that little lieutenant from the other day… is it all over with him? Such a handsome boy. A little frail perhaps, but very stylish! You know what he reminds me of? A violin! And here he is!'

Lieutenant Roberti was standing a step away from Emilia. He bowed slightly towards the ladies, then greeted the Commendatore and the colonel. At which he asked Emilia to dance.

'Lieutenant Roberti appears to be wildly infatuated,' the colonel's wife commented, raising her voice as soon as the couple had left the table. 'My dear Commendatore, it seems Emilia has stolen his heart.' The colonel's wife could have talked about love all night long. But following a subtle nod from Emilia's mother, she kept her mouth shut.

Commendatore Curzi disdained the silence cowards use to keep danger at bay: 'If the world, such as it is today, were governed by peace and harmony, instead of by strength and willpower, that little lieutenant over there might get along just fine. But peace and harmony have no place outside of the dance floor.'

The colonel's wife laughed, amused. 'Just look at them – they're so made for each other. Emilia looks so pretty tonight. Very pretty indeed.'

The mother kept her eyes fixed on the young couple. She might well have been saying goodbye to him at that exact moment. She might have been explaining why they couldn't be together. She might have been employing noble phrases, along the lines of, 'I'll always respect you.' In fact, given that the waltz's heady notes can play tricks on one's mind, she might have even gone so far as to say 'I'll never forget you.' Nevertheless, if she had something to say, then she should have gotten on with it: after all, how long could a waltz possibly last?

Even the father's eyes were fixed on Emilia. The couple entered his line of sight and then suddenly left it again, swaying back and forth as though being swept about by the waves. What was resoundingly clear, however, was that Emilia was not talking. *Good girl*, he thought, *no point in sweet nothings, promises, or tears*. He was proud of his daughter's silence. And since a string of pearls had been mentioned, he would make a point of buying her one as a present. One with two strands, or three, maybe even four… He too was gripped by the waltz's rhythm.

When Major Maiorana approached to invite the colonel's wife to dance, the latter leapt up, as light on her feet as a little girl. Once out on the floor, her eyes met Emilia's. 'God how I love to dance!' she exclaimed.

The Commendatore was still examining the lieutenant's uniform. He still couldn't fathom how that uniform could be kept so rumple-free, as though it wasn't hanging off a human body, a warm body made of muscles – no, it was as if he were a glove or a soap bubble. He didn't even seem to be breathing, his nostrils didn't seem to flare, his chest didn't seem to be rising and falling. *If life was as harmonious as this waltz,* he thought to himself, full of melancholy, *then this little lieutenant would have been a perfect match for Emilia, they're very similar and cut from the same cloth. But life isn't like that: it would be like giving Emilia a pheasant for a husband, a nice little golden pheasant…* Having grown irritated, he turned his head away and stopped looking at the dancers.

Maybe they'll run off to the terrace. As soon as the dance is over, Emilia's going to drag him out onto the terrace. And once they're alone, she'll tell him… But what will she say?! What could she say? Her mother was wringing her hands.

Like a troupe of incompetent actors, the orchestra musicians adapted to the atmosphere on the floor, playing at faster tempos, playing the last notes as loudly as the room allowed. Right on the final beat, just as the couples were slipping out of their embraces, Emilia addressed her first words to the lieutenant that night: 'Keep dancing.'

One spin, two spins, three spins. The couples had all unclasped, some were still standing immobile in the middle of the dance floor, while others had already headed back to their respective tables. Right in the middle of it all, keeping its distance from the couples still standing and those leaving, one last couple kept spinning along.

The Commendatore's eyes had turned into fangs. As for Emilia's mother, she was barely able to restrain herself as she raised her hand to cross herself. *Don't let anything happen, God, don't let anything happen, God.*

At this point the dance floor had emptied entirely. Yet the lieutenant with agate eyes kept spinning about with his girl in his arms. 'Pretty, really very pretty…' the colonel's wife murmured. The Commendatore stood up, but nobody paid him any attention. Everyone had stood up by then, neatly arranging themselves in a square around the dance floor. 'Look!' said the colonel's wife, 'the hall is ready for the cavalry lancers.'

Only the orchestra players were still moving. They were miming a bizarre comedy, which is to say that they didn't know what to do, whether they should keep playing – but if they did, what would they play? Yet the young officer and his girl didn't need them at all.

Then, right on the other side of the orchestra, a passageway swung open. Somebody was on their way. All eyes turned to that opening, and the General in Chief of the army corps emerged at the other end. It was as though the rows of guests had taken up formation so that the general could review his guard of honour.

One spin, two spins, three spins. Then the young lieutenant and the girl came to a stop. The girl bowed deeply before the general, while the young lieutenant stood to attention. The General in Chief of the army corps dismissed them, and his hand betrayed a trace of kindness.

CAPTAIN RENZI

Captain Renzi's gaze was lifeless. Instead of establishing a dialogue with his interlocutor, he'd been tasked to ensure it wouldn't happen. Even his way of talking put people off: he meticulously avoided any kind of intimacy, which made any dialogue with him as abstract as a carpet's geometric patterns.

Major Anastasio claimed that Renzi was a mercenary – he never gave his opinion on any matter and limited himself to performing his duties to the letter. Even though he'd only just arrived, he knew the outskirts of the city better than any of the other officers, all of whom had been in Africa far longer than him. He appeared sensitive to the beauty of their natural surroundings, at which point his typically unyielding composure would vanish for an instant.

Yet when it came to his relationship with his fellow soldiers and subordinates, appealing to that aforementioned sensitivity was bound to end in failure. Other officers were far stricter, some were even intractable, and a few were even cruel. Captain Renzi, on the other hand, was fair-minded, yet one couldn't rely on his indulgence, understanding, or pity. He was simply calm and collected, in full mastery of his feelings.

Privates Danisi and Ranieri had no luck with him. They happened to infringe one of the military's rules and wound up being judged by the very same Captain Renzi. Sergeant Major Sanzogno burst into Captain Renzi's office in a state of obvious excitement. He had caught the two soldiers in an indecent act. Truth be told, he tried to blame it all on Danisi, who was a bad egg and whom he'd kept his eye on for a while. Ranieri instead was a good soldier, honest and sincere, and he honestly had no idea how he'd fallen into such a trap. He wasn't very sociable or outgoing, but was serious and honest. (Sergeant Major Sanzogno had actually played no part in the discovery; in fact, most of the soldiers had known for some time. Yet a certain Capresi had snitched to the Sergeant Major. This Capresi didn't like Ranieri at all.)

The Sergeant Major's excitement led him to overstep his bounds and advise the Captain to punish Danisi and forgive Ranieri. It was a groundless hope. While still in the midst of talking, the Sergeant Major confusedly began to realise this: if he'd been truly invested in the matter, he should have brought it to the Captain, but should have resolved it in his own way; if there was no way to exonerate Ranieri, then he should have kept his mouth shut. But now it was up to the Captain to decide – and Renzi would certainly not keep his advice in mind. Not that he allowed his real intentions to transpire, just that there would be no surprises.

Nevertheless, the Sergeant Major was to be surprised regardless, not that he dwelled on it much, given the disappointment he experienced the moment the Captain opened his mouth. He cited the rule the soldiers had broken verbatim from memory – and this act of total recall did surprise the Sergeant Major – but merely by reciting the flouted rule he made it clear he would not be indulging either of the two privates. The rules had to be applied.

By the time Captain Renzi should have reasonably forgotten about the entire incident, a high functionary from the administration whom he'd met in Italy happened to walk into his office to talk to him about Danisi and Ranieri. Unlike the Sergeant Major, the functionary had come to exonerate Danisi, who was his son. After all, they were merely twenty-year old kids (in actual fact Danisi was twenty-two and Ranieri was already twenty-four), it had all just been a mistake. What point would there have been in casting a light on a momentary lapse of reason, instead of turning a blind, indulgent eye to the whole affair and dropping the matter entirely? That punishment would just ensure they were publicly pilloried, and what was the point of mortifying them like that instead of trying to reach out to them? Why bring them to the brink of desperation and make their mistake seem even bigger in their eyes? Would it really help put them back on the right path?

The functionary had very little sympathy for Renzi. It had required some effort of him to come all the way to his office; all the more so since he had now realised that while Renzi was listening to him attentively. He nonetheless did so in the coldest manner possible. Had he spent an additional hour making his case, he would have still walked away empty-handed. Thus, cutting himself off randomly in the middle of a sentence and attempting to strike a cordial tone, he asked Renzi: 'Well, what have you decided?'

Captain Renzi appeared slightly surprised by the question; the functionary's thoughts were on an entirely different wavelength since he had not given this particular question any consideration. Sure enough, he said:

'The punishment I've dealt them is a disciplinary measure, just as though they'd left their barracks without leave, I didn't attach any moral judgment to it. We officers must ensure that the rules and regulations are followed, we haven't been charged with looking after their souls. Once they have received their punishment, they will return to their usual ranks as ordinary soldiers, and if they won't make any further mistakes, I'll think of them as exemplary soldiers…'

'What do you mean?' the functionary exclaimed, suddenly frustrated, 'do you really not understand the implications of your judgment? Do you really believe that this kind of punishment has nothing to do with their being morally judged? This may very well be true as far as you're concerned, but you do not seem to grasp that by revealing an indiscretion which others tend to judge not only from a regulatory, but above all from a moral point of view, you have assumed a great responsibility here. By dealing with the matter publicly, you have encouraged others to think along these lines, and it was wholly in your power to avoid that.'

'I am profoundly and sincerely sorry for the way in which the situation unfolded. As I have already mentioned, this was not my intention…'

'Do you finally see how flippant you've been?' the functionary passionately interjected.

'I haven't been flippant,' the Captain sternly replied. 'I only did my duty. I wouldn't hesitate to do it again. Discipline is…'

'But no,' the functionary bitterly retorted, 'you're mistaken, because–'

'Perhaps my one mistake was to consent to talk about the matter,' the Captain calmly replied, and that sentence brought the conversation to an end. 'It is the strict purview of my superior officers to judge my decisions.'

'So be it, even if I have to take this all the way to the King,' the functionary bursted out, 'but I'm not prepared to let this go.'

He left without even saying goodbye. The Sergeant Major entered simultaneously through the door opposite the one the functionary had used. He had also come to discuss the matter of Danisi and Ranieri. It appeared as though he was no longer kindly disposed towards Ranieri. In fact, the two soldiers had been caught while attempting to communicate with one another in prison. Having intercepted a message – which for that matter contained nothing important – the Sergeant Major had called them into his office. He couldn't say that they'd been too brazen or impertinent, instead they had been calm. It looked as though their punishment had lifted a weight off their shoulders.

'My actions didn't go far enough.' The Sergeant Major concluded, 'they must be permanently kept apart.'

He was giving the Captain advice again, and he bit his lip, vexed with himself. The Captain said nothing, neither yes nor no. It seemed as though Sanzogno's words had left an impression on him, but in a completely different manner to the one the Sergeant Major had expected. In fact, he didn't seem displeased in the slightest. He dismissed the Sergeant Major without saying anything, headed over to the mirror to ensure his appearance was in order and left to inspect the troops.

He mulled over what the Sergeant Major had told him. Hearing the functionary speak, one might have believed his account of the soldiers' desperation, and if he didn't experience any regrets it was only because he was convinced that he'd merely done his duty. However, the Sergeant Major's speech had agitated him. His observation that the soldiers looked as though a great weight had been lifted off their shoulders had struck him as truthful and accurate. The Captain secretly envied those soldiers for having found peace and solace in their punishment.

No pleas or supplications were forthcoming from Ranieri, and there wouldn't be any either. When he had seen the functionary before him, he had originally assumed that Danisi had sent him to intercede on his behalf. Instead, he had been mistaken – they had accepted their punishment. In fact, as the Sergeant Major had so eloquently put it, they felt liberated.

That evening, Captain Renzi headed over to the Officers' Club. On the night of his arrival from Italy, Colonel Tarenzi had invited him there. He hadn't returned to that place since. He had been expected to attend a lunch with all the other officers to mark the visit of two navy units to the colonial city. Ever since then, he had become a tireless devotee of the club. He arrived punctually each day at nine, headed over to the bar – from which vantage point he could see who was coming and going – strolled through the rooms, climbed up one of the turrets, and then went home. More often than not he didn't exchange a single word with anyone. At first he had become an object of curiosity, but as time went on nobody paid him any heed.

Once he reached the club, he went to the bar and asked for gin with a splash of orange juice. This was his favourite drink and the bartender would prepare it for him as soon as he saw him enter the establishment. He was always one of the more elegant officers – except that he lacked the fatuousness which distinguished all the others – and he wasn't smugly proud of his appearance. One only had to look at him when he stood in front of the mirror: meticulously well-kept, but absent-minded, he seemed no more interested or pleased than if he'd been putting his desk in order. Two officers made for the bar with the sole purpose of greeting him.

'Do you know we're leaving?'

The regiment had been transferred to the border. In those days, there was constant talk of war brewing on the horizon, and their orders appeared to confirm this.

Captain Renzi was keen to know all the minuscule details of their departure date, taking the two soldiers by surprise. Yet his curiosity stopped short there. He merely wanted to know at what hour and on what day the regiment would be departing. Nothing more.

'He's such an oddball,' one of the officers said as they walked away.

The Captain remained sitting at the bar for a half hour. Then he stood up, ambled distractedly from one room to the other, and then went up to the terrace. He left shortly afterwards and swiftly made for a corner of the garden. There was a group of officers there talking animatedly. They were exchanging confused comments about the war, of the lodgings they would find in that distant border town, of the families they would have to leave behind. As for the younger officers, they commiserated over having to leave their city and club behind. Everyone had drunk their fill and conversation flowed easily.

'Is it true that you're leaving?'

'Of course! You heard that too?'

'I did, Major Fontana told me.'

'Some pretty excellent news, eh?' the young officer said sarcastically.

'Why do you say that?'

'What do you mean, why?'

'Are you afraid of war?'

'Not at all. I don't have any confidence in this war. They'll leave us stranded out there for a year or so, to rot.'

'Are you upset you're leaving the city?'

'But of course I am,' the young officer answered, off the cuff.

The Captain observed him for a moment. The young man was twenty two years old, he was a second lieutenant in the artillery. He wasn't very tall, and his hair fell over his eyes. He wore his uniform with elegance. There was only that hair, dangling above those always alert, darting eyes, which stood in stark contrast against his regular features, and otherwise serene, limpid eyes. They betrayed the fact that he was still oscillating between restlessness and mischief.

'I heard the regiment is leaving on Saturday.'

'Right, but I have to leave tomorrow. It's either going to be me or Lieutenant Fermi, since he's still not feeling well.'

They were still standing in the midst of all the other officers. Captain Renzi would never have talked to anyone in a secluded space. He didn't indulge himself any further. He addressed a few words to one of the officers in his regiment, and then withdrew.

It was almost midnight. The officers were talking loudly, and laughing even louder, and they were no longer as composed as they had been earlier in the evening. Captain Renzi never stayed up that late. He always went home at ten thirty. Instead, on that night he stopped at the bar on his way out and ordered another gin. Yet he was composed as ever, and he was the only one who had remained cold and distant while the ghost of general excitement stirred everyone else's spirits. There was more commotion than usual, since the officers who were leaving for the border were being feted by their comrades.

'Won't you toast our companions?' Colonel Tarenzi asked him, slapping him on the shoulder. He was a very cordial officer, they called him batiushka[ii] because everyone said he was more like a priest than a commanding officer, as had been the case (as far as some were concerned) with all the colonels serving under the Russian Tsar.

The Captain raised a glass to the health of the departing soldiers. The young second lieutenant wasn't there, he must have still been outside in the garden. Once the toast had been drunk, Colonel Tarenzi told him:

'By the way, dear Captain, come to my office tomorrow morning. I need to speak with you.'

The Captain replied that he would do as ordered. It struck the good Colonel that the Captain took to his tasks far too seriously. 'But don't give it any more thought,' he added, as though wanting to reassure him, 'it's nothing important.'

At that exact moment, the Captain spotted his young friend leaving the club. He treaded lightly, as though he'd been an officer from a distant bygone era, when a military commission was still a worldly career. He was still brushing his hair away from his face with

---

ii Russian: 'Little Father'.

that same impatient gesture: it looked as though he was ruffling it up rather than smoothing it out. For the past few moments, the Captain had experienced a kind of envy at the thought of Danisi and Ranieri, who now felt liberated, as though the punishment had freed them from a terrible burden, just like the Sergeant Major had said. *Scandal is necessary*, he thought to himself, *and while one probably shouldn't go looking for it, its arrival is still a blessing.*

The following day, at exactly nine o'clock, the Captain was standing in the Colonel's waiting room. He had to wait for him for an entire hour. The Colonel never arrived before ten. As soon as the Colonel had entered, he greeted the Captain amiably and personally ushered him into his office. He talked about his various illnesses, of the city's humidity, which wasn't doing his health any good, and that he had in fact already put in for a transfer. The Captain listened to him respectfully, and gave a brief reply when appropriate.

'By the way,' the Colonel suddenly said, as though he'd just remembered the reason for having summoned the Captain into his office that very moment, '– came to see me…' meaning the high functionary who had paid Renzi a visit the previous day. 'That incident between the two soldiers has become the biggest piece of gossip in the city. I'm not quite sure how that happened, and who took it upon himself to ensure everyone heard about it, but there's hardly anyone who isn't talking about it. Nobody really knows the two soldiers in question and nobody bothers to try to. But we've heard about your refusal to… deal with the man who took an interest in them. It's not worth our while to squabble with this man. Naturally,' he quickly added, in order to forestall the Captain's objection, 'the matter is under the purview of army discipline, and they shouldn't stick their noses into these affairs. But there we have it, dear Captain,' and here the Colonel resumed his captivating, almost embittered, paternal tone, 'we've had to make so many compromises already that it wouldn't make sense to dig our heels in on so trifling a matter. We can either agree or mutiny, and since we have no intention of mutinying, let's agree to this request. As such, you must rescind your order and let's not discuss the matter anymore. I don't like that bastard at all, probably more than you do, and I would like nothing more than to keep those two in prison just to vex him, but…'

Having realised that the Captain didn't feel the need for that conversation to continue, the Colonel suddenly stopped short mid-sentence. Especially since he had been compromising himself by making all those statements.

'Are we in agreement?'

The Captain hadn't liked the Colonel's speech, but there was nothing left to discuss, this was an order, and the tone in which it was delivered was beside the point. Had he refused the Colonel's order and taken the matter up directly with the General, the latter would have invariably taken the Colonel's side. As soon as he got back to his office, he would rescind his order. However, he was still certain that he'd done his duty and had applied the rules as intended. Colonel Tarenzi, on the other hand, was a bad officer.

'We are.' the Captain said, taking his leave. The Colonel observed him. He looked as he always did, and he didn't betray any peevishness. He was calm, in that cool manner for which he was universally known.

THE PRINCE OF CLEVE

I

On seeing Lieutenant Nemiri standing before him, the President of the Shopkeepers Association seethed with rage. The young man's presence was simply intolerable to him: it was an outright provocation.

It had proved impossible not to invite at least a few young officers to the annual ball, alongside higher-ranking civilian and military officials. Yet why Nemiri? The President replied to Nemiri's greeting with extreme coldness.

The lieutenant however behaved obsequiously, he kissed the president's wife's hand and complimented the reception hall's splendour. His submissiveness betrayed a cruel and sarcastic attitude. Being of noble birth, it was as though he'd wanted to express how honoured he was to join that colonial club.

The lieutenant had entered alongside the young Berto. The President asked him to keep an eye on Nemiri. 'I'm sorry your father's no longer with us, Berto. If he'd lived to see this sort of man step foot inside the club, he would have instructed the waiters to kick him out.'

'But no,' Berto said. He was a young man completely devoid of any spontaneity and was furthermore pensive and reserved, almost like a priest. His father had once been the President of the local Chamber of Commerce.

'He's a dangerous man,' the guest insisted, keeping his eyes fixed on Nemiri. 'You're a good lad, Berto, and there are some things you just do not understand; but when it comes to business I've developed an infallible eye for these things.'

'People have surely exaggerated…' Berto's answers were always defeatist, and served only to cushion against the impact with reality.

'He who is offended never exaggerates. Please spare me the unpleasant task of having to recount his adventures.'

Berto kept quiet.

'If I see him strike up a conversation with a girl,' the President added, his vexation growing with each moment, 'I'll challenge him to a duel.'

He kept his arm hanging by his waist, ready to unsheathe his sword. There was something impetuous to his behaviour, as well as solemn and serious. He hadn't seemed to account for the fact that his hand laid nowhere near a sword's hilt, but rather a large golden watch with its visibly sumptuous chain. Standing next to him, Berto felt as though he was merely adding a little decorative value to the scene. He was a witness to events he was not fated to take part in; just as was the case in crowded frescoes, where people are depicted despite the fact nobody knows their respective dramatic functions. 'Come on,' he sullenly added, 'he won't get that lucky.'

At that moment, the Governor entered the hall. Although his presence had been assiduously requested, his arrival had remained a maybe. The President instantaneously cheered up, as though a divine blessing had been bestowed on him.

'He's as handsome as the Duke of Mantua,' one of the ladies admitted.

The excitement among the shopkeepers prompted by the Governor's presence was intense. The whites of their starched shirts shone on their chests like medals.

The Governor smiled, decreasing the tightness with which he shook those men's hands as he went along and cast an indulgent glance around the hall. Then, just like Lieutenant Nemiri, he paid the place a few compliments. The President felt oppressed by all that courtesy.

A group of officers standing in a corner surveyed the scene.

'He isn't a good governor at all,' Captain Sorrentino said irritably, turning his back to the illustrious guest, 'but he got lucky. The hard part of the job, in this colony, fell on others' shoulders. He reigns on the foundations of the sad peace that they forged. Cruelty has been exiled because it is no longer useful. The indigenous resistance has given way to resignation. Considering the situation, the police itself would do; the army is only here for the sake of appearances. It serves no purpose.'

'This is the original sin of our presence here. But surely, Captain, you don't intend our lives here to be spent meditating on that original sin…'

In contrast to the Captain, Colonel Verri made an ostentatious show of his indifference. 'A governor's worth lies in compensating resignation with humanity, or to borrow from our propagandists, progress and civilization.'

'As for me,' Major Borghi's wife said, 'I don't give a fig for progress, it's nothing but a bit of theatre, propaganda. I admire this governor because he amuses us.'

'This is where we exorcise the political meaning of our presence here,' Captain Sorrentino retorted, sarcastically, 'with a bit of music and elegant dancing.'

'When there's no injury there's no tragedy,' said the lady who had compared the Governor to the Duke of Mantua, 'everything is both easy and insignificant. The curse is missing.'

'A curse?' Captain Sorrentino exclaimed. 'The injury occurred when we first occupied this land – that is the original sin. Anyone who can't see the curse looming over us cannot see the path we're walking on.'

Calm and indulgent, the Governor was seated at the top of the room. The members of the club had especially welcomed one thing: the simulation of power. The Governor flaunted his presence there as though he was an actor. Meanwhile, the orchestra played courtly arrangements that were both depressingly slow and sublime. It contented itself with merely ensuring its presence for the moment. It would only begin to play in full swing later in the evening – mediocre melodies to be sure, and yet they were also magical. If only the Governor himself had been able to hear the music, instead of being dragged hither and tither like a page boy.

The Governor raised his gaze. The shopkeepers were entranced by that gaze, and followed it like a magic wand. The violinist who led the orchestra pulled his bow away from the string, which groaned. The pianist punched the final three chords of the tune they had been playing. Sound emptied out of the hall.

The full orchestra, comprising the violin, the double bass, saxophone, piano, drums and chimes, launched into it. It was a feast of colours: a joyous, sensual rush, an echo of the sea and its nocturnal abandon. The Governor looked at the beautiful Princess of Cleve sat in a corner next to her husband, a second lieutenant of the third artillery regiment. Yet the dancing couples, like a colourful festoon, took center stage and the Princess vanished behind them.

'Berto,' the Princess's mother said, taking the young man's hand as he passed by, 'why don't you come and sit here next to me? There's simply too much excess in reality and I find it overwhelming.'

She raised her eyes, two slits. Two tiny sparkles of light shone out. Were they tears?

'These old tear dams have grown weak these days, but what can I do about that?'

Like an astronomer high in her observatory, the old woman studied the room. Her eyes were fixed on the princess, while also keeping track of Nemiri's movements. She couldn't deny the overwhelming evidence: they were like stars that belonged to the same constellation. The lieutenant was dancing with a woman not much younger than him who walked around him in circles as though trying to tie him up. The confusion, the randomness of movements, was obvious. The mother could read people, and could spot the obvious – and fatal – relationships that linked them together. It left her feeling distressed.

Once the tango was over, the Governor's eyes snuck around the couples still standing in the middle of the hall and finally reached the Princess. She was so fragile and tiny that her stillness appeared like a gracious and vain attempt to lend herself a heavier, more important presence. She looked like a little girl at a carnival, wearing a costume meant for someone older. The violinist observed the Governor. He couldn't follow his gaze and discover the object of his attention. He was boldly prolonging the duration of that silent interlude to please his master, to conceal his stare and allow it to slip past the couples and find its desired target.

Lieutenant Nemiri accompanied the young lady back to her seat. Stopping, he shook the strings she'd tried to tie him up with off his shoulders. When he bowed towards her, she squirmed in a prudish, bashful way. 'The angel who bowed before her seems to have filled her with fright!' Princess Cleve's mother exclaimed.

Her awareness proved to be an inadequate bulwark. 'Berto,' she said, showing her the tortured slits of her eyes, 'that Nemiri…' but she didn't finish her sentence.

The movement in the hall was like a battlefield, and the waltz's notes flew like flags above that tangled mass.

The Governor stood up. The orchestra slowed the waltz's rhythm. It was an invitation.

The Governor authoritatively left the dais, but then stood still, as though lost. Between him and the Princess, whom he'd been able to spy from only a few feet away, lay a kind of labyrinth, from which he was unable to extricate himself. The waltz's notes were like magic circles.

Instead he invited the Podestà's wife to dance. A woman who nursed a constant fear in her eyes. The Governor was circumspect. He tried to keep up with the music, zig-zagging instead of going in circles. He suddenly began to spin too, and the Podestà's wife shuddered, as though the strings had snapped and she were falling into the Governor's arms, or who knows where…

The Prince of Cleve was standing anxiously next to his wife. He kept bending over to her in order to talk to her. The Princess's stillness (her face was split in two by her perfect stillness) was a vain attempt on her part to resist. The Prince's words assailed her like flames: '*All you can offer me is a kind of goodness which cannot satisfy me: you know neither impatience, nor restlessness, nor pain. And you're not unsettled by my passion…*'

Having emerged unscathed from the waltz's waves, the Governor had come to a stop right in front of the Princess. He gazed at her admiringly, now that she had begun to move – barely at first, as though neither her heart nor brain were responsible for putting her in motion, but as though she were being articulated by an intricate alien mechanism that allowed two or three movements at a time. He looked joyfully amazed. He had once seen two similar-looking figurines perform a couple of little movements each time the clock struck the hour, although he couldn't remember where. The Princess was performing her mechanical dance in front of the stupefied guests.

The Governor was easily moved by the Princess's fragile grace, and her pointed little face, like a swallow's beak.

When the wicked Lieutenant Nemiri appeared in the group's midst, the Governor immediately realised he was the second figurine. He experienced a curious feeling: the years that had passed stood between him and the luminous shore of youth, and age blocked his path like an interdict. At the same time, he felt a slight pleasure that was precisely linked to his age. Lieutenant Nemiri's presence had stolen the Princess away from him, but it had given him something equally precious in return: a couple. *The gracefulness of youth is a mystery*, he thought. It was at this point that he felt that he could only overcome being excluded in a single manner: by wanting what was fatally bound to happen anyway.

'The young people aren't dancing?' he asked, with slight irritation in his voice.

A prodigious dissolution ensued. As though he were the mechanism guiding their movement, Lieutenant Nemiri bowed and invited the Princess to dance. The Governor's command had marked the stroke of that hour.

The Princess of Cleve and Lieutenant Nemiri took over the room as if it was their own private garden. The Princess's mother felt that they were running away; it didn't much matter that they occasionally brushed past her as they danced, that was just a ruse, a trick. She would have wanted to hold her arms out and stop them. What antidote could possibly make them stop, what could possibly break the magic spell that the Governor's order had cast?

The civilians in the crowd could already detect the incipient affair: they believed intrigues and scandals were embedded in the regulations that governed military society – their mirror opposite.

The Governor looked at them and the perfect harmony of their movements – as though they were being coordinated by a single device, as well as the proportions of their bodies, as if they had been cast by the same mould – left him feeling excluded, brutally so.

On the other side of the hall, the Prince of Cleve, who was still standing, kept his eyes fixed on his wife's agile feet as they ran around to who knew where. The suspicion of adultery was far from his mind. He was looking at the tiny golden shoes, which barely touched the ground as they moved, and he felt the distance between them grow wider, a nocturnal separation, immeasurable. It didn't matter much that they were kept contained by the frame provided by the club's dancehall, which was richly decorated with fanciful stuccos.

The dance came to an end, and the Prince's wife was returned to him, her chest barely moving. She leaned on the Prince's arm, first lightly, then slowly with her entire weight. She sat down, and something about her movements had retained the lightness of that dance, as though it had never come to an end. The Prince looked at his wife's shoes, which were now immobile.

He suddenly rose and bowed before her. The Princess stood up, barely smiling, laid her hand on her husband's shoulder and followed him into the next dance. The Prince pressed her tightly against himself, as though frightened that she were about to flee – in fact he held her so tightly that she could barely breathe. Nevertheless, she said nothing, and kept following his lead, despite being nearly deprived of air. It was a complete reversal of the earlier dance between Nemiri and the Princess, unravelling the tangled mass created by the Princess and her knight.

A few minutes later, once the party's luminous energy had exhausted itself. The Governor – paying some hurried compliment to the club's president, who had accompanied him out onto the street – took his leave and left.

II

Inside the immense amphitheatre, the group of people following the Governor around resembled a flock of birds that had perched for a moment to recover their strength. Nothing remained of the *skēnē* – the edifice which encloses the *proskenion* – aside from a little door. The landscape beyond was unscathed: it replicated the theatre's structure at ample intervals along the coast, a staircase leading down to a nonetheless invisible boundary, the sea.

The morning was clear and the sky limpid.

'Professor,' the Governor called out from atop the steps, addressing the archaeologist who had accompanied them to tour the excavation sites at Cyrene, on the high plateaus, and who had remained standing in the orchestra pit because he couldn't make it all the way up the steps, and go to and fro like the rest of them. 'Why don't you recite something for us?'

It was an order. The archaeologist looked around.

'Ερως ἀνίκατε μάχαν, 'Ερως, ὃς ἐν κτήμασι πίπτεις,
ὃς ἐν μαλακαις παρειαις νεάνιδος ἐννυχεύεις,
φοιτᾳς δ' ὑπερπόντιος ἔν τ' ἀγρονόμοις αὐλαις:
καί σ' οὔτ' ἀθανάτων φύξιμος1 οὐδεὶς
οὔθ' ἁμερίων σέ γ' ἀνθρώπων. ὁ δ' ἔχων μέμηνεν.'[iii]

The amphitheatre was a port, and those sailors had come from distant countries. The goods that the merchant-archaeologist was offering them were alien and incomprehensible to their ears, as well as faintly ridiculous. The old man himself looked ridiculous, weak and overly serious, so that the assembled visitors could barely contain their laughter.

'*O Eros, invincible in strife*,' Lieutenant Nemiri thundered, throwing everyone's thoughts into disarray:

'*Eros, thou who hurlest disasters,*
Who in the soft cheeks

---

iii 'Hymn to Eros' in Sophocles's *Antigone.*

Of the maiden liest in ambush,
Who rosiest beyond the sea and rustic cottages
Neither any among the Immortals can escape thee,
Nor any of the short-lived mortals;
and whoever has thee is mad!'

'That's absolutely wonderful, wonderful!' a lady who was sat next to the Governor exclaimed.

Were the words fashioned by the era's great charismatic poet, Gabriele the Prophet, sufficient to explain their perplexed amazement? The presence the young lieutenant commanded had played a determining role. Unfamiliarity, and the blind fumbling around in the dark which had characterised the previous hours, had now given way, vanquished by the swell of emotions.

'*Behold me, O citizens of my native country*'

(Lieutenant Nemiri was reciting the poem only a couple of steps further down from the main group. He was so close that they could almost touch him; his capacity to play any role given to him was now defying verisimilitude. Like a ghost resurrecting old customs, the young man played the part of the young maiden.)

'*Entering upon the last journey,*
Looking at the splendor
Of the sun for the last time,
And hence forward never again!
Hades, who stills everything, conducts me
To the shore of Acheron alive
And deprived of marriage…'[iv]

[iv] Lines drawn from Gabriele D'Annunzio's play *Città Morta*, or *The Dead City*, Act 1, Scene 1. Gabriele D'Annunzio, G. Mantellini

Behind the archaeologist lay the hills and the immense necropolis which housed the area's only inhabitants. The graves were square black boxes, cavernous holes that looked like windows carved into the hillside.

They climbed their way up to Apollo's fountain. Water was dripping down from the rocks. The Princess of Cleve was immobile: she filled the hollow of her hand with water.

'What are you doing?' Colonel Ajello asked her.

'I want to see if it's fresh,' the Princess hurriedly answered.

Truth be told, she was petitioning the local gods. Apollo, the city's founder, had chanced upon this place when pursuing a nymph. Kyrene, *the mistress of the land*, as Pindar contents himself to say.

At the evening banquet, the Princess was sat with the Prefect to her right, who was trying to ensnare her in the web of his conversation, like a spider. She couldn't even keep up with him: all that administrative jargon, those snippets of gossip burrowing their way into reality like worms, all of that oppressed her. Instead she tried to listen to what the archaeologist was saying, but she could only grasp whatever he said in Greek. In order to help the Governor understand what he was saying, the old man would raise his voice whenever he uttered a word of Greek. Those words lingered in the air, like breadcrumbs marking out a magical road.

The Prefect's tactless speech was laying reality to waste. On the other hand, the guardian of that ancient city used reality to

---

(tr.), *The Dead City: A Tragedy* (Chicago: Laird & Lee, 1902), p.13-14.

help one pay attention, as though one were a neophyte searching for a hidden, invisible realm.

Lieutenant Nemiri's recitation in the amphitheatre had had the burning immediacy of a religious revelation. That celebration of Eros had been an externalization of his own feelings. The Princess was certain that nobody had understood the meaning of that ceremony. Nemiri was the object of desire, he was desire itself. A single person, and the intensity of their presence, can be a key to reality. The Prefect's words were ashes that reality was scattering around as it ran by, while Nemiri's presence sent reality up in flames.

'*You have for some time now developed a taste for solitude, which both shocks and worries me, because it comes between us.*'

The Prince's reproach had made her shudder. He was sat far away from her, but he was keeping his eyes on her. His words lay in the dark oblivion of her memory, until they suddenly resurfaced to assail her once more. She lingered immobile, as though attempting to hide, or conceal her tracks.

Yet the Prince never took his eyes off her.

The Princess left the hall. She hated that pretentious hotel, the wasteful marble, the columns, the arches, the dome, the giant staircase. Just like the previous day, time had flitted away on pointless chatter: it all felt like a game of cards that would never end.

A few pines, planted far from one another, just a few feet from the hotel. To the left, the incomparable ruins atop the mountain. Up ahead in the distance lay the terraces facing the sea.

The Princess descended the steps. She walked slowly, even though it seemed to her that each step was taking her very far away, as though she weren't wearing sandals, but seven-league boots.

Solitude already constituted a kind of distance.

She crossed the deserted square. She descended the steps that led to the woods. She sat in the shade. They couldn't see her from the hotel. That, too, was a kind of distance.

The ruins of the ancient Greek city were simply marvelous. The presence of the others had bothered and exhausted her. All emotions, when truly present, have to find an outlet in order to be expressed, or concealed. As was often the case, when beheld by our immediate consciousness, emotions tended to be laid to waste.

Lieutenant Nemiri's vitality earned him diffidence and libel just as in the same way it simultaneously earned him favour with others. It was said that a woman would compromise herself simply to speak to him; in truth, nobody eluded his grasp and the Governor had kept him on as his ordnance officer. Being everywhere at all times seemed to amount to a constant flight from anywhere specific.

The Princess was playing with a branch when she suddenly felt something pulling at its other end, as though a bird had grasped it in its beak. She raised her gaze, frightened. It was the Prince, the same sad restless bird he always was.

They entered the pine grove, walking alongside one another. A road that led to the port of Apollonia once passed through there. Half of the small commercial outpost had sunk into the sea centuries earlier due to an earthquake. One could admire the seaweed-covered ruins from atop a boat.

The port lay almost twenty miles from Cyrene, and the road that led there was on a steady decline and was pleasant to walk.

The tombs had been carved into the rock, on the hillsides facing the sea. They had eaten through those hills like termites through furniture. The square black entrances were windows into an invisible world.

The Prince sat beneath the portico of a tomb which mimicked the architecture of classical temples with moving humility. There was nothing except two columns, each slightly taller than a couple of feet. At the top, above the tympanum – a bunch of purple flowers. Its simplicity, even more than its venerable age – the tombs had been built in the 5th century AD – made that place a wellspring of time. The Princess sat in front of her husband; inside the tiny portico, they looked as though they were inside a carriage.

The impression she'd had after leaving the hotel – of having worn seven-league boots instead of sandals – came flooding back to her.

The dead were spying on them. Now that the sky had turned lilac, they had all come out into the open. They were an invisible public, and they formed a crowd around them.

The Princess recalled a popular fairy tale: It was said that the dead would throw themselves under the path of the living at night in order to be trampled on. Obviously, they don't suffer any pain. Yet they still want to feel the weight of something. Weight is one of the markers of living things they are most sensible to, and the one they have irremediably lost the most. Weight excited them more than colours, which really excited them, and even more than words and music.

The Princess experienced the admiration of those spectators as though she were an actress. There was an obvious connection between that necropolis, which took up more space than the city itself, and the city's four theatres. She knew they were grateful to her for having worn that dress with its cheerful patterns, and they were looking at her sandals and her little string of pearls. Their steps, the sound of their steps, must have been like a triumph.

The necropolis was the city's fifth, and most important, theatre.

The scene was silent, the Prince gazed into the distance, while those terraces were engulfed by the dark, one after the other. The Princess straightened her tiny bust, as though wanting to take a proper breath of air.

Acting, she thought, *means putting on those seven-league boots.*

They weren't more than a couple of hundred feet away from the hotel; it had been a specific, initiation-like journey, and now they stood on the slope of death itself. This was a place where one could come and look at life and gain perspective; it is for this precise reason that it is called the slope of death. A city which had honoured its dead in such a manner was necessarily loyal to the arts of the theatre.

The Prince and Princess had been embroidered against the backdrop of a temple that could have fit in the palm of their hands. The Princess decided that she would confess. It appeared as though she was being driven by a fatal strength, as she recited a text she'd nursed in her mind since the start.

'*I ask for your forgiveness a thousand times over*,' she said, '*if my feelings have upset you in any way. But I'll never offend you with actions.*'

The Prince (*so the wife loves someone else – and who was that? Who?*) leaned his back against the rock face. Having endured two thousand years, it was damp to the touch.

The play was growing ever more tiresome. He too wanted a tomb like that, by the sea. The only true interactions would be with the sea, the limpid sky, and the terraces on which lights and shadows undulated. Neither did he want to see any of the living – apart from the old archaeologist, with his loving hands and beautiful, mysterious verses, as well as the stories of ancient kings whose moves were governed by the sovereign mechanism of Fate.

The Princess nursed an acute sadness within her; yet she also exhibited the same determination as the Greek maiden whom Nemiri had evoked in the amphitheatre. The itinerary through the pine grove and then through the paths of the necropolis had made what had previously appeared impossible or unthinkable seem simple and easy. Amidst those clear, pure eyes lay in fact this certainty (and she would have wanted to confess this to her friend, the archaeologist, and entrust this certainty to the care of his delicate hands). Standing on the slope of death, (and here again the connection between the four theatres and the necropolis appeared obvious to her), the only true mistake one could make would be to lie.

'*Once upon a time I used to be very curious about the future*,' the Governor said, pushing back his chair and standing up, '*but I've been told so many lies and so many unlikely things… I convinced myself that one can never acquire any authentic knowledge*.'

The dinner guests stood up in a hurry. The Prefect's gaffe was irremediable; being a stranger to that court, he had no understanding of its secrets.

The Governor was omnipotent, and unlike the ones who had preceded him, he trusted and had sympathy for the country and land he had been sent to govern. His approach to reality was natural and immediate. Instead of being oppressed by his powerful role, he played into it with a beguiling and cocky display of bravado.

He had been foretold that he would die *by accident*. The most unlikely of circumstances given it would have been very difficult to kill him voluntarily. He had rejected the prophecy with a smug laugh, as though a horse had just neighed.

The Prefect never managed to strike a natural pose in the Governor's presence; instead, he looked like an embarrassed lover poiselessly offering up his devotion and, to capture his attention, the sinister products of his imagination. He had taken his cup of coffee and placed it before his wife's eyes so she could divine the contents of its slimy grinds. The Governor had immediately stood up and pushed back both his chair and the offer. He was horrified by prophecies – as if someone had just told him that the lord of this land was unpopular with the gods.

The assembled crowd dispersed.

Whenever he was reminded of that prophecy, the Governor felt pestered by the court and the guards. He dismissed everyone and went out onto the street by himself, as though he wanted to expose himself and defy fate; but fate was hiding in a mysterious place and would only come out at an unexpected moment. *You won't sleep where you like on the day that you die*, went an old snide, gloomy proverb he'd once overheard. Was his careless behaviour actually a case of him showing off his virile courage, or did it instead simply betray his desperation?

The solitary walk unfolded in the most tranquil of manners. He crossed paths with only a few people who greeted him respectfully: his subjects would protect him. He went back to the villa he'd had built for him in an unspoilt bay east of Cyrene, and shut himself in his room. Yet he didn't love solitude – it was a waste.

The Prince of Cleve was headed in the villa's direction. He turned around before reaching it. He always kept his head low whenever he walked. Not by chance, the pavement rocks had been laid haphazardly and he appeared to be adjusting his walk to tread exclusively on them, as though it were a test. The Governor despised the Prefect's servility, that bottomless desire of his to delight and entertain him; yet he also felt a kind of dissatisfaction if he felt excluded from someone's thoughts, his existential anxiety would gnaw away at him. Why did the Prince not look up at the window from which he watched him?

He recalled having seen the Prince and Princess an hour or so earlier as they headed in the same direction that the officer now took in the opposite direction, on his own. He descended the stairs and went out onto the street. Leaving, he dismissed all who offered to accompany him.

He furtively took the path that the Prince and Princess had taken earlier. The valley was so narrow that nobody could see him, and the path remained hidden. At the bottom of the valley, a clear stream flowed past the smooth white stones only to eventually spill into the Halfmoon, the deserted gulf he could admire from his white villa. It was the only stream around for thousands of miles. Long ago, the region was crisscrossed by mighty rivers, but now only the terrifying magnificence of their dry beds remained. Devoid of water they were now barren, as mysterious and *incomprehensible* as the archaeologist's verses.

The villa had been built on a ledge atop the mountain, where the valley opened into the gulf's pincers. It was the only building in the area, the only rocks which had been picked up and purposefully arranged. The ruins of the Greek city lay forty miles in the distance. Its presence made the Governor uneasy: he ruled over a colony where the natives had been exterminated, and he could not bear the physical reminder of other rulers and predecessors, and the tombs left behind to mark the vanity of power. Those dead were the priests of a cult which contradicted the reality he presided over.

A cursed day! The Princess was in the company of the old archaeologist. They were sat on a boulder which formed the northern boundary of a tiny lake, where the water was only a few feet deep, where the stream pooled before moving on. The Governor knew that lake well; it was tiny and narrow, like a funnel; he often leaped headfirst from atop that very boulder into the water, to swim above the smooth white stones.

The archaeologist was wearing shorts. His legs were scrawny and worn. It was an intolerably ugly image, which he chose to reveal instead of concealing, almost as though he was trying to show them off – the exact opposite of when a priest dons his sacred vestments – however, just like the Governor, he too appeared to belong to another order.

During the previous day's lunch, the Governor had noticed how the Princess had listened attentively to the archaeologist's words. At first, this had brought him pleasure: the archaeologist was a buffoon, and he was providing the court (of which she was the guest of honour) with entertainment. Yet he also just as easily noticed that the old man and the Princess appeared to have embarked on a secret voyage.

The Governor had no time for priests and their rites, and he nursed a hateful attitude towards the archaeologist as though the latter were conspiring to bring about his demise. He was a sorcerer, in possession of powers beyond the Governor's control, and which in fact actively worked against the Governor's authority. His archaeological science was nothing but a symbol of that power.

If the Governor had taken a leading role in the revolution of 1922 it had been because its celebration of youth and strength had seemed to place man at the center of the universe once again. He detested the occult, the invisible: youth and strength seemed to him the only realities that could confront constant collapse. Yet he had also been among the first to see through the ridiculous masquerade. He had travelled further along the path of revitalization: he loved prestige and success, and he worshipped the present, all of which swelled his frame. Against the black warp of his desperation, he weaved intricate, deceitful plots. He was horrified by death, by solitude, by silence, by secrets – old age seemed to him like a church, which came with wisdom and dangerous powers of the occult.

The colonial government was spending fabulous sums to facilitate archaeological research. He favoured this approach in order to encourage tourism, instead of purely relying on those deserted beaches. If he had been able to follow his instincts, he would have had the ancient city buried again, concealing all trace of its existence. An uncontaminated landscape filled him with a vital sense of the eternal present, the ruins created a temporal perspective that oppressed him.

The Princess finally stood up. Her gaze fell in his direction. The Governor hid behind an olive tree.

They had taken a path that would bring them in his vicinity. He would only have to advance a step or two, and hide at the top of the path, in order to swoop down to kill the archaeologist. The Governor's high place in society wasn't the only consideration keeping him from committing that violent act, nor was it pity. The old man certainly knew some terrible, evil secrets – he was an enchanter.

The archaeologist and the Princess passed him by, heading towards the villa. They had their backs to him now.

The Governor left his hiding place. Only then did he notice that the Princess was limping. Whenever she placed her left foot down, he would hesitate and then grimace as she tried to alleviate the weight on her aching foot. That rhythmical movement was as graceful as a dance. The Governor experienced a confused surge of pity and he ran down the path. He burst onto the scene like a bandit, being so big, formidable and excited. The Princess, frightened, took a step back, but the archaeologist didn't seem surprised in the slightest.

'May I offer you my arm?' the Governor brusquely asked.

The Princess slipped her arm through the Governor's. Her touch was so light that it certainly wasn't helping her keep any weight off her foot.

The archaeologist walked ahead, discreetly.

Guided by the archaeologist, the Governor felt that the procession carried an evil omen with it. Her slow pace was exasperating him. He felt as though he was imprisoned in an order, like when he was forced to pay the archaeological digs an official visit, so that the photographers who followed him everywhere could snap their pictures for propaganda purposes. While he was hidden amidst the trees, his presence had been charged with an unequivocal intensity; walking in the sorcerer's footsteps, while wearing vestments fitting for the ruler of that land, the Governor followed with the wounded Princess on his arm. They looked as though they were taking part in a rite.

Ever since the day that he had been told he would be killed by accident, he detected vanity and treachery in everything that was shown to him, in all the gifts that men and women and nature itself offered him. The days assumed the vain, deceitful and malleable shape of his death, a sort of itinerary, a calendar whose final date had already been set. Even the Princess's melancholic dance, light-footed and yet desperate, was a kind of death, an escape.

III

'War,' Colonel Verri said, gravely and ironically, 'we'll have it, there's no doubt about it, we'll have it.'

The officers had taken refuge in the kitchen. They had carefully ensured the door was shut.

'And we'll lose it!'

'Of course we're going to lose it. But we'll give them hell!' the Colonel retorted.

'For honour!' the Captain exclaimed, as though laying the winning card on the table.

'That too,' the Colonel cheerfully conceded, 'Honour means style. We don't have any weapons or any kind of organization; we have only our education to aid us in this brewing war. When we come face to face with our enemy, our actions won't be spurred by our means, which are modest. Our collective aim, our love of the motherland, would throw us into utter desperation in the face of so much confusion and so many lies: but here we have a chance to renew our individual valour, or better yet, our knightly valour, when a man measures himself up against a human ideal, rather than a collective pursuit.'

The Prince of Cleve lay stretched out on a bed, dying, two rooms away from the kitchen where the officers were located.

'You'll see how far we get, you'll see!'

The kitchen was the only place they could speak without being heard in that small house. There were many people there, and in such a restricted setting, they were pressed shoulder to shoulder.

'We're in for the long haul,' the Colonel declared, 'we'll give them hell! Do the English really think they can swat us away like flies? As if!'

The door swung open and the Princess appeared. All the officers stood to attention.

'Please, be seated.' The Princess only needed a little relief in the shade. The officers provided a comfortable arbor, their shadows provided her with shelter. She sat down at the table. All that white hair on the Colonel's head looked as though a painter had imprinted their bizarre signature upon it. There was something rather pathetically excessive to it, ridiculous perhaps, and yet consoling – that white hair brought the Princess some relief and the Colonel kindly consented, as though he were carrying her upon his back.

'We'll show the English what we're made of, yes we will,' the Colonel added, bitterly.

The future had arrived, and one could already hear it ringing. The Princess made a despairing gesture. The future! It too was atrocious, unbearable. She stretched her hand across the table. The Colonel hurriedly grabbed it and hid it in the palm of his.

Silence had spread its spider web. All was still, except the boiling coffee maker, the desperate lament of a beast everyone ignored.

The doorbell rang, incredibly loudly. Lieutenant Rossi hastened to open the door.

The officers were all on their feet, immobile. The Governor was barely able to squeeze through all the assembled men. The Princess concealed her hand in her lap, and lingered motionless. A smile so brightly white it was as though someone had shone a spotlight on it. She looked incredibly gracious, despite hiding her hand in her lap like a cat.

She stood up. She smoothed her skirt with her hand and then took a deep breath: the ceremony was about to begin. The Governor had come to greet his officer. There was no doubt that this greeting was like a Sacrament of Extreme Unction. The Princess gathered her strength, and led the procession.

The Governor's frame was so large that he looked like an eagle that had been stuffed into a small room. His face was almost six feet away from the Prince's. There was something limitless and hard-edged to his presence.

Diligent when it came to fulfilling his duties, he had come to take his leave from Cleve, and stifling his instincts, he carried himself with a paternal and vigorous calm.

The Prince had taken to dying with cool modesty. That motionless eagle a few feet from him was a theatrical conceit, a lavish kind of decoration, a shadow. The Prince refused to accept the mundane, sentimental comfort that the Governor had come to bring him, the pompous goodbye gesture from the Supreme Authority of the land.

At this juncture, the Governor, the mighty eagle that had filled the room with his presence, hung his head. Power and all Supreme Authorities are humbled before Death. This was also the reason behind Youth's humiliation (the four young lieutenants could barely stay still, they were worse than choirboys).

What did Colonel Verri's presence represent? His hair was white. And what about the two officers standing to the Governor's right, the ones nobody had seen before? Captain Sorrentino was as restless as a racehorse. He was a generous, violent and ironic man who had lost himself in the attempt to re-conciliate himself with the ungallant era into which he'd been parachuted. He kept the Prince's gaze with a kind of furor. Then, as though an executioner had just lopped his head off, he bent his neck into a deep bow.

Space in the room was restricted, and the assembled gentlemen's faces were bunched together, like on a canvas. The dark background gave the silence an aura of solemnity.

The efforts to save Cleve's life had been abandoned. The Governor's visit had only occurred on the condition that the doctor would be sent away. The ceremony in which Power, Youth, Strength, Courage, Wisdom and Order had been humiliated would have lacked any meaning if there had been any hopes of saving him. The presence of science itself would have been an attempt to mediate, and the religious solemnity of the scene would have been lost.

Colonel Verri ran a hand through the white river of his hair, as though trying to dry it.

The Princess took a step forward. Her features were closely guarded, secret. The Governor observed her. Would she drift into a monologue? She was so little and gracious and yet was always dealt a difficult role to play! The Governor would have gladly laid himself at her feet like a carpet, she was so delicate that he would do everything in his power to… the Governor put all his means into transforming himself into a beast – a loyal and ferocious dog.

'*I feel so close to death*,' the Prince said, '*that I don't want to see anything that might make me regret leaving life behind*.'

The Princess wrapped up her words again, crumpling up the page she would have wanted to place before her husband's eyes, the concluding act of that earlier confession, and her pleas for forgiveness. Her face, as tiny as a swallow's beak, was clean, and would be forever sealed. She left the place of honour, by the top of the bed, and resumed her seat to the Prince's right. The officers all took a step forward. Those faces coalesced into a gloomy, virile chorus that sang of blind melancholy – a lament for horns lost in the valley.

MILITARY MANEUVERS

'I don't know if I saw any ancient tombs on those mountains. Those tombs also belong to warriors, *condottieri* whose actions have been celebrated by history. They came from the East and their tombs mark their journey's exact itinerary. I retraced their steps in the opposite direction just six months ago. I had to stop at the colony's border, instead of retracing this mighty river to its source: the black stone of Arabia, the mecca of devout pilgrimages. Regretfully, I had to stop my journey far sooner than that. Yet I can't stop thinking about that long strip of tombs. On days like this, when I hear the general command shouting for war, I see yet another strip of tombs, superimposed on top of thousands of similar strips. The earth, for those who are not ignorant, like the general command, which insists on trampling on virgin lands, is a tangle of roads. Roads that have been travelled on by others before us, and which others will travel on after us.'

Dismantling the camp took up the entire day. General Desiderius Occhipinti didn't seem to be in a hurry to return to the city.

Atop the camel-hump of a hill, surrounded by a wall in utter disrepair, lay an arid cemetery, where the soldiers had thrown the remains of their peeled oranges. The General hopped over the wall, followed by Captain Valentini. The General approached a tomb, which resembled a sword blade, and using his hand he carefully wiped away the dust caked around the stone. He had knelt down on one knee. The tomb was bare and porous.

'I explored up and down the entire littoral in the past few days – there are few signs indicating our presence here and they are all superficial. The arid earth, the desert, and these useless shrubs: everything here contradicts our vision of the world, which, despite Fascisms' guise of idealism, remains positivist at heart. There is a profound harmony between the native's vision of their world and their natural surroundings. Our efforts, to borrow from our propaganda efforts, all go to waste in the midst of nature's solemn silence. This land doesn't want us here.'

The General stood up. Captain Valentini helped him up with his arm. The youthful Lieutenant Rossi was waiting for them at the bottom of the cemetery.

'What's your opinion on this, Captain? Will the English be the ones who turf us out of this colony, or will it be it the natural violence of this very land that chases us away? Last Saturday's sand storm, just before the maneuvers began, was truly frightening. One day I think we'll disappear in exactly the same manner: as though the earth had swallowed us up, or as though the winds had hurled us into the ocean. The colony is an artificial organism, and we are destined to die.'

COURTLINESS

Professor Favagalli's conference passed through the club's ballroom like a Corpus Domini procession in a cathedral: all expressions employed were *in costume*, whether historical or traditional. The Professor had been invited by the women's committee to celebrate the hundred and fiftieth anniversary of Alessandro Manzoni's birth.

'When we talk of words, we are talking merely of style,' Colonel Verri said.

'There's only one way out of all this, except silence of course,' Captain Sorrentino impatiently insisted, 'and that is through irony.'

The hall was crowded. At a glance, it looked as though the entire city had squeezed its way in, like a civic assembly. Why had General Occhipinti offered to play the role of King Desiderius? Professor Favagalli had announced, in the letter in which he had accepted the ladies' invitation, that his conference would be restricted to Manzoni's play, *Adelchi*; yet he had also requested, as though asking for a down payment, that four officers be present to voice the roles during the tragedy's final scene. General Desiderius Occhipinti was an introverted man. Yet all of a sudden, like a guilty man who consents to confessing his sins in public, here he was stepping onto a stage of his own free will.

Incapable of accepting the fact that some phenomena cannot be explained, Mrs Betti remarked that General Occhipinti had agreed to play the role of King Desiderius because they shared the same name: 'That coincidence must have sparked his idea.'

'But why did he accept?' Captain Sorrentino thundered. He was a restless officer and he couldn't stand it whenever someone cheapened an event by providing a mediocre explanation for it.

Professor Favagalli perfumed his sentences with the most pretentious words and colourful combinations. Nobody had ever seen such a waste of precious materials – or such excess – in that colonial city. Yet all that overabundance – like in a church filled to capacity where one then stubbornly attempts to exorcise *horror vacui* – actually came off as rather depressing. Manzoni's sentences allowed for few breathing spaces, like placid notes played on an organ. Captain Sorrentino, who was having a hushed conversation with Colonel Verri, as though ensconced in the secrecy of the confessional, automatically stopped speaking and began to listen. It was as though he was reluctantly and distractedly watching a funeral procession pass by.

Professor Favagalli's words flowed as warm as tears. He loved to recite passages from plays, but he lacked the talent for it. Phrases crumbled on his lips. He was drawn to the theatre, and he would endlessly speculate over betrayals and martyrdoms – but the era he lived in was averse to all forms of excess, and thus kept them out.

Nobody found the courage to clap when General Desiderius Occhipinti, Captain Valentini, Captain Landucci and Lieutenant Ross stepped onto the stage.

Professor Favagalli slinked off into the audience. The four officers were the royal carriage everyone had come to see, or maybe the *charrette des condamnés.*[v] The public eagerly awaited that reading as though an abdication or regicide were about to be announced.

General Desiderius Occhipinti's recitation immediately left everyone in the public both disconcerted and disappointed.

'*O, hand of God, How heavily*
have you descended on my ancient head!
In what condition do you return my son to me!
My son, my only glory, I am overcome,
And tremble to see you.'

The small handful of copies of Manzoni's *Adelchi* found in the city were passed around. The readers searched for the General's confession, where the last scene was stretched out. Their efforts bore no fruits: every single verse appeared to contain the key to the whole text, but all the possible interpretations cancelled one another out. They were now waiting for the actor to settle the matter.

Desiderius Occhipinti's transformation into a vanquished king, who wept over the loss of his kingdom as well as his son, fired up their imaginations. The examples of Ernesto Rossi and Tommaso Salvini[vi] were brought to mind. Dragging the impassive General into a delirious, Verdian conflict was the only means to compromise him and thus understand him, or better yet, it was the only means by which to defeat and kill him. That secretive man was planning an attack on the entire colony's happiness and

---

v French: 'cart of the condemned,' a cart used to transport condemned prisoners to the place of their execution.

vi 19th century Italian actors.

its self-satisfied serenity: one couldn't help but want to overcome his silence, as though it were an evil spell.

Occhipinti's reading was cool and collected. The desperation he voiced couldn't have been less immediate, his phrases were nothing but mere academic posturing, like a neo-classical frieze.

'*And now you will die,*
not as a king, but deserted, in the hands of your enemy,
without lamentations, except from your Father, and thrown
before a man who exults to hear them.'

Captain Landucci proffered his reply, in a completely unembarrassed manner. It appeared as though he had seen through the General's intentions on the spot: '*Old man, your sorrow deceives you. Pensive / And not exulting, I contemplate the fate of a valiant / Man and a king...*'

Made nervous by the long wait, the audience could barely conceal its bad mood. The way these officers were interpreting Manzoni's play, which had been transposed to the years of the Cisalpine Republic, seemed of little consequence. Yet having been assembled to hear a confession, they had instead been shown an inscrutable mask. This chaste and reserved recitation and the way words were spoken without explaining their meaning ultimately emptied them of any communicative value – as though they'd been speaking another language, even though it was still sprinkled with familiar sounds. The effect was labyrinthine: like starting upon a path to nowhere.

The authorities were perplexed. The General breathed in the air of conspiracy and often scanned his surroundings suspiciously. It was as though the actors were squandering the meaning of their lines. The Prefect, the supreme guarantor of law and order, could not comprehend any reality unless it was endlessly repeated to him. He abhorred anything that was new and mysterious as though they were fatal flaws.

'So, this is theatre then?' the Prefect asked Colonel Verri, who was sat to his left.

'I tend to find dialogue difficult to follow. Or rather tiresome,' the Colonel replied. The way the room itself had been decorated, with pictures and festoons, appeared to exclude the possibility of all dialogue. 'A grown man hardly ever puts up with listening to the sliminess behind most confessions.'

Nevertheless, their appeals fell on deaf ears, and the Prefect was used to the clear paradigms presented by order.

The public could no longer follow the recitation. Just like at the opera, they caught a few stray words here and there: *woeful... pity...never...hope...arm...place...*the kind of words made popular by nineteenth century librettists.

'*O father, I see you again! Come close.*
Touch the hand of your son!'

Instead of expressing love and resignation, Lieutenant Rossi's words unleashed a sort of violence. The General had pronounced King Desiderius's desperate words with a stiff upper lip. Rossi's vehemence was commensurate to the role. Instead of ending with a confession, the reading of the text was about to conclude in forgery.

'*It is dreadful / To see you like this*,'[vii] General Occhipinti said, in a detached manner.

[vii] Michael J. Curley (tr.), *Alessandro Manzoni, Two Plays* (Oxford: Peter Lang, 2002), pp.216, 217.

Colonel Verri observed the Prefect out of the corner of his eye.

'It's all wrong,' the other snapped, albeit taking care to protect himself from Mrs Spada's careful ear, who was sat to his right. 'Rossi just doesn't get it,' he added.

Mrs Spada gave a nod in agreement.

Professor Favagalli was extremely agitated. This performance contradicted all his instructions. Yet this was not the chief cause behind his feverish state: rather it was the gall with which those actors were turning everything to a lie – both Manzoni's intentions and the words they were voicing. He wouldn't have much minded if the pillars supporting the great hall they were in suddenly began to show cracks. Everything had fallen apart.

Rossi voiced Adelchi's lines, expressing anger and desperation.

'*Lament no more, / Father, no more, for God's sake / Was this not my time to die?*' The young man died, cursing: '*Rejoice at not being king, rejoice that every path…*'

'Do you hear that?' the Prefect exclaimed, horrified, 'this is a man who is cursing life!'

'He's certainly not going to Heaven,' Mrs Spada calmly replied, passing sentence. 'I see neither peace nor resignation in this man's soul. It's a gloomy death.'

'*If I lose you, / My son, who will console me for it*?' General Occhipinti asked. The young man was dying surrounded by three priests, who were as cold as statues, and who were furthermore confusing – or purporting to confuse – the youth's death rattle with a prayer.

'We no longer have any real aims except to fulfill our promise.' General Occhipinti said.

Captain Sorrentino raised his head in a jerk and called out: '*Call it not patience, Gaunt; it is despair*'[viii]

Once the performance was over, the club's assembled guests dispersed into its other rooms and gardens.

'Captain, do you think,' Desiderius Occhipinti asked Valentini, 'that we truly have a purpose in today's world, meaning do we have a real political-military role to play?'

'I think there isn't even much style left to it as it is,' Colonel Verri grumbled, 'The Napoleonic eagles felled by the soldiers of the Seventh Coalition were picked up by antiquarian dealers and lovingly restored. As the Empire becomes fashionable once again, the prices go up. Professor Favagalli, do you think we'll one day see the Fascist eagle lovingly stuffed in some lady's sitting room?'

Favagalli smiled awkwardly – banter was not his forte.

The vapid notes of a military march broke into the great hall. At the Berenice Cinema, five German girls had shattered the calm that reigned over the colonial city. The curtain-raiser's finale, which had involved those girls sitting in a papier-mâché train, wearing sexy military uniforms, had been an overwhelming success. Now one could hear that little tune everywhere, whether played on a piano or whistled by a soldier as he passed by. 'What a brothel rat,' a lady hissed, as though addressing the insult to a rival.

'An officer,' General Occhipinti said, 'is a courteous man. Our ethos no longer serves any political or practical function: it has become an absolute.'

'I, Captain Luigi Sorrentino,' the impetuous Captain proclaimed, 'find myself here in Africa to brave the adventures

---

viii From Shakespeare's *Richard II*, Act 1, Scene 2.

that Fascism strews across my path in order to test me, in order to allow me to know myself and realise my potential.'

It was as though he were suggesting a toast.

Turning his brightly-lit face to scan his surroundings, Favagalli ran into Captain Valentini's silence and was left dumbfounded by it. The man had a penchant for subtracting himself. 'When he doesn't know what to do,' Lieutenant Colonel Fontana said in a good-humoured fashion, 'he just takes himself out of the picture.' Yet Favagalli detected different intentions in that man. All that chatter, even if voiced far away from the Fascist authorities, could nonetheless (if maliciously referring to someone higher up) cause someone huge problems.

'Fascism is a world of wonders,' Verri pressed on, as if having divined Favagalli's suspicions, wanted to provoke him: 'in which the knight is presented with fabulous perils and encounters, which are artificially created and very large indeed. The trials which Fascism places in our path won't manage to bring down a giant like Albion, nor will it make our diet more curious – it is a path of gradual self-affirmation, and by walking it, we will fulfill our destiny. Fascism is the face of the present, whereas we try to resist with virtues from our remote past: honour, loyalty, mutual respect and gentle manners. In fact,' Verri concluded, whispering in Favagalli's ears, 'all you need to do to fight Fascism and overcome it is to be courteous.'

'If our social class doesn't wish to identify with Fascism, it will have to reject the entire narrative of our history and settle for the rigidity of the mask,' Fontana held forth.

Sorrentino broke into the restless circle.

'One day we'll recite Europe in the same way one recites lines from *The Trickster of Seville*[ix] or *A Month in the Country.*[x] The declarations of war will drop down like a curtain and there won't be anything left of our world. Our life here is regulated by the distant echo of mannerisms and traditions that went out of fashion decades ago in Europe.'

Verri looked at him. The Captain's fiery temperament amused him. 'Theatre,' he said, 'is an ironic form of communication. It is the only kind of confession befitting a grown man.'

'…Whom Fate has already torn from its book,' Captain Sorrentino cheerfully asserted, stamping the seal of that evening shut.

[ix] A play by Tirso de Molina.

[x] A play by Ivan Turgenev.

THE FORT AT RÉGIMA

Captain Valentini received the order to join the regiment stationed at the Fort of Régima, to the south of the city. 'Everything's missing in that fort,' his predecessor had warned him, 'not just danger or action, but there isn't even a reason for keeping a garrison there. Orders never reach you. You must look on the High Command the way one beholds a higher power. It's useless to ask for a sign or an explanation. The High Command won't remember you until it needs you to go somewhere, or want you to come back, that is if it remembers you're still out there.'

The Captain was nevertheless glad to go. His departure for that fort essentially presented itself as an opportunity to subtract himself from everything: General Occhipinti and the military parades, the Officers' Club, the speeches by the Secretary of the local Fascist party, the five German girls and their papier-mâché train at the Berenice Cinema and the evening walks alongside the main avenue…all would be swept away. *Solitude*, he reflected, *is the epitome of subtracting oneself from life and for this very reason it is blessed.*

The fort was situated on a hill. The brief walk one had to take to reach it was pleasant. The path was slightly uneven. Not a single tree in sight for over thirty miles. The fort, one part of which lay in complete abandon, had a medieval feel to it – a feature the original builders had probably wanted (first the Turks then the colonial government) and had decided to enhance it with pointless battlements. Yet time had worked its magic on those imitation battlements, and the inclemency of the elements had endowed the fort with a hard-edged, aristocratic sheen. More than Western medieval structures, it recalled the castles the knights had built in Greece during the Fourth Crusade. The landscape was identical. The Captain's armoured car tottered along a path strewn with stones. Sometimes it ventured into the open fields, where the ground was often more level than the path itself. Had I come on horseback, the journey might have been more comfortable. As with the celebrated Knight of La Mancha, he had many famous examples in mind: Anseau de Cayeux, Thierry de Tenremonde, Orry de Lisle, Guido di Conflans, Macario de Sainte Menehould, Bègue de Fransures, Conon de Béthume, Milon le Brèbant, Païen d'Orléans, Peter of Bracieux, Baldovino di Beauvoir, Hugues de Beaumetz, Gautier d'Escornai, Dreux de Beaurain…the Captain proved unable to stop thinking about the legacy of those knights. They had occupied Constantinople, made and unmade Emperors, and had divided the vast empire into feuds; they had scrambled hither and tither throughout the lengths of the Empire in the vain attempt of keeping alive a system, which, lacking any roots in that country, was ultimately fated to die.

All that remained was their fortresses, like the gigantic carcasses of vanquished animals. Nothing had linked those knights to anything that had come before them, and nothing survived their slaughter. The Empire had simply swatted them away, like flies.

As the Captain bounced around in his armoured car, it struck him that repeating the same sequence of events so many centuries later was both cruel and unbearable.

A SOLITARY DUEL

'Literature is reality's dress uniform,' Major Morelli's wife said, slipping her foot into a purple velvet shoe.

Reserved and aloof, as though on display in the shop windows, the ladies were selecting their footwear for the New Year's Eve Ball in Treni's, the cobbler. Mrs Occhipinti had a golden sandal in her hand.

The cobbler, a ridiculous and repugnant-looking little beast, was sat at Mrs Borletti's feet. He always struck a gracious pose, light as a pixie. These movements were his exaggerated way of recognizing how ridiculous he looked. There was something pathetic and heartrending in all that ostentatiousness. The ladies were nevertheless drawn to it, as they slipped their feet into the shoe held in his hands, cupped with sensual repugnance.

Mrs Borletti laughed. 'There's something death-like and funereal about literature…' she said, somewhat embarrassedly. 'Truth be told,' she added, lifting her index finger, 'the spirit freezes life in time. My dear,' she exclaimed, leaning her upper body forward, 'aren't you feeling well?'

'I'm fine, I'm fine,' Mrs Occhipinti calmly replied, raising her hand. She hated compassion. She had spent two months in the hospital; she had been released against her doctors' wishes so she could celebrate Christmas and New Year's Eve with her husband, the General of the Army Corps, Desiderius Occhipinti.

The hospital's head physician had stammered when he'd told the General: 'I refuse any and all responsibility…' Occhipinti had shot him a cold stare. Then he had given his arm to his wife, and as though he could barely notice the pitiful effort it took her to walk, he had left alongside her. The General's orderly, standing to attention out on the street while holding the car door open, was filled with terror at the sight of that woman as she walked along in tiny, mechanical jerks.

'Are you sure you don't need anything, darling? Maybe you're tired?' The General asked.

Mrs Occhipinti thrust her leg forward, as though kicking away her friend's pitiful voice, or wanting to prove her strength. The sandal flew off her foot and landed in a corner.

Lieutenant Mazzei appeared in the shop window's frame, looking as though he wanted to smash it and step inside.

A couple of days later, during the Christmas dinner held at the Prefect's house, the guests paid particular attention to her. Mrs Occhipinti remained impassive and her sentences were cold and curt.

The Prefect's wife had welcomed Mrs Occhipinti with the most unrestrained and intense pity imaginable – as though in a romantic novel, it was to be the highlight of the day. Yet she had been rudely refused. Mrs Occhipinti was a dark guest: aggressive and hard-edged, she had not come to put her agony on display, but rather her strength. The Prefect's wife was convinced that Mrs Occhipinti's illness was merely her just punishment for her sins. Thus, her strength – a blatant display of pride and presumptuousness –

struck the Prefect's wife as completely sacrilegious. *Our house has been profaned*, she thought to herself, alarmed.

General Occhipinti hadn't kept track of his wife's mistakes. He refused to connect her mistakes to her illness, or to think of her condition as a form of punishment, like the Prefect's wife did. In the same manner, he also allowed her to suffer while he sat next to her, silent. Only his behaviour had been normal when he'd accompanied his wife out of the hospital, or taken her to the Prefect's house for dinner, free of all bother and orotundity. It appeared as though he knew nothing of the devils looking to waylay his wife on her path.

The Prefect, who perceived the General as enigmatic, had once asked him why he'd opted for a career in the military. 'Because it's the only way of life that is scientifically precise.'

He abhorred confiding in people, as though doing so would violate a rule.

The halls of the Officers' Club were brightly lit and empty. They would remain open until four in the morning.

The Cathedral was crowded with people. The Bishop had already made his entrance, having been preceded by his priests. Having descended from his palace and crossed the square, the Bishop had entered through the large gates. All in black, and lined up in serried ranks, the nuns sang choir.

The officers were wearing their dress uniforms.

'His Majesty doesn't speak,' Captain Sorrentino said. 'We would just need a nod of his head to sweep Fascism away like dust.' He took in the club's hall, crossing it in great strides. He was irritated and restless. 'Well, what's stopping him?'

'He would certainly prefer a more cautious kind of Fascism,' Colonel Verri said, having a penchant for indulging the Captain's temperament, 'and an even falser and more hypocritical one too while we're at it. In other words,' he added with a smile, 'one that is both more civic and cynical. But maybe he's worried that any attempt to perfect it will ultimately weaken it, and make it incapable of withstanding an opponent's blows.'

'Why doesn't the army take the initiative? If the King is unable to lead us, he will at least follow us.'

'Alas, my dear friend, don't fill your head with too many delusions. Nobody's going to make a move. We have compromised ourselves too much already. The declaration of war is like a messenger who can no longer be stopped. We'll fight that war, for better or worse! Then, one after the other, the king and his subjects, the army and the fascist dissidents will start to make their move. Or maybe it will happen the other way around, meaning everyone will show up late! By that time, we'll probably be able to prove that we had never wanted the war in the first place.'

'But why are we just accepting all of this? Why?' The Captain's irritation was sharply in relief, and the Colonel observed him indulgently. He was a man at his peak who was hesitant to squander his energies in a time of mediocrity. This contradiction held the key to his destiny.

Captain Sorrentino stopped in the middle of the hall. 'Our only hope then is for Mussolini to come back to his senses and stop before he falls over the precipice and just sends us home.'

The Colonel smiled. 'Opinions!' he said cheerfully. 'Because it might turn out to be the worst solution, prolonging slavery for an indeterminate amount of time. Our lives grow ever more inward and empty. If he pulls back from this abyss, the Duce might assume greater powers for himself. We'll owe him for that too, for defending us from Fascism's fatal outcome.'

'So we don't have a choice!' the Captain exclaimed in an excessively cheerful manner.

'You're wrong there,' the Colonel retorted, 'if we manage to save our skins, then we'll have saved everything. There are always plausible reasons for coming to terms with one's past. If in the end we don't come to war, we'll keep living as we are now forever: the king, his subjects, the army and the fascist dissidents. There's an empty void inside me and I don't know how I'll ever fill it. I don't expect anything out of war. But if I have to survive it, I don't want the price to be an apology! If they are willing to forgive my sins, then I won't bother them with my explanations and justifications. Maybe I just don't love life enough – trials and explanations strike me as utterly ridiculous.'

'This Christmas mass has been going on for ages,' Captain Sorrentino said, returning to his seat. He didn't feel like singing hymns anymore.

'The Christmas mass and the military review to mark the anniversary of the Charter, the ball in the Governor's palace and the great maneuvers: without these spectacles, life here would become unbearable. Mussolini keeps us entertained as though we were courtesans.'

'Go on, I said, I don't need anything.'

The voice hailed from beyond the tomb. Colonel Verri and Captain Sorrentino jumped to their feet. They were barely able to nod their heads to the General of the Army Corps Desiderius

Occhipinti, who was on his way out. His wife lay seated in a corner of the sitting room. The dinner at the Prefect's house had been a challenging trial. The tension caused by the people around her was consuming her.

Colonel Verri crossed the sitting room. He bowed. Captain Sorrentino stood next to him, lingering impassively like a guard. The General's wife observed them without moving. She then extended her arm so that the Colonel could hold it devotedly in his to plant a kiss on it.

The General's wife hadn't left the hospital in order to be pitied, as some of the Prefect's wife's guests suspected, but merely to be able to watch and listen, so that life could start flowing freely before her eyes once again, instead of going around in circles at the hospital.

The Colonel took a seat next to the General's wife. Here they were: Counsel and Strength, the two last loyal men. The General's wife eyed one, then the other, as though probing them.

The sitting room's emptiness was as heavy as sleep. The General's wife felt like giving in to it. The compassionate attention the Prefect's guests paid her had nevertheless irritated her and thus reawakened her strength. The chatter at the Officers' Club was a spider-web, and it wasn't strong enough to keep her for long.

She suddenly dropped her neck, like a swaying drunk. The Colonel smiled kindly at her, and interpreting that nod as a sign, he turned to his friend and said:

'To tell the truth, my dear Captain, we are unable to overcome the *petty religious root of our problem*. From a social point of view, it's a mistake. Few among us are in fact citizens. The army is a mystical body. Hierarchy aside, the exceptional importance we give to form and following the rules imply faith as well as a *common faith*, which we nonetheless lack.'

The General's wife's eyes grew wide. She had grasped the last sentence, like an image caught immediately after waking up, and she had mulled on it without managing to penetrate its meaning. She felt such an intense and unbearable solitude that a cry almost escaped her lips. She pressed a handkerchief against her mouth. Silence! Silence!

The Captain looked at her admiringly.

'Among the most passionate of us, opposites become interchangeable,' the Colonel said, 'dread and restlessness for war, execration and indifference towards fascism, the anxiety for a renaissance and the certainty of not being up to its task. Even if *good* manages to triumph, meaning that the righteous win (or at least the ones closest to righteousness), can such an outcome change destiny and allow me to reconcile myself to life? I am dutiful when it comes to my work, just like others are. But it's nothing but pride – or just an easy solution. In this confused war, many of us will serve with great dignity, and perhaps even with heroism when the occasion calls for it. But what will all this praiseworthy behaviour really mean? Selfishness is foreign to a religious soul. I shall calmly trust what my superior officers tell me. What others will go looking for when we begin to move towards the enemy, I don't know. But look they will.'

The sitting room was deserted. The stuccoes on the ceiling and walls had a sepulchral magnificence to them. All in all, the room's decoration was of a funereal character, and exaggeratedly consoling.

'What will humanity's fate be, then?' The Captain asked. He nevertheless lacked the earlier spring in his step. The appearance of the General's wife had left him distracted. Was all that agony – the General's wife clung to her willpower as though it were a sword – noble or sacrilegious? What sense was there to all that effort?

'War is a game to change the way the world is ordered,' the Colonel insisted, 'but neither camp is capable of reconquering my faith in life. The impulse to commit suicide springs from an inability to hold a dialogue with the events of the world around us. *Self-awareness* is a prison into which we threw ourselves while waiting (or looking) for a purpose. This is as far as our education allows us to go.'

'What fruitless effort!' Captain Sorrentino angrily exclaimed, coming to a stop smack in the middle of the room. The General's wife was motionless. The Captain looked at that silvery face: he watched it float against the wall like the moon in a limpid sky. 'We should instead seek to reach a positive solution, one azure enough to spread around the entire world.'

The General's wife smiled with joy. That word – azure – had stirred her.

The Captain crossed the room with only a few steps. 'I'm going to tell you a story,' he announced.

'This,' he said, laying the palm of his hand on the table in front of him, 'is the Fortress.'

He showed her. 'It's an orderly and isolated complex,' he explained.

The General's wife listened attentively. His words seemed clear enough to her. That clarity already heralded the aforementioned azure. The Captain didn't bandy on about what that Order might be, it wasn't necessary. The story would have the brevity of dreams, and share their burning immediacy.

'Opposing the Fortress, is our Hero.' The Captain took two paces to his right, and looking inexplicably youthful, he bowed before his public. Then, standing erect, he headed towards the little table.

'A conflict is born when a hero can no longer endure his isolation, and the repugnance he feels for the intangibility of Order. Owing to its isolation and immobility, the Fortress stands outside of time and experience.'

The Captain walked around the table three times while keeping his eyes fixed on it. With each turn, he bent his knees a little further. Then suddenly, he stood up to his full height and turned on his heels.

'The young man escapes!' he took a couple of steps away, approaching his spectators and thus subtracting himself from their gaze. The table had been left behind in the middle of the room.

'The people of the Fortress refuse to take note of this flight and feign ignorance, but time and experience seep through and infiltrate the gaps left by the Hero's escape.'

'That departure was a wound,' the Colonel burst out.

The General's wife was following the story very attentively.

'But the young man,' the Captain resumed, stepping back on the scene as though having just returned from a trip around the world and had wound up at the starting point again, 'comes back and stays. The opening created by his departure is plugged up by his return. The Fortress welcomes the young man as though it had just emerged from an illness, or freed itself from the germs of an infection, and recovers its initial harmony. Life in the Fortress carries on, in a repetitive circular motion, including: the addition of another young man.'

The image of the circle pleased the General's wife. The present was only the darkest hour of the night. But azure was a path. She smiled cheerfully once again. Growing calmer, she nodded: the Captain was free to continue.

Sorrentino launched into it again, yet this time in a threatening tone, and laying his palm on the table again, he said: 'The Fortress has been besieged.' At which point he accosted the spectators to explain. 'This time it has nothing to do with germs of an infection, or an illness of the organism, or rather one of its cells (the Hero): it's an external force.'

With soldier-like, booming steps, the Captain advanced towards the Fortress. Once he'd arrived in front of the table, he suddenly turned around. His features were tense. 'The young man defends the Fortress with incredible doggedness.'

The tension in his features left no doubt as to the young man's determination.

Then, loosening his arms, which had previously lain still, he added: 'All one needs to notice in this edifying turn is the young man's exaggerated effort, which is vaguely ambiguous, and his careful violence when faced with the enemy; it is so different from the cold, calculating and impersonal determination of the others.'

The Captain repeated the same movement many times over: he would spin around halfway and then stop and show only his face. Another half turn and another stop. Both spins were so similar that in the end, partly owing to the speed of his movements, they came to resemble one another.

'The external force, the only external force, appears to coincide with death: and as it happens the young man is killed. His heroic behaviour shares the same enthusiasm as the moment of escape. When that journey has failed, especially as an experience meant to renew the Order of things, death appears as the only force, or reality – and *place* – that is foreign to the Fortress. From the enthusiasm of the journey, and optimism, to the pessimistic heroism of the final battle, polluted by romantic leaps and moody suicides.'

'Very good,' the Colonel said, smiling indulgently, 'that's exactly what I meant to say: you never know what the Hero is looking for when he moves towards the enemy.'

The General's wife looked at the Captain with her icy eyes, she could barely even move them anymore, like a puppet whose strings have all snapped. She nevertheless kept her head straight and her eyelids open.

Once they had left the Cathedral, the officers poured into the club. The ballroom was still empty, and people milled around in the large entrance hall.

The young lieutenant Mazzei crossed the ballroom. For a moment more, he lingered like a lost messenger in a crowd. Behaving as one who reaches the end of a road, he went to stand before the General's wife and there came to a stop.

After a dramatic silence, he directed his eyes towards hers, which looked away.

The eye staring straight ahead allowed her to see what she was about to lose forever – youth, beauty and life – the other eye remained enigmatic. She had used up all her strength on the eye looking straight ahead without bringing the other eye in line with it. She made a supreme effort to keep them firmly fixed in the direction of Lieutenant Mazzei's eyes – maybe this was the solution to all enigmas.

The public flowed towards the ballroom, where a banquet had been laid out.

Now that he had been left alone in the oblong hall adjacent to the main ballroom, Captain Sorrentino crossed it in a pacey manner. Surly and incredibly highly-strung, he had finally found an outlet in the parody of that tragedy.

'I am convinced that Fascism is unequal to tragedy! And it is frightening, frightening! Not only is nobody making a move here, but even the Great Powers aren't moving.'

'We do not have a destiny,' he added, disdainfully.

'What a great bargain, eh?' the Colonel muttered.

'Without Nazism, Fascism wouldn't be able to bring us closer to tragedy. It's nothing but a minor, mediocre scandal. Without the Nazis, we'll be forced to side with the powers of democracy against the Soviets. And if the Nazis are defeated, the Fascist remnants will be incorporated by the democratic powers in their struggle against communism. Nazism is the barrier holding back the tide of that disgrace. We the oppressed will never rebel against the regime, neither will the latter ever exceed the colonial confines of its misdeeds and boldness, nor will our friends make war upon us, since it would be seen as unforgivably impatient to waste any soldiers' lives in our national comedy, which is so provincial – Hitler will declare war and it will be fought against him. *That* is a scandal, but Fascism isn't. At least it isn't considered a scandal by our collective conscience, which is so accommodating, nor is it deemed so by those well-disposed towards the compromise made by the democratic powers. Hitler has overstepped, and the fire has been lit. Our neighbour's house is about to go up in flames, and we'll wind up burned alongside him. Deceived by the nature of that fire, we drew close to it in order to conveniently warm ourselves up, but by the time we'll want to leave it'll be too late. In other words, we'll suffer the same fate as that of a stupid servant who is in thrall to a diabolical master. Only when our entire house has gone up in flames will we be able to rediscover ourselves. Even the king, who binds us all together via that solemn oath of loyalty, will manage to do this.'

General Occhipinti appeared on the scene. 'Darling, do you want to come into the next room? A service is being held by the Christmas tree.'

He offered her his arm. The General's wife concentrated all her energies on that spot. Her hands stirred on the armrests, and blood slowly flowed through her whole body again. She looked like a snake exerting itself. Yet she stood up, and took her husband's arm. She crossed the sitting room and entered the ballroom.

A few chairs had been positioned right in front of the orchestra. In the middle lay a gigantic Christmas tree. Slivers of silver foil hung from its branches. The General's wife sat down. She was alert and felt that she was being watched, just like at the Prefect's house. The presence of people gave her strength – and gnawed at her. She composed her features into a smile.

In order to make the Christmas tree stand out even further, the ballroom's lighting had been arranged in an unusual manner.

Almost all of the available light shone on the tree and the few guests of honour. The other guests were nothing more than an iridescent dust cloud of jewels and decorations. The stuccoes appeared to be hanging like festoons off the azure strip running alongside all the walls. The orchestra, which was only composed of string instruments, played a slow, melancholic melody, yet did so discreetly in order not to disturb the mysterious, nocturnal harmony. There was a strong visual character to the service, while the music was instead merely secondary, complementary. Yet the General's wife nevertheless listened to it attentively.

A male voice rang out clear, filling the room and dominating the sweet sounds of the string instruments. The General's wife felt she was hanging by that thread. There was no doubt that this service aimed to bring her in the direction of that divergent eye, to the blue spot that the latter was pointing to. Her composed smile dissolved into cheerfulness. 'Aren't you feeling well, darling?' The General asked, bending down towards her.

> '.......................*sparget sonum*
> ....
> ....*ante thronum*
> ....*et natura*'[xi]

The General's wife was hanging by the thread of that hymn.

To the right, the young officers were lined up like priests. The General's wife's gaze examined them one after the other. It seemed to her as though she was moving, carried along on a stretcher towards the destination which her sight had denied

---

xi Excerpts from the Latin Christian hymn, *Dies Irae*, or *Day of Wrath*.

her, but which her ears had already found. The General, who was now sat beside her, waited for an answer. The General's wife replied with a nod. She feared being distracted, and the service required all her powers of concentration. She kept her arms along the chair's armrests, and followed the slow, musical rhythm of the priests' footsteps. She looked to the left, at the officers and the ladies. The dress uniforms and all that impeccable grooming charged the scene with tension. The General's wife straightened her bust. She dominated the scene with her head.

The General's wife was hanging by the thread of the singer's voice. She barely caught a few words. Maybe she distorted them or misinterpreted them, since she alone heard other words being sung. All of a sudden, making a convulsive gesture, she recognised that hymn, which they were trying to pass off as a sweet, innocent Christmas song.

'*Judex ergo cum sedebit*
Quidquid latet apparebit…'

The procession came to a sudden stop, the line of young priests broke up, while the officers and ladies on the right took a step back, frightened.

The singer took a single step forward on the stage and the General's wife was filled with terror when she recognised Lieutenant Mazzei's divergent eyes. She kept her lids forcefully open. There could no longer be any doubts: that young man was her death.

'Do you want to leave, darling?'

Here was the warrior who had come from afar, the Guest calling out for her, for whom 'the use of darling and excuses' were worth nothing at all. The doors swung open, and the Fortress' inhabitants held their breath.

Victory belonged to the other. The fatal duel – the General's wife nursed no doubts as to the final outcome – thus boiled down to an attitude problem. When it came to duels between knights, reason and outcome had no bearing, but one's attitude, which equaled one's honour, did have bearing. One could move against the enemy with the kind of loving leap that Captain Sorrentino had described. Or one could oppose the cold light of self-awareness, and push the limits of life to the extreme.

The azure point, the supernatural, is merely death – a door which opens only to reveal nothing, a loss which doesn't match up with any purchases. How does one enter through that door?

A lover's tremour, a prisoner's dignity…

A warrior clutching a sword stands by the door.

The General's wife straightened her bust, kept her head level and her eyelids open. The procession of priests reassembled itself. Then it began to move.

The lifeless body of the General's wife was carried out. The General dismissed those friends who had offered to accompany him.

Colonel Verri and Captain Sorrentino were sat on the last empty chairs. 'Mazzei disappeared,' the Captain said. The Colonel smiled. 'I can't think of anything more irritating than this music,' the Captain remarked, irked. 'I was in the other room when Mazzei started to sing. He took my breath away, and now we're listening to this garbage again!'

'Oh yes,' the Colonel replied, 'but did you notice the damage those musical notes inflicted? They cost The General's wife her life!'

'So let's re-immerse ourselves in this garbage then,' the Captain said, scanning his surroundings. 'At least it won't cost anyone their life.'

Vexed, the Captain stood up and left.

JUNE 1940

If war can bring one to suicide, it can also replace it, Lieutenant Cossa soberly commented, folding up the newspaper announcing the death of a great writer. The thought that war was a kind of solution in its own way had crossed his mind several times. Although he nursed a horror of war, he had nevertheless been surprised to have often desired it: *in order to drown myself in it, like that great writer did in the river.*

Stepping out, he happily breathed in the evening's mild air. He felt in the highest of spirits. One could even say that he was on affectionate terms with the notion of suicide, he even called it his secret friend. This was why the thoughts which had crossed his mind in the wake of the writer's death hadn't unsettled him at all. He hardly ever betrayed the melancholy that guided his thoughts when it came to his public discourses. Even though he struck most as cordial, he was incredibly reserved, and despite his melancholy, he was perceived as cheerful.

The Fatherland, for which he had donned his army uniform, certainly animated him. Despite his ability to have himself recalled back to Rome, he had passively allowed himself to be assigned to the African Army: once the conflict finally erupted, he would be sent to the front lines, ready to sacrifice himself. Not that this future sacrifice warmed his heart, or rather, since he could not say he was truly indifferent, it warmed his heart but in completely the opposite manner: instead of rekindling his love for life, it had brought him a step closer to suicide. He was only capable of feeling certain emotions when his mind was on this particular track.

What a strange fellow that Pietro is, he thought to himself on entering Major Brivio's house, *sometimes he strikes me as stupid in such a way that I don't know whether he amuses me or irritates me; other times I pity him intensely and he makes me feel uncomfortable, blackens my mood, so why do they keep him on in that house?*

In the meanwhile, Pietro ushered him into the sitting room and then withdrew.

'I don't know if you realise this, Eugenio, but you always show up late. Do you think it makes you look more interesting or desirable? Or is it some other silly reason? Maybe you just don't want to come here anymore… so why do you show up regardless? Come on, I want to introduce you to Colonel Boninsea's wife, you'll see what a cretin she is! My dear Colonel's wife…' he loudly called out, employing a formal tone, 'May I present Eugenio Cossa, and if one is to believe all my female friends, the most brilliant officer in the entire army!'

'Enio,' he hurriedly added in that curt, almost irked tone with which he had greeted him, 'I'll leave you here on your own as I have to tend to the others, I'll see you again later.'

He seemed to want to embarrass me, Cossa thought as he took a seat next to the Colonel's wife, *but I felt he quickly lost interest in it. He's running away from an explanation – he too! – because soon we'll be moving into such a void that it'll make our hearts skip a beat, the emptiness of our feelings, of our actions, fake jealousy and an insincere explanation. This was why he cut his speech short and dropped in this 'cretin's' lap.* As for the Colonel's wife, employing the calm of one who is about to enter a long conversation, she began asking him a series of questions.

'So, do you like Africa?'

How I love those questions! Cossa energetically wondered, *how they let us sleep so comfortably at night, now we can sail for a couple of hours down this conventional canal of conversation, without needing to give it neither sense nor direction, since they are dead-end conversations. Nor do we have to worry about making any effort since the tide will carry us along.*

The Colonel's wife talked about the city, which she didn't like very much.

Yet the bare landscape surrounding that city exerted a great fascination on her, the Greek and Roman ruins were simply superb, while the Libyan littoral was far more unspoiled than the Riviera. Nevertheless, much was missing, there wasn't much entertainment to be had, and since this conversation had provided her with the perfect platform from which to voice an invitation she had prepared herself to make since they had been introduced, she asked: 'Would you be free to dine with us next Saturday?'

'Ursula and the Major will also be joining us,' she quickly added, acting like someone who had fired a first shot, but being unaware of its effect, then fired another for good measure.

See? Cossa thought to himself as energetically as before, *she too wants to host a young officer at her house, and since Ursula told her that I was the most brilliant officer in the whole of Africa, she picked me.*

However, isn't it probably our fault? We shut all the windows and then moan about suffocating to death. We throw our interlocutors in the conventional canal of conversation and then weep when we see him drown. The poor Colonel's wife had just arrived in that city, and she would have had a tough time finding somebody ready to hazard even a few words of conversation in that living room. *We all want to live, with a finger firmly planted in risk, and one's feet firmly rooted on the mainland, with those formidable roots we call habit, wariness and laziness! But what should I do about it? What should I have done?* Even before he had set foot in the Major's house, he had known that Ursula's unenthusiastic reception probably awaited him – at which point, after this, that and the other, he would embark on a conversation that would sail along the coast of Africa, and all the Greek and Roman ruins, and the city's surrounding countryside, before sailing into the bay of boredom and other distractions. *Did I show up late precisely because I knew exactly what lay in store for me? And isn't this exactly what I'm going to get today, tomorrow and forever after?* Once again, adopting conventions seemed to him the only way out: *I must go back to being the brilliant officer they say I am. In fact, I need to be brilliant within the confines of this conversation's prison, I should make up some fact about the Greek and Roman ruins that nobody has ever heard before, something new, but it nonetheless should be something that doesn't try to exceed the limits of that prison, it's important that I play the game and show off some wit. There's no other alternative: there is only suicide and conversation. I reproach myself for all this sentimentality, and yet I find the Colonel's wife is braver and more coherent.* For her part, the Colonel's wife was now asking him to tell her more about ancient Greek civilization ('Only the Greeks,' she said, 'because despite all my respect for the Romans and for Fascists, I think Greek art is simply superior to Roman art.'), expressing her surprise at having found such enormous and well-kept Greek ruins in Africa, where she had instead believed the Greeks had never been.

Cossa replied to her question in an offhand manner and reverted the talk back to the city, the Officers' Club and the various entertainments on hand.

The Colonel's wife had been waiting for exactly this kind of encouragement, and like the navigators who once circumnavigated the Cape of Good Hope in order to reach the Red Sea, she loosened up in order to speak of trite things, she unfurled the sails of a long conversation, using Africa as a metaphor to talk about herself, her life and her principles.

Cossa slept, his cheek resting against the warm, soft pillow of the Colonel's wife's conversation. He dreamed of a third kind of life, one situated between suicide and conventional life, between the river where the great writer had drowned herself and the conventional canal of the Colonel's wife's conversation. He dreamed of finding a free country there, where man could be himself, allowing him to actually live his freedom rather than be forced to suppress it with suicide or stifle it in conversation; a country where one is capable of putting up with risks and adventure because risk and adventure are no longer a one-way road to either resignation or convention. *A place where I won't sleep and dream as I do now, but where I can talk, risk and maybe even die, but where I won't kill myself, or think about killing myself, or think about all there is left to do while I await the moment to become the most brilliant conformist in the whole of Africa.* In the meanwhile, the Colonel's wife stagnated in a conversation woven by personal reflections, a few sighs, a little nostalgia, some pride, regrets, a great deal of severity and the unstoppable desire to give up – all that baggage, all the contradictions that result in the shipwreck that occurs when people turn fifty. Yet the Lieutenant was the one who was truly shipwrecked, even his lover looked at him amused. *My poor Enio, maybe I was a tad too cruel in offering him up to the Colonel's wife as a snack. But she's my guest of honour and isn't Enio the most beautiful gift to offer a woman who is anxiously searching for the ultimate adventure? She'll even go as far as to lick the shadows and footprints Enio will leave behind on her carpets. At that age, one easily becomes as demoralised as that.*

'And you won't forget to come by on Saturday?' the Colonel's wife insisted.

Why is she asking me that again, Cossa asked himself, *didn't I already show great pleasure when telling her that I would go to her house? Does she desire my presence so much that she is willing to compromise herself over it? Can someone conquer their freedom at fifty?*

His eyes widened with surprise and he looked like he had just woken up. Yet in doing so his eyes appeared even warmer, and the Colonel's wife passionately dove into them. *Oh life*, Cossa thought, *how marvellous it must be at fifty! Oh youth*, the Colonel's wife thought, *how beautiful it is!*

They danced a single waltz, at the end of which, Cossa bowed and took his leave.

The Colonel's wife saw him step out onto the balcony, lean against the railing, and stare into the distance. *How romantic he looks!* she thought, *Speaking with him was the first time I've had any love for this land where they stranded us. I hadn't talked so passionately in a long time, and though much of it was wasted on futile, banal things, it still made my heart sing. And he listened, I'm sure he didn't miss a single word, but while he listens and dreams, he nevertheless grasps what someone is trying to tell him. The next couple of days will seem so unbearably long ... will he really show up on Saturday or will he forget?*

The Colonel's wife saw Pietro, the Major's handsome adjutant, draw near to Cossa carrying a tray topped by some trembling glasses: the Colonel's wife kept her eyes peeled. Cossa selected a cognac. *On Saturday he'll come to my house and drink the finest cognac there is to have in Africa; despite Mussolini's righteous campaign against importing foreign goods, I'll be able to offer him some Courvoisier, even if I have to put up with the entirety of the army criticizing me*. While she thought all this, she scanned her surroundings with a fiery glare.

In the meanwhile, Cossa was agonizing over the dinner invitation on Saturday night. *Do I really have to go?* He detested extravagant attitudes, although he liked being sociable and fulfilling his obligations, thus ensuring that people wouldn't become overly curious towards him and he could therefore preserve his freedom. In fact, those very people tended to envy him: because they found him too easygoing, too happy, and too fortunate. *I am who they would like to be, and thus if their envy sharpens, their curiosity becomes dormant. Nobody suspects that affectionate friend who accompanies me to the club, or around the barracks, who even makes me yearn for war. Nevertheless, the misunderstanding must persist. To find this sort of courage, instead of trying to slip out of the shell of one's solitude like the Colonel's wife did tonight.* While he thought about how he had to keep up appearances at all costs, Pietro came to tell him that the lady of the house was looking for him. Cossa smiled. He knew all about Ursula's overindulgences. Ursula also obliged her husband's adjutant to attend the tea parties she held for her friends, not only so he could help her serve said tea, but also so as to then leave him standing in a corner, even when he wasn't needed. Ursula would offer her friends tea and biscuits alongside Pietro's beauty, which the assembled ladies were free to admire while they nibbled on their biscuits and sipped from their cups. Pietro was exceptionally handsome, and one would have had to have eyes made of stone not to see that. Nevertheless, it had taken Ursula's genius and penchant for overindulging herself in order to remove all obstacles to adoring his beauty, and they had now all run off to go see him. Pietro noticed Cossa smiling at him without betraying any embarrassment or annoyance. Having noticed that the Lieutenant was observing him, Pietro stopped. *Is he a complete idiot? And yet he immediately intuited that at this very moment I have ensnared him in my gaze, while all the other times he drew close to me he walked by discreetly. Even now there's no vanity at all in the way he's standing there stock-still in front of me. As if he were beauty himself, or rather as if he and his beauty were two separate things, meaning he could leave his beauty right here in front of me while his thoughts fly far away without betraying themselves, without his face expressing any emotion at all. And yet this cheekily insolent Pietro is now the very same man who sometimes comes to open the door for me with a sad air about him that makes everything awkward and makes my heart ache. Yet all one has to do is notice his beauty for him to then hide behind it, the Pietro that makes one's heart ache then hides behind Pietro's beauty: the one I'm looking at right now.*

'Careful you don't make the Major jealous,' Lieutenant Marchi told him ambiguously.

Cossa calmly looked at him. Was he alluding to his relationship with Ursula?

'What do you mean?'

'Pietro is very special in this house.'

Cossa shrugged. *What could he possibly mean by that?* he asked himself, completely disinterestedly.

'You seem pensive, my dear Lieutenant,' the Colonel's wife told him, given that he'd almost involuntarily headed in her direction. 'Is there something wrong?'

'Pensive? Let's not exaggerate! I was only asking myself what role beauty has to play in our lives, if it's right for one to admire it without feeling awkward about it, or if one should instead distrust it, if the person who displays said beauty really thinks of it as a mark of distinction, and what such a soul could feel in relation to that beauty in which its body is imprisoned.'

Meanwhile, he thought to himself: *When that silly Colonel's wife asked me whether I was pensive I felt as if someone had been spying on me, and had peered through the cracks. Thanks to that lyrical sentence I fed her, I can now disappear, the rhetorical exercise has been picked up again, and now there's nothing for me to do except to let her ramble on: after all, who among us has nothing to say about beauty or the soul?*

What a sensitive, intelligent man, he's brave enough to talk about beauty and the soul, the Colonel's wife thought to herself at that very moment: *I used to have these conversations with my first fling thirty-five years ago*. Yet while on the verge of replying, she suddenly felt hindered, and blushed a deep crimson, *just like that first time*, she thought, and then the commotion made her heart melt.

Sensible and clever, Cossa behaved generously at that point and feigned not to notice her increasing unease and carried on talking:

'I wonder whether if our admiration of beauty, in the restlessness for the role that admiration plays in our soul, we don't actually wind up making the mistake of forgetting that this very beauty is connected to a soul, and whether we don't end up demeaning that soul and treading all over it while wrapped up in adoring that beauty: meaning that a person can be both adored and demeaned, and maybe that person carries a secret sadness or secret shame within the locked treasure chest of their beauty.'

At that very moment, he suddenly noticed – was it really a surprise? – that his thoughts had turned to Pietro, the Major's handsome adjutant, the same man Ursula offered up to her friends in the warm and cosy setting of her tea parties, putting him on display like her tray of biscuits, the very same man whom he'd admired earlier, and whose soul wasn't looked after by anybody. It suddenly seemed to dawn on him why meeting that young man had prompted both admiration and discomfort in him, because Pietro often burdened him with his inexpressible sadness. *We've all wronged him, and Pietro probably hates his beauty due to how his soul is constantly demeaned as a result: yet he doesn't react, he doesn't even seem to realise that he could react, instead he obliges people as much as he can, offering himself up to my gaze like he did a few moments ago, resigning himself to satisfying the appetites of anyone who desires him, demeaning his soul by making a gift of his beauty. Maybe Marchi meant to imply that Pietro's even been sleeping with the Major!*

The Colonel's wife was waiting for him to start talking again, she had been waiting for thirty-five years for someone to talk to her again in that way. In those few minutes it took Cossa to gather his thoughts, she didn't show the slightest impatience: in fact, she liked even more when he seemed distracted, when he simply followed his train of thought, and forgot to speak, when his face grew more open and intense, allowing her to understand him more than when she lingered in silence when he spoke, even though she truly loved to hear him talk.

'I witnessed an injustice and it troubles me,' Cossa picked up again, employing an actor's tone, 'we often demean with our admiration those who would instead wish to be questioned and understood, our respect and admiration merely conceal our indifference, we pick a flower and tread on the plant; I feel I played my part in this injustice tonight, and instead of whispering these thoughts to you, I would like to scream so loud that even the deaf would hear me.'

The Colonel's wife looked at him, both excited and frightened: would he really start screaming? She decided she would echo his scream, even though she didn't know what he was talking about and which point he wanted to make.

'But who would understand? Who would be ready to take the first step towards redressing this injustice? It would imply a new way of thinking, a new way of feeling, and people aren't up to that task, either they can't or they don't want to, and if that's the case why not say it? Why should one fear expressing romantic thoughts, given that admiring someone's beauty and respecting someone's soul can only be reconciled in love.'

That word so resonated in myriads of different, intense ways throughout the Colonel's wife's soul that Cossa deemed it useless to carry on that conversation, and instead he let that word linger in her ears without bothering her by taking his leave or making up an excuse, and so he left, for the second time.

A grave injustice had therefore been committed in the Major's house, which served as a temple of Pietro's beauty. It was a prison in which the flower of his soul was being unfairly made to wilt away. Having left the Colonel's wife behind, Cossa crossed the room with the fervour of a Don Quixote, even though he thought so himself. Yet on finding himself face to face with Pietro once again, he laughed: two abstractions, beauty and the soul, were substituted by a person, Pietro.

And whenever one compares what one had imagined with what is really there, the fragile designs of our imagination against reality's sculptural evidence, the comparison favours the latter, until one felt entirely ridiculous. Cossa hadn't yet reached that point. Talking passionately while employing an actor's tone, he had managed to express himself, something he couldn't manage to do without that reserve. Yet it was this very reserve that was now defending him from reality's attacks: as a matter of fact, during his conversation with the Colonel's wife, he hadn't wanted to interpret reality, but to substitute it, like any good thespian. Or rather, having downgraded reality to a pretext, he would place a second reality next to it, one peopled by characters called beauty, soul, injustice and rebellion, meaning that this second reality was free to completely disregard any attacks from that first reality since the contact between them was both decisive and irrevocable. Nevertheless, Pietro, who was now suddenly standing before him again, absorbed by the task of looking after the Major's guests, had aroused these considerations (meaning the interpretation of reality) in him, as well as the creation of a new, independent reality – Pietro immediately surmised that Cossa's laughter was directed at him, even though he had no idea what kind of cartwheels he'd had to in order to catch his attention. He suddenly transformed into what Cossa imagined him to be, his soul flitted away the moment it had captured the other's attention, freeing his beauty to shine even brighter. Pietro, who had struck Cossa as a simple soldier when he'd first laid eyes on him, was now being divided into those two components which Cossa's imagination had previously reduced him to. Neither the first nor last were confirmation that reality offered the imagination – in finding itself spied upon and in fleeing away, that departing soul had left a painful expression on Pietro's face. *I must save that man*, the lieutenant thought, feeling thespian-like again, even though he was no longer performing before the audience of the Colonel's wife's eyes, sighs and desires. *I must restore this man's dignity, given all the offenses caused not only by Ursula and her friends, but also by the Major (if what Marchi said is true) and myself. Pietro must rise above the pitiful solitude in which he lives, and he must be able to have his hopes and illusions, just like anybody else – do I have any? – and he must also stop being the humble guardian of his beauty. This transformation must first occur in the souls of others before it can take place in his – shall I lead by example?*

'Idiot!' the Major, an incredibly irritable man, shouted, calling for Pietro a second time. The latter hurried over to serve him, but as he didn't know what the Major wanted, and since he was carrying a tray of pastries, he offered him one. The Major let out a hearty laugh and with a lightning-quick gesture, he tipped the tray onto the floor. The atmosphere was tense. Pietro was falling headfirst into the void created around him by everyone's curiosity, their need for entertainment, and their disdain. He knelt down to pick up the pastries. Some had even fallen between the Major's feet. Pietro drew close to them, but the Major instead gave him a furious kick, which ended up hitting the open-palmed hands Pietro had raised to defend himself, and he fell on his back, his mouth agape. The Major always enjoyed toeing the line, yet once he finally crossed that line (for example by kicking his adjutant), all his irritation remained intact – which was why he was laughing, as though he'd just absorbed all the vexation he'd wanted to inflict on Pietro. The Major found himself face to face with the desire to kick somebody (it was both a temptation and a warning) – he would have liked to kick Pietro's face, but he couldn't, which was why he had done so right away; but all he had gotten out of it was a profound sense of annoyance, an even gloomier despair. If he was looking for an infraction of the rules, this was a really paltry one, the Major confessed to himself, while his eyes – which had shone excitedly a moment earlier in the heat of the challenge – now looked disheartened by their own boldness, because if one gives in to an urge that nevertheless fails to satisfy, it proves demoralizing. *One must try harder and commit to compromising oneself further, until there is no escape, until one finds oneself in an experience where there is no way out. Is war the experience I'm looking for?*

Dissatisfaction and the inability to adapt to one's life (or of finding and accepting compromises) was leading everyone onto the path of war. *I'll wind up killing a man on the street, just the first man who passes by, that is if war doesn't create the kind of opportunities that my desperation is craving.* As though life had trampled on some of the pages of his youth, possibly because all of his life had turned out contrary to his wishes, even though everyone was daunted by his willpower, the Major's dreams (and even war is a dream, because it seeks the solution to all problems from a diverse, collective reality, the fulfillment of all of one's desires, the most complete manifestation of oneself) were that of an adolescent: that a man should resolve to do things with absolute passion, that one should face one's experiences without considering failure, except the ultimate failure, that one could hold all of one's cards in one hand, either to keep multiplying them forever, or to lose them on one's last hopes. Yet this was exactly the reason why war was looming, why war was brewing, for the ways in which one wanted to justify that war didn't ultimately satisfy the very reasons why it was being clamoured for. *I despise Mussolini's stupid war to steal a strip of desert away from the English,* he pondered, while looking into the void of Pietro's mouth as the latter knelt at his feet, *and to kick the French out of Nice and Tunis – if we'll go to war it should be either for total annihilation or a complete renewal. And if Italy winds up annexing Tunisia, Nice, Corsica and Savoie, and if we'll drive the English off a few beaches and into the sea, what will I have gained out of it? How will my life change? Will it be easier to live? Will I – once I've helped throw a few Englishmen off some beaches – know how to live?* As for Pietro, that kick to the mouth had left him feeling just as deluded: the Major had humiliated him, but what did it matter, how would that evening be any different from all the others that had come before it? He was the same Pietro as always, more humiliated perhaps, but still the same man, in the same situation, with the same thoughts, and even his life was the same, even though – when the Major had shouted – he had experienced a sharp sense of fright as though it were an enormous sense of hope, maybe over the course of that soiree which Ursula had organised, his life would be hurled (by someone else of course, given that Pietro was a pessimist, and didn't believe in the virtues of his own willpower, or capabilities, and whenever he said yes to the Major, it wasn't because he was a soldier and the latter was his superior officer, but because everyone had their own destiny and his was to simply say yes) *beyond the river*[xii] from whence he would never return. Was he also thinking of murder, and that he would be its victim just as the Major would be its perpetrator? Instead they had both been tricked in the same way and with the same gesture, everything had been mediocre and their lives had gone back to square one, the unruly hopes of arrogance and fear having been betrayed, they were incapable of realizing themselves, even though thanks to that kick, which one had vulgarly given the other out of sheer caprice, and which the other had accepted with senseless submissiveness, both men had managed to profoundly express themselves.

Cossa was tired and he would have wanted to go home, but he had been the last to arrive and thus didn't want to be the first to leave. Thoroughly rebellious, when it came to relationships

---

[xii] Reference to the River Styx, which the Greeks believed formed the boundary between world of the living and that of the dead.

with other people and with society at large, he was a conformist at heart. He pushed his conformism to the limits in order to please others, possibly even cater to their stupidity, and this in turn led the others to call him splendid. He admired the Major's strength, which allowed him to throw himself into the thick of the action, and to dominate it: whereas he would just stand there, frozen, feeling that he could only ever be a spectator, as had been the case when the Major had kicked Pietro. In fact, instead of intervening, as his thought a moment earlier had led him to suppose that he would, he had instead gone out onto the veranda, finding that scene distasteful, and experienced a kind of regret over those pointless hours he'd been forced to live. Once again, as though answering a call, his thoughts turned to the definitive gesture the writer had made when she'd wound up in that river.

Even though – and he demonstrated this when he re-entered the room a few moments later – he was capable of overcoming emotions, or at least hiding them, the Major was drinking alone in a corner, with a gloomy sadness imprinted on his face, as though he'd been the one who'd received that kick instead of giving it.

Cossa approached a group of his fellow soldiers and was surprised to see Pietro among them. He was at the centre of the circle standing next to an officer Cossa wasn't acquainted with. Amidst the confusion of tins, herbs and filters, Cossa immediately realised that none of these items belonged to the Major's house, and in fact he noticed a small suitcase propped against Pietro's feet. He had already caught wind of this new obsession making the rounds of local drawing rooms, which had just been brought into the country by the officer who was now standing in the middle of the circle.

Magic, like war, is a way of shuffling the deck, to overcome the obstacles that left us to drown, romantic unruliness against the wise, prudent life, a leap into the unknown, a re-evaluation of passion, ideals, sacrifice and risk. While this desire for war runs through our minds, with so much hope being placed on magic, our moral structure announces it has failed.

A girl facing him gripped an elixir of love. Perhaps she wanted to employ the elixir's deception to resist the science of cautiousness, of matrimony and all of her mother's conventions, the imaginativeness of courage, love and passion. The world is suffering under the weight of its rationality; having banished the irrational from our lives, we shall now drown in war, and beg magic to give us the breath of life. Guilty?

Cossa sat in a corner and opened a book, the first one he chanced across: La Rochefoucauld. Cossa was lazy and didn't read much. The pleasure he derived from literature rarely rewarded him for the effort it took to read it in the first place. If what he happened to be reading stopped interesting him as soon as he shut that book, he would walk away disappointed, thinking the author had deceived him. He loved La Rochefoucauld because he could talk about himself with the author by way of their common interests. On these occasions, reading became a way to transcend his solitude.

Cossa felt a warm gust of breath – maternal, and even sensual – breeze past him. The ambiguous feeling it engendered left no doubt that it was the Colonel's wife. He felt her hand slip off his shoulder to turn the pages of the book still in his hands, until it stopped and her finger pointed to a passage: 'Love alone has caused more evils than all other passions put together. Nobody would be capable of listing them all. One must nevertheless recognise that love has also produced some of life's greatest blessings. Thus, instead of speaking ill of love, let's keep quiet, let us fear and respect love forever.' While he read, he also thought: *It really is curious how this woman has noticed how extraordinary these words are when written by a man such as him, how pathetic it is to be kept company by all these other thoughts.* Yet blocking the path to such considerations was a question: *Are you sure that the Colonel's wife read this passage and attributed it to La Rochefoucauld, instead of finding it in a collection of thoughts that were both difficult and incomprehensible to her, finding only one single thought among them that she could adhere to – in other words, she found some quote by Rousseau or Lamartine that suited her purposes?* But why had the Colonel's wife showed it to him? What meaning had she assigned to that particular passage? Cossa tilted his head upwards to look at her. Seen from below, she had assumed otherworldly dimensions, she looked like one of those allegorical figures that people Tiepolo's ceilings. Yet just as was the case with those figures, any interpretation put forward might be the right one: Time, Virtue, Moderation, Glory, Wisdom – any of them would do. Thus, the Colonel's wife was merely a golden cloud hovering above his head, he could interpret her whichever way he liked, he could look at her as a woman sensitive to literature and the complexities and finesses of the soul, or he could see her as a colour-blind woman who could have a man dressed entirely in black standing in front of her and still only spot the pinkish hue of his clasps, or, finally, as his third alternative, he could see her as a sensual woman who nonetheless employed third parties (in this case, La Rochefoucauld) to voice her flirtatiousness, probably out of shame. Naturally, he could ask her about it, and he knew he would be shrewd enough to unmask her. But was it worth the effort? Wouldn't the Colonel's wife subsequently lose all her appeal? That golden cloud would flatten into such a banal figure. *Even though you're waiting so anxiously, I'll spare you: I'll let you shine on that ceiling instead of dragging you down with a string.*

What is he thinking? the Colonel's wife asked herself in the meanwhile. *What thoughts are running through his head? After he read out those lines, he turned to look at me – and I suddenly felt in the grips of vertigo when I saw my reflection in the abyss of his eyes. There was even a shade of irony in his gaze, and it is this very irony that keeps me suspended in the air. How long will this misunderstanding last? Why are you looking at me?*

Look at that idiot, Ursula mused while she observed them, *she's lost all restraint, she's madly in love. And Eugenio is so lazy that he's fully capable of becoming her lover! When he eventually realises that it'll be too complicated to slip out of her grasp, he'll wind up becoming her lover*!

Ursula is watching us, Cossa noted. *Is it jealousy? Oscillating between irony and jealousy, her gaze envelops us, my dear Colonel's wife. Using her jealousy to prop you up, you feel closer to me. She finally found the courage to trust her feelings at the age of fifty, but she has simultaneously lost faith in her virtues and powers of seduction. You would find the strength to leave your husband tonight and run away with me, if you could only be sure that I loved you in return. On the other hand, if the girl who was laughing while holding that elixir of love found herself in the exact same situation, she would debase such a beautiful adventure with all the rules her mother had inculcated her with! The result is always the same: impotence. O, why does nobody have any virtues anymore, why does no one trust their natural gifts and talents, why aren't we capable of heeding our impulses? Everything is always wretched and miserable.*

The Colonel's wife straightened herself with a sigh: a shadow of sadness fell on Cossa's handsome face. *He's sad and I'll never know why. He's sad and I probably wouldn't be able to do anything about it. Why did I run into him?*

'A curious thought,' Cossa commented, casting judgment on the entire scene. 'Do you not think it's true?' the Colonel's wife asked him, as if she hadn't showed it to him in order for him to see how curious it really was. 'What are you discussing?' Ursula asked, drawing closer. Yet instead of stopping, she passed them by: she wasn't interested by what those two could possibly be discussing in the slightest. The Colonel's wife asked herself whether it was decent of her to spend all that time with that young man. She looked at him as though imploring his aid. Yet Cossa was still observing Pietro, who having entered the circle that surrounded the officer-magician, was picking up everything around him and stuffing it back into that little suitcase, which he then deposited in the waiting room.

Why did I meet him? Why did I meet him? The Colonel's wife asked herself, despairing, while her heart melted into tears. In the meanwhile, an officer had sat himself next to Cossa, and was explaining to him how that comrade of theirs prepared his filters. *While we talk to others,* Cossa thought, *we feel more intensely alone.*

And if this conversation doesn't take a distressing turn, it'll be quite pleasant. This comrade's conversation protects me and shields from the indiscretions of others. His thoughts suddenly turned to Pietro again, who having picked up all the odds and ends belonging to that herb-rolling officer, had gone into the kitchen. *What should I do now?* He would have liked to follow Pietro into the kitchen. Instead, he lingered impatiently while waiting for the other to finish speaking. *There are those who are greedy for time, who live it out in a solemn way, who spend a minute as mindfully as though it were a gold doubloon. Then there are others who crush it under the weight of facts, and the busier and more industrious they are, the more they feel that their time has been hollow and meaningless. I prefer squandering time: for instance, while I wait here for this fool to stop talking, even though I would much rather stand up and go to the kitchen. Not doing what I want to do makes me aware of the passing of time, a feeling that usually makes people impatient, but since I do not suffer from impatience in the slightest, I actually find it very pleasurable. Now I can feel the passing of time like sand through my fingers, whereas whenever what I want to do and what I am actually doing overlap, time becomes imperceptible. Barring off the path of life with his conversation, this chatterbox caused a traffic jam. While stuck in this traffic jam, I am experiencing life intensely (or rather, more intensely). The kitchen where Pietro has (probably) fallen asleep, while I sit here listening to this chap, has now been brought into sharp relief, and given Pietro, while he stands next to the window (I am certain that he's standing next to the window, every time I entered that kitchen I always found him next to the window), such an intensity of meaning that I would vainly search for, if I could get up right now and step inside that kitchen.*

While he lingered, wrapped in his thoughts, cradled by his comrade's conversation, Cossa observed Luisa, Captain Carli's wife, who was sat in a corner leafing through a magazine in order to decorously uphold her silence. She was the victim of a prank. Ursula had decided that she had to find Pietro a girlfriend (the fact she'd made love to him herself didn't mean anything to her). She had chosen Luisa because, as Luisa herself had put it, she didn't have anyone. Thus, she had employed any pretext available to send Pietro to Luisa's house at all times of day – in fact, at some rather odd hours – while simultaneously telling everyone that they were lovers. On seeing him entering and leave her house all the time, nobody entertained any further doubts in that regard. Pietro, who knew all about that prank, was very embarrassed by it. Luisa had noticed Pietro's embarrassment whenever he came to see her. At which point she would become very deferential and would use all her courtesy to try to put that poor boy at ease – he would then feel even more embarrassed. Ursula no longer needed any pretexts to dispatch Pietro to Luisa's house. Luisa had taken over that task, and if Pietro tarried in showing his face, she would go look for him herself. Naturally, she was sensitive to Pietro's incredibly handsome looks, and she never failed to attend Ursula's tea parties, when she would find herself unable to tear her eyes off him (Ursula would comb his hair before said parties, she found grooming her husband's adjutant incredibly amusing). Yet Pietro's embarrassment in Luisa's presence made his handsomeness touching, almost pathetic – and Luisa was very drawn to the pathetic. Did he love her? Luisa asked herself that every day. What did Pietro feel for her?

Who or what could give her such an answer? *What do yes or no really mean?* Whenever she looked at him, her eyes probing him for answers, Pietro would turn suddenly pale, lowering his gaze and sighing, fiddling with the buttons on his uniform. *What do yes or no really mean, what does love mean, how do people interpret it?* When she was at home, Luisa's gaze was always directed towards the street. And whenever she saw him approaching her house, she would run off to ensure she looked presentable, even though she'd already prepared herself for his arrival. While standing in front of her mirror, she would only grimace, being far too confused to attempt fixing a loose lock of hair or ribbon. When she heard the doorbell ring, she would sit down. She would sit down to prevent herself from running over to the door. Then she would suddenly stand up, run panting down the stairs and open up, so they could both stand there, while he stared at his feet and she gazed upwards at the sky, waiting for the spirits to return. This would carry on until Pietro opened his mouth and told her that the Major's wife wanted a needle, or a croquis, or that she wanted to know whether they would be going to the Officers' Club that evening. Luisa would slowly climb the stairs while the adjutant remained on the ground floor. Luisa was perfectly aware where she kept her needles, or what specific croquis Ursula was after. However, she was in no hurry. Once she'd arrived upstairs, she would lean against a wall and slip into a reverie. Whenever she returned downstairs, Pietro would take the needle or croquis, allowing their hands to touch lightly, at which point Pietro would give her a military salute while Luisa gave him a slight nod of her head. *What is love and how do people interpret it? What do yes or no really mean? Go ahead and ignore reality, Luisa thought to herself, ignore what can or cannot happen, sacrifice all the opportunities that reality seems to have placed before you – reality is only doing that in order to blackmail you – ignore all that filthiness that usually goes with love. That filthiness is always easy to pursue – Ursula being a perfect example of that – even without being in love. I don't need anything. Except maybe silence, just like now. All I want is to sit here on my own, safely ensconced behind this magazine. I don't give a damn about reality, I detest it. Pietro can be anyone's lover for all I care. Yet what would he mean to them? What does Pietro mean to them compared to what he means to me? If we hold the two ends of a needle just for a moment, our hearts bleed. Ursula, who has certainly gone to bed with him, would have been left entirely indifferent by the whole experience, and she would have to employ all of her genius in order to feel any kind of emotion, while if we found one another standing face to face, even the tiniest of non-events leaves us feeling overwhelmed.* This particular thought buzzed around all the others in the manner of a large fly, pestering Luisa: *Are you afraid of reality? No*, she finally replied, regaining her self-confidence, *I know nothing can give me what I want, reality is for people who lack all imagination. People of this sort usually only allow their imaginations to take a few, measly steps – while when it comes to people like us, reality only blocks our imaginations, it debases our dreams, our encounters, and even love itself! Why is Cossa looking at me?*

Is it true that Luisa is in love with Pietro, like Ursula says? And yet I kept an eye on them, and they didn't exchange a single word all evening. Have they made love? Because so many stories have been told about Pietro in this regard that I no longer know what to believe. What does this woman love about Pietro, if she loves him at all? This woman is brave enough to keep quiet, while I need someone to talk to me in order to do the same. After all, her silence is more meaningful than mine. Will I find it possible to overcome the barrier standing between me and life, to cross the river of suicide that separates me from real life? What price will such a possibility exact? What made this possible for Luisa? Or did I begin my suicidal vocation from a disadvantageous position? What is love? Have I ever experienced it? Will I be able to answer that question myself or am I only capable of making an inventory of all these questions that torture me? Do these questions really torture me or are they merely a symptom of my curiosity? Outside of suicide, what is serious about me, what are the real, sincere questions I am asking myself?

At that exact moment, the officer who'd been chatting with him stopped speaking. Cossa had voyaged in the dark, and he had no idea what the other officer, once the magic had started, had actually said to him. Yet crashing against the man's sudden silence, Cossa woke up; and since the dam which had kept him contained had now been removed, he forgot about all the questions he would have attempted to answer if that chatterbox had preserved the silence around him, protecting his isolation in the way that magazine defended Luisa's. He stood up. He turned the hands of his soul's clock back, and stepped inside the kitchen where Pietro had fallen asleep. And as he was now performing an action which corresponded to a past desire – he had, in fact, been very distracted when his fellow officer had been speaking to him – he could observe himself fully, as though the action he was about to perform had already been accomplished by someone else. The detachment that this created allowed him to analyze himself with clinical objectivity. *Why did you go to the kitchen? There he is, snoozing next to the window. Everything is precisely in its proper order, just like you had anticipated. When faced with such conformity, what is one to do? Why does the meaning of our actions disappear even before we've fully accomplished them? And what is – what makes Pietro so wonderful?*

I want to understand the mystery surrounding this adjutant, around whom the entire house revolves! I want to cut right to the heart of that mystery, which the others don't seem to perceive beyond the fascination it exerts on them – he was thinking with the same Don Quixote-like attitude with which he had earlier crossed the room. *I want to bring the light of reason into the semi-obscurity surrounding Pietro, in the kitchen where he shuts himself away to sleep next to the window. I want to understand if his seductive powers are owed to his extraordinary beauty, his stupidity, or the purity that keeps his beauty stupid; or, if stupidity has a limit, meaning Pietro is capable of understanding he is loved and adored – but also despised – and a shadow of his wounded humanity sometimes fell over his face, and which also settles (for instance) over my heart. It is the same shadow of sadness that I saw on his face tonight when he opened the door to let me in, and which I've often mulled over in my head.*

Pietro is asleep. He's so handsome when he sleeps. Ursula apparently often goes into his room to watch him sleep while she knits. Did Pietro dream? And if he did, what did he dream about? Why does he always linger by that window? What does he see in that night, what does he see when he dreams? Even now that he looks as though he's sleeping, he's abandoned his beauty and left it behind for all to see, like a lifeless body so that people – like me? – who love to watch him sleep can admire it. Pietro lives hidden inside his dreams, and I am very curious about that secret life (or am I jealous?). Pietro's true beauty lies in his humanity, which is concealed by his (physical) beauty. I understand him when I feel upset and perturbed by the sadness that suddenly engulfs his features. He can immediately make me aware of a feeling, and when that feeling fades, and I start to think again, everything becomes garbled up again and I can't understand anything anymore. Intelligence is a highly valued trait, but it comes with limited powers. Intelligence can be a terrible obstacle to knowledge. Intelligence constructs its own world and then superimposes it on reality, believing the former could help illuminate the latter, but in the end it only distorts that reality. Intelligence is useless unless it functions in tandem with another intelligence, in a world achieved through reason. But, lo and behold: stupidity is already an insurmountable wall; and feelings remain a mystery. Intelligence does not dwell in the world that it has created. Yet our ultimate humanity, the meaning of our life, the unanswered whys of most of our actions, strength, depth, character, flavour, limits, the roots of our emotions – all remain unintelligible and it despises it all for being unable to comprehend them. Intelligence does not bring a man out of his shell, in fact, it imprisons him in the world it has created for him. Intelligence can reveal how extraordinary it is through the sheer magnificence of its creations, and for the acrobatic leaps that it is capable of performing in that very world. If we instead try to evaluate intelligence according to the function most appropriate to it, that is of penetrating a given reality – oh what a useless, imprecise instrument, oh what a mess, what impotence – simply consider my little performance here, consider how much useless effort I wasted erecting an edifice on top of Pietro's slumber and his dreams, look at how intact and impenetrable his sadness – or how he lives his dreams – remains to me.

In the meanwhile, Cossa watched Pietro as he slept, just like Ursula did whenever she knitted. Yet just as there was much to laugh about on Ursula's account, it was also the reason why he could watch the young man sleep as long as he did. Without this precedent, without being able to mock Ursula, he wouldn't have hesitated and he would have left immediately. And in order to prove to himself that he still had all his wits about him, to satisfy the needs of reason by interrupting a contemplation that grew deeper and more relaxed as the memory of Ursula faded away, he called out: 'Pietro!' Yet by attempting to prove his resolve, he only betrayed himself. Hearing a different tone than he was used to in that voice, one neither angry nor disdainful, nor ironic or authoritarian, Pietro didn't stir, but instead kept dreaming, or looked as though he'd kept on dreaming, and it was only when the officer shook him lightly by the shoulder that Pietro regained his wits and jumped to his feet: 'Yes, sir, lieutenant!' he exclaimed. Cossa was holding a glass of cognac in his hand, he had chanced across a full one and had started sipping it while he was watching Pietro sleep. 'It tastes quite strange,' he said, putting the glass down on the table. Pietro picked it up and downed it in a single gulp.

'My cognac!' a girl exclaimed on entering the kitchen at that exact moment. 'My elixir! Pietro, what have you done?'

She ran back into the sitting room to tell everyone that Pietro had drunk her elixir. She had slammed the door behind her.

Lieutenant Marchi crossed the same threshold a moment later: 'We've got to go, Cossa,' he said, 'it seems our orders have arrived and we're due to leave tomorrow at dawn. The war has begun.'

The young officer who had announced the news stood in a corner. It appeared settled that the regiment to whom Boninsea, Cossa, the Major and Lieutenant Marchi belonged to would be leaving at dawn. The war would probably break out soon. In a matter of a few hours, or a few days. France had given up, and Mussolini wanted to take full advantage of that. The declaration of war would be greeted with statutory enthusiasm, but at that exact moment, since the final decision hadn't yet been taken, they all felt guilty and anxious: just like death, war forced one to rethink life. The Major was the first among them to recover from this, and he was the first to start chatting; in fact, although he'd spent a great deal of time prior to that huddled up and worried in a corner, he now appeared to have regained his vitality. At that precise moment, he did not consider that he could well die in that war. However, they had resolved a great problem for him: *how he should live*. This was why he felt in high spirits. The others' expressions betrayed their fears over their destinies (*Will I survive*, Lieutenant Marchi asked himself, *will I outlive this war?*), the Major's face beamed with great confidence. On top of that, he burst into a huge laugh, which annoyed everyone else.

Everyone except Mrs Boninsea, who hadn't heard the Major. She lingered immobile in the middle of the sitting room. All her thoughts spilled in tears. The lights were going out in the great theatre of the world: *And when four or five years from now they'll switch them on again, I'll be an old woman!* With a single gesture, Mussolini, like a greedy croupier, had taken her last years away from her, scooping up those casino chips she'd risked with such fear and hesitation.

Standing next to her, by the window, was Anna, the Major's daughter, who was biting her lip, angry at the prank which had been pulled on her. She was sixteen: *Must the war really break out now of all times?!* Mussolini had set her back by three or four years, even though she was finally old enough to go to the club, she would be forced to stay at home, now that she was finally old enough to have an officer accompany her on her walk down the main boulevard, there soon wouldn't be any officers left in town, *and I'll be fourteen again!* She was in the grips of despair.

Once the coming of the war had been announced, which would probably be officially declared in the coming hours, Luisa had left her magazine behind; if the latter had proved an effective shield in protecting her from the chatter of Ursula's guests, it would no longer suffice, the war had splintered that shield, exposing her to the shocks of life. *War!* Now Pietro wouldn't go see her anymore, and Pietro would leave along with all the others. The idea of having to say goodbye to him that very evening – *and here of all places, with everyone present* – was breaking her heart. They probably wouldn't see one another until the end of the war. Which was the same as saying: *In heaven!* Luisa stood up. Her heart really was breaking now. She had always despised reality, but if she despised it, it was also because she was happy with what she had, since reality was abundant enough as it was for a sensible soul such as hers. In fact, for her to understand and accept reality, it was necessary for reality not to run her over, but rather to barely graze her as it flew by; it did not please her to be in the eye of life's storm, but rather she wished she could observe a sleepy, peaceful, familiar landscape from behind the safety of a window – the same window that Pietro appeared in once a day, almost every day. Those few seconds for her were enough – searching for a needle for Ursula while Pietro waited downstairs – to feel her heart swell, leaving it worn out and exhausted for the rest of the day. How could she possibly survive the war's vicissitudes? She could barely tolerate life in the colony, which everybody complained about due to how boring it was, and everyone there seemed impatient and crazy to her. They set everything they found and lived in on fire, as if it had nothing to do with them, but it was instead a novel or a play. Were they completely insensitive? Or was she the one who was truly impatient and restless, so much so that she could never endure anything, except the tiniest of emotions – Pietro appearing at the end of the dusty road – had he also become unbearable to her? If peace-time scared her, how could she possibly put up with war, which frightened everyone who found peace boring? The mere news that all the regiments still stationed in the city would have to leave for the front had thrown her soul into confusion, so much so that she suddenly – like a scream – recognised a feeling she had never thought herself capable of, which she had hitherto been certain she would never experience during the course of her life. A feeling which had never even occurred to her: regret – for never asking that boy whether he loved her or not! She lingered in the middle of the sitting room, but nobody paid her any mind. *The rivers have run dry, the roads have been blocked, the doors shut, the windows bricked up, everybody keeps what they already have, and what failed to happen will never happen* – she stammered on in this manner inside her mind, until she could no longer see anyone around her – *it's over, over, over!*

Ursula allowed herself to fall into an armchair. War! Her calculations had panned out, she had lived her life all too lucidly aware of what was lying in store for them, and she had drawn the most extreme conclusions. Not being a religious soul, she had prepared herself for the deluge in her own manner: in other words, she'd accumulated such an excessive number of crazy incidents that thanks to all the scandals her husband had been threatened with repatriation. When it was announced that war would likely be declared in the coming hours, she had felt her knees buckle, as if she had hitherto borne a weight which had drained all her strength. The others were in the grips of regrets, fears, hopes and delusions: whereas she had squeezed all she could from peace-time, and she had enjoyed her life on the brink of scandal, and now felt spent. As though it had suddenly dawned on her that might prove calmer than peace-time, and its obsession with 'living it to the full,' because it was not fated to last.

I'll go to bed with him tonight, the surly Anna thought to herself, *and if the war can wait until dawn to break, then I'll be Pietro's lover tonight.*

The messenger stood on the door's threshold talking to various people. Having hurriedly accomplished his fatal task, he had resumed his usual role: that of a young officer, just like all the others. They had dispatched him to the colony in order to take part in the war and he had arrived there as though it was already the front. He was the son of anti-Fascists, and fully aware that he was being kept under observation, he behaved prudently. While he conversed with the other officers, or rather while he pretended to follow what they were saying, he mulled over this thought with nervous intensity: *That's it! This is the moment to obey our orders, now there's nothing left to do but to heed our Duce. We must even show some enthusiasm, so that his ambition may grow, so that he'll take even greater risks over time, so that he refuses any and all compromises, so not a single door will be left open. He has poisoned peace-time to the point that we've decided to throw ourselves headfirst into this war: because even if it proves atrocious, it'll be our way out.*

All of a sudden, the Major drew near to the group the messenger was socializing with, carrying a glass in his hand. A toast? A war song? A pathetic farewell to peace-time? A joke? Pietro looked at the Major with painful curiosity, since he always expected that man to do something to him, he expected him to somehow express his state of mind – just like his earlier kick had revealed his desperation.

The Major never spared a thought for what he was about to do. Thus, he had decided to kick Pietro at the same time that he actually kicked him. His state of mind for the time being was that he was blindly searching for a way to express what he felt on the inside. He wasn't intoxicated, but he had drunk quite a lot. Standing right there in the middle of the room, he raised his glass. He still didn't know what he would do at that point. So he started to sing; it was one of Schubert's beautiful *Lieder*[xiii]: 'Im Abendrot'[xiv]. He sang as though he were proclaiming, mouthing those words that nobody understood, since no one there spoke German except Ursula, and the Major had chosen that mysterious way to bid goodbye to his youth, to his wife, who knew what he was saying. That scene was truly pathetic as

[xiii] German: 'songs'.

[xiv] German: 'at sunset'.

the warrior, who was meant to be on his way, instead hesitated and was now stretching out his goodbye to unrealistic proportions – one can see such scenes in a number of operas. Using the reference her husband had provided her with, in the shape of a *Lied* he often sang in his youth, Ursula could thus relive the past twenty years of her life, when she had so feverishly experienced all that remained of her youth, in the manner that other people interpreted youth – and which in her, thanks to that instinct for exaggeration owed to her German roots, or maybe inspired by her husband's example, she took a path which lay in between tragedy and farce (everyone apparently agreed that her adventures fell into either of those categories). Planting one of her feet in her past – in the *Lied* her husband was singing – while keeping the other firmly fixed in the present, in the concrete announcement of the coming war, Ursula looked at her guests from atop those twenty years of peace as though one were watching a river's leisurely flow from atop a bridge. The river mirrored her reflection, and more than disgust, or horror, she felt happy to finally be outside of it. Seeing as she also knew a bit of Latin, a famous passage by Lucretius, it was the first that she'd used Latin to express herself, for the first time Latin became the ultimate expression of her soul: *Suave mari magno*, with all the verses that follow[xv]. And while she talked to herself, simultaneously listening to that *Lied* which her husband had chosen from thirty years of memories, she had rediscovered her former virginal, prudish attitude. She looked like a girl who was going to be serenaded by her first love, the kind of girl that first love would express his feelings to, that song cleared the air, it restored something both

---

[xv] Latin: 'Pleasant it is, when over a great sea,' from Book II of *De Rerum Natura* by Lucretius.

indefinable and yet necessary. Everyone felt it, through what one of them – the biggest bully, and the one with the most overabundance of character – was expressing: the Major was the group's poet, he had earlier given voice to their desperation with that kick and was now expressing the overflow of emotions affecting all present with that mysterious song. Once he had finished singing, the Major stiffened up once again and approached his wife, whom he kissed, then approached his daughter, whom he also kissed, then, having bowed to kiss each lady's hand, he turned to his men and said: 'Let's go.' He departed in sure-footed manner, as though heading off to a parade rather than to war. One by one, his officers followed him, planting kisses on the ladies' hands, smiling to the girls – all the while losing none of the rigidity and form which the Major had inspired in his own final goodbye. Despite there being a great many of them in that room, the scene was nevertheless very poignant, and emotions were running high when the last officer left, just as they had been when the Major had led the way with his goodbye. The men were going to headquarters to receive their orders, while the women headed home to prepare everything before their arrival. After the great peace-time feast, the soldiers only had a few hours at their disposal, and they all had to leave on time, while the women stayed behind: 'It's like coming back from a really long party at the club.' Mrs Boninsea said with a sob in her throat.

Pietro had gone upstairs to his bedroom. He was readying himself to leave.

Ursula and the Major never saw one another again. Sure enough, the war had started a few days later, and the Major experienced an adventure – whom men with little imagination thought was simply unbelievable, while those who appreciated the bizarreness of life deemed it completely unique; others, who read mysterious meanings into facts thought it tragic, while those who understood that facts meant nothing at all saw the comedy in it. The matter had been officially hushed up, given that the war was only a few days old and the requisite regulations for hypocrisy hadn't yet been drawn up. The Major had been wounded while inspecting the southern front lines in his jeep. Such was the confusion along the infinitely long sandy front that the Major had quickly found himself behind enemy lines, inspecting troops he believed were his own. That he'd gotten out of there alive was in itself a miracle, given that two of the men who had been with him were killed and then immediately used as human shields by both the Major and his driver: the only one who could be said to have truly survived the incident, given that the Major (following two months in the hospital, and despite the intensive care devoted to him due to his having been the highest-ranking officer to be wounded on the front lines) died.

'If he'd known that the area he was traveling in had fallen into enemy hands even though it was still technically supposed to be behind our lines, he would have gone there anyway, just to discredit the entire High Command.' This was a comment made by the Major's superior officer, the general, whom knew the Major well. It appeared that the Major insisted on leaving surprise and scandal in his wake even in death. He had even been ready to sacrifice his life in order to further discredit himself: even though he was a romantic, or rather, precisely because he was such an incurable romantic, he therefore behaved cynically, unmasking mediocrity and fraud wherever he found it.

The Major's death had left an even greater impression on Pietro than the war's outbreak. He had always respected him greatly. He looked to him as a real master in that authoritarian world they lived in. He struck his fancy, and he felt, without really knowing why, that the Major belonged to a different breed: those who know how to act, taking a feeling, desire, or caprice and then imposing it on others, regardless of what those others thought. Thus, given that Pietro found it easier and more congenial to obey and follow, without the Major he would have felt the void around him. Instead, when the Major moved, he had made Pietro move in his own turn, since the mechanism that set the Major's will in motion apparently regulated Pietro's will too; in fact, Pietro needed the Major in order to function. They had long since joined into a single, symbiotic being.

The war had broken out to save him from that tea party, during which time he'd felt as though he'd been drowning. It had broken out so he could finally step down off that pedestal where Ursula's friends had placed him. Then the Major had died, freeing him from the hindrance of his will. Had he longed for the war's outbreak? For the Major's death?

Pietro lingered while looking at the Major as he lay stretched out on the field hospital bed. He sat next to the Major in the same way he'd once sat next to the window. He stared out into the Major's night, like he had once observed the starry sky. Amidst the dark depths of the night, Pietro had once dreamed many dreams, the very same ones that Cossa had so torturously spied on during that last night of peace-time. Maybe they weren't even dreams, but rather states of mind, a kind of peace made possible by the dark. And ever since Cossa, no longer satisfied with observing him, had started strolling with him, Pietro had surprised himself thinking that he now wanted to die in the same way he once used to desire nightfall. Ever since that memorable night when they'd met, when he'd still been warm with sleep and Cossa had been troubled by his obstinate observation of the boy, Pietro had nursed the desire to definitively cross the threshold of the night, instead of being stuck on the exhausting see-saw that life forced him to ride. And if he had first ventured into the night on his own, he now thought he would share that adventure with Cossa forever. He peeked at the dead Major, buried in his desperation. He, on the other hand, no longer felt desperate, as if the only desperation were the one brought about by living, and that he would die in the same way others decide to save themselves.

Death caught Cossa on the fly, as his aircraft burst in flames as festively as a firework. The officer shocked everyone with his courage. It was said that he had followed orders irrespective of danger, and according to Marchi, he had followed those orders obtusely. *I don't avoid danger when following orders, rather, I follow orders to find danger.* Death appeared before him now – not as his salvation from desperation and solitude, but as a means to re-conciliate all the contradictions in which his soul had found itself once he'd moved beyond desperation and solitude.

Cossa managed to pilot his craft a few moments longer before the plane wound up with its nose stuck in the sand between two enemy lines. 'A mock landing,' an officer soberly commented while he observed the scene.

Cossa managed to emerge out of his cockpit. Yet after a few feet, his body laid on the ground:

'It-is-over!' Cossa mouthed in a different voice to the theatrical tone he used to employ when being ironic, the glove his consciousness needed to wear in order to handle a feeling or an emotion.

His life amounted to a long, grey road along which he'd travelled in absolute solitude, and his surpassing of solitude coincided with that great, blue lake, that midnight blue in which he was drowning.

From the grey of solitude and suicide to the blue of love and death! In order to accentuate the theatricality of that comment, he wanted to accompany the sentence with a gesture. He tried to raise his arm. Yet it appeared to have sprung roots, and refused to budge. It was the kind of feeling that wasn't even unpleasant, since the connection between his willpower and hand had almost been severed, and his hand appeared to be reaching out to something else, something far away and still uncertain, but already very intense in its own way. Indeed, while all his life he had considered reality too clear and too miserable, everything now seemed simultaneously intense and uncertain.

He had written to Ursula that the Major hadn't donned his uniform when about to die. He had given the world one last great kick with his last letter. Cossa felt that he was also cut from the same cloth, and even though he was alone in the middle of the desert, he behaved as though he'd been sitting in the Major's living room, when the Colonel's wife had gazed at him lovingly.

What is that boy doing now? Is he sleeping or did he see a plane fall out of the sky? Did he know it was mine? And what are they so worked up about, shooting in this way? What are they firing at, deep in the night?

His vision misted over. *Is this the end?* he asked himself, employing his consciousness's final effort. Pondering that question, he breathed his last.

The fusillade was intense. The soldiers on either side of the lines didn't move: and yet they kept firing as though they wanted to fill the night with their sounds. Yet the night was a sack full of holes, and it remained peaceful and serene.

New Officers' Tales

A DARK THING

'What we need here is a pleat,' Antonio's mother said.

Having stood up, she fixed a pin to the side of the pseudo-Polish woman's flower-patterned dress. She took a step back, took a better look, then, opening her hands in a gesture of valediction, she said: '*Voilà qui est fait!*'

'You're an artist, my dear lady,' the dressmaker said, vexed. Just as Antonio's mother had so happily intuited, all one needed was a pleat. 'I can't even see straight anymore!'

She laid her fingers upon her eyes: the gestures were merely rhetorical, as though she were illustrating her words.

'The hems appear to have been stitched hastily, watch out for the smaller one, it's coming undone.'

The pseudo-Polish woman looked beyond the mirror at Antonio, who, having sunk into an armchair, and having discarded his school-bag on the floor, looked like he was growing increasingly bored.

'Why don't you come tell her yourself? The girl tells me you're one of our nicest customers – could you please also tell her that stitching hems requires enthusiasm?'

***

'Only amateurs have any flair these days,' the dressmaker said, having reappeared with Mrs Boncompagni. 'Just like adulterers,' she hissed. She kept fiddling with the thimble on her finger.

'Darling, you never did tell me,' Antonio's mother said to her friend, 'whether you're happy.' She picked up a scrap of cloth: 'Drama, so much drama. You know,' she said, turning to the dressmaker, 'Elena hates surprises. She's secretive!'

Antonio suddenly stood, took the pseudo-Polish woman by the hand and dragged her outside.

'Elena and Antonio… have run away! Yes, it's a fantastic cloth, these large bloomed flowers… I don't like the outline Elena picked for the dress: it tries to imprison this cloth and deprive it of all its fragrance. Yet she didn't manage to, since these flowers simply cannot be repressed. 'Look,' she said, unrolling the cloth, her eyes were clear and held a marvellous light, 'I would have done it like that. You need to let necklines hang. But what good does it do?'

The dressmaker displayed great surprise.

'Of course,' Mrs Boncompagni said, letting the cloth sample fall on the chair, 'Elena would never wear this.'

Having stepped out onto the boulevard, she looked for her friend and Antonio. She found them at the corner of the Officers' Club, and Antonio was sat on the second step, which was a little larger. He held up a closed fist at the pseudo-Polish woman.

'There's nothing prettier than a North African autumn,' she said, delighted, 'in this light, the streets become as intimate as private gardens.' She seemed to know everybody, and she greeted them all with a smile or a nod of her head, as though she was at a gala.

They entered a haberdashery under the portico of the Sisters of Charity of the Immaculate Conception. Having dipped her hand into a cardboard box, she began picking colours. 'This ribbon,' she said, showing the pseudo-Polish woman a pink ribbon, 'has such a delicate, tender colour.' Everything that passed through her hands appeared inimitable to her – or at least she managed to give it enough importance to make it inimitable. 'I would just pin one to my dress, and go around dressed up like a gypsy: with bows, ribbons and flowers everywhere.'

'If you come next week,' the shopkeeper said, 'I'll have some new stock in – and,' she added, leaning over the counter, 'very refined stuff at that!'

'Really?' Mrs Boncompagni asked, slipping two spools and a ribbon into her purse.

The boulevard was crowded owing to the ritualistic pre-prandial walk. Mrs Boncompagni observed the interminable and joyful procession with curiosity, as though she's released all those people from cardboard boxes. The electric lights severed the sun's severe stream of light during sunset, as if a long series of candles had been lit.

'When will you learn to run errands calmly?' she asked her friend, 'New things scare you like thunder and lightning!'

Antonio, absent-minded, walked behind the two ladies, carrying his school-bag. A hoarse klaxon beeped at them aggressively as they crossed a tiny street.

'The presence of objects brings us comfort,' Mrs Boncompagni said, taking the pseudo-Polish woman by the arm, 'their variety serves to distract us. Fashion is my private theatre, a goddess who is a sister to dreams.'

'Mrs Boncompagni,' the dressmaker exclaimed, on seeing her walk back in. Her shop occupied two window-spaces under that portico, not far from the Piazza Ammiraglio Cagni. 'What a miracle…'

Mrs Boncompagni smiled – the shopkeepers' punctual exaggerations brought these quotidian scenes to vivid life, like festive music. Yet it was useless to try and encourage Elena to participate – the present was hopelessly inert, and the theatre was the exclusive prerogative of the past. This was why she still hadn't gotten married, despite being close to forty! She wasn't pretty, with that wan, pallid skin, and those features (which didn't leave a lasting impression on anyone), despite her being both delicate and sensible. 'She could make a man happy,' Mrs Boncompagni would say, 'if only they found an appropriate place to meet, between the past and the present, between great models and quotidian banality.'

Centuries experienced as intensely as her own personal vicissitudes had made Elena's gaze weary, like that of the old.

'You know,' she said, in order to soften her friend's discomfort in the face of the shopkeepers' verbal excesses (the dressmaker had disappeared in the back of the store), 'Antonio came running in yesterday, and he slammed the door so loudly that Attilio, the orderly, and Margherita and I ran over to see what had happened. Just in time to catch Antonio's triumphal cry as he returned from his walk with you in the municipal garden. A royal bill to settle with history, fabulous sums! My dear Elena, my beautiful princess – that boy loves you dearly and it makes me happy.'

Mrs Boncompagni selected a black hat. She looked at her friend in the mirror. 'I won't have Antonio looking to the party secretary, or the prefect or the Podestà as role models,' she whispered to the pseudo-Polish woman.

Standing under the hat's brim, the two ladies appeared to have entered an imaginary scene. The dressmaker's movements and those of the store clerk constituted a kind of counterpoint, a director's ingenious trick to force the spectator's attention to focus on those two heads. 'Tell him all about the Polish King, my dear, so that Fascism will strike him as utterly odious: *How a Balilla or a Piccola Italiana*[xvi] *can contribute to the victory of the Axis powers!*'

The dressmaker emptied all the white tissue paper out of a purple hat. 'This is the secret: novelty.'

Mrs Boncompagni forgot her disdain and the problems of Antonio's education.

She devoted herself to her sitting room's decoration with tender care: 'Did you notice that I lowered the wall mirror a little?' she asked her friend. Everything had been moved, meekly: a wall mirror had been heightened or lowered, the carpets laid out lengthwise or crosswise, and the round coffee table had been moved from the right to the left. 'Today, the teacher gave them a lesson on Julius Caesar, a pompous and useless icon. Antonio was bored. I want to read Shakespeare to him. He must see Caesar through the eyes of Brutus, or Mark Anthony, and not Mussolini's, or those of his teacher.'

Having come to a stop in the middle of the sitting room, she leaned against a mahogany Liberty console, and as though she'd just approached a rostrum, she began to proclaim the

---

[xvi] Italian: the name given to, respectively, boys and girls aged 8 to 14 during the Fascist years, similar to the Hitler Youth in Germany.

following lines, while the pseudo-Polish woman, doubling up as the Roman public, sipped from the cup of tea Margherita had offered her:

'*As Caesar loved me, I weep for him; as he was fortunate, I rejoice at it; as he was valiant, I honour him; but, as he was ambitious…* But it's impossible,'[xvii] the orator exclaimed, having grown angry. Antonio had, like a latecomer to the theatre, furtively snuck into the room and was now sitting on a satin armchair. Who knew that filth had clung to the boy's shorts throughout the day's adventures, and now he was sitting on satin? The boy's mother grabbed him by the ear and held the prisoner in custody.

'I hate your sitting room!' Antonio shouted, exasperatedly, 'I hate it, I hate it!'

He then proceeded to swear, convulsively, that he was going to cut up the satin chair with a razor blade, shoot at the canvases and the chandeliers.

Antonio only needed the pseudo-Polish woman's presence to convince himself that everything the others said was debatable and ultimately of secondary importance – or so his mother believed. Elena's past was a voyage he intended to undertake in order to bring back startling discoveries. Uncovering the stories of the Polish King was like discovering the New Indies, or rather his New Indies, a new way to embrace the world. The pseudo-Polish woman had also imprudently spoken to him of a suicidal Countess: from that day on, Antonio shadowed her every step, sort of like descending into the netherworld, a dangerous path for a ten year old boy.

[xvii] Lines from Shakespeare's *Julius Caesar*, Act 3, Scene 2.

The one responsible for saddling Elena Guastalla with that nickname had been Lieutenant Colonel Boncompagni; Elena hailed from very aristocratic stock, even though many of the links in the chain that bound her to the old Polish King were, according to the easy-going Boncompagni's judgement, rather vague.'

'Exaggerations, all exaggerations…' he would say whenever his wife reminded him of her friend's illustrious ancestry.

Antonio loved the solemn and profound shadow Elena cast; in fact, Elena's past became the basis of his apprenticeship, where, as Mrs Boncompagni was fond of saying, he would learn to make sense of life. This explained his bizarre behaviour on occasion, as the present proved too insignificant for him.

The Boncompagni family was assembled in the sitting room, on the ground floor. The radio was on. The mother held a piece of embroidery in her hand. 'Antonio, lower the volume, daddy is reading.'

'Thank you, darling,' the Lieutenant Colonel said, raising his eyes from his newspaper, 'you really do look after everyone.'

The ostentatiousness of petit bourgeois courtesy was one of the Lieutenant Colonel's pastimes. Making an equally ostentatious display of loyalty to the Duce was another. 'One must play the game,' he used to say.

Mrs Boncompagni sighed. 'Isn't it time to go to bed, Antonio?'

The boy peevishly stood up and ran off to his bedroom, on the first floor. His mother followed him, waited until he had undressed, tucked him under his covers, and switched off the light. The teacher had said that he was apathetic at school. 'I think,' she had petulantly added, 'that his indifference will gravely hinder his development.'

The remark had left her indignant: did that woman wish to write the novel of Antonio's life? Was this what they called *educating*?

'It's useless for us to try and weigh in on his education by trying to interest him in Tarzan's adventures, Balilla gatherings or Meccano toys,' she said, entering her bedroom. They inhabited the west wing of the villa, which had two turrets on either side and was ugly, isolated and intimate.

'Meaning,' the Lieutenant Colonel replied with a bow, 'that I should no longer take an interest in his education.'

He didn't seem that surprised by the sudden way she'd begun the evening's conversation.

'Instead of enriching those boys' lives, that teacher just flattens it with her explanations. But what does it matter,' she exclaimed, irritated, 'if Antonio knows that London is the capital of Great Britain? The multitude of people in possession of that same fact is so stupid and suffocating and…'

'Darling, aren't you in favour of universal suffrage?'

He had removed his shirt and was now in his undershirt. He still looked svelte and elegant despite his forty years. He had started to put on a belly, but it was a kind of addition that didn't impair his figure. He had regular features and he wore his hair in a lateral parting.

'Antonio is restless,' Mrs Boncompagni said, 'he can mysteriously intuit that our vision of the world does not include him entirely, but rather maims and saddens him, asks him to make fatal sacrifices. *Expelled, is what I call a man denied the protection of the law*,[xviii] Kleist warned, he who never came to terms with anything.'

Evening conversation was a mandatory rite.

'Why are you saying all this?'

'When Antonio will *grow into himself*, he will become an outlaw. I've always had a serene relationship with reality. But the light of Antonio's life is different, and a mother is rarely wrong when it comes to her intuitions and premonitions.'

'Whereas I think you want to make Antonio into your doppelgänger and thus use him in a dialectic manner, a task I failed you in. When all is said and done, what you're doing to him is very selfish: you task Antonio with living out the difficulties and hardships you've barely experienced thanks to the excellent, serene education your own family gave you.'

The Lieutenant Colonel had always loved parroting people, imitating with admiration and irony. On occasion, Mussolini himself would become the object of his pantomime, or, at other times, like in this instance, he would mimic his wife. He never expressed what he was really thinking, or rather the only way he could express it was to reflect what the other had said in his own manner, examining their turns of phrase, their tone. It was a constant, playful parody. Maybe he simply had nothing to say, like a mirror lacks any image or colour of its own on its reflective surface.

'Elena hasn't found her footing in society, and her independence – which is the subject of so much of your irony – immediately captured Antonio's imagination.'

[xviii] David Constantine (tr., ed.), *Heinrich Von Kleist: Selected Writings* (Hackett, 1997), p.237.

'All this is very ingenious, darling, very ingenious indeed…' the Lieutenant Colonel said, 'When all's said and done, you're the little boy. I think you'll wind up turning him into a writer, this is what I think the Polish woman's throne alludes to. My Lord, why have you inflicted this new punishment on me?'

The Lieutenant Colonel lingered self-contentedly in front of the mirror. He loved to admire his own body, it was a way, he said, *to plant his feet firmly on earth again* – and looking at his body he felt that it was restless to receive his orders, loyal as a dog, he added sarcastically, and as imperious as a demon, he added yet again, feeling happy. Whenever one of his comrades mocked him over his vanity, he would gravely reply that sports were nothing but a rather ingenious and completely hypocritical variation of his so-called vanity, since it involved the pleasure of looking after one's body while out under the sun.

'Whenever you speak,' he said, 'I always feel as though you've got a tail, your movements are so sublime and theatrical. At other times, what can I say – I experience a maddening desire for lightness. Now the idea of having not one but two such creatures moving around with their tails in this house frightens me to the core.'

'For that matter, the boy already has a very long tail. The Polish King, the suicidal Countess, the officer who died at the battle of Auerstedt,[xix] these are all keys, links in this golden chain.'

'But you're the one who laughs at her, calling her a dancing bear and a talking dog!'

[xix] One of the battles of the Napoleonic wars (1806), which ended in a French victory. The officer mentioned is likely the Duke of Brunswick, one of the Prussian commanders.

The Lieutenant Colonel was irked. He put on his pyjamas.

'He's very proud of her, and very jealous, too,' his wife pointed out, 'Elena is his most prized possession: he torments her like a prisoner, but she's a hostage of the highest value. Today he came back from their walk and very excitedly told me the pseudo-Polish woman's secrets. He was acting so spasmodic as he described it to me, that it scared me.'

'It didn't scare you, darling,' the Lieutenant Colonel corrected her, 'in fact, you enjoyed it.' He opened the bathroom door.

'You'll only bring him to the brink of despair…' the Lieutenant Colonel exclaimed, coming back into the bedroom, refreshed by the shower. His movements were exaggerated, it was his way of stretching before bed. The excited confusion of his movements brought his utterances into sharp relief. 'You're wearing him out. Mind you, I don't want to concern myself with the boy's education, believing I would simply be wasting my efforts, and I wouldn't be more likely to succeed than his teacher. Yet when one suffers from *grandeur*, when the tail is ostentatious, when every gesture becomes a ritual or symbol: life is curtailed until it's as brief as a libretto. One must pay up by the end of the third – at most, fifth – act!'

'We can't seriously consider letting him become a balilla!' Mrs Boncompagni exclaimed, dismayed.

'The ancien régime is as responsible for fascism as are you romantics,' the Lieutenant Colonel retorted, 'fascism may well be protecting feudal interests, but its strengths lie rooted in romantic myths, and the degeneration of romanticism is an excellent mask for the safeguarding of feudal interests.'

'You're quite eloquent this evening,' Mrs Boncompagni said.

'Antonio isn't very interested in his parents, and as you put it, he rejects the order we embody, just like he rejects school; that's something, especially for his age. Especially since he has also displayed a febrile fascination for certain facts, complete devotion to a royal spectre, he's trying to find a new scale of values and he disdains the destiny of the balillas. Not bad, not bad: I see the complete makings for a total ruin. My only hope, darling, is that you're wrong, that Antonio will suffer uselessly for some time and then it'll all be over. In fact, one day he'll leave the pseudo-Polish woman behind the way one shuts a book, he'll take a few steps, and then having reached the other side of the garden, he'll go and play football with boys his own age. It'll be like it was in primitive societies, when the young man underwent the initiation rite and left female society to enter the world of men. Of course, we don't live in a warrior society these days, when eight million bayonets are nothing but a muscular prompt to be deployed at will by the theatre directors of politics, thus the world of men is the world of sports.'

In order to better illustrate what he was saying, he opened and shut his arms in a sudden jerk, standing on the tip of his toes.

II

'You have such a beautiful home!' said the Baroness Sanjust of Teulada, the Podestà's wife, once she'd stepped inside Mrs Boncompagni's sitting room. She had brought her son along with her. 'Go play with the lady's son. And remember,' she added menacingly with her finger, 'behave!'

Antonio and the boy went out. The Baroness was visiting the Boncompagni house for the first time. The sitting room had been subjected to maniacal rearrangements for the occasion: it looked fake.

As soon as they had gone outside, Antonio grabbed his accomplice by the hand and dragged him to the bottom of the stairs. There was nothing to fear from Margherita and the orderly, who were busy in the kitchen.

Antonio pushed the boy past the door, and standing overbearingly close to him, as though wanting to choke him, he laid out his plan. His guest was frightened. 'Shut up!' Antonio exclaimed, 'You stay here. When my mom leaves to make the tea, I'll whistle. You'll flip the electric switch off. Careful: if you do it wrong you'll burn your hand. This is how you do it. Got it? Now go!' he exclaimed, holding the swinging door against his chest.

Margherita and the orderly were going back and forth between the kitchen and the buffet set up in the sitting room, which had been designed to resemble the imaginative geometric designs of carpets: here were some cakes shining like medallions, here were some tarts lined up in long rows. There was such an obvious ceremonial detachment in the manner those two carried one dish after another back and forth, while the ladies, sunk in their armchairs, lingered oblivious to it all, so much so that the Podestà's wife made a graceful gesture of wonderment and asked: 'Who's all this for?' The scene appeared to have been reduced to one of those delicate porcelain depictions popular in the eighteenth century.

The mother, the orderly and Margherita were busy in the kitchen, standing over boiling water as the steam passed from receptacle to receptacle. By the time Antonio barely whistled, more cautiously than a swallow, leading the other boy, broken into submission through fear, to pull the power. The house was cast into pitch black, as was the sitting room when Antonio burst into it, like an impetuous knight, the ladies imprisoned in their armchairs, completely at his mercy.

The spectacle that unfolded, after the orderly managed to find the oblivious little prince in his hiding place and switched the lights back on, was truly frightening. Meringues had been squashed, cakes vandalised, flowers trampled on. The ladies looked bewildered. When the sitting room had been plunged into the dark, neither of them had noticed the knight's intrusion.

The mother commanded the orderly and the maid to clear the table. She additionally had the orderly go fetch some crackers and biscuits from the patisserie on Piazza Cagni.

The Podestà's wife barely drank a few sips of her tea and contented herself with placing a single biscuit on her saucer, without bringing it to her lips.

Knowing that the pseudo-Polish woman was still in the sitting room, the Lieutenant Colonel went to join her. 'My dear princess!' he murmured, planting a kiss on her hand. He cast a glance over what remained of the earlier buffet: a few crumbs of cake and meringues, looking like the eviscerated remains of sacrificial animals soiling the high altar.

'Quite a bit of commotion today. What's new?'

Margherita had already told him everything.

He looked at his wife. The impression she'd left the Podestà's wife, and worse still, the profanation of the ceremony in which her house was being celebrated had left her looking aged.

The Lieutenant Colonel approached the buffet. He was nibbling a few things, picking them up from plate to plate, even picking at the crumbs on the tablecloth. He kicked the crumbs on the floor under the table with his foot.

'You know what I think?' he asked, turning to his wife, 'Antonio did this for Elena's sake: a memorable gesture in honour of his beloved. You didn't understand him at all. Antonio was right to feel aggrieved, you mistook him for a simple little thief! What an inadequate audience... Deep down, I find all this highly gallant, and most ingenious!'

Having left the table, the Lieutenant Colonel went to sit between the two friends. 'What exquisite cakes! Antonio is being incredibly impertinent by screaming that they're disgusting, you did well to give him a good hiding. Whose is this cup of tea?' The Podestà's wife had used it. The Lieutenant Colonel stirred its contents. 'Cold tea is very refreshing.'

He was in the mood to talk.

'You didn't love Tommaso until he had played his last card, and you love Antonio who still has all of his. Quite a careless, foolish act. Antonio is what Plato – or whoever – once called *a dark thing.*[xx] My dear princess, you've taken on quite the risk.'

Tommaso Marinoni was a reserved sort of officer, around forty years old, still a bachelor, who had once carried on a long conversation with Elena one evening at the Officers' Club, attracting the guests' curiosity. He had been killed a few days later, after an accident on the mountains, when his vehicle 'flipped over, executing him,' as Boncompagni had put it, incapable of talking about a tragedy without enforcing an ironic distance as though it was something he'd read or thought. 'Tommaso was able to bring Elena from the distant centuries of her ancestors'

xx Reference to Plato's Cave.

times and back to the present: but lo and behold those very same ancestors steal that distinguished officer away from her to keep him imprisoned in the cold mansions where they dwell…' he had then added.

'At times I feel as though I am saving the tragic Tommaso and the restless Antonio, as far as our friend is concerned, we are interchangeable apparitions. All this is arrogant and offensive – what do you think, darling?' he asked, turning to his wife who was sat on his right. He felt young and alive, pleased by the fact he didn't have any powerful ancestors lurking in his past, his nature fled from the drama: 'only he who lives in here and now manages to steer clear of them,' he said, facetiously. He distrusted Fascism's tendency to invoke the past in the anxiety to bring it back to life. As in Tommaso's case, he feared that the Roman Empire would bury fascism in its ruins, contrary to the former's idea of resurrecting that old world.

'I don't understand, should I punish Antonio or not?' the Lieutenant Colonel asked, impressed by the ladies' silence.

III

On the walls of the city, posters had been put up announcing the forthcoming season of opera at the Berenice Cinema, an exceptional event in the colony, and one on which the administration counted to augment the golden aura of their prestige. It was a symbolic gesture, a kind of consecration for that distant land: what could be further removed from the boundless, deserted Africa, devoid of social artifices, than an opera? The playbill included *Andrea Chénier*, *Rigoletto*, *Madama Butterfly*,

Cavalleria Rusticana and *Pagliacci*. The piece which had been picked to open the season was Lucia di Lamermoor, starring Mercedes Capsir,[xxi] a soprano whose glory was fading, and whose portrait, where she appeared smiling and all powdered up, could be seen in all the shop displays along the Corso.

A week prior to the season's inauguration, at a conference held in the great hall of the Municipality building, a teacher from the Giosuè Carducci[xxii] secondary school had employed seductive slides projected on an immense canvas to illustrate the majestic ruins of the Greek and Roman amphitheatres in the colony.

Quicumque mundo terminus obstitit
Hunc tangat armis, visere gestiens,
Qua parte debacchantur ignes,
Qua nebulae pluviique rores.[xxiii]

The over-attentive audience in the auditorium broke into frenetic applause, those Latin verses which nobody understood were a kind of patriotic mass, where they bore witness to the past rather than the great beyond, given that this past was the source of the legitimacy of the new colonization of the African mainland. The hall was full to bursting, and the heat was stultifying.

'One of the colony's health-stimulating effects,' the Lieutenant Colonel jovially commented while he and his wife returned home in a rented carriage, which was as black as a gondola, two

---

xxi Mercedes Capsir (1895–1969) was a Spanish opera singer.

xxii Giosuè Carducci (1835–1907): leading Italian poet of the 19th and early 20th century who was also the country's first Nobel laureate.

xxiii Horace, Ode III: 'whatever limit confines the world/may Rome storm it by force and see/where the fire rages the brightest,/and the clouds, the rain and the dew.' (My translation).

flames throbbed in the headlights atop the driver's seat, 'is to make one proud of its past civilization, even someone like me, whose gaps of knowledge extend to entire centuries. Here in the colony, we are all rewarded by our illustrious heritage: this is why the pseudo-Polish woman didn't make much of an impression on me. She numbers a King among her descendants, while I – going by what the archaeologist said – can count Pindar, Plato, Callimachus and Emperor Hadrian among mine, all of whom also took part in public assemblies of colonists.'

He coughed. 'Nobody had realised that our colonization is a sublime theatrical event. The *Mal d'Afrique* is a period, darling,' the elegant officer added, taking his wife's hands in his, 'just like the baroque.'

Stimulated by emulation, the women of the city were in crisis. Mrs Boncompagni had managed to send for one of her mother's evening dresses in Italy, given that her mother had once been an incredibly elegant woman in her time. It was made of black silk, with sparkling sequin *paillettes*. It clung to her sides a little too tightly. The dressmaker didn't seem to be bothered at all over having to modify an old dress rather than creating a new one. Having been pulled out of a chest, the dress was worn, but thanks to the confluence of clout it exuded, it ennobled her profession. 'I feel as though I'm preparing you for the stage!' she said, enraptured.

During the final fitting, which had unusually taken place in Mrs Boncompagni's sitting room rather than the shop on the Corso, Antonio lingered in mute, agitated contemplation: his mother was thus becoming a character. It was as if an alien, magic hand had lain on her. Thanks to that dress, she had transcended everydayness, it was a kind of elevation – perhaps a metamorphosis. The dressmaker was kneeling before her, mumbling about something or other, looking like a devout worshipper before a sacred image.

Maybe Antonio identifies with me as the suicidal Countess, his mother thought, experiencing a mixture of vanity and pain, and by pain – *with all the wasteful, sentimental excess typical of suicide*s – she meant the Countess's, her son's, and her own.

Antonio was taken to the performance of *Rigoletto* by the pseudo-Polish woman (who was wearing a long dress, which was diaphanous, and looked like a larva that had come from another world, or had just simply landed on the scene, as Lieutenant Colonel Boncompagni put it) who paid her many compliments when accompanying her to the theatre along with his wife, but which he quickly turned inside out like a glove as soon as the aging miss disappeared with his son into the illuminated atrium as though they were the ones about to step on the stage.

However, Mrs Boncompagni's attention was fixed on the little knight who was entering the theatre, beaming with pride at the damsel on his arm; there was something false or unreal about it, which appeared to allude to something difficult and non-adaptable in Antonio's soul and nature.

What is an officer, which characteristics define him?

The Corso was bustling with activity. The last latecomers who were arriving at the theatre, the multitude of curious onlookers, the people on their customary evening perambulations: it looked like an immense miniature, or a scene set in an Africa crowded with bit players.

The season of opera had reanimated the night, the windows on the Corso were brightly lit, and the colony performed that ritual with a kind of consecration, celebrating their ancestors, the sacred remains had been brought over and ritualistically exhibited on the new African land. Who would have imagined that one day, the abandoned coastline where the Expeditionary Corps under General Caneva had landed, would see a theatre built on it, where a play set at the court of Mantua would be performed!

Having retracted their steps, Mrs Boncompagni and the Lieutenant Colonel sat at the open-air café of the Hotel Italia, situated in the Piazza del Re, where the little orchestra, whose stage was situated among the trees of the Municipal gardens, played a pot-pourri of excerpts from famous operas, as though wanting to please the clamouring crowd of those who had been excluded from the entertainment inside the theatre.

Once midnight had passed, the couple, comprising the diaphanous princess and her tiny knight, reemerged from the Berenice's dark, silent parterre and reappeared in the piazza. The Lieutenant Colonel and his wife were waiting for them on the sidewalk of the garden overlooking the theatre. Antonio gave his mother his hand, his fist tightly clenched, a ritual gesture introducing something difficult, and he talked and fell silent again in a feverish state of excitement. It was as though the pseudo-Polish woman, having spent a great deal of time preparing him, had brought him to the temple, where the setting of his mind and the past, a golden tail, had, thanks to the stage décor and music, been magically pushed out of the invisible world into the visible one. In the meanwhile, they had headed towards the crowded, festive Corso, and Mrs Boncompagni and Antonio walked slightly behind the pseudo-Polish woman and the Lieutenant Colonel.

Fragments of a cheeky, tight-lipped conversation, whose thread was entirely clear and indescribable, infantile and inscrutable, Antonio's words projected themselves on the stage of the future, drawing out his *silhouette* as a man, his destiny. It was as if the knight had offered the palm of his hand to an expert fortune-teller. Antonio had been elected to suffer constant discord, this is what his mother had read in his palm. The violence of feelings as performed on the stage was devastating and had nothing to do with real, everyday life: the boy had seen figures flash before his eyes, egged by passions similar to his own, or with the same intensity of passion as his, perhaps even sharing the same excess that typified and moved the characters in his mind. The theatre's magic circle as the metaphorical objectification of the mind and its unruliness, where life remains warm at the core.

Provided, therefore, that he could become a character from an opera – whose secret lies in the brevity of life, in fleeing the reckoning of the road for that of the stage – the brave knight Antonio had been finally allowed to undergo a rebirth, even though it occurred as he raced towards catastrophe. This was why the Polish King, the suicidal Countess, and the gentleman killed in a duel depicted in the little golden oval miniature (or bauble, as the Lieutenant Colonel put it) that Elena wore pinned on her tailleur's label, as well as all the other characters from the pseudo-Polish woman's past, were metaphorical configurations of Antonio's destiny, illustrating all the possibilities lying before individuals which everyday life appeared to exclude. Thanks to the power of alienation, the fact that the actors sang instead of talked also alluded to their rejection of society's rules and its deadly magnitude. Elena's past had been a prelude to the opera, into which the boy had finally been admitted, having moved up a rung on the ladder of consciousness. Opera was the twin of history: a triumphal confirmation of the lessons the pseudo-Polish woman had taught him – in fact opera acted as a safeguard against history.

The Corso was teeming with people, and the party carried on: only on the occasion of His Majesty Victor Emmanuel III's visit had the colony experienced such long nights. The seafront promenade, which ran parallel to the Corso, was as brightly lit as the latter: three-pronged cast iron lanterns were hanging from columns of Roman travertine, their light gently skimming the water's trembling surface.

The Lieutenant Colonel and the pseudo-Polish woman in her *crêpe georgette* dress, now a little rumpled, were walking a few steps ahead of Antonio and Mrs Boncompagni. It looked as though the officer wanted to draw everyone's attention to how they looked like a couple while he walked alongside the old miss, who resembled those tempestuous characters in those old operas which always ended with a sacrificial offering. He had thus been granted the pleasure of walking along the Corso, a real place, with a character that was both imaginary and musically seductive. For the first time, he found it ironic – irony being his sole means of even approaching the truth – that he finally understood Antonio's fascination for that boring, penniless woman.

Mrs Boncompagni didn't miss a single opportunity to nod her head at someone she knew with a smile on her lips. Her social conduct, even in the most extraordinary situations, followed a musical rhythm, just like that walk along the Corso. Once upon a time there were dances that resembled soft, lavish strolls. What did it matter if thanks to some incomprehensible spell, her knight had been reduced to a midget?

After all, her thoughts were not directed to the Corso, still heaving with people at this late hour owing to the opening night of the opera season. Amidst that festive, restless sea, all that interested her was the island constituted by her son, Antonio.

Only a small incident occurred. Having almost reached the end of the Corso, they had crossed paths with the dressmaker, who wasn't far from her shop. The poor woman was left speechless after she greeted Mrs Boncompagni and failed to be greeted in return. She was one of her few clients who said hello without first being obsequiously prompted: and now she didn't even answer anymore. She experienced a moment of spite and disappointment, which was immediately negated by the sudden fear that her most generous client had found herself in the middle of some drama. She had seen her gallant husband walking with the Polish woman a few steps ahead of Mrs Boncompagni and her boy: but it simply couldn't be that the old Miss Guastalla could cause the beautiful Mrs Boncompagni any jealousy. Or perhaps, just like during the nights of the carnival, people's faces had been replaced by masks?

The agreement struck at home had stipulated only a single outing to the theatre for Antonio, given that the cost of a season ticket was *a tad exorbitant* (as Lieutenant Colonel Boncompagni snidely remarked) simply to fill a little boy's evenings.

However, when Antonio learned of the ban, he was seized by such an excess of frightening anger that his mother, knowing the performance would begin in not too long, offered to give up her own seat so that he (meaning Boncompagni) could accompany the boy. The morning had already been tense, and he had already heard the doors being violently shut on several occasions – one of Antonio's bad habits, for which she always reproached him – but he had taken it too far that morning and it made the house seem haunted by ghosts. She had spent the rest of the morning in a pensive mood, but she hadn't questioned Antonio. She had been so distracted that she'd forgotten her appointment with the dressmaker, and when she realised it, she took it as a bad omen. It was as though a placid, serene plane of her life had just flitted into nothingness.

All of this had taken place in the morning, when the Lieutenant Colonel had been away.

Now they were all at home, while the beginning of the performance drew nearer and nearer.

'That boy's an idiot!' the Lieutenant Colonel thundered, one could have heard him all the way out on the street, or on the terrace. His voice, almost always eloquent and ironic, was completely suited to his martial profession. 'A nervous breakdown just to go to the opera! What are we going to do with a boy like that?' he asked, beside himself with rage. 'I'll give him an opera!' he screamed, wearing the most evil expression worn by baritones as they skulk off backstage.

That vain man also knew how to be incredibly ugly. It struck Mrs Boncompagni that her husband's voice was a sound triggered by the same forces she'd seen earlier that morning in

Antonio's slamming of the doors – or a different force entirely, yet one which nevertheless existed on the same dramatic plane.

The orderly appeared, looking spooked, believing himself to be the object of the officer's ire. The young man spoke the dialect of the rural valleys around Bergamo, a tongue suffused with guttural sounds and glottal stops, Mrs Boncompagni often guessed at what he said, rather than truly understand it. Yet on that day he sank even deeper into his accent, and she couldn't make any sense of it.

The opera in the house: while the Lieutenant Colonel makes every room reverberate with his yells, one can still hear Antonio's desperate, combative cries, sounding like a tenor in the final stretch of the performance. However, the drama wasn't over, far from it.

Her motherly foreboding received its confirmation: that boy was destined for a difficult life. It had already been made obvious by Antonio's zealous devotion to Elena's past, a kind of swashbuckling drama where every adventure was always sealed by a death.

All palliative remedies would be useless, as would deferments: the tragedy of Antonio's path to self-awareness simply had to play out.

She had gone to the hairdresser that morning, who was incredibly busy, as all the ladies wished to look seductive at the theatre, propelled by the desire to emulate one another. Amidst that domestic din, masterfully curled locks were entirely extraneous to the scene, just like wigs. *Today marks the beginning of Antonio's drama*, she told herself, as though she was staring into a mirror.

The orderly's tender heart couldn't bear it any longer and he rushed over to help his young friend. He crossed paths with the Lieutenant Colonel at the door and barely moved aside in time.

Boncompagni reappeared in the room where he'd left his wife. He was calm and had a wry smile on his lips, it looked as though it was all over.

'From now on,' he said, 'I'll be seeing to the boy's education.'

THE DARKROOM

Colonel Baldassare Rossi was especially known among the idle, frivolous members of colonial society for his passion for photography. He would rest his camera on a wooden tripod. He didn't take photographs on the spot, but rather focused on shooting well-prepared scenes – like those pictures of public ceremonies taken by official licensed photographers, or slightly morbid portraits, ones where the subjects' heads were encircled by a milky or sulphurous halo. Whenever he was wholly engrossed by his work, he would give orders with irritated severity: he appeared to want to bend the will of others and present his camera with his model's inert remains.

His portraits were anything but inert or monotonous: his array of pictures featured all imaginable kinds of moods and personalities. At times, he seemed to – and this was the highest form of praise – aspire to the model, or want to fall victim to the inspiration of the moment. Nevertheless, he was the sole author of the script that the model read while striking a single pose, and it was useless to try to convince him to take pictures in that way or the other: one had to surrender oneself to him.

Possibly owing to the fact that he wore a glass eye, the essence of his face appeared to be reserved to his right side, where the immobile eye lay in its orbit, which remained subject to the other side where a useful, working eye furnished him with all the information required for everyday life.

Rossi was a bachelor. That aside, nobody knew anything about his life.

There were those who insinuated that his passion for images concealed repressed or frustrated desires: that man could possess souls through his camera. Others, employing a softer tact, suggested that it was his way of conversing and communicating. A witty soul explained that Rossi's photographic eye was merely a replacement for his glass eye.

Some women had taken fright when the Colonel, who was usually so measured with his movements, suddenly disappeared behind his instrument with one quick move: instead of his head, all they could see was a piece of black cloth. Thus armed, he looked as though he might attack them. Instead, he contented himself with opening his additional eye in the dark and capturing the desired image.

Which he then returned to his subject, having immortalised her into stillness, as if said woman had fallen under a spell.

One lady, who was devout if nonetheless possibly victim to morbid fantasies, had remarked on leaving Rossi's studio that she felt as though she'd just left her lover's room after committing adultery – she had added in her husband's presence, leaving him to gaze at her with an awkward expression. This might explain why she never showed the portrait the military man had taken of her to anybody, including her offended, curious husband. Strange rumours regarding that portrait made the rounds, which the lady never bothered to deny. Loyal and honest, she was pleased by the strange adventure caused by that photograph.

The Colonel refused to move the farraginous instrument elsewhere, he wouldn't even consent to take it to the Officers' Club, which he steadfastly attended. Anyone who wanted their portrait taken had to go to his house and enter his studio on their own.

This was why people were astonished to see Baldassare Rossi head over to Mrs Campana's house one day, schlepping his instrument and all the big light bulbs to her place on Via Regina Elena. Curious passers-by stopped to watch as the officer ordered the camera and its tripod, which were semi-wrapped in that piece of black cloth, to be brought out of the car. However, the gossipers had no reason to grow suspicious: helping the Colonel in his task (in the absence of Captain Campana) was Campana's orderly, as well as his son, Natalino.

Mrs Campana welcomed the Colonel with a conspiratorial smile. Despite it being two in the afternoon, she was in evening dress, wearing makeup and jewelry. Truth be told, she appeared more drawn to the shapeless body hidden under the black cloth than its military escort. There was a brightness and sonorousness to her, and the makeup she wore at that unusual hour turned the house into the corridors at the opera.

The orderly had watched her, astonished, while Natalino was excited and jealous. He was ten years old and had just begun classes at the local middle school.

Poking his head out of his room, the tutor, Klaus Lichtenberg, a man in his thirties who was giving him German lessons. He discreetly helped the Colonel with his equipment, wordlessly substituting the orderly, who was clumsy and in a hurry. But why all these ceremonies?

The only one who knew that secret was the photographer. The previous night, Mrs Campana had gone up to him in the Club's great hall on Corso Italia.

'Colonel,' she'd said, 'I'm forced to confide in you in a way I've never done before. But I know it's the only way to overcome your hesitation. I'm doomed, the doctor said I simply must return to Italy right away. He made it clear to me that there's no hope left. I told my husband that I had to go home because my mother had been afflicted by a terrible illness… it would be useless to torture him over this, he'll know everything *after the fact*: not even pain managed to bring us closer together. I'm going to leave my son here. I know that these are my last days with him… the mail boat for Naples leaves next Saturday. What am I going to tell him? Offer him some moral maxim? There will be plenty of people who will do that, in fact they'll associate those maxims with his dead mother as if I was giving him those lectures myself. It'll be the most boring part of all this, I don't want to start now. I've got another plan in mind. I want to leave my son a lot of photos. So many photos. I want you to come to my house and photograph me in various poses and different clothes: it'll be like living all the years stolen away from me here in Africa in the space of a single day. But I can't come all the way to your house dragging a trunk full of clothes, people will think I've left my husband for you. It'll be so much easier to bring your celebrated camera to my house. You'll hand the photos over to my son when I'm dead: you'll tell him that his mother sent them to him, instead of the letters she'll never write.'

Baldassare Rossi displayed no emotion whatsoever. 'When would you like me to come?' he asked, giving her a slight nod of his head.

'Maybe it would be best not to waste any time: come tomorrow.'

'At what time?'

'At two in the afternoon, I think we'll have enough to keep us busy for a while.'

'Will the Captain be there to help me?'

'The Captain is off on a mission. His orderly and my son are here with me. Then there's a young German professor. He knows more about music than electric instruments, but maybe he'll come in handy. He's writing a thesis on the Greek ruins of Cyrenaica and the studies carried out by Northern European scholars: from Thrige to Bates and Wilamowitz, of whom he speaks almost every day as though he were preparing us to sit an exam.'

As it turned out, Herr Klaus was of great help. He wasn't acquainted with the camera's workings, as he knew nothing about electricity, but he was diligent and promptly obeyed orders. In half an hour's time, the studio had been reassembled in Mrs Campana's sitting room. Mrs Campana posed for her first photograph.

Then she disappeared. Amidst the silence that ensued, neither of the two men exchanged a word. Mrs Campana reappeared another half hour later wearing a different long dress. A new pose. One time while wearing black gloves. Then she slipped her arms into long white ones. She even displayed a range of moods: cheerful, melancholy, alert, pensive, aggressive, absent. She almost always heeded the Colonel's suggestions. On a single occasion, she insisted on being photographed in a strange pose, her naked arms distended in an arch in front of her, or as Herr Klaus thought, as if she was trying to embrace the invisible.

When Mrs Campana left the sitting room, the German was shocked to see a tear, a single tear, leaking out of the Colonel's working eye.

He took a step back, embarrassed, when he realised that the Colonel's other eye was fixed upon him with a glassy look of reproach, as though he'd committed a faux pas with his curiosity.

He went into the corridor. He saw Mrs Campana, who was coming towards him while wearing a close-fitting black taffeta dress. While he backed up against the wall, the lady walked past him like a ghost, and for the final time, she stepped inside her sitting room, which had been transformed into a darkroom.

Lichtenberg went downstairs. He didn't want to see his pupil, he didn't want him to see he was scared. He felt guilty, even though he didn't know the reason why.

His heart skipped a beat when he saw a ghost wearing a black hood leave the sitting room and descend the stairs while being carried on the shoulders of the Colonel and the orderly. It wasn't even as if he'd seen Mrs Campana's lifeless body. He went out onto the street and started walking hurriedly.

Natalino was right behind him, looking even smaller while he chased that six foot-tall man, mocking and restless, he wanted to know why his lesson had been interrupted that day.

That evening, Natalino learned that his mother would soon be leaving; as for him, he would have to go to boarding school. He immediately connected the announcement of his mother's trip with that afternoon in the darkroom.

'Why are you crying now? You're a big man, come on! You know who I took all those photographs for? For you!'

Natalino allowed her to console him. Recalling fables he'd heard years before, he said, fearfully, that the Colonel's glass eye seemed to him like a clock that marked an hour that could not be exceeded.

On the day of her departure, Mrs Campana confided in the foreigner. He lived in two of the rooms on the ground floor, which had been given to him in exchange for his services as a tutor. She told him that she didn't want her son to associate her image with the arduous road that led to the graveyard, but instead the downhill path of life: 'Life must seduce him into living, and I want the image of me to reside in that flux, I don't want him to situate it in a cemetery, where life has come to an end.'

From the window, one could see all the passers-by from the waist up.

'Here's what all those photographs depicting elegance, desire and vanity that I'm going to leave him will achieve. His mommy will lead him into the light by the hand: and when I'm gone, the images will do it for me.'

Her figure was harmonious, her features delicate, she was carefully composed, and she lingered for a moment, immobile.

'Make sure he keeps up with his logical analysis…' she enjoined him.

Lichtenberg's thoughts turned to the secret tear in the Colonel's eye.

On that day, the scrappy bits and ends of his thesis lay dormant before him, they looked like tombstones. Natalino surprised him while idling in his room downstairs and having walked up to him carefully, shook his elbow.

WEDDING MARCH

Terzi was a haughty man, whom nobody had ever managed to humble. He struck one as a remnant of that era of duels, when a man could strike fear into the hearts of many with his anger, his umbrageous sense of honour, as well as his dexterity and confidence with a sword or pistol. Lieutenant Miccoli used to say that Terzi's head was made of stone, exactly of the kind used at the top of the architraves in old palaces: if he never bowed his head it was simply because it would have probably snapped!

His daughter, Elda, was his spitting image. She was highly vivacious and generous, but she also shared his indomitable willpower. Terzi used to say that if only his own soldiers had had her temperament, their enemies during the war would have had a much tougher time. This ridiculous sort of praise was the only kind of approval anybody had heard him give a living soul. 'Elda is his Achilles' heel,' Miccoli insinuated. He swore that he would court her in order to mock her statue-like father, but then pulled back and declared that he wasn't in the mood; truth be told, he was frightened.

The son, who had arrived ten years after Elda and was in his second year at middle school, was also afraid. Terzi was very hard on him. Claudio was an excellent student at school and submissive at home. He only seemed to really be alive, just like at school, whenever he stood outside of his father's shadow.

Mrs Terzi often had an opinion, that is, until her husband expressed his: his mere appearance in an affair would cause her to vanish. Resentful, Elda would say: 'It's like we don't have a mother.'

'I'd like to see how you would handle it if you were his wife…' Mariangela Terzi would say while sobbing.

'He and I will have our reckoning one day.'

She seemed to be waiting for the opportunity to challenge that man and his pressing sense of honour to a duel.

The opportunity finally arrived, and it was as banal as it could have possibly been.

Elda had fallen in love with a young man of obscure origins, who had *emigrated* to the colony just like people used to head over to America fifty years earlier. He apparently aspired to be an artist. Nobody, of course, had ever spent a cent on any of his sculptures. He made a living by giving drawing lessons.

The Colonel's wrath exploded right on time. Nobody knew what he might have wanted in a son-in-law, but needless to say, the unlucky wretch couldn't aspire to the role. He hadn't expressed any particular reservations in regards to the young man, whom he'd barely seen: it was as though he were dealing with the ghost of a dream, the kind one chases away, annoyed, when one wakes up. Nevertheless, while he had woken up, his daughter was still submerged in her dream, where the ghost was still alive.

Much drama – or indeed, melodrama – erupted in that house. Mrs Terzi seemed so scared that she displayed the most severity towards the young man. She constantly talked of the matter and let herself slip into hysterics, as though that odious young man was a brute who was trying to rape her.

Claudio was well aware that there wasn't room for another man in his father's house, and the rejection of Elda's beloved offered virtual proof. His nose was always stuck in a book, as though he was hiding in them. Every time he sat for an exam, he got a higher grade: every ceremony or honourable mention was a mockery, as if the spirit of knowledge had understood that he studied so excessively because he was afraid of real life.

The wicked affair unfolded along predictable patterns, with a crescendo of tension but no new plot elements. The young man didn't seem so indolent at all, and had found himself a good job with a well-respected local businessman. No unflattering rumours circulated about him in that colonial city. He was reserved. However, none of these efforts had yielded any fruit: Colonel Terzi's opinions were autonomous and irrevocable.

The wedding day eventually arrived. Elda made herself a short white dress.

The only people present at the ceremony were the friends of Attilio Rossi, the groom. Terzi ignored the event altogether. Instead, he showed up at the Officers' Club with his wife at the same time they always did. The guests' curiosity was intense; yet that expression of his gave them no satisfaction, he seemed to use the same expression for everything. Claudio arrived at the church looking very pale, but well dressed. He had disobeyed his father's orders for the first time. If he had managed to slip out of the house, it was only because nobody dared imagine he would attempt to take part in that ceremony. Was he challenging his father, perhaps? Truth be told, he was absolutely convinced that a tragedy would occur: either when the couple entered or left the cathedral, his father would be lurking in wait in the parvis, or he would have summoned his soldiers to appear and then gunfire would have ensued. His melancholy mood seemed to be troubled by those deranged visions: then it would finally be over, and his father would triumph once again, but by then he was no longer there, having fallen into the heap of bodies alongside his sister, still in her wedding dress next to Attilio and his friends, whom nobody knew.

The gunfire did not transpire, neither before the ceremony, nor after it. Claudio hesitated for a long time before going home. When he finally appeared, exhausted, nobody thought to speak to him.

Terzi was convinced that even his daughter's studies – a thesis on German philology – would soon adopt the *bohemian* bend her life had taken. In Colonel Terzi's dictionary – nay, his cosmology – the word *bohemian* indicated a realm of absolute evil.

Claudio was horrified to notice that his parents no longer mentioned their daughter's name.

Nevertheless, one day, after months had passed, the Colonel found himself face to face with his daughter and his son-in-law when attending a dinner party at his friends' house by the sea. It wasn't a trap, the host hadn't been in the city for long and knew nothing of the complicated matrimonial affair.

Colonel Terzi experienced a surge of pleasure: just like him, his daughter always held her head high. She had never asked to come to the house, and she'd never sent an ambassador to plead pity on her behalf. That surge of pleasure unleashed an unwilling smile. As for his wife, who thought she'd stumbled onto the drama's climactic moment, her blood rushed through her veins. She embraced her daughter. The Colonel looked at them ironically: his teary-eyed wife on one hand and on the other Elda, shirking away from curiosity, and her graceful face, which sat gently atop her long neck, concealed all sentiments.

Claudio had gotten lost as soon as he'd entered. He had been invited too, but on seeing that Elda and Attilio were there, he had fled.

After that casual encounter, Elda and Attilio began visiting the house. Only Claudio and his mother feared that the situation could take a dramatic turn at any moment. As for Attilio, he never once dredged up the subject of his pointless humiliation – and Terzi approved of his tact. As if the showdown had always only involved two opponents: the colonel and his daughter.

It was at this time that following a brief sojourn in the motherland, Elda returned to the colony armed with a degree, having received the highest possible marks. The Colonel decided to celebrate the occasion by holding a reception in honour of his daughter's success. He appeared impatient to brush all those past misunderstandings under the carpet.

'How would next Saturday suit you?' he asked her, affectionately.

'It's better than Sunday,' Elda replied.

'Do you want a public reconciliation on top of the one that just happened behind the scenes?' Elda explained to her brother later that evening, her brother being the only one who was still truly in her confidence, as though she wanted to educate him. 'And so we must pay the price, and start from scratch all over again. I went to the church on my own, and my father refused to accompany me, acting as though Satan himself had stood at the altar to consecrate my doom. Yet when the organ started to play, by which time I was halfway between the doors and the altar, I felt that someone was accompanying me: there is a father who stands behind all fathers, and who is never wrong about the purity of one's heart, that's what the music was telling me – in fact it was a fearless witness. Now that daddy understands that being a sculptor is not such an infamous trade, and that the world of *bohemia* is vast and varied. He's proud of my degree, and he's even taken a shine to Attilio: for once, he's been forced to take it all back. Attilio pretends as though he's forgotten all about it but I'm cut from the same cloth as daddy. He wants to re-conciliate? Fine: but on my terms.'

Elda drew close to her brother's ear, as though fearful of spies. She knew perfectly well that nobody was eavesdropping on them, they were in Claudio's bedroom, on the first floor.

'Do you understand?' she concluded. 'These are the symbols that can bring some ceremonial relief to life, otherwise it really would be what he calls bohemia, a random sequence of colourful, meaningless facts. My father didn't attend my wedding, as though I wasn't anyone's daughter: the damage done by this image (me entering the church on my own) must be repaired. This was the sequence of events that led to my father walking away from my life: how does he plan to stroll back into it?'

***

The sun was blinding that Sunday, the piazza was teeming and the cathedral was crowded. Elda had told her father that she wanted to attend mass with him and he had told her to meet him at the foot of the steps. At eleven o'clock, sharp.

The Colonel was already irritated by Elda's tardiness. The fatal, all-embracing *Bohemianism* he had detected in his daughter's life was now resurfacing through that insignificant detail – her tardiness – and was causing him infinite vexation. Once the reconciliation had taken place, Elda should have resumed her place as her father's favourite and returned to being the person she'd always been: a flawless machine, a paragon.

However, there she was, finally. Terzi stiffened: for the first time, he lost control of his stony features. The mother was following them, from a distance, she wasn't sure whether they would get into it. Perhaps her husband's wrath would implode in that very church. Hidden behind a column, Claudio watched the couple advance. The church was already teeming with people, and everyone remained focused on the ceremony, as though a rehearsal for a theatre performance was unfolding in a real place. Those who knew about the family affair whispered details to the uninformed. The real – and the sacred – seem to appear and disappear in sequences rooted in both the past and present: it was as though time had suddenly shuffled the deck of cards and had started to play, or had gotten confused.

The duel that Elda had always foreseen was taking place at that moment. Elda was challenging her father. Hiding behind the bright marble column, Claudio asked himself whether he would ever dare to do so himself.

Elda had therefore triumphed, the mere fact that her father was walking next to her while she all dressed in white heralded his defeat. Yet with every step he took, his face appeared to relax into greater and greater joy. Were they witnessing that scowling man's metamorphosis? It was as though he was the groom, while the congregation had assembled in that sacred space to witness their union. At this point, the Colonel identified with his daughter, the willpower that belonged to that tall, beautiful girl with the restless eyes, was all a result of him. The *bohemian* girl whom everyone feared was now as placid as the bouquet of flowers she held in her hands. The realm of willpower that the ceremony Elda wanted consecrated, was the opposite of the realm of *bohemia*, where everything was interchangeable. *Bohemia* had been vanquished, and Elda had returned to her father's ordered world. Thereupon he would be happy to give her away to another man, given that her education was finally complete.

Having reached the far end of the church, he saw Attilio, who was waiting for them at the altar. There was nothing unusual about that nice young man, he wasn't tainted by original sin. The Colonel slipped his arm loose from his daughter's and gave her away to the man she had chosen for herself.

Claudio fled. He walked alone along the piers by the docks. He looked at the fish in the water. His suicidal impulses had reawakened. He would drown himself. He too seemed seized by his father's measureless pride: only that his was rooted in negativity.

THE ASTROLABE

Major Lanzi dawdled in front of the mirror, it was as if he wanted to walk into it. He resembled an art critic keenly examining the particularities of a painting to ascertain its paternal origins were different than previously believed.

He had been told his son would be arriving on the next mail boat from Naples. He hadn't seen him in four years. He couldn't recall his son's physiognomy: he was looking for clues in the mirror.

In order to shoo away indiscreet or perhaps even malevolent questions, he would say that his wife never came to the colony because she couldn't put up with the climate, which was sometimes too humid, sometimes too dry – whenever the winds from the desert swept wrathfully along the coast. It was a widely-known fact in the city that the Major kept up a relationship with a widow who managed a milliner's on Corso Italia.

It had been his wife, Elvira, who had revealed the existence of a rival to him. Arrogant and capricious, she had refused to follow him to the colony, where he had been transferred. It had been a humiliating scene. The son of a modest servant of the state, he had married a woman of noble origins. The first time he had set foot in his betrothed's palace, he had been immediately impressed: he had been admitted into a different world and his path had reached a fork. 'It's as if I had been caught in the clutches, or rather as if I'd fallen into the quagmire of that love affair,' he would explain, years later, recalling the episode.

Once one climbed the staircase, one entered the arcade, where superb and enigmatic life-size portraits could be distinguished in the scant light: as if the corridor opened a window on the invisible, it looked like the interior of a mausoleum or the secret headquarters of a sect. Inside the ballroom, there was a single three-pronged chandelier of Murano glass, whose milky glow stood out against the dark, almost nocturnal colours of the ceiling. The inlaid doors were complex surfaces that looked like board games. Yet the furniture in the actually inhabited part of the building was an ill-assorted bunch, which included a few deformed modern pieces. This impression of disorder was a bad omen – almost a prophecy. When Elvira had revealed to him the presence of her lover, declaring that she would not be going with him to the colony, Lanzi had recalled that very house, where it seemed three centuries vied with one another for the available space in order to profane it.

In a sense, it was his youth that was arriving on the mail boat. Having grown, Arturo's resemblance to him would have certainly grown more marked. Yet he had his mother's restless eyes, the only trait of hers that was nevertheless dear to him. Perhaps he was finding it difficult to conjure an image of his son because some trait of hers always interfered. The sad shadow of a broken marriage had descended on the son. As if one of the characters had leaped out of one of the large paintings in the dimly-lit arcade and hit the ground: he was haughty and enigmatic too, and while still being incredibly young, their features were bound by a strange and fatal mimetic synchronicity.

What would the boy say about the banal little villa on the African coast in which he lived, surrounded by a desiccated, dusty patch of garden? His guest's face – where every detail could be read one way or another – concealed his own: as if he had slipped on a mask. Elvira used to say that Arturo had large hands, just like him, which were rough and possessive: a merchant's hands, she would say, suited to whoever sold and purchased goods, not the kind of hands that beamed beauty or authority.

If Lanzi dawdled in front of the mirror it was also because nobody in the city was in his confidences, not even the widow – an exile, a peroxide blonde – whose tiny house doubled up as a storeroom for her shop: all those hats sitting in rows on the shelves looked like the heads of gods whose faces had been cut off. He had made some ironic remarks about the presence of those heads in their love nest: in order to put him at ease again, the widow said that they all had their heads turned to the wall. Lanzi asked himself why every love affair he'd ever experienced had contained a mysterious third presence: the outsized, vindictive portraits that had so disdainfully welcomed him into Elvira's home and the empty hats in the milliner's bedroom.

He went out onto the street. The sky was limpid and serene. It was midday. The mail boat transporting his son wouldn't arrive until four. There would be no difficulty spotting him from afar: the port was often deserted and the mail boat would slide into the docks slowly like in a procession, leaving behind a bright, foamy wake.

***

The meeting between father and son unfolded in the most natural manner possible. If anything, there was an excess of discretion on both sides, as though they hadn't wanted to attract anyone's attention. However, in that small colonial city, which was excitable enough despite its military idleness, their meeting failed to elicit anyone's notice. Perhaps the African landscape had, like a painted backdrop, given them the theatrical impression of an invisible public.

The widow saw them passing by her shop. Hijacked by the demons of his past, which had reappeared in the shape of his son, Lanzi wasn't right there on the sidewalk – his spirit was far away. The young man's presence was like an epiphany: *his wife has come to Africa!* She thought to herself deluded as she watched the couple walk by.

The blank faces underneath the hats smiled malignantly, as if they already knew what was going to happen, not only in the future, but also the past, which is devastating and which nothing can erase. *We've said all we needed to say*, the widow sadly thought to herself. Yet her disappointment was being held back by the surge of an opposing feeling: that the younger version of her lover couldn't compete with the older one – she had been enchanted by Major Lanzi's stern, reserved expression, which his son completely lacked.

Reconciled, she smiled, happy with her lot.

The Major observed his son insistently: it seemed that he and his wife had to divide their estate between them – and this estate had a face. He didn't ask the boy any questions, let alone any about her. From the moment of the revelation of the rival's presence, one silence had been quickly followed by another in their relationship, like a book devoid of text.

Major Lanzi exhibited an exaggerated interest in Arturo's studies. He had enrolled in the faculty of law. All of this was to avoid more sensitive topics to argue over, and in order to give their dialogues a little vivacity. He went so far as to become menacing and authoritarian whenever the subject arose.

In their sitting room at home, which was also enshrouded in a penumbra, or the feast of light at an outdoor African café, they looked like characters who had met in a scene that was altogether different to the one they should have met in: their conversation was swamped in tediousness, as if they were still in the dressing room, before the terrible, bombastic verses of the tragedy began to be sung. Was the drama in question the one between Lanzi and Elvira?

No, Lanzi thought, *I am talking to my son, who is as distant as the image left by a painter of a man who belongs to another era. Only that this different era isn't the past, but the future: Arturo is my heir*.

While he was sliding back in time, observing his son in the light of his slight resemblance to Elvira, the image headed towards the future, *like a document, the page where the story has been written* – he thought, ironically.

Not that the boy's mother had instructed her son to reject any intimacy with his father: Elvira never took an arduous path, and it was this very arrogance that always led her to choose the path of least resistance. Neither had he expected him to be the one to discover the rival's presence, he had led him by the hand to face the other. Her illustrious ancestors had allowed her to walk across the scene of the present nonchalantly, given that they didn't attach much importance to it.

Arturo had arrived sealed up, as if the artistic spell which had captured the likenesses of his ancestors unto canvas, and had transformed their physical bodies into powder, had kidnapped him too: Elena had sent him a portrait, with whom dialogue would prove impossible.

In order to pull himself out of the unnerving morass of soliloquies, the Major tried to imagine his son's difficulties; he told himself that he had to take an active hand in that life, but he didn't know how or what he should say. Arturo didn't seem to be hiding any secrets or irresolvable dramas. However, he was evasive, a sealed treasure chest which could have been either full or empty, nobody knew. Nothing indicated that Arturo needed him, nor that he would push him away.

Maybe it was the way he had grown used to those faceless hats, to those mute masks that now made Major Lanzi look upon the simple sound of another's breath close to his as a deafening din.

Another river flowed through the microcosm of that house, close but invisible – a current similar to the unruly realm of dreams. Alone, each in their room, Lanzi was finding it impossible to distract himself. He felt *responsible for that destiny*, even though he didn't know what that turn of phrase really meant. In a way, it felt as if his doppelgänger had taken up residence in the adjacent room: that little villa was straining to contain both of them.

When, having given in to his impulses, he would appear in his son's bedroom, he would look visibly marked by fatigue. Yet nothing in his speech justified the tension.

Proffering some excuse or other, he would occasionally go out on his own. Or he would persuade his son to go out on his own. Yet he would draw no relief from it, as though he'd been split in half. It was far better for them to go out together, either on a long walk, or to sit at the cafés on the Corso: the presence of other people minimised the stagnancy of the situation. They delegated all chatter and movement to others, as though they were reading a novel or watching a film. Or as if they had both taken up residence in the realm of dreams.

One night they headed off together to the Officers' Club. Arturo had made some friends and Lanzi saw him swapping jokes with them, looking free. Whereas he saw his son as an impregnable fortress, in the presence of his friends he transformed into a peaceful garden. There was a redheaded girl with him, who had cheerful freckles on her skin. *She seems to bring Antonio to life better than I do* – he thought, as though his son were a puppet made to move on command.

Major Lanzi was now observing his son's legs, which were as long as his, and they looked a little goofy when he danced, moving in unnecessarily large steps. The fragile ballerina had to take a step and then slide with her feet the rest of the way to cover the same distance. These imperfections made the young couple look very graceful indeed.

Comforted, Lanzi smiled and raised his glass of wine. He asked himself whether Arturo's liberation hadn't been caused by the link that bound father and son, to the fact that Elvira had been substituted by the redheaded girl with the cheerful freckles. It was as if by dancing, Arturo had lost his resemblance to his mother. His wife's *palazzo*, which was the word he used to coldly describe everything concerning the woman who had refused to follow him to the colony, vanished from his mind. The austere and intimidating portraits had cast a spell on him and his son: the redheaded maiden was the fairy who would set them free.

He smiled awkwardly, he had the confused and metaphorical imagination of a young boy. It was so weak and fragile… it was two-dimensional, thin as paper. She looked at him playfully, as if amusing herself by trying to find the features his son had inherited on his face, as though she were chasing a third image, produced by the convergence of the two of them.

Lanzi stood up and grabbed the girl by the waist, drawing circles upon circles on the dance-floor, like an endless festoon: the waltz's notes made that movement all the easier, as if they were being swept along by the wind. This was why he'd had that impression ever since he'd entered that circle: that music had replaced words and they were being carried away by a constant, indomitable flux. Having climbed onto a mail boat, they had begun a journey towards a distant port: the music was water.

The Major was stunned when, having come to a stop, he saw his son standing still and mute next to the doorpost: his face was marked by the painful concentration that characterised many caryatids. He wanted them to leave. *More for him than for me!* he admitted, as if quoting someone, *we are divided because we are not the same person.* A malignant smile: the phrase recalled the Lord of La Palisse,[xxiv] *the only credible philosopher because he never deviates from tautologies.*

---

xxiv Lord of La Palisse: Protagonist of a French chanson that has since become famous. It was inspired by a French nobleman killed in the

He was called away by a superior officer and disappeared with him into the garden, onto which the Club's inner facade opened out. From there, one could see the silhouettes of all the assembled guests and one could hear the little orchestra's overindulgent notes. The Colonel was talking irritatedly about the *binding necessity* – and he constantly used that legal term – of repairing the roof of the Moccagatta barracks in the one of the city's suburbs. 'The rain spills into my office!' he exclaimed disdainfully. The Corps of Engineers were taking their time, claiming they were urgently engaged elsewhere. The Colonel wanted Lanzi to take charge of the situation: 'I'm counting on you!'

It struck Lanzi that he felt like a prisoner of a palace, just like Elvira, who had never torn herself away from those regulation portraits. Yet instead of life-sized portraits, there were now the silhouettes of dancers as they glided back and forth past the French windows, which gave out onto the African night. Amidst those shadows, he thought, while taking care to answer the Colonel's questions, was his son. If Elvira had been imprisoned by her ancestors, he had been imprisoned by his son. The phrase meant nothing at all. Yet meaningless things often carried the greatest weight, since the knot could not be untied.

The Colonel looked at Lanzi, astonished: the Major was smiling while talking about all the endless bureaucratic hurdles that would have to be overcome, which couldn't possibly justify his good cheer.

***

Italian Wars in 1525. The lines from the song 's'il n'était pas mort,/ il ferait encore envie.' were successively misread as 'if he wasn't dead,/he would still be alive' rather than the original meaning of 'if he wasn't dead,/he would still be envied.' Thus, Spina's meaning here is to use him as a symbol for tautologies.

When his son left, given that the autumnal season of exams at the university required his presence, the Major once again became the lord and master of his little villa.

His relationship with the widow resumed its usual flow – as well as its *function*, so to speak. The widow, Carlina, never set foot at the Club, which was a kind of military court, and where it was rare for civilians to be admitted, and the fact she was a simple milliner was an unbridgeable disadvantage.

His life, which was monotone, in fact monochrome, as he put it – given that he had a penchant for precise and metaphorical expressions, seemed even emptier now. He had taken a step forward – or rather, a step back, just like when Elvira had announced the presence of a rival. Even his son had abandoned him: the curled-up ball that was his son had silently rolled past his house and was now far away.

He would occasionally go for a stroll along the white seafront. The water was barely moving and it shone. It looked like a gigantic mirror, but it only ever reflected the constantly limpid sky.

He had had the idea of buying an astrolabe, an instrument which could work out the position of the stars. However, would he be able to find one or had they become museum pieces? *The stars don't care about human affairs, he thought to himself, and hats and life-sized portraits are just as indifferent. Even though they're the ones who plot the destinies of human beings with their enigmatic games. They are omnipotent, but nevertheless display no curiosity for human events.*

Lanzi, the father, the star, could very well be the architect of his son's destiny, but contrary to the stars, his own curiosity was eating him alive. His son had fallen from the sky in a distant land, amidst a dark night, and he was now vainly trying to find a trace of him in the universe of his mind. There had always been an occult and determining presence in his life: *hats, portraits and stars*, just like the milky chandelier hanging from the ceiling of the palace's great hall, constituted the trinity of his life. *It is said that the stars influence the destinies of men*, he thought, stopping, while his shadow on the ground looked at him, as though it wanted to talk to him, *but it's just a mechanical fact: oh how I envy you star, you're never weighed down by the burden of destiny*! He appeared to want to detach himself from his shadow. Yet this inescapable twin simply strolled alongside him.

My head has been aching for a while, he thought. However, he felt an upsurge of annoyance: why was he trying to deceive himself?

One evening, along the Corso, he had been walking past the milliner's shop – where he never set foot in order not to set the rumour mill running again – and casting quick glance at the window display he noticed that a hat studded with shiny flakes which he'd already once noticed due to its veil, which was blue instead of the usual black, was now missing from the display and could be seen inside the shop itself, atop a woman's head. *Who could it be?* That question was like a switch that set his mechanism in motion and he soon found himself inside the shop.

Imagine his amazement when that head turned, revealing the deception: it was the girl with the freckles that were as festive as confetti, who was looking straight at him. She wasn't smiling, like at the ball, quite the contrary: as soon as he appeared, an expression of painful concentration had settled on her face, which the hat's veil couldn't entirely conceal. It was as though he'd tripped, just like when she'd danced with Arturo, who took gigantic strides, leaving her to glide across the floor to bridge the same distance.

Why am I so surprised by it? Didn't they come in pairs? At the Club, he had detected the same painful expression on his son's face. It was simply natural for the couple of caryatids to wear similar expressions. *Why am I so surprised by it?* He asked himself again. It was like facing the echo of a scream.

Inside that shop, all the characters had arranged themselves in a triangle, and the apex at the top of that triangle wasn't the milliner, who was smiling behind her counter, but Arturo's shadow.

'Why don't you ask me to dance?' the girl asked him. She had repeated what she'd told him at the Club, like a wind-up doll who could only mouth the same words while the music played. The Major bowed. *Yes*, he thought to himself, *there's that smiling girl, that look of painful concentration I thought I had detected and had assumed it was a message from my son – turned out to be all in my head.* He reproached himself for always being hot on the heels of what wasn't really there. Yet the feeling of being unable to be a part of his son's destiny tormented him, as though he was standing right there, in front of him. *Every mind is a labyrinth*, he thought, and *to love is to fall into someone else's labyrinth…* Yet irony gave him nothing but momentary, useless relief.

'Do you know what Arturo told me?' the girl asked him, immediately adding, as thought to dash the father's hopes: 'He told me that the light is really blinding here in Africa!'

What silliness! What banality! Lanzi glared at her sternly. Yet a thought flashed across his mind like lightning: Had Arturo been using the metaphor of the blinding sun to refer to his father? Of course not! Now he was the one being silly and banal. The girl then lowered her veil, which she had lifted in order to let her words through. She then removed the hat from her head and returned it to the milliner, who was still behind her counter. She then fled from the shop, but turned around as soon as she was out on the street: as if she'd just decided to finally say what she knew – but it was late and she vanished as though she'd been spirited away.

'The light is blinding in Africa,' the Major repeated out loud, as though reading an epigraph. Yet he nevertheless made small talk with the milliner. Only his right shoe still pressed against the counter, like a desperate, loving wave crashing against a reef.

'I'll dine with you tonight,' he said.

The woman's face lit up. Yet the officer was annoyed with himself: it was as though he'd given her an order.

Out on the street, where the light seemed different to him, he started on his usual evening perambulation, a ritual of the military court. Lanzi nodded a greeting.

His mind wandered off, as usual, and his thoughts turned back to the stroll along the seafront. *Idleness is the poison of military life*, he concluded, as though putting a seal on the entire affair.

'Precisely…' the Major loudly confided that night as he addressed all those hats lined up in rows in the devout milliner's little house, a theory that belonged to priests who held voluminous scrolls of knowledge in their heads, in fact it was all-embracing knowledge. As for the stars, high up above, they remained silent, distracted.

SILENCE

'The army is the aristocratic form of emigration'
Gottfried Benn

The black cockroach on the stage threatened all of creation.

'*Mon cher ami*,' Colonel Verri said to Captain Valentini, who was standing next to him, 'my ears are crying.'

The Captain didn't reply. He kept his gaze fixed on the stage, but he wasn't listening.

The piazza was crowded. Infantry units had been deployed in rows in the middle of the square; on the right, towards the lagoon, stood the youth organizations; on the left were all civilians, and there were a great many of them. The piazza's architecture was funereal.

The sky was blue and the sun was fixed in its middle. So much indifference didn't bode anything good. The local party secretary's threats hadn't shaken up the ranks, it had instilled fear in them. Lost amidst the peacefulness of their natural surroundings, his threats had had a sinister effect.

'One can only be a good fascist on condition that one feels an intense loathing for oneself,' Colonel Verri said, closely observing the party secretary. 'Captain Valentini,' he cheerfully added, 'I'm proud of how observant you've been. You haven't missed a single word, not a single word…'

The frenetic applause of the assembled civilians, as well that of the youth organizations' initiates, drowned the party secretary's words.

The army stood immobile in serried ranks, like a funerary bas-relief. Colonel Verri turned his head: he looked at those soldiers and those officers.

'What are we going to do? What are we going to do?' he muttered, 'It's over, Captain Valentini, it-is-ov-er!'

THE SOUL OF ANOTHER

In that foreign surname, Mrs Bellotti recognised a sign that was even worse than a bad reputation and should have instantly put her on her guard. The announcement that Lieutenant Wojciechowski would come over for tea had thundered in her hostile ears: that scoundrel had set his sights on Giulia. Having been in the colony for a decade, she showed no indulgence towards the officers there: their foreignness to the place was all too obvious. Those barbarians turned life in the city upside down, and then lost sight of it amidst their luxurious idleness. The Officers' Club functioned like a public square. Mrs Bellotti hardly ever set foot in it, and when she did so it was with the greatest reluctance. In that place, everything turned into theatre, and then dissolved into febrile obviousness. The presence of Gianbattista Serra, an esteemed professor from the Giosuè Carducci secondary school, whose visit had also been announced, was simply a mask which Wojciechowski used to trick people, given that he was friends with the professor. That Serra read a great deal, pedantic subjects that belonged to different times, a kind of invisible city as opposed to the real one. *Yet he who reads too much*, Mrs Bellotti thought, opening the French windows of the three tiny balconies that gave out on the Via Regina Elena, *becomes a stranger to the environment where they live, and lives on their own terms.* She had met Lieutenant Wojciechowski only once, at a café on the Corso after Sunday mass at the cathedral. Nevertheless, she occasionally saw him walking down the street, an aura of nothingness about him, just as though he were a spectre or a demon: he appeared to share the peculiar nature of the books Serra read.

Mrs Bellotti was also a teacher, at the secondary school on Via Fiume, in the new neighbourhood that the colonial government had built on land it had reclaimed, to the south of the Ottoman-era citadel. The streets were wide and they intersected at right angles.

A quick getaway which had taken place half a century earlier had brought the Wojciechowski family to Italy. It had taken Serra a great deal of reading to reach what Wojciechowski had simply inherited: *foreignness*. Having sacrificed the harmonious strictures in which he had pursued his education, he now knew a great deal without ever seeming to make much use of it. Despite the fact that the colonial city was rather small, nobody knew anything about Serra's life. Whoever walked by his house often heard animated, heart-wrenching notes of music. Prior to meeting Wojciechowski, it seems his only friend had been his piano. He was a wiry man, as if he'd been carved out of wood, his height was slightly below average, and his nose was concave, allowing his little oval-shaped golden glasses to constantly slip further down.

Serra taught French, while Mrs Bellotti taught natural sciences. She occasionally looked on Wojciechowski as a poisonous flower, which while being beautiful, its seductiveness ultimately meant death: the flower's caducity was a sign of that. If the scoundrel got his hands on another victim, it wouldn't have bothered Serra at all, and perhaps his intellect compelled him to respect Wojciechowski's freedom. Nevertheless, it certainly mattered to her: *Giulia is my daughter*! Once Wojciechowski had appeared, the invisible city had become a real-life character, as if the baby grand piano had taken on a human form instead of just sitting there in the corner of Serra's little villa – and had started going everywhere, on the streets, shops, sitting rooms, and at the Club – and as if that wasn't enough it had even started wearing that woeful, elegant uniform, similar to the military marches that fascist militants sang in the streets about violence and heroic deaths.

Despite Serra's presence, a kind of Trojan horse which Wojciechowski had used to bring his wicked plans to fruition, she would have nevertheless greeted that guest with open hostility: after all, what did the army have to do with school, or soldiers with books? If she ever saw Giulia walking with Wojciechowski from her window, she would think that Giulia had read the other's secret books in a single sitting. At which point she would begin to heed her colleague's words: being highly intolerant, he had told her that Serra belonged to that perfidious race of intellectuals 'who are completely unrelated to us as educators; educators,' he explained, 'are people who transmit knowledge, and they devote themselves to its destruction and reinvention every decade or so with the zealous treachery of sorcerers.' It was a pity that his words sounded as though they'd been coined in a cheap inn: overweight and little loved by his students, her colleague's breath always stank of alcohol, even in the mornings. Why did everyone seem to tarnish their not completely undignified positions with some aspect of their behaviour?

Ever since Giulia had grown up, she'd felt constantly apprehensive, as if she were travelling on a remote and dramatic itinerary, where people had replaced places. As for Serra, whom she allowed to go out with Giulia, she thought he had started behaving hypocritically ever since Wojciechowski had arrived in the city: as if everything he taught his students or told his colleagues took him further away from what he knew.

As for her, she preferred to look on all of them – the meagre ranks of intellectual citizens and the army's officers, who were garrisoned in the colony but were as foreign to it as though they were mercenaries – from the safety of her windows, rather than inviting them into her house. The music in Serra's cottage, whose interior always looked like it was night-time, in a neighbourhood on the outskirts of the city, had nothing to do with military bands: yet even these, vivid and shrill, wrapped in the sumptuous mantle of glory and the unknown, spoke of death. Ever since Wojciechowski had appeared, she felt as though she could hear a funeral march take over that house, a spell that didn't herald immobility, like in so many fables, but of endless flight.

As though she'd wanted to erect a dam inside her four walls to act as a bulwark against those changes, she had meticulously reconstructed all the elements of her home in Lombardy in her apartment in Africa. Positioned next to exquisite objects were counterfeits or surviving relics of bygone fashions she held on to all of them with the zeal of a memoirist transcribing all of life, saving it from falling into certain oblivion. As for Doctor Bellotti, who was in charge of customs at the docks, he assisted his wife in her quest for a mechanism or ritual that would bring time to a stop, just as had happened in other eras when people had employed science, madness and fraud to turn base metal into gold. All their nice furniture belonged to his wife's family, to whom he was rather devoted; being a keen nationalist, Doctor Bellotti looked upon the reconstruction of his Lombard home as the symbolic confirmation that the colony had enlarged the motherland's hallowed ground.

Mrs Bellotti was making a cake. The eggs hadn't been whisked properly, her hands were nervous. *Is Wojciechowski coming to tea? Good*, she would even bake him a cake – so that he would witness the strength of habits and traditions: if he thought he could turn the house upside down with his presence he was dead wrong, but a murder would still get a slice of cake, just as a boyfriend would. She would have done anything in her power to keep that young man from crossing her threshold, his presence inspired the same disdain in her as the filthy, smutty book she'd found in the hands of one of the boys entrusted to her care (or, in her husband's case, whenever he came across unsavory contraband at the port). But since Wojciechowski was bound to come in, she had decided to welcome him with great care and consideration, placing an emphasis on her every gesture, word, the very presence of things, like the cake's exquisite taste, it was the only shelter she could seek: harmony repels deceit.

While she was alone in the kitchen, whose window gave out on a small courtyard (which was as spartan as a prison cell and just as silent), her thoughts seemed to go around in circles restlessly, like the egg that the spoon in her hand chased around the bowl: it was like she was miming her mind's confusion to an invisible spectator. A single fact left her speechless: the colony had been conquered by the Italian army after many years of fighting against the natives' desperate resistance; now the former enemies had become obedient subjects, and the colony had been pacified. One could go out for a walk along the endless plains at any time of day feeling as safe as along the narrow, shady, familiar banks of a Lombard lake.

Nevertheless, danger had finally reemerged, this time in her own sitting room: the man who had turned her house upside down was from the North – with blue eyes, greyish, slick hair, perfectly parted, his face deceptively limpid, just like in those portraits from the early nineteenth century, whose canvas always looked lacquered. The war front – she thought in an ironic, bitter start while her hands came to a rest – had shifted to the North, in fact it now cut her sitting room in half with its invisible line. Perhaps in bygone days her family's ancient furniture had seen the shadow of a Wojciechowski in her grandparents' home on the shores of Lake Como, perhaps in the shape of some minor Austro-Hungarian officer who had appeared at a lunch or party, his visit prompted by dark, secret sentimental intentions.

The young man had an incredibly thin waist, looking like one of those Venetian goblets whose extremities almost protrude into nothingness; as for his movements, they were naturally harmonious, *but disturbed by a restless will*, she thought, *a kind of presence within presence, yes, a temporary presence, indeed, a provocative presence*, which could nevertheless be amiable enough except when it furthered a man's unchaste desires. This ductile will, which was emphasised by an obvious precision with his movements, made that relatively small officer more fearful in war than some of his burlier comrades: his aim was more precise and his bullet would strike first. Mrs Bellotti would have liked to see him in a duel, and as soon as she realised that she would have rooted for him (her nervous hand started whirling around to whisk her eggs), she looked as if she'd lost her mind.

Having removed her apron, she went from the kitchen to the sitting room, it seemed as if the preparations for the visit knew no end, like when a director stubbornly insists that his cast reshoot one scene or the other: she had barricaded herself behind bourgeois intimacy against the assault led by powers from the North which, amidst the slumber of African powers, was attacking the colonial house where she had lovingly reconstructed her ancestral home – just like when backdrops depicting the time-honoured Nile are hung when performances of *Aida* are staged in Italy's opera houses.

She carried the silver tea service to the kitchen so that the maid could polish it, once she'd finished washing the stairs where a thick film of red dust had settled; two days earlier, the city had been blasted by scorching winds from the south, as though it had wanted to sweep the city into the sea, or sink her like a ship. She removed the slipcovers from her Louis XVIII armchairs, made of dyed maple inlaid with rosewood, which were upholstered in olive green silk. Her ancestors' home, even if situated in Africa, was an earthly paradise: Lieutenant Wojciechowski would enter it like a tempter. What was at stake wasn't innocent happiness, but the bourgeois order from which he wanted to take Giulia away – that officer was looking for a brief fling without being forced to pay any tribute to the law; he wasn't Adam, he was the snake. Nevertheless, this time, the cherub who stood guard at the gates of order, *with a flaming sword which turned every way.*[xxv] In other words, Mrs Bellotti would appear before the fact, and not after it; not in order to chase away the sinners, but to vanquish the tempter.

While she was robing her sitting room in its dress uniform, she felt a kind of intoxication. She rolled a carpet down the stairs until it reached the bottom of the landing, the ceremonial effect had to be noticed as soon as one crossed the threshold. She polished her Empire-style mirror, which was framed by a gold fillet studded with acanthus leaves.

She walked along the ancient carpets as though listening to a fable, or telling one. But which fable was it? The story of her family, which adhered to set guidelines.

II

Mrs Bellotti presided over everything in silence. Serra was talking about something, one of his programmes, which everyone was acquainted with and which they thus hardly paid any attention to; programmes which had nothing to do with the painful, dramatic notes that one could occasionally hear while walking by the isolated little house, where dreams transformed into sounds, into a chilling, meandering Chopinesque, once the mask of mundanity had been dropped amidst unbearable memories. It was as if Serra had sent a bland body-double around the city in order to deflect the curiosity of others from himself. Serra never invited anybody to his house, but Wojciechowski had been spotted leaving his abode on several occasions.

[xxv] Genesis 3:24.

Mrs Bellotti had carefully brushed her hair, had put on a black dress, which was elegant as if straightly-cut as a uniform: not a military one, but one which adhered to faith and a sense of order. She wore a beautiful string of pearls around her neck, which she'd inherited from her mother, the pearls were small and irregularly-shaped, and they almost reached down to her waist. She stood up to pour the tea. Her maid had begun to do so – but as if she'd prearranged the unexpected twist – she had stood up to do it herself.

Giulia kept her eyes fixed on her mother. The latter's hand was still, but her heart, buried underneath the black cloth, trembled with anticipation. Her eyes were moist.

He's late! Giulia had the habit of using the style of opera librettos even in her inner monologues. Now she couldn't find the right affectation to express her thoughts, the pang in the pit of her soul. She cited works of opera, but her ironic intentions had yielded pathetic results. She'd forgotten the gesture the soprano usually made at this point, during the final act of *La Traviata*. Wojciechowski smiled, the incomprehensible gesture was incredibly graceful.

The Lieutenant was sat on a small, Neo-Classical chair, whose backrest was decorated with crossed arrows, and he had crossed his legs, resting his right ankle on his left knee. The chair creaked under the weight. It wasn't an elegant pose, but there had always been an ironic sense of exaggeration about that man, as though he too were quoting characters from various operas. Mrs Berlotti felt as if he'd converted their home into a stage, so that he could then abandon it, allowing reality to split into two, and the foreigner, like the actor, constituted an alternative to an established set of values.

Why was he being accused of such horrible things? Why did nobody know anything about his past? His ancestors belonged to a different community. It was said that Wojciechowski had put out a rumour that he'd once killed a man. Whereas he had in all likelihood refused to squash the slander in order to make a mockery of both reality and the present.

'And now Serra will play something for us,' Wojciechowski announced.

Serra, who had already stood to his feet, headed to the piano. Nobody had ever seen him play, and he shielded himself with irritation. Yet in Wojciechowski's presence, it was as if everyone's automatic instincts were stuck, just like we're capable of flying in our dreams, or how we do things that would seem heinous to us in our waking life.

'Do you like Wagner?' Wojciechowski asked the mother, completely unmoved by what he'd just heard, the finale of Liszt's arrangement of *Tristan und Isolde*. He then mockingly added that those last ten minutes, where Isolde 'tried to dissolve herself like a pill into the warmth of Creation' were rambling and stifling. The phrase shared the nature of his gestures, borrowed from a secret repertory of punctual exaggerations devoid of any elegance, in fact they were wilfully rude and antagonistic. Serra, who perhaps had grown used to hearing him speak differently when they were alone, suddenly stood to his feet, irritated. Thanks to one of Wojciechowski's diabolical tricks, Serra's irritation hadn't manifested itself when he'd been invited to play, but was instead showing up now. He shut the fallboard with an awkward gesture and there was a loud thud: it was as if the gesture had been performed not by the highly courteous pianist, but rather by Wojciechowski, who had nevertheless not budged from his seat.

This continual recourse to theatrical expedients, like his rude comment about Isolde's song, left Mrs Bellotti chilled to the core. That man, just like an artist – not in the service of knowledge and beauty – exaggerated life in any way he could whenever he could. The same legend that accompanied the little Lieutenant was nothing but a manipulation of texts.

Giulia had lingered in surprise when she'd seen her mother open her mouth, presumably to compliment Serra, who had stood up from the piano, but had then closed it again, as though struck by the comments made by Wojciechowski, who both desired and hated his friend's musical talents. She stood up to offer her guests some multi-coloured pastries, trying to distract everyone. The plate was made of silver, with a kind of knotted cord wrapped all the way around it, it was rather elegant. There was a piece of pink organza shadow work embroidery underneath the pastries' fluted paper.

Seduced by a foreigner! Giulia thought, putting the plate back on the console. Whereby the scandal (she was making an aside, like in the old comedies) didn't lay in the seduction of which her mother was wholly ignorant, but rather in the person who had seduced her: *a foreign character, whose very presence is a sin!* The act became less important than the person who perpetrated the act, who attracts all attention. Yet what sense did it make to think of Wojciechowski as a foreigner? After all, even though his parents were foreigners, he was born in Italy and wore an Italian army uniform. Or was anyone who had a different past automatically a foreigner? She had been seduced by the devil!

The officer accepted the cup of tea from the mother's hand as though he were signing an oath of loyalty. Yet Giulia had no doubts: she would betray him. The law had been converted into comedy, an example of infinite human possibilities. In order to guarantee a pact, one had to guarantee one's presence: yet who would vouch for the foreigner's presence? He could easily be elsewhere just as much as he was here. Using that name to refer to an Italian officer struck her mother as a lie – and his court was a lie too: she had, if anything, learned the truth of the facts and people on the stage, which was dazzling and ephemeral.

After all, isn't an actor on a stage perhaps nothing more than a metaphor for the foreigner? Reality vanished in references and mirrors.

The mother offered him some tea. No, Wojciechowski took his without. Something bothered her about his gaze. The people the officer drew close to him changed. Everything happened very quickly, but something (in those people) never returned to normal, as though part of their mechanisms had malfunctioned.

Mrs Bellotti straightened her bust and lingered in that pose for a moment. *But the soul of another is a dark place,*[xxvi] she thought, unwittingly quoting an old Russian master. She was torn between piety and diffidence. She picked up the plate with the lemon slices on it and slid it into his cup of tea as though she'd wanted to contradict the guest who said he liked his tea plain, or had wanted to poison it.

[xxvi] Complete Quote: 'But the soul of another is a dark place, and the Russian soul is a dark place – for many it is a dark place.' from Fyodor Dostoyevsky, *The Idiot* (London: W. Heinemann, 1915), p.227.

Lieutenant Wojciechowski smiled. Weapons were useless. *Home is a sacred place!* Tall and upright, Mrs Bellotti looked like a priestess. *You'll be sorry!* her wrath made her golden bracelets tremble. But was it really wrath? If his sacrilege appeared fatal to her, she could nevertheless see – just beyond it – the punishment. The war will sweep everything away: people, things, traditions, laws, intrigues – as well as that Lieutenant who wore a beautiful uniform, whose extravagance was probably nothing more than an ironic way to emphasise the pointlessness of vanity and the interchangeability of everything.

For the second time, she felt torn between piety and hostility.

Another spoonful of sugar?

She bent over. Her face was now a few inches away from Wojciechowski's. They looked into one another's eyes while the mother, who wasn't paying any attention to what the officer was saying, spooned up some sugar and put it in the waiting cup which he had held out.

Serra picked up a subject which he thought would prove a distraction and defuse the ceremony's tension: 'Why go through all this trouble? Please sit down…' and he stood, only to remain standing awkwardly in the middle of the room, holding his cup of tea. The mother barely managed to tear her gaze away from Wojciechowski's blue eyes. *Go away, go away!* She was willing to forgive all his transgressions if he would only leave her house. Wojciechowski's eyes were still. Yet again, she refused to meet his gaze, no matter what they offered. *I only care about one little thing, to divert your destiny away from this house; as for reforming your character, only God can do that.*

Having returned to her seat, she asked Serra if his mother had made up her mind to go live with him in the colony. Why was she hesitating?

Conversational conventions: this particular question blended in with the silk of the armchairs and the silver multi-pronged candelabras on the console. She tried to make an impression on Wojciechowski. The silver tea service appeared out of the grotesque.

No, she didn't try to impress him with her possessions (Just a few moments earlier, Serra had said: 'Foreigners have gone to the ends of the earth in order to collect antiquities,' God knows to whom he was alluding), but rather by trying to show him that: *this is a house and every house is precious, just like individual lives.*

The only plausible guarantee at Mrs Bellotti's disposal was what was similar, or rather what was recoverable through an analogue process, or better yet what was identical, for what is real is normal: otherwise what we inherit loses its value and once disowned it becomes a hostile force. Hadn't she strived to avoid exactly such continuity by bringing all her Empire, Charles X and Louis Philippe-style furniture to her house overseas? This was the reason behind their presence, and not the magical suggestion of Bonaparte's Egyptian expedition, or the conquest of Algiers desired by Charles X and his successor. In that sitting room, hostile to Wojciechowski's presence, were the objects and symbols of unity of the house. And it didn't matter at all that their style had spread across Europe, right up to the frozen lands of Wojciechowski's ancestors. Sacredness wasn't intrinsic to the beauty of the model, but rather it was conferred by their daily use, the precious patina added to it by her family and by her native land. Thus, a memory that is dear to us isn't connected to the maker of the object, but rather the one who gave it to us. She didn't want to inspire admiration in her guest – *admiration*, she would say, *restrains one's greed and wealth redeems all vices* – but her piety, possibly mixed in with some fear which Wojciechowski no longer remembered, hidden in the pleats of his soul, which they hadn't yet reached, to extirpate all his willpower and wickedness.

Yet the silk didn't seem to put up a sufficient resistance, the immaculate candour of the maid's bonnet and pinafore – which was embroidered – was evanescent: everything appeared weak and open to attack, anything that this scoundrel left untouched would be ravaged by time or its unholy servant, war, which was now drawing near. The mother saw the tea service taken to another house, and her armchairs would soon be gone, as would everything else, including the four of them as they sipped their cups of tea. Nevertheless, she wanted to resist the Lieutenant's acceleration of that ruin.

Once again, the instinct to get up and threaten him took a hold of her: *Easy, easy…* – but she didn't know how to follow that up.

Serra was complimenting her on the cake. In that sitting room, he behaved as though he were in the mess hall: every movement and sentence had been fixed and predetermined, adhering to a ritual which he was well acquainted with, and closely observed. Yet did the symbols in this mess hall of his have any meaning? He was an incredibly erudite man, yet he didn't involve himself much in his culture. In fact, he looked like a priest of social conventions,[xxvii] an erudite man who wore the garbs of Leporello as he chased that reckless Don Juan, reciting the words of the dead.

For your mother, for your mother… – yes, because even Wojciechowski had to have a mother, who feared for her son, who was perhaps even more exposed to danger than others. The thought of another mother softened her heart: giving life to a creature is not the same thing as signing a deal with the devil, but God forbid, it was still a risk regardless.

She recalled what people had said about Wojciechowski. He had been accused of horrendous things because nobody knew anything about his past; one can corrupt one's descendants, not one's ancestors, jealous hands that worked in secret. Perhaps it was nothing more than slander, the result of the envy of his less fortunate comrades. It was even said that he'd been sent to the colony as punishment (so that, perhaps, he would be immediately dispatched to the front lines once the war had been declared, the body of the nation being impatient to rid itself of that defective addition). There were also those who said that he had been posted there by highly-placed people to spare him the consequences of a mistake.

Whichever prologue had prefaced his story, *this man*, an appellation she employed with extreme denigration, was now in her sitting room. If the Italians were defeated in the war and the enemy army occupied the city, she would be forced to host a barbarian in her house, and she would no longer feel horrified by that presence. The Lieutenant's real or presumptive sins smeared

---

[xxvii] Don Juan's servant in Mozart's *Don Giovanni*.

his uniform like blood stains. The felony – the word she used to describe Wojciechowski's designs on Giulia – seemed to her as irredeemable and fatal as death.

Her behaviour became apathetic, having lost her willpower in the way one abandons a ship's rudder when tired of fighting against the sea's fury. It didn't matter much that no image was further away from the sea than that of the meagre space which the officer took up: yet that name was a kind of codex, subject to shadows and madness, like the keyboard of Serra's baby grand piano, from which he extracted notes that perturbed oblivious pedestrians as they passed in front of his little villa.

Space and the fury of movements are occasional by-products of violence and shadows, the void and the abyss can co-exist in an elegant uniform, or a pentagram.

III

The Giuliana beach[xxviii] was the pride and glory of the Municipal government, which had built three rows of multi-coloured wooden beach cabins, where one could both change one's clothes, just like in a theatre's dressing room, as well as cook or rest. The lunch offered by Colonel Colombo was held in the Air Force's blue chalet. This served to put Mrs Bellotti at ease, given that Wojciechowski was assigned to the infantry, and thus there would be no danger of running into him. It seemed Mrs Bellotti only moved around the city in order to avoid something or someone, like in some children's games, where fatal mistakes committed on a multi-coloured, bizarre board led to esoteric itineraries.

[xxviii] One of Benghazi's main beaches.

Nevertheless, there was Lieutenant Wojciechowski standing right at the chalet's door: bare-chested with his greyish hair and blue eyes, he looked like a parody of African savages with their dazzling ebony skin.

His beautiful uniform hadn't led anyone astray, the young man was perfectly chiseled: there was something truthful to him, and he wasn't entirely deceitful and fake, as she thought. She was shocked, her mind procrastinated, maybe she had seen demons in the guide of puppets or ghosts. A human body always gave her some guarantee of truth. Yet there was nevertheless something unusual to his body's shape, which shared the unusual gracefulness of Cranach's nudes,[xxix] turning to the North for some familiar reference to describe those inanimate wonders.

'Look at that fool,' Doctor Bellotti said, irked.

Wojciechowski gave him a military salute as though he'd been in uniform; he looked like a little rascal poking fun at the adults' pompous ceremonies.

While they were sat at a table, some distance away from the others, and while Colonel Colombo was politely entertaining them, at the same time that Wojciechowski, Giulia and the Lieutenant appeared almost completely naked, one could notice the big blue sea behind them like a bed in the background.

Truth be told, it had been Doctor Bellotti who had discovered them, but Emma had only seen one of his pupils burst into flames, a concave mirror that metaphorically dilated the scene.

The chalet was full of people coming and going, some were dressed in bathing costumes, while others looked as though they

---

[xxix] Lucas Cranach the Elder (1472–1553): German Renaissance painter and printmaker.

were backstage at a theatre, mingling with the characters and ghosts of other plays. It was one thirty in the afternoon, but the sea breeze kept the bathers' faces feeling fresh, just as moving, colourful lights at a theatre often add a veneer of magic to the actors on stage.

Mrs Bellotti noticed that her husband's irritation was about to cross the point of no return; she had been told frightening stories of whenever the man in charge of customs, whose office was situated at the docks, had discovered illicit contraband. He was a robust man with a round face. A keen nationalist, when his wife had mentioned that the little Lieutenant could pose a small danger to Giulia, his knee-jerk reaction had been to exclaim: *that name!* going blue in the face. What would he do now? The same rigidity he demonstrated in his defence of the laws of the State reflected itself within his family environment, order meant harmony of the whole. Yet could he, a mere civilian, order an army Lieutenant to be arrested? And on what charges?

The conversation at the table carried on, but Bellotti got muddled up whenever he tried to proffer a reply, and each time his gaze turned towards the entrance, where the forbidden couple stood, his gaze became entirely distracted. Holding his knife and fork in his hand, he looked like a man who was either intoxicated or traumatised by dreadful burst of pain.

Emma felt that she had tortured her husband over Giulia's sentimental life, her daughter's drama had been augmented by the love her husband felt for her, and his rather ridiculous passion for appropriating all her feelings. Colonel Colombo was struck by Bellotti's agitated state. The other dining companions, two couples who had just moved to the colony, and ironically resembled one another, looked like theatregoers who had shown up late to the performance and were thus finding it impossible to understand what was going on. Yet while inevitable, the drama was in no hurry, it had taken root inside that chalet, and it was letting *time* slide slyly by, like a god from the underworld who, having emerged into the light, stops to bask in the sun, before fulfilling all the destruction it carried in its heart.

For instance, nobody ever found out what Doctor Bellotti said to Wojciechowski in a fit of anger barely an hour later, once the lunch hosted by Colonel Colombo had drawn to an end. It was as though the sea-breeze had either carried his words away or muddled them up: in the same way that a spectator's untimely cough at the climax of a drama often deprives the other listeners of a key sentence, the drama's final seal, which had been long awaited, and thus the whole play is left acephalous.

The two men had found themselves face to face on the smooth planks of the chalet's entrance. Doctor Bellotti was attired in an elegant white linen suit, while the young man was semi-naked, as though someone had stolen his uniform.

Save for the colour of their skin, hair, the clear blue of their eyes, their encounter on that African beach looked like it was mimicking one of those yellowed photographs or oleographs that once graced the covers of shiny illustrated weeklies: here was the colonist, dressed, and the native, naked, in the same way sumptuous altar pieces often show how the divine and the human are separated by two planes, or the way their cautionary frescoes separate the saved from the damned. There were those who later said that Doctor Bellotti had rubbed the foreignness of

Wojciechowski's name in his face, in fact he'd distorted his name, which was in itself barbaric, as though it bore all the resounding proof of Wojciechowski's betrayal.

Others instead said that he had pronounced Wojciechowski's name correctly, but that he had mocked him over his incredibly thin waist: he too had noticed that the young man had been shaped with the same freedom with which Venetian glassblowers modelled their glass – they spun the hot fibre into a thread, pushing the glass to beyond the laws of physics. It therefore seemed that the Doctor had levelled heavy insinuations against that artistically-shaped physique.

The only sentence which had been distinctly heard had been the following: 'But out blood will never be one!'

It was at that moment that, given that Mrs Bellotti had not left her table, Giulia, still in her black swimming costume – which emphasised the rosiness of her skin, her hair hanging loose on her shoulders, her gaze clear and limpid – suddenly appeared next to her mother, just like sirens, whose bottom halves are never clearly perceived, and she whispered: 'But now our blood is the same, in a single new creature.'

Then she hurried away, not because she feared her mother's brutal reaction, or the insufferable questions she might ask, but in order to show off her full figure.

In the same manner that an art critic can immediately recognise that two paintings created at different times in fact constitute an unnecessarily untidy diptych, Mrs Bellotti finally realised that her daughter had been shaped by the same hands as the one which had crafted Wojciechowski; her waist was thin and narrow, like the incredibly pale figures in Cranach's canvases.

While her husband (and Giulia's father) went about rodomontading on the beach, refusing to sign the pact (mostly to please her, since he was obsessively loyal to her), a creature in Giulia's womb subverted the pact, nature had triumphed over laws and religious ceremonies.

She stood up, looking as though she'd been pierced by a sword. Here comes the first victim, Giulia thought to herself, half-moved, half-mocking: in that delightful setting, bathed in the immaculate splendour of the African coast, they were living out a conventional tragedy.

Emma crossed the chalet, whose floor was composed of long, varnished planks of wood; she looked like the messenger on whose arrival all the characters' confused heads turn to look at.

Having reached the two rivals, she turned towards Wojciechowski and said: 'Lieutenant, we'll expect you over for tea tomorrow.'

Wojciechowski stiffened into a military salute, like when he had seen them enter. Yet his gesture no longer looked like a provocation, and the person who had performed it had lost his brattish aggressiveness, it was as though that brief sentence had defused the tragedy.

The small gathering of onlookers who had assembled broke up in a flurry of ironic comments, looking like spectators drifting towards the exit once the curtain had fallen.

Taking Doctor Bellotti by the arm, Colonel Colombo was reminiscing over his time in the military, telling him atrocious, pointless stories.

They strolled along the shiny beach. There was Serra, right up ahead, sat in a *chaise-longue* over which a festively-coloured cloth had been draped. Despite the fact the chalet was only a short distance away, he never raised his eyes from his book, which was tiny and very old, a kind of cult-like object, all the more surprising in a crowded beach of loud sunbathers where everything was new, fresh, colourful and sonorous.

Laughing, Colombo ripped the book out of his hands.

'What's this, what's this? The *s*'s all look like *f*s, and the *v*'s look like *u*'s, what the hell is this, professor?'

The Colonel showed the book to Doctor Bellotti, but he couldn't see *s*'s, *f*s, *v*'s and *u*'s, what he read was a story. Serra was friends with Wojciechowski: the damned devil had leapt out of one of the Professor's books. His wrath was already on the lookout again.

The Doctor took the book from the Colonel's hand as though he'd wanted to throw it into the sea. At that moment, Serra's eyeglasses slid down his nose and fell. As though having emerged out of the sands, Wojciechowski appeared among them, knelt down, picked the glasses up, and handed them to Serra.

The tea that took place the following day, a Monday, was brief. It looked as though the Bellotti sitting room had been converted into a public notary's office, where three parties (Giulia being absent from the proceedings) had agreed to meet to stipulate a contract.

It was decided that the engagement would take place a month later, and in the meanwhile the youths could be seen together in public, given that a hurried announcement would have raised unnecessary suspicions. For the first time in his life, Doctor

Bellotti felt as though he'd taken part in a secret criminal meeting, similar to the one those smugglers who infested his ports must have attended. Yet this wasn't about saving some merchandise or seizing illicit profits, it was about his daughter's honour. It was also the only time in his life when the line between the legal and the illegal looked like it hadn't been neatly cut by a sword, but rather was a slender thread that shook with the changeability of the wind.

Mrs Bellotti thought that the Lieutenant had committed another crime on top of seducing her daughter, given that her husband was near collapse, an earthquake had destroyed his ordered, geometric conception of the world. Sat in that sitting room, they looked as though they were drifting away from the mainland – where they had lived happily until that day – while atop a boat.

Doctor Bellotti said that they would use the gravity of the situation as an excuse to avoid attending the wedding reception.

As it happened, the war was announced just three weeks later.

Just as a lady who had proved not entirely indifferent to the unpronounceably-named Lieutenant's charms said, Wojciechowski was one of the first to leave. She hadn't known that he'd gone to the front, where the army had already been deployed, but the *other world* – where new arrivals, especially in the early phase of the war, weren't that frequent yet.

As far as the director of customs Bellotti was concerned, that *fallen soldier* was more like a deserter. Even he had been called up to active duty, as if he'd been forced to take his son-in-law's place. Before leaving for the front, where he might meet the same fate as Wojciechowski – yet without giving rise to atrocious, obvious rumours – he had decided, right there in that sitting room (the designated location for the declaration of such lawfully-binding sentences) that the unborn child – which was the first time he'd ever referred to that strange guest in his daughter's presence – would bear the name of Bellotti. (Or rather, Bellotti-Riva, he added, combining his wife's name with his own, in tribute to the family which he'd been honoured to marry into; a tribute which, when mouthed by that portly man who'd aged so much during those last few weeks, which had seen so much trouble to befall both his home and motherland, sounded rather pathetic.) The Bellotti name? He seemed to prefer that the unborn child should endure the shadow of incest over his conception, as if he himself, the director of customs, had been the boy's father, or by the unknown, anything was better than that barbaric name, which was as tragic as destiny itself!

His wife didn't intervene, even though Doctor Bellotti appeared to be desperate for her to do so: yet ever since the drama had started, Emma's vitality had entirely vanished. He had seen this before on numerous occasions.

Even Giulia, who wore a little cotton dress and colonial sandals on her feet, remained silent and said nothing at all. What point was there to sharing one's secrets with other people? Had Tadeusz Wojciechowski ever done that?

Twenty-four Colonial Tales

BOOK ONE

1

ON THE SHORE

1939

'Africa is a giant riding-stable, the ideal place where one can train and hone the ancient art of horse-riding,' the General said, shattering the silence.

They were standing by the shore, on the boundless plain. The palm trees, few and far between, looked as if they'd been planted by an invisible hand to mark out paths that knew no end. The General was fond of spending time with Captain Valentini, who was a reserved man and always on the alert, but who carried on the conversation on his own, inside his head, where there was never the bother of having to listen to a reply. What good would it do anyway?

They had been riding for two hours. The sun was oppressive, but a sonorous breeze was rising from the sea (it felt like the plain's invisible twin, a continuous flowing) – like how music, sometimes, which is a movement in itself, ensnares our immobility, while we're sat in the profound recesses of a theatre or a closed room. There wasn't a single structure in sight: neither native and wretched nor colonial and optimistic. Nothing except the littoral's expanse – 'one of the great wonders of the world,' the General sternly commented, as though he was mocking his listener – that extended for thousands of miles along the colony's coast, a testament to the fact that it wasn't inviolate. Nothing could be seen along the greyish strip, neither man nor machine: as though it had been created for ghosts.

The General took to horse-riding with his customary ceremoniousness even in that deserted place, as though he were at a parade and was busy inspecting the troops. His bearing was always proud and erect, a joker had once said that he'd resembled *the Four Horsemen of the Apocalypse*, as he frighteningly held four fingers up.

'Do you know Professor Curri?' the General asked.

Changing his tone, which grew a little more irritated, he added: 'Yesterday we dined together at the air force's *chalet*; I don't know who invited him. He said that Montaigne once questioned an Indian chief who was held as a prisoner in France what prerogatives he enjoyed in his country. The chief replied that he had the right to be at the head of his troops when leading them into battle. What else is new? That's what history teaches us.'

Valentini nodded his head very slightly.

'Professors always talk such rubbish when they speak of battles.'

They carried on riding in silence.

'Come on, there's no need to drag Montaigne into this; even heroes in action films put themselves first and drag everyone else along.'

A pause.

'Who knows where? Needless to say, the "enemy" is nothing but a metaphor.'

Just like the sea-breeze, they too looked like the victims of a kind of perpetual motion owed to atmospheric events, fated to always keep floating. The breeze was the wind generated by the unequal heating of different zones.

Even the littoral carried on sliding towards the East.

'Captain!' the General exclaimed, as though his comrade was far away and he was calling him back. Instead, their horses were right next to one another, just like during the ritualistic military exercises where they weren't free to heed either their own caprices, or their knight's.

'Do you know what a chief's prerogative really is? To fall from even greater heights, the highest possible heights is what I mean.'

Valentini raised no objections whatsoever. His silence had a soothing effect, leaving something unexplored, unfinished. This was why the General loved talking to him.

'Anyone who doesn't understand that doesn't have the right to lead anybody, because he is oblivious to his tragic privilege. Bloody hell! I would have liked to tell that chap that tragic destinies were the exclusive prerogative of kings in the old plays of antiquity!'

He suddenly spurred his horse into a gallop.

Ready to follow him, Valentini leapt after him.

However, the littoral looked like an infinite thread, and it too ran alongside them, with all its unrivalled reserve, overwhelming them.

2

BLOOD MUST FLOW AND YOU MUST DIE[xxx]

Her name was Elena Petrović, and just like Her Majesty, she was born in Montenegro, the ancient Illyria, and she had married an Italian man who wore a uniform, but the similarities ended there. The Captain was a man of average height, portly, optimistic, and his character was entirely different from Victor Emmanuel, who sat on the throne so diffidently, as if he didn't actually wield supreme authority, but rather feared it. Captain Andolfato on the other hand liked the world he lived in, and everything seemed beautiful and well-disposed towards him: nature, the State, the Fascist party, the colony, the Army. If one put a problem before him, he would try to minimise its importance, to dismiss it, and this appeared to free him from the need to try and resolve it. He wasn't held in especially high regard by either his superiors or his underlings, but neither did he have any enemies, since everyone recognised the goodness of his soul and his inexhaustible human sympathy.

[xxx] Lines spoken by Anckarström, a character in Giuseppe Verdi's *Un ballo in maschera/A Masked Ball.*

In the midst of that pleasant life – the Captain also enjoyed perfect health, despite being quite the drinker, and the alcohol accentuated his good cheer – only a single eccentric detail stood out: his wife's extraordinary beauty. That such an exquisitely sculpted woman had married a man who was the epitome of banality itself had stirred much disbelief in that small colonial town. 'Mentally and physically banal,' the skeletal Professor of Natural Sciences sarcastically commented, lusting after the man's wife.

The woman had composed an elegant and devoted letter to the Queen, in which she had bowed before Her Majesty to proudly inform her that they shared the same name, and that she had also come from Montenegro to Italy, in fact to the colony, a land which had been restored to Rome under the reign of Victor Emmanuel III, the Victorious King.[xxxi] The letter sent by one of the ladies in waiting at court had been accompanied by an official portrait of the Queen, which Her Majesty herself had so graciously signed; having been slipped into a silver frame, the letter could be admired in the sitting room. The Captain made a point of bragging about it: as if he and Victor Emmanuel were in-laws now.

Nobody understood what sense it made, once the incommensurable difference in rank was accounted for, for him to call himself the King's *brother-in-law*. Had he married his sister, or was the King perhaps his wife's brother? Someone put the question to him and he had replied with a laugh; at times it seemed as though he didn't understand the way the word

---

[xxxi] Popular nickname granted to Victor Emmanuel once Italy emerged on the winning side after World War I.

should be used, in the way one doesn't know the various names of animal species, and he therefore formulated his answer with a gesture of laugh.

'He's the only animal who laughs,' a shopkeeper angrily commented, passing sentence on the man, Mrs Andolfato – who had never laid eyes on him a single time – being one of his customers. It was as if the Captain and Victor Emmanuel had married the same woman, who had somehow – as if magically – been split into two identical copies. The dictionary, while being vast, did not account for the relationship between two men who had married different models of the same woman, Elena Petrović. 'It's a neologism that idiotic Captain came up with,' Strino, the Professor of Literature mockingly explained. 'But doesn't neologism mean a word borrowed from another language?' the Professor of Gymnastics asked, proud of his strapping physique, but devoted to the arts of the spirit, to culture, which his education had forced him to *abstain* from (as Pirovano Maria, the Professor of French, put it).

'A neologism can also indicate a new meaning for a word already in use, my dear colleague,' the Professor of Literature replied, placated.

If the professor nursed an opinion *on this*, it was because the beautiful damsel lived in a building at the bottom of Via Fiume, on the second floor. In order to reach the Corso, she therefore had to walk along the pavement beside the secondary school. Thus, while a professor would be explaining one of Horace's odes, or complicated equations, they would see this image on the street pass by like a vision, in a white, straight-cut princess dress. Elena wore no jewellery, neither real stones, nor fakes, 'in the same way nobody looks at an old canvas painted by the hand of an artistic god and thinks of adding some trinket to the picture,' the Professor of Philosophy explained in his baritone, *comblé*.[xxxii] He too – all the while never losing the thread of his lesson on Kant's philosophy, unlike his thirty-odd students, who understood none of it – would follow that lady's steps with his eyes, as she strode hurriedly along, as if fleeing from something. It felt as though she wasn't a material presence, but rather a collective dream conjured by the male teachers who were crushed by the boredom of their lessons. Even the headmaster, a furtive man, often cast a quick glance across the street, and if he happened to cross paths with her on the street, he would rapidly remove his hat, enraptured, his reason flitted into smoke.

It was as if a tragic fact from historical memory had slipped through the fingers of the magician illustrating his point in the classroom, as if it had leapt out of the book and jumped onto the street, sorrowful, inscrutable, excited and lonely; it was right there, in that secondary school, that the details of the epilogue of that story were first learned.

'Of turning point in that story,' the scowling Professor of Mathematics corrected, still jealous of her looks, despite the fact they had faded.

The beautiful lady had killed herself.

She had done so right there in that apartment on the second floor of the building at the bottom of that sun-drenched road. Her eldest son, barely twelve years old, had found the door shut on his return home. He had jumped from the stairs up onto the

---

[xxxii] French: 'satisfied'.

building's ledge and had climbed into the bedroom through the open window: in front of him lay his mother, in a pool of blood.

The Professors all talked at the same time, one was still sitting down, and another was on his feet. The council had been adjourned, and the day's agenda lay inert beneath the headmaster's glassy eyes: what was to be done?

Truth be told, nobody expected those eggheads to do much about anything.

However, the man who stood stridently up from behind his desk, like a Captain who leaps upon his saddle when the decisive hour has come, or so his loyal accountant said, was a businessman, who was bound by ties of friendship to the Andolfato family (the beautiful suicide had been his youngest son's godmother). He was a man in his forties, robust, authoritarian and generous. He had burst into the Andolfato home, being among the first to arrive – having been warned by a mysterious phone-call, it was later said – and had ordered the bereaved husband and his two sons to follow him back to his own house. In fact, he had basically kidnapped them.

As it happens, events had unfolded in a far calmer manner: yet following the customary formalities, the Andolfato family had actually spent various weeks living in the houses of close friends.

The city was very small and everyone knew that the woman had committed suicide. The official version of events was that she had suffered a sudden stroke. 'She suffered a blow, a blow!' people constantly said.

'Yes, she suffered a blow to the heart,' the Professor of Mathematics and Physics creepily added; she was skinny as a rake, and had no heart.

The unhappy woman's son, the one who had found her in a pool of blood, would go suddenly pale whenever he heard those words – *a blow, a blow!* The lie was meant to protect the boys from their classmates.

They played together in a group of four – the Andolfato boys and the Mariani boys – now that tragedy had united them into a single house. Yet it was always as though a dark cloud hung over them. In the way that music is sometimes like an invisible plain, an alternate reality to the slower passing of time, where nothing happens.

The youngest of the Mariano boys, Albertino, who was ten, always seemed to run along a secret track. He was the only one in that group who had noticed his friend's *binary* pain: he wasn't merely suffering because his mother was dead, but because her blood had also been concealed, and while he hadn't been obliged to lie – and to say that she had suffered a stroke – he was required to keep quiet whenever anyone voiced that lie. The authority of his elders had therefore been compromised: it was as if they were the ones who were children, incapable of living without the help of consoling lies.

Albertino was proud of his father's gesture. The latter had wanted to host them all in his house and he had therefore spared the Captain the need to ask. What should he have asked for, after all? That man also looked like a little boy, and was now both taciturn and dazed. Mrs Mariani, who had always been friends with the deceased, gave him some comfort; she was a woman who possessed a soothing lightness, even in the midst of tragedy. It was as though the Captain had become her third child, *her big boy*, as the Captain himself bitterly commented.

A blow!

If Elena's final gesture had been rescinded and re-written, the adults had nevertheless failed to take sufficient precautions. After a carelessly mislaid sentence here, and an allusion there, either from relatives, strangers or classmates, in the end even the boys – the two Andolfatos and the Marianis – found out the truth: the beautiful woman had had a secret affair with one of her husband's colleagues.

Adults and children alike were certain that Captain Andolfato was innocent, and the road to her suicide had taken other paths, which had had nothing to do with his thoughts, actions or words. Had he known about the affair? Nobody had had the regrettable idea to ask him, given that even baseness has its limits. There had certainly been no outbursts or threats.

On the husband's part.

If anything, the more sophisticated ones tended to say, it was worth looking into whether any threats had been launched by the invisible man on the scene, the woman's lover.

Whom nobody ever questioned.

Mariani protected the Andolfato family, his friends. Everyone was aware that Mariani was a Don Juan, but nobody had ever insinuated that he had had that woman in his sights. He would never have dishonoured that friendship – just as he always kept his word when it came to business. It appeared as though he felt it was his duty to take charge of the situation and keep his friend and his sons on the painful path of continuity. At the table, he would talk of trite and even bizarre subjects, as though wanting to use the quotidian as an antidote. The widower was very grateful to him: he had never thought such a tragedy would befall him.

He would facetiously say that 'there's no need to prepare oneself.' He looked like a man who walked along carefree singing his way through life while death had already left to hunt for its victim.

Mariani's youngest son, Albertino, Elena Petrović's godson, wouldn't let himself be. He wanted to help his friend, Peppino. He certainly understood that it was necessary to banish that unbearable memory – that is, the suicide – but he found it naïve and rude to merely say that it had been: *a blow, a blow!* He had also understood that his friend was suffering because of it, as though the adults had wanted to make him – the first person who had witnessed the event – out to be a liar.

It took him a few days to wrap his little head around all his thoughts.

Apparently, the day had been proceeding without a hitch in that house, which was now shared by two families: if Mariani had decided to impose *normality* on the tragedy's victims, his wife was offering them *levity* in the form of playful, affectionate conversation. As for Albertino, he had not only understood that Elena would live through a passionate affair, but that his friend had known all along. Maybe his father didn't know, but he did. Thus, he had seen the lover's secret face in the pool of his mother's blood.

They often read adventure comics together.

Slowly, Albertino was able to see the wood for the trees. To start with, he had managed to get his friend to admit that there had been another man in his mother's life. It seemed that confiding in someone did him much good, as though he had been freed from the weight of being the only one to know something, or being unable to talk about it with anybody – *children shouldn't get mixed up in affairs such as these, this was his mother they were talking about, a sacred image who was now dead…* As if being forbidden to talk about her could change any of the details of the facts already known to him.

Albertino had some talent when it came to sketching, and his teachers praised him for it. He decided to avail himself of it. That evening, when they were alone in their room, he pulled a sketchbook out from under his bed and began to draw, beneath his friend's attentive gaze. He even drew a speech bubble, just like in their comics, but he only mouthed the words, without writing them down. Perhaps because the words were superfluous, or because he feared someone would find the sketchbook.

The ceremony had been going on for several evenings, without anyone ever noticing that the light would stay switched on for a long time, because the room gave out on the terrace.

Drawing took up a great deal of time, and thus the narrative progressed slowly. This helped the young novelist to unravel its thread.

The plot twist happened all of a sudden. It wasn't a piece of fiction, but rather a memory. He had read a sentence in one of their comics, 'Cino and Franco,'[xxxiii] the adventures of two friends, *a hand covered by a piece of cloth…* Just like in the comic book, the murderer had faked his beloved's suicide, secretly gripping the gun that had killed her. This was what was being revealed to him. It hadn't been a suicide, it had been a murder. His mother had betrayed her husband, but she would have never abandoned him by killing herself.

[xxxiii] Italian translation of the adventure comic-strip *Tim Tyler's Luck*, which ran from 1928 to 1997. Many of the stories were set in Africa.

Peppino listened while holding the comic book in his hand, which Albertino had even taken the trouble to fill with colour. Peppino didn't seem to want to substitute one lie with another (a murder instead of *the blow*), or to want to be cheered up; but Albertino seemed to be the only one who had understood the question that had been nagging him all that time: *why did she leave me?*

Albertino's answer was wrong, but he had in some way at least heard his question: this was what truly cheered him up.

'Can I have it?' he asked his friend, holding the comic book in his hand. 'So, do you think I should avenge her now, is that it, should I kill him?' he added, pointing to the handsome lover in the book, whom Albertino didn't know: he had sketched a tall, blonde man with an Olympian physique. Whereas he was actually (given that Peppino knew him) a Lieutenant of average height with elegant features who had something restless or musical about him, as if his mind was always somewhere else. This had endowed the Lieutenant with a childish immediacy, which had struck Peppino, as though he'd found himself before a playmate his own age. Whereas he was in fact a man in the midst of a baleful tragedy. Everyone knew that his mother was plagued by nerves and mental afflictions, even though her beauty always distracted them from his and left them ensnared.

Ever since the day Elena had killed herself, her lover had also apparently vanished, as if they'd eloped.

Peppino loved his father, but he also knew that his mother had hailed from a different world. Not because she'd shared the Queen's name, which was a meaningless coincidence. Besides, she didn't look anything like her: if there was something statuesque or matronly to the Queen, it was an effect that existed only in the ambit of her public appearances, while his mother instead had been shaped so simply and yet so gracefully that she appeared ethereal. At times, his father had seemed genuinely embarrassed to have such a beautiful woman by his side.

If anything… the title of happy couple suited her only when in the company of that Lieutenant with his theatrical – nay, musical – elegance.

That man had killed his mother because it was the only way, the only way to run away together to that elsewhere where they both hailed from. There was a kind of consistency to the affair, even if the others had turned out to be inadequate spectators. Peppino felt complicit.

At that moment he understood that he was forgiving his mother – not for having betrayed his father, or for her relationship with his fellow officer – but him, because she had abandoned him to the world where he could still embrace her venerated shadow.

Peppino appeared relieved and glad when, the following day, beneath the heavy African sun, the azure sky which was a little whitish in parts, but entirely cloudless, he rode in the shiny, black rented carriage as it brought him back to his own home. Not the one where the tragedy had occurred. Mariani, an energetic man, and lightning-quick when it came to making decisions, had seen to all the arrangements: they now lived on the other side of the city, on Via Roma, on the third floor of a building owned by Mariani, where all the furniture had already been moved from the house that had been abandoned. Mariani had been the one to convince the Andolfato's previous landlord to terminate their contract. After all, that tragedy had been absolutely dreadful, and men needed to stick together in such times, it was their duty to do so.

Next to the Queen's official portrait, bearing its kind inscription, there was now a smaller portrait of Elena, also in a silver frame, in the new house on Via Roma, a picture that showed Elena in profile, showcasing all her unblemished beauty, it looked like a painting. Anyone who stopped by the Queen's portrait noticed that her expression was rather conventional, whereas Elena was staring at some invisible point, out of sight for anyone looking at her portrait.

Just like Peppino, who often stood in front of the portraits whenever he found himself alone in that silent house. Something troubled him: he had for some time suspected that he resembled the vanished Lieutenant.

As though this metamorphosis was the secret thread of willpower.

3

THE SEDUCER

Being the fourth offspring of one of the more notable bourgeois families in that colonial city, the boy was feeling restless: well, his two older sisters were practicing a role and would soon tread the scene. It was as if a bare wall had grown a window onto a boundless landscape – as if the ceiling had collapsed and *unknown constellations had appeared in the celestial sphere*. This was uttered by the boy's mother, who was playfully illustrating her son's restlessness – or rather, metamorphosis – to her friend. There were no important roles to play and the modest stage was provided by the convent of the Sisters of Charity of the Immaculate Conception of Ivrea, which was situated on the Corso. In order to celebrate the carnival, the school had put on a play. 'What amuses me is that they all have different roles on the social ladder. Go figure, at my table is the *Countess* – for whom I modified one of my evening dresses, taking it in, and even the *prison warden* – I had her maid's apron dyed black. Yes indeed, I've got quite a lot to do. I complained about it to the Mother Superior: my name isn't even on the playbill. It seems the Prefect's wife will be in attendance – as well as other esteemed names.'

They were sipping their tea in the sitting room's penumbra.

'But the men have been confined to the orchestra,' she told her friend, 'I didn't read the play because they only gave the girls the pages with their lines. I nevertheless managed to piece it together. The story is *très larmoyante* and it's about a fallen woman who's led back to the right path. However, the entire plot takes place in the absence of men: fathers, husbands, brothers, even the priest, and it's even missing the kind of character who matters most in these dramas, the seducer, the men who have gone out, they're on a journey, or sleeping: but they never set foot on the scene, not even the postman or coachman. As if! Imagine putting together men and woman on the same compromising, pandering boards of the theatre: who knows what authentic dramas would ensue, it would be like leaving young people alone on the Giuliana beach by the light of the moon. The theatre is a full moon and the nuns won't let themselves be duped. So, they threw out *all the men*!'

The boy hadn't even noticed the spell that had been cast by the nuns, who watched over the order of things. He attended the local secondary school. He too was acquainted with *La Traviata*, the daughter of Manzi the jeweller, who was good friends with his sisters, and who had been entrusted with the title role, even though he'd been unable to read many of her lines, since he could only read the brief scenes in which his sisters appeared. He hadn't even understood that she was to play a *fallen* woman.

'He's the only one who sees things as they really are,' the boy's mother explained, 'that poor girl has fallen in love with a man she cannot marry, and who is promised to another. The fatal word – *fallen* – is never mentioned in the text, it's implied, just like the presence of men. I haven't really understood what is going to happen on the stage, because the nuns want to put on some theatre, to reflect life, cutting out real characters and dangerous words. There's a real risk that the public will rise up and rebel: *come on*, they'll shout, *how about performing a real drama with the right characters and the right words?* Picture the Mother Superior's embarrassment! Maybe she'll call the police or sink to her knees to pray. Maybe she'll start to think the theatre is the devil's playground and she'll have it demolished.

'My wife is talking nonsense,' her husband said, having entered the room without either of the ladies noticing him.

'Go on now, go on,' Mrs Gilberti replied, laughing, 'I don't want to see any men in this sitting room – which is our stage – just like the nuns with their play. Plays can only occur thanks to those who are absent, since whoever generates drama is condemned to absence!'

On the day of the performance, the boy was sat in the orchestra. While it was true that opening night had been reserved for the adults, the entire city had turned up, but since his sisters had roles in the play, it was decided to make an exception for young Giovanni. One of the sisters, the *Countess*, had been responsible for persuading the Mother Superior to consent. She loved that dreamer and said that she wanted him present in the theatre.

From the moment that the lights came on and the curtain rose, the boy seemed to hold his breath. He was struck by the presence of his sisters on the stage, they seemed enchanted and more in the moment than he'd ever seen at the house – in fact, it was as though they had hitherto lived incognito, lodging at that hotel, their house, but without ever revealing their true identities. Thus the performance desired by the Mother Superior had been a kind of favour, as if the good Mother had called him over to a dark corner of the house to tell him exactly who he had been living with. There are no adventures without revelations.

However, the boy made another discovery. The Mother Superior's revelations were reticent: there was evil, but there were no servants of evil. For instance, the seducer – why were they keeping him hidden, or worse, maybe he was hiding of his own accord? It was as though the boy wanted to challenge him to a duel, despite the fact neither of his sisters had been seduced, instead it had been a friend of theirs.

The play was a cheat, just like when one plays poker with an extra card, or rather missing a card.

He too began to applaud, although he didn't know whether he was applauding the play, his sisters, the Mother Superior's reticent revelations or himself, now that he'd discovered the trick – or maybe for a different reason entirely.

All appeared to have drawn to a close when, on his way out, Giovanni caught a quick glimpse of his mother standing slightly to the side next to an officer who looked roughly her age, around forty; the pair were talking. His sisters' triumph on the stage appeared to be fading. The real actress was his mother, as she stood on the boards of her stage, her dream – she looked elegant and smiled, but something stirred in her in a manner that he'd never previously seen.

That realization quickly led him to understand that the seducer was standing right in front of him, and it left him stunned.

Everyday life was not an ordered world, with steely rules, and the theatre wasn't a world of boundless excess: the latter was nothing but the spy-hole one used to peer into the hidden dramas of everyday life – then he went out onto the street and resolved not to spare anyone or anything, including his house.

He wanted to call the Mother Superior over so she could chase that man away. Instead he started crying and ran away.

4

THE STOLEN MANUSCRIPT

Once he had finished reading the manuscript, *the little professor* – as they called him in the city, because he was blond, thin, almost childlike, with a lock of loose hair always hanging over his eyes – placed it on the table. It was bizarre that that woman hadn't seen anything but old age and death in that industrious Italian colony. She hadn't written about his city, but rather about the colony's capital – which lay roughly a thousand miles away; roughly because precise measurements were careless in Africa, and those spaces – the ruthless southern winds that seemed to want to obliterate everything in their path to restore the landscape's primeval innocence – made any notion of precision nothing but wishful thinking, if not in fact ridiculous. Whenever he looked at the windbreak hedges outside, which had been planted to shield the areas of cultivated land and vegetable patches, his mind turned to the Justinian walls which had failed to protect the cities of the ancient Pentapolis[xxxiv] from the blind impulses of the tribes from the interior. Scorched by the sun, one could still tour their ruins along the coast: Ptolemais and

---

[xxxiv] Pentapolis: informal league of five cities in the western part of Cyrenaica, named after Cyrene, the leading city of the Pentapolis.

Teuchira. All this appeared to justify the utter absence of joy in the author of the manuscript, now that, as she put it, war had been consigned to *the winds and the barbarians*: the Italian colony was on the verge of slipping away, of being hurled back into the sea.

The author had indulged herself, for example lingering on the almost ethereal receptionist at a hotel, a parody of the confident army officers, in his uniform and his incredibly pallid skin, as though he'd just emerged from a dream. Or the incredible story of a baroness who was on death's threshold in some room, even though nobody was allowed to know which: people said one day a guest would place his hand on the wrong door handle and on entering would come face to face with death.

Her death.

Truth be told, the entire manuscript was riddled with sepulchral indulgences, *which is rather natural when all is said and done*, the young man thought, *because it's a kind of last will and testament: it doesn't deal with any material possessions, but rather with the past, a past which that woman didn't know who to entrust with.*

She had been a friend of his mother's, while in the *other* city, Tripoli. A city whose incredibly long history – the Phoenicians, the Romans, the Arabs, Charles V, the Hospitaller Knights of St John of Jerusalem, the Sultan, the Barbary corsairs, Count Volpi,[xxxv] all stood on that scene like in a kind of eighteenth century *Singspiel*[xxxvi] – appeared to guarantee both its reality and

[xxxv] Giuseppe Volpi, Count of Misurata [now Misrata] (1877–1947): Businessman who governed the colony of Tripolitania in the mid-1920s. He was also the founder of the Venice Film Festival.

[xxxvi] German: 'sing-song,' a kind of opera.

its continuity, thereby devaluing the city he lived in, which was as intimate as one's home, having been nearly conjured out of thin air by the industrious colonial government two or three decades earlier. However, surprises abounded whenever one tried to circumscribe a complex reality: the narrator knows that well, it resembles the confusion and embarrassment that a tourist guide experiences in a historical city where monuments crowd the proscenium like characters, all wanting to tell their own stories, which are often heartbreaking because they're in ruins – and all the more seductive for that reason. It is difficult inside a theatre to obtain the silence of a librarian, where every book is like a cell where the prisoner inside is a mute.

Carlino sighed and smoothed back his hair, without touching it, simply by tossing his head back, as though turning the page.

He was a bastard, and thus a secret.

Whenever she went to see him, his mother would introduce him as one of her sisters' sons, and nobody ever got suspicious. Especially in the colony, which filled with people from all parts of Italy, thus allowing them to reinvent their pasts: there was no such thing as a constrictive, collective, communal memory, just like in America, of which the North African colony was a mere parody, albeit only a stone's throw from Italy's doorstep, on the other side of the Mediterranean, or *Mare Nostrum*. The mother owned a dressmaker's. Needless to say, there were three characters in this drama, naturally the secret familial nucleus, there was a father; a married man who'd had a long relationship with Teresa. He belonged to higher circles and was well-to-do. 'Rather well-to-do,' the malicious gossipers stressed. Carlino had no love for him: he was a despot, *with a beast's dangerous narcissism*, as he would say. Teresa did nothing to adjust the father's image in the boy's mind – given that Carlino had after all barely seen him, and ever since he'd lived in the colony, for the past five years, he hadn't seen him once.

Carlino was twenty-nine years old.

He was esteemed and respected by all at the secondary school on Via Fiume: he was steadfastly diligent in carrying out that ancient and noble profession. The students occasionally took advantage of him, they weren't afraid of him. He hated to experience or inspire such a sentiment – fear – in anyone.

He had lain the manuscript down on the small iron table, which stood atop three curvy legs, and had lingered there motionless. At which point a German man with a grey beard, who had landed in the Italian colony to venture with a colleague towards the heart of Africa, where they intended to carry out geological surveys.

Geology is concerned with the origins of the Earth and its composition and structure as well as its history as it changes over time. Carlino, who taught mathematics and had never even heard of geology, the notion struck him as very curious and he told the German as much, which made the latter shudder – who nevertheless being courteous, smiled. It was *funny*. As Carlino knew German, he had offered to serve as their interpreter during the few days they would be in that coastal town to prepare their expedition along the old caravan routes of the desert. They were punctilious, they wanted to prepare everything, even though Africa tends to scoff at anyone who makes plans, just as it did with all those efforts to catalogue and 'circumscribe' everything, the mathematician ironically explained.

They were sat on Carlino's modest veranda – which he'd erected at the back of his little villa, in the shade, under a sloping glass ceiling, a corner of Oriental taste: the divans were strewn with cushions, bleached mats on the floor, painted peacock feather protruding out of *cloisonné* vases, yellowish ostrich eggs decorated with leather trappings, as well as a whole assortment of Oriental knick-knacks on the walls. He had never managed to come up with a plausible explanation to himself – the others never asked him anything about it, since that kind of taste was particularly in vogue at the time – as to why he kept indulging himself in *reconstructions* which strived towards being museum-like but wound up being dreamlike instead.

The geologist, for his part, had been very taken with that corner, it was the complete opposite of the gargantuan natural structures that were the object of his studies. He had wanted to show it to his colleague and he had taken advantage of the situation to quote some noble verses from the *West-östlicher Divan.*[xxxvii] It was as though his soul had stumbled, just like our ears can sometimes hear strange, mysterious, elusive sounds: an unperceivable shadow had danced through his knowledge-cluttered mind.

Doctor Batisti, a friend of *the little professor*, appeared at the garden gate. He too wore a grey beard, which had been trimmed in the same style, leaving the two – the physician and the geologist – to look at one another somewhat embarrassedly, as though one was mocking the other. Yet neither truly knew who among them was the fake, and thus they both kept quiet.

[xxxvii] *West-östlicher Divan:* (*West-Eastern Diwan*) a collection of poems by Goethe inspired by the Persian poet Hafez.

The fact the Doctor didn't know a single word of German brought some lightness to the situation. Carlino, who spoke to one first, then the other, felt like he was walking on two different roads.

'Did you read it in the end?' the physician asked, having noticed the manuscript on the table as he took a seat.

'I finished it just a moment ago.'

'Was I indiscreet in giving it to you?'

'No,' Carlino replied. 'The manuscript was addressed to a person. Well, I am that person. I am Antonio's friend…'

'Let's go back a few steps…' he began, as though standing in his classroom, whenever they had to summarise a certain notion, the students' memories suddenly became wobbly. 'I first made the acquaintance of Mrs Manzi in Paris, several years ago. Having always been close to her, my mother finally convinced her to come in winter to the colony. The old woman appeared to be close to the end of the line, or was at least unable to avoid it. Nevertheless, Africa saves only whoever she wants to save, and is as inscrutable as Providence itself: it can seduce one, destroy another and bore a third… it hardly ever repeats itself and it laughs at all our plans, even the flamboyant ones our Generals cook up.'

The woman had lodged at the hotel, the Mehari, which was situated by the shore: a low, well-structured edifice, which looked as if it wanted to playfully and elegantly recreate the bazaar's winding labyrinth. So long as she'd been able to walk, the old woman had dined at her friend's house; later she did so at her hotel, a ship she could no longer abandon at will: amidst Africa's blinding light it was slowly carrying her to her final port of call.

'I'm disappointed that the manuscript was left unfinished: she had promised in her *incipit* that she would explain why she had felt the need to talk to me of all people, but she wasn't able to do so. Time laughs at me while I wait for clarity on my own life,' at which he stood up, as if he'd struck at the heart of the matter, or had wanted to impatiently emphasise, either *jokingly* or painfully, his appearance on the manuscript's stage. The physician followed the words, while the scholarly German observed his movements, the former looked like he was in a library, the latter as though he were at a cinema – and they were both engrossed: 'She wrote the manuscript for me because we both nourish *unlimited ambitions* for the people we love: a kind of violence that demands a theatrical intensity in life, which is the only plausible release one can experience, however ephemeral. The beloved is unable to be satisfied by any old plan, our love suffers because of it, as though it was devoid of justifications, derided, and even if it doesn't perish, it never knows peace. All of this gave us a language, a system of values, reactions in the face of others' victories or defeats. That woman was deluded by the four men in that *drama*, the husband and the sons – even handsome Antonio, whom she told me one time she hadn't even been able to profit from his ruinous fall in order to grow. But let us leave that ghost alone, it's an insatiable spectator and it is offended by the lives of others, indifferent to its torments, yearnings, just like nature, which has its own dramas, which are always independent from ours: didn't you promise me that you would tell me how you managed to get your hands on that manuscript?'

The physician was astonished by *the little professor*'s revelation, that he himself had been the intended recipient – every event results in a revelation – and thus that he would ultimately in his own way be a character in the manuscript's narrative. 'Easily done,' he confided.

He instinctively stood up, while Carlino sat back down. The scholarly German stood there watching them without understanding anything, although he was far from embarrassed. The different languages had created scenarios that overlapped, just like the real and the unreal, sounds and sights, or the present moment and one's memories. Perhaps he understood geology as a metaphorical science. Regardless, all he had to do was think that he was standing in front of animals that belonged to some odd, unclassified species, which was devoted to idle meanderings.

'I bore witness to the agony of her death throes, in that colonial hospital,' the physician said, 'she'd shown up all of a sudden and there weren't any of her relatives there: having been called from the motherland, they hadn't had time to get there yet, the mail boat operated according to fixed schedules that were indifferent to all the (occasionally hurried) tragedies of human affairs. The old woman was nearly immobilised, but I had the distinct impression that using her hand or her eye – don't ask me how, when reality has reached a turning point one can't take note of everything – she would start to fiddle around with her diary: I should have hidden it.

'Maybe I made the entire thing up: but one page I read, almost without realizing it, and maybe some phrase that was specifically directed at me, which foreshadowed the rest of the text, convinced me that she hadn't written her diary for her husband or her sons, and that they couldn't be allowed to get their hands on it. It might be true that it hadn't been written for me either, but a stranger is in a privileged situation whenever one looks for a confidant, and can provide a confidential service: I took the diary without bothering to conceal my actions and stuck it inside my bag. From that moment on, the unhappy woman never looked at me again. Four days later, her family arrived, the father and his three sons, but by then she had slipped out of consciousness.

'So what should I do now? Should I return the manuscript to them?

'Having placed it in your hands, I feel relieved of any sins of indiscretion, it's as if you were the one responsible for the theft now. At least… what I mean… that my good cheer comes from the fact that I fulfilled the mission, however casually, by placing the diary in the hands of the person it was destined for. Keep it, burn it – or hand it over to your German mentor over there.'

The geologist nodded with his head, possibly because the physician was looking at him.

Only then, having regained his calm, did he ask what had happened – and he pointed his finger at the manuscript, having understood that the real story lay in there, and not in the conversation between the two friends.

Carlino tried to sum up the entire affair, but whether he was distracted by other thoughts, since it was difficult to tread slowly when the past transforms itself and returns with all the violence of the wind, or perhaps the geologist had remembered an unresolved detail from the trip, the German had therefore mistaken one thing for another: an old woman had died, and this lady – which the manuscript mentioned, where maybe a last will and testament had been concealed, not once concerned with worldly goods, but with the interpretation of old, painful memories – had actually been the doctor's own mother. He immediately stood up and offered the newcomer his condolences – who in his turn stood up, smiling and failing to understand why that distinguished gentleman, who wore a beard like his, was congratulating him.

Carlino didn't translate a single word, and that was fine. After all, when the past returns, it enchants us and steals us away. Inside that manuscript was his own story, lost in the wake of others' stories.

Now all that is left is to explain how so many different events can be interconnected.

Carlino's mother and the manuscript's author (as was to be expected, this was a story of disillusions, not that it had anything to do with love or money: that woman had *unlimited ambitions* for the destiny of others and none of the men in her life stuck their necks out or took risks; but she was wrong, there was something captivating about Antonio, or at least this was the opinion of the woman who had loved him for a while) were therefore not the same person: they were childhood friends. Just like how Carlino and one of the woman's three sons, Antonio, had spent parts of their youth together.

This wasn't what had misled Carlino, it had been a sentence which had slipped through the author's fingers. Perhaps her illness had reduced her faculties. She had therefore revealed that Carlino wasn't the son of that industrious businessman who'd carried on a long-term relationship that everyone knew about, a man he hated – Carlino had in fact, her friends had confided in her, been fathered by an army officer with whom she'd had a brief fling, a man of whom she'd then never heard from again, there was little more to his memory than his uniform. It seemed like the same old story that rose out of a conquered town, when soldiers ran loose through the streets, having been given a free hand. An officer had come into her home, he had forced himself violently on her and then had vanished. In actual fact, the event had taken place in a hotel where the mother had been staying.

What truly embarrassed Carlino was the hate he'd nursed for that devastating father of his, with his beastly narcissism, who believed himself master of the entire universe, having confused the former for his factory: he had *blamed* an innocent man. Thus, he too had been betrayed in his turn: his real father was a uniform. His childhood drama was either absent or was headed for other destinations.

He could run over to his mother, erasing the thousand miles of distance that separated them, and ask to know more. But hadn't she confessed to her friend, who didn't seem to know much about it anyway?

What about him, *the little professor*, wasn't he a grown up man after all?

What did it matter to men who their fathers were? Fathers are figures who belong to the world of infancy, of adolescence.

The geologist was observing his guest and nodding affirmatively with his head.

The physician looked at both of them and didn't understand what had happened. It seemed as though the manuscript belonged to the two of them, and that he was being kept in the dark, the situation had been turned on its head.

'Today,' Carlino mockingly announced, '*the little professor* has died: the manuscript was my initiation rite, marking my passage from youth to adulthood: I will now begin my second life.'

The geologist didn't understand what the guest had said about him, he had merely grasped the word *professor*, which was used in both languages.

5

WHAT ARE YOU GOING TO BE WHEN YOU GROW UP?

It was the oldest game in the world. Every boy has been asked the same question: a playful and troubled echo, every boy has therefore asked himself that very question.

'Things were easier during the times of the barbarian hordes,' Colonel Varzi said in a good-natured manner, 'one knew that one was fated to follow in one's father's footsteps, whether he was a hero or a thief.'

Sat on the tiny jetty on the beach, the three officers were listening to the groups of boys busy *playing the future game* on the sandy shore. Their answers to that question didn't vary from the usual: one wanted to be a pilot, another a sailor, a third an inventor, while the fourth wanted to be a racing car driver. 'Funny,' the Colonel commented, seemingly the most alert among them, 'none of them seem to be interested in any kind of productive enterprise.'

'Nor moneymaking!' the General added, without bothering to explain if he considered this a sign of maturity or ignorance. They were in their bathing costumes, their uniforms had been hung up in the bathers' chalets as though it was a storeroom for theatrical costumes. The men were all of average height, with rather slender physiques and tanned skin.

In that group was a blonde boy who said he wanted to be a poet. Turning to the Colonel, the General asked him: 'Should he be counted among those who chose a productive enterprise?'

Perhaps because the people around them were in their bathing costumes (save for a few who were in their pajamas or their bathrobes, as though they were priests of some kind), and thus, surrounded by a reconquered primitivity – they looked like a barbarian horde that had chosen to strike camp. The three men on the jetty began to talk about the scattered fragments of history relating to the Vandal invasion: had it reached all the way to Cyrenaica, or had it stopped short at the perilous gulf of Sirte?

'Carducci's history teacher said that, having come down through Spain, the Vandals stormed Tripoli, where they subsequently lost their way, and inexplicably dispersed, like a stream of water. Besides, nobody ever said they'd reached the Nile.'

'Why don't you ask Garibaldi about that?' the General, who hailed from Pinerolo, in the Piedmont, haughtily said.

The conversation languished. The three *historians* seemed more interested in the redheaded lady who, having stood up, was taking tentative steps along the shore. They looked like hunters, ready to pounce on their prey.

This too was one of the oldest games in the world.

'Let's play the game in reverse: what sort of past would we have liked to have?' the Colonel asked. 'Or better yet, what would we have wanted to be as children?'

'Where would we have liked to live as children, you mean?' the General corrected him, a little dryly. But no answer was forthcoming. Everyone seemed wrapped in his own thoughts, memories, longings, delusions and lassitude.

Nevertheless, there was that blonde boy, slender as an eel, the one who wanted to write daring verses as an adult, perhaps to bring the unspeakable to life, and who was now, having distanced himself from the others, stood up to his ankles in water and staring straight at the blinding sun: the legs hanging off the jetty, the three officers looking like bored schoolboys, who instead of sitting in class and listening to their teacher, preferred to dream of games, lying on the beach, fishing and sleep – which only generates even more dreams.

6

FROM THE STATIONER'S

Christmas, nor any other holiday was being observed that day, and yet the excitement and the aura of sacredness which reigned over the family environment was similar to it: on that afternoon, Mrs Ruffatto had gone out with her four sons to pay the Pavone stationary shop a visit.

It was difficult to understand why the boys experienced the inextricable tension – made of lights and shadows – that comes with embarking on a journey only while at that stationer's. That first day of school at first appeared barely distinguishable from the rest: their imaginations weren't being fueled by the prospect of meeting new classmates, teachers, the new classrooms or subjects they would be studying – it was being moved by coloured pencils, compasses, rulers, copybooks, erasers, pencil sharpeners, and 'all the other accoutrements of the hand,' as Mrs Ruffatto, who knew how to crown the most everyday occasions with a halo of unreality. She certainly ensured her boys were up with their studies, but she nevertheless didn't let those studies take up the entire day; instead of forcing them to *observe reality*. She kept a door to a lighter world open, which was real and invisible in its own way, thus allowing external elements to mix with others, thus helping to avoid the pernicious tendency to oversimplify reality.

Owing to his profession, Doctor Ruffatto had gone inside all the houses in the city and had been able to see those families in the midst of their daily routine: there were messy houses and very strict houses, as well as those that were ruinously nervous or completely devoid of any intimacy. None of them felt like his own, which was pleasant and serene. Fairy tales, in that house (which had its fair share of problems like all the others: the children's health, school, daily errands, cooking and cleaning rituals, washing, hanging the laundry out to dry, making the beds, keeping all the drawers tidy…), once the boys had outgrown their childish naivety (all except the youngest, who was almost four years old), had returned in the form of *theatre*.

Even at the theatre we can see what everyday life looks like, but events are naturally accentuated and the rhythm of those sequences of events are accelerated, transfiguring them. Instead of demeaning reality in order to prepare the boys to look after themselves in the social jungle, the boys' mother instead sought to poke fun at it, or to exalt it by derailing it off its boring, grey tracks. As if she wanted to educate them in the art of dreams, to keep that dream alive in their everyday lives – to feel at ease in those dreams, without being stifled by them. 'I always come to your house at different times, Doctor, and without any advance warning: I've never seen your wife annoyed with the children, or tense, or quiet; there's something… colourful about your house, as if there was always enough light, as though nothing or nobody ever tripped up,' a friend of his – who was also a patient who suffered from asthma – once told him. Everyday actions can claim a number of meanings, in the same way that fairy tales have blurry confines, because they are simply able to do so.

Thus they had visited the Pavone stationary shop on the lively and narrow Via Torino. They weren't merely buying the usual instruments of their apprenticeships, it seemed as though the boys had forgotten that in the space of a few days all of them would be finding themselves in a new classroom, where they would be expected to cram some knowledge – which was old, obvious, worn out and for the time being entirely useless – into their heads while sat alongside thirty-odd classmates. Instead, it seemed as if all those instruments – the golden compass, the shiny ruler made of fake ivory, the copybook with the aggressively coloured cover, the pencil sharpener that was shaped like a sea shell, the exotic-looking eraser, the ink which looked like it was a liquid metaphor of the night, the pencils that yearned to flush out the unspeakable through words, drawings or numbers – had been designed to allow alchemists, astrologers and other secret conjurers to make mysterious and decisive discoveries.

The youngest boy, Stefano, appeared torn between the excitement of being in his brothers' company, who were busy preparing for a long journey, and the suspicion that he would be left behind *on dry land*. He was a delicate child, in some ways his father's favourite, probably because he shared his fatal uncertainties. He wore spectacles, which made his face look somewhat fake. Doctor Ruffatto often left him to orbit around his mother, who was more suited to ensuring his happiness: the boy always seemed to get excitable whenever he entered the room, as though his clout was inauspicious.

Perhaps the boy was aware that his mother was certain that he would soon become similar to his brothers, Doctor Ruffatto thought, and that he would share their inventive, serene outlooks on life; while he himself feared that everything would soon become complicated and his own uncertainties would accentuate the boy's own. Stefano had often alternated between mimicking his father and his mother – which had led to the previously mentioned arrangement.

Doctor Ruffatto watched his wife and sons while unseen behind one of the windows of the twin buildings at the top of Via Regina Elena, as they made their way to Via Torino, which began a little further on. The boys were talking tirelessly: even Stefano, who probably didn't have anything to say, but who didn't want to be *left out*.

His mother held him by the hand.

This was the portrait of his settled life. He had raised a family, he was a cherished husband and father, and even more ambitious people than him seemed to envy him his simple, happy house, and the harmonious, exciting flow to the passing of time within its walls. The ceremony of taking the boys to the Pavone stationary shop had traditionally been reserved for his wife, both of them having tacitly agreed to the arrangement. This allowed them to walk home together in the evening, when all the boys would want to show him everything right away, all at the same time. This too provided proof of his wife's gracefulness in bringing a spark to everyday life and giving it a different light. *He who doesn't know what to do with pennies will end up wasting millions*, the Doctor thought melancholically.

He had been standing by the window for the past half hour. He wasn't waiting for his wife and children to pass by, even though he knew at exactly what time the procession would appear.

He had taken a day off from the hospital, since he had to clean up, or rather pack up, the apartment his brother – who had died two months earlier – had lived in.

He had repeatedly postponed the chore, as if fleeing from the responsibility of writing the final act of that life.

His brother had been separated from his wife, who had long since returned to the motherland.

Owing to some childish impulse, he had always kept a trunk full of family papers – mementoes of his youth and some old letters – at his brother's house instead of his own. Not that he would have expected his wife to stick her nose into that sort of business, in fact she even knew about the trunk in his brother's house. It was as if the Doctor wanted to protect his house from the (possibly malicious) influence those papers might exert on it. He had buried another version of himself in that trunk. Why he didn't just burn it all, nobody knew. His brother had been a discreet man and he had never asked him any questions. Besides, the apartment was very large, it took up an entire floor, and thus the trunk had never been in the way.

A smooth plank had been placed on top of the trunk and this had then been covered by a piece of red velvet with golden rickracks which hung all the way down to the floor.

It looked like an altar.

Or a sarcophagus.

He never opened the trunk, and having finally decided to dedicate that entire day to packing everything in that apartment up, or rather, to working out how he would pack it up, given that the owner was already demanding it be turned over, on his way to the apartment he had wondered whether the trunk wasn't already empty, maybe he had thrown everything away one day and simply forgotten, or perhaps his brother had thrown it away, it had been years since they had given any thought to that *legacy* (of his former self).

Apprehensions or vain hopes: they were all present, just as he had left them. It was thus up to him to free himself from those shadows – it was out of the question to bring that trunk home and foolishly entrust it to someone else yet again. Besides, who would he be able to entrust it to?

Those papers had nothing to do with colonial life, which had begun when, as a newly-married man freshly armed with a degree, he had accepted an offer of work from that hospital in Africa. In fact, just like his marriage, Africa had also kept him away from those papers.

Now the velvet cloth with golden rickracks had been thrown on top of a chair and the trunk was finally open, a metal box full of letters, all of which were bound by a singular passion, a longing…

Sacrifice? Was he carrying out a ritual? What possible meaning could he draw from erasing all the traces of a relationship, especially now that his brother was dead? What did his brother have to do with it all anyway? He had never learned anything regarding its contents, despite having been its loyal custodian.

It was as if the calendar wanted to make fun of him. The word *end* – which had been written so many years prior to that moment, before his blessed marriage, his career – appeared to have run away: the letters were there and they were reclaiming the present.

Ruffatto sat down and started reading.

When he returned home that evening, there was an unusual pallor to his face, and the boys welcomed him boisterously.

His wife noticed his troubled state of mind, but she didn't say anything, packing up an entire house must have been exhausting, and it wasn't the right moment to discuss the contents of that trunk – truth be told, the thought of that trunk didn't even cross her mind.

Ruffatto listened carefully to all that his boys were telling him, displayed amazement at each object he was shown, his amazement being both ironic and loud, since the game of exaggerations is inexhaustible and makes everything precious, even unique.

Later that night at dinner, a friendly couple had been invited over and so the boys had calmed down a little, but the festive echo still reverberated throughout the house, even the newcomers – an army doctor and his wife – felt it.

Only little Stefano with his mercurial genius had understood that his father was absent, *empty*.

Affectionate at times and capricious at others, and always unpredictable, Stefano was ever careful to reaffirm his will in front of his brothers, especially when around his father, who probably favoured him above the others because he needed more protecting, but on that night it was Stefano who was protecting his father, even though he didn't know why.

The eight people in that room took up all the available space and the table had been extended to make room for the guests. Yet it seemed as though six of them were on one plane, while Doctor Ruffatto and his bespectacled clone were on another. It was if the boy had wanted to show his father that he was acquainted with suffering too.

Or better yet, what it means to suffer over dreams. It was as if he too had re-read those three hundred letters from the past, to take his leave from every single one of them, forever.

7

PTOLEMAIS

The beach umbrella was blue with stripes of white. A breeze rose from the sea, the current of an invisible river, which had either evaporated under the sizzling sun, or laughed the sun off entirely. The party had reached Tolmeita, the ancient Ptolemais, roughly a hundred miles east of the city.[xxxviii]

There was a white lighthouse on the top of the little rocky promontory.

A soldier had died a month earlier while taking a dip with a friend west of the lighthouse, in a seemingly tranquil bay where the undercurrents often carried one far from shore. That stretch of water was treacherous even for the local fishermen's ships.

The beach was deserted: the umbrella stood out like a sail.

It was said that there was an ancient theatre lost somewhere amidst those barren hills, but nobody knew its exact location, since the excavations hadn't gotten underway yet. After pondering the matter, Professor Berioli said that the theatre 'couldn't be anywhere else'. He had offered to act as a guide for the party, but nobody had wanted to follow him: he was a boring

---

xxxviii Whenever Spina mentions 'the city', it is meant to indicate Benghazi.

man, read extensively and indefatigably, and ceaselessly quoted the authors he'd read.

'He has such a sepulchral mind,' Mrs Lozzi said, 'who brings books to the beach? Does anyone go swimming completely clothed?'

'You'll see, you'll see, he knows everything by heart.'

'I would love to test him.'

The Professor had disappeared, only to show up again two hours later. It was midday by then. Yes: the location of the theatre in those hills was just as he'd guessed down below. His sandals were dusty, he looked like a wayfarer from the old fairy tales.

'So, you share the same rare and exalted tastes of the Greeks when it comes to locations, eh?' an officer attached to the party mockingly said in a loud voice, he had just graduated from the Military Academy of Modena.

'We will never again attain the heights reached by Greek knowledge,' the Professor modestly replied, 'if anything, I can only brag about having been educated by them just a little.'

'As for me,' Major Lambertini said, both solemnly and menacingly, 'I was educated by the Romans.'

It was an invocation of Fascism, but it only served to generate a great deal of embarrassment, nobody ever understood what that officer really meant whenever he spoke, the truth was always theatrical, as if it was a quality to be attributed to a specific character. Only that he had *forgotten* to let everyone know which character his mind had summoned at that moment.

Perhaps the Professor already knew that, since he nodded at that remark, rather than being frightened by the Major's threatening tone.

'Anyone who wants to play at acting can go up there – so long as you leave us in peace down here.' Mrs Lozzi said. She had been the last to slip into her bathing costume, but not without first going through the very time-consuming poses and rigmaroles involved when revealing one's nakedness – it looked like a ballet.

'What if my head isn't at peace?' Major Lambertini asked, pained.

'Then throw it away,' Mrs Revelli said, 'throw it right into the sea.'

Lambertini vanished into the sea.

'It would have been far better if he'd thrown that sandal-wearing Professor into the water.' Mrs Lozzi confided to her friend, in hushed whispers, 'One never knows how to… handle these men, nor, by extension, how to chase after them. Sometimes I dream about stupid, mute, deaf and handsome men – in other words a man fit only for the darkness of one's bedroom.'

The Professor, whom everyone had forgotten about, cut in.

'In Goethe's *Torquato Tasso*, when the poet asks the Princess if she considers all men to be 'unfeeling, wild and rude,' she replies: *Not so! But ye with violence pursue/A multitude of objects far remote*.'[xxxix]

'What a bore!' Mrs Lozzi exclaimed, having lost her patience.

Lambertini called out from the sea, making it look as if the current was dragging him away. He faked everything, even being in danger.

'You're such a comedian!' Mrs Lozzi yelled from the shore, while smilingly replying to the Major's call, all the while baring

---

[xxxix] J. Goethe. *Goethe's Works, Volume III* (Philadelphia: G. Barrie, 1885), p.119.

her body, which was still seductive and alluring, under the sun (as if it had nothing better to do than illuminate her).

'You can go ahead and read out loud Professor, the ladies have gone in the water,' Major Lambertini said.

The first picnic, a light one, had come to an end.

He was sat on a deck chair, over which he'd draped a brightly coloured towel.

The Professor was wearing shorts, which looked faded, and a white shirt, which was all creased. He was the only one who wasn't in a bathing costume. He scanned his surrounding, suspiciously.

He read in a low voice, as if looking to isolate himself:

'The Khalif, likewise, during his residence in Egypt, the present year, erected a tower, or castle, on mount Al Mokattam, which he called Kobbat Al Hawa, the tower of desire; and permitted two of the gentlemen of his bed-chamber, who were Christians, to build a church, denominated first from them *the church of the two gentlemen of the bedchamber*, and afterwards the church of the *Romans*, upon a spot of ground at a small distance from it. He also erected a *Mikeas*, or *Mikias*, or measuring pillar, in order to determine the gradual increase of the Nile, at *Shurat*, a place belonging to the village of *Banbanudah*, in the country of *Al Sa'id*, *Thebais*, or the upper Egypt; and repaired another of the pillars at *Akhmin*, in the same region, which was gone greatly to decay.'[xl]

'What century are we in?' Lambertini asked.

'The twelfth.'

---

xl Anonymous, *Modern Universal History, Containing the Most Genuine Life of Mohammed, Vol II* (G. Kearsley, 1762), p.403.

'Go ahead and read, Professor.'

Berioli had the habit of writing down phrases which he collected here and there into notebooks that were considerably smaller than the kind used by scholarly types – he taught at the Regio Liceo Ginnasio Giosuè Carducci. It was as though he dreamt of reducing an entire library to microscopic proportions. It struck Lambertini as a funereal dream, like the ones the Pharaohs used to have, who wanted representations of the entire cycle of life painted on the walls of their tombs, or maybe even as a vainglorious dream, one shared by those who sought the formula to transform base metals into gold. His taste for the bizarre had been piqued.

'*I wanted to outrun my desire for you,*
but my desire carried the day'

'It's such an absolutist dream, it's unacceptable, it's sheer blackmail,' Lambertini exclaimed, standing up. 'Who said that?'

'Al-Mutanabbi, a poet of the tenth century.'

'Right. I had thought it was some librettist from the mid-eighteenth century. If it's from the tenth then it's fair enough…'

He sat back down.

'Keep reading Professor!'

'*The dress of the bride, during this procession, entirely conceals her person. She is generally covered from head to foot with a red cashmere shawl; or with a white or yellow shawl, though rarely. Upon her head is placed a small pasteboard cap, or crown. The shawl is placed over this, and conceals from the view of the public the richer articles of her dress, her face and her jewels, etc., except one or two 'kussahs' (and sometimes other ornaments), generally of diamonds and emeralds, attached to that part of the shawl which covers her forehead. She is accompanied by two or three of her female relations within the canopy; and often, when in hot weather, a woman, walking backwards before her, is constantly employed in fanning her, with a large fan of black ostrich feathers, the lower of the front of which is usually ornamented with a piece of looking-glass. Sometimes one zeffeh, with a single canopy, serves for two brides, who walk side by side.*[xli]'

'And what's a kussah?'

The Professor seemed reticent.

'But this is an eighteenth century Englishman describing a bride's bathing rituals!'

Lambertini didn't press the issue.

The modern women were in the water, far away, growing smaller and smaller in the distance, until one could only see their heads.

'Keep reading Professor!'

'*Often I sang this, and even out of the grave*
will I cry it: 'Drink, before you put on
this raiment of dust.[xlii]

'This is Julianus Aegyptus, we're in the Justinian era (527 to 565), the very same Emperor who had the walls of Ptolemais rebuilt – can you see them down there? It seems the walls had almost been entirely destroyed by Khosrow I, before the time of the Arab invasion. Have you seen the mausoleums strewn along the coast?'

---

xli Thomas Patrick Hughes, *A Dictionary of Islam: Being a Cyclopaedia of the Doctrines, Rites, Ceremonies, and Customs, Together with the Technical and Theological Terms, of the Muhammadan Religion* (London: W. H. Allen, 1885), p.324-325.

xlii John William Mackail, *Select Epigrams from the Greek Anthology* (London: Longmans, Green, 1906), p.289.

'I don't want to see anything, keep reading Professor!'

'*The Prophet said: If anyone introduces an innovation, or gives shelter to a man who introduces an innovation, he is cursed by Allah, by His angels, and by all the people.*

'*The Prophet said: the innovators are the worst of all of God's creation.*

'*The Prophet said: the innovators are the dogs of the inmates of hell.*

'*Al-Hasan said: The most detestable creatures are those who seek the most insidious answer to blind the servant of God.*

'*Al-Hasan said: The more innovators redouble their zeal to save God, the further they leave Him behind.*

'*Muad said: The hand of God lies upon the community, when a man separates from it, God abandons him.*

'*Al-Fudayl said: Do not trust the innovator and do not seek his advice in your affairs, and do not sit with him since whoever sits with an innovator – Allah will cause him to become blind.*

'*Al-Fudayl said: O Allah do not let any innovator give me anything so that my heart should love him.*'[xliii]

Lambertini remained quiet.

Standing up in the sea, the two ladies were admiring two slender officers as they swam in butterfly strokes, their arms rhythmically leaving the water in unison while kicking their legs like frogs. Their performance struck Lambertini as failed attempt at flight, and most ungraceful. *The spitting image of this entire century*, he thought to himself, vexed.

The sand on the beach was scorching.

'*You won't sleep where you like on the day that you die.*'

[xliii] Sayings of the Prophet's companions.

'You made this one up, didn't you?' Lambertini exclaimed, pointing his finger at the Professor.

'No, no… I just don't know whether it's a proverb or whether I lifted it from a book, I don't even know if it's a sacred saying…'

'If you can't give me the century it was written in, then don't even mention it at all: anything that isn't signed is a fake.'

They lingered in silence.

Someone from the group – there were five or six couples – shouted something at them from the shiny, wavy water.

'Yes!!!' Lambertini shouted, even though he hadn't understood a word they'd said. He then made a sweeping gesture with his arm, as if he'd just caught something in the air.

'Keep reading Professor!'

'A demon lurks inside solitary travelers.'

'What century? What century? The tenth?'

'No,' the Professor said, as though he were some antiquarian in his shop, frustrated by his customer's inability to grasp the quality of an object from the *Haute époque*:[xliv] 'it's from the ninth.'

The waves washed ashore in a sweet and mellow way, not too dissimilarly from the conversation taking place.

They looked like a book-cover to Lambertini, who felt that he was holding the precious, invisible book in his hand. The swimmers lay even further away, their voices could no longer be heard, and one could only see their gestures, as though it was a series of muted paintings. That moment already felt like the memory of a distant past, and the world assumed the slow rhythm of memory.

[xliv] *Haute époque* is a term employed by antiquarians to refer to furniture and art dating to the Middle Ages, the Renaissance and the 17th century. Not to be confused with Belle époque (1870-1914).

'Keep reading, Professor!'

'The portion of the earth which is inhabited is reported to be estimated at a hundred years' march, that is to say, eighty years for the countries inhabited by Gog and Magog, sons of Japheth, son of Noah, a region (Siberia) which, situated at the northern extremities of the earth, is bounded by the sea of darkness. Fourteen years are required for the countries occupied by the Blacks, which comprise all that is beyond Mogreb, (Western Barbary), and extend along the same ocean.

'And finally, the six remaining years' march are required for the countries of Northern Africa, Egypt, Syria, Arabia, Persia, the land of the Turks, that of the Khazars and of the Franks, China, India, Abyssinia, the country of the Selavonians, that of Rome, as far as the great city of Rome, and other countries; in one word, all the countries occupied by infidels.'[xlv]

'Africa has taught me that space is an immense proposition,' Lambertini said, melancholically.

'Well, that's exactly the same lesson reading imparts,' the Professor muttered in a low voice.

'Do you think you'll discover something here?' Lambertini asked, growing annoyed.

'He had stood up and was waving strange signals to the bathers out at sea as they bobbed up and down.'

'Why didn't Khosrow's armies reach these shores?'

'It appears that the entire Persian army vanished on one occasion while crossing the desert between Egypt and Cyrenaica.'

'Do you think we'll share their fate?' Lambertini asked, his tone serious, as though subjecting himself to a difficult trial:

---

xlv The *Atheneum*, Issue No. 520, Saturday, October 14, 1837.

world-wide war was at their door. It was as though he was petitioning a saint inside an empty church.

'I don't know anything about war,' the Professor answered, lowering his gaze.

'Caution is cowardly.'

'Yet arrogance is a sin.'

'There you go: drop it all into the hands of the army… Picture yourself as a Greek hiding inside his Justinian walls as he sees Khosrow's armies on their way. A picture as strange as the surrounding plain, where five hundred people lived, at most, as if it was one of history's theatres. But of course: the desire to miniaturise an entire library in your notebook is a similar game to the one they played in those times, which involved putting everything in a single place, just like they did here.'

'It seems that during the Christian era the citadel was home to an important movement of heretics.'[xlvi]

'The stones are characters themselves. I tried to explain that to Lozzi.'

'Is that the blonde?'

'Occasionally, I feel as though I was the sun,' Lambertini said, 'who rises alone each morning, looks at the world, observes the ruins of times, and then vanishes, still alone. Do you think I've stretched that metaphor too far?'

'Anyone used to reading isn't surprised by much.'

'I've never been able to find an answer to this question: *what do you wish to see when you open your eyes*? If you were to answer that question I assume you would say a library as big as the world, everything is inside books.'

[xlvi] The followers of Arius (256–336) who was born in Ptolemais.

'What has already existed anyway, time resides within books, that's not much of a discovery.'

'Nothing, that's what I see.'

'What about the rest of you?' one of the ladies in the sea shouted, 'Aren't you coming in?'

'The landscape's beauty, with the Greek temples' white ruins, the Justinian walls, Khosrow's shadow, the Christian heretics, the Arab invaders, the mausoleums carved out of porous stone on the shores, the theatre buried in the hills, etc., etc., the landscape's beauty is a *bookish beauty*.' Lambertini leaned his head over. 'Tell me, did you like that last thought at least?'

It seemed that tall, self-assured man was agonizing over something. He moved his arms, as though he was talking to someone – but there was nobody in front of him.

He sat back down. He shut his eyes. Then once again, without opening his eyes, he raised his arms, like a clown or a bronze statue whose arms are always up in the air:

'Keep reading, Professor!'

'*It is night, so arise, because the night is when lovers talk,*
Crossing the threshold of Friendship's door.
The night shuts all doors wherever it finds them,
All except for Friendship's door, which stays open at night.'

'Naturally, God is the friend in question.' the Professor added in a hushed tone.

Lambertini made an irritated gesture.

'Of course! I was just waiting for you to teach me that! Everything here speaks of God, the space, the emptiness, the sky, time, and all the history that burned to ashes…'

Yet he then resumed his inquisitive stance.

'Where did we get to? Are we still in the eleventh century or have we gone further?'

He was holding some sand in his hand, which he slowly allowed to slip out of his fist, looking distracted. The Professor thought he was looking at an anthropomorphised hourglass.

'Who knows?' the latter said, somewhat embarrassedly. 'It's by Abu-Sa'id Abul-Khayr,[xlvii] but I don't really know who he is.'

'So we've gotten lost then!' Lambertini concluded, mockingly. 'We don't know where we are anymore!' and he raised his hands into the air again, like a blind man.

During that afternoon, after the ladies had flicked through all their magazines ('and scored a few points,' as Lieutenant Rossi said, being a young man who knew a thing or two, having been born with the mind of an adult, just like an elf), the semi-naked ladies – some of whom were wearing straw hats, others wore brightly-coloured veils – all allowed the Professor to speak. One needed to reshuffle the cards in order to keep their husbands entertained: there were fifteen people and the scene was composed of several juxtaposed planes, some of which were secret, while others were singular or dual, if not plural.

They were walking along the coast, heading west.

'After the death of Alexander the Great, when his empire crumbled, it was Ptolemy II Philadelphus[xlviii] who gave the city the name of Ptolemais.'

[xlvii] Abu-Sa'id Abul-Khayr (967-1049): Persian Sufi poet, often compared to Rumi.

[xlviii] Son of Ptolemy I, one of Alexander's companions and the founder of the Ptolemaic dynasty in Egypt.

'What century was that, Professor?' Lambertini interjected in an authoritative tone.

'The third century before Christ.'

'We've got a long way to go!' Mrs Lozzi exclaimed, shaking her sandal, which was covered in wet sand, 'to get to the present day…' she explained to her friend.

'It prospered during the Roman era…'

'Why don't you tell us a little about the monuments? Let us leave history to the side for now, it's always the same,' Mrs Lozzi said, bursting out in a laugh.

Lambertini laughed too, but he appeared distracted.

The Professor picked up his pace, as Rossi put it, whispering into a comrade's ear, and sped through the classical era as though driving a Fiat.

'Then the Vandals laid it to waste.'

'What was there to destroy?' Mrs Lozzi asked, looking at the bare landscape, where there was nothing beside the sky, sea and hills save for a few scattered hovels, some palm trees, and finally the lighthouse, which stood behind them atop a rocky promontory, like some solitary romantic character.

'Then, well, Justinian came and raised some new walls,' Lambertini concluded, as though talking to someone he'd met just the previous day and to whom he was now re-explaining himself.

'Ptolemais was marked on all the ancient maps, even Muhammad al-Idrisi's,'[xlix] the Professor announced, seizing Lambertini's attention.

[xlix] Muhammad al-Idrisi (1100–1165): Arab Muslim geographer from Ceuta.

'Are those the Justinian walls?' Mrs Lozzi asked.

'Don't confuse those, signora, those are ours, we had them built in the early days of the occupation, when the revolt had broken out, almost twenty years ago.'

'Using old stones, however!' Mrs Lozzi exclaimed, who was keen to chat with the Major.

They had arrived in front of a mausoleum, which was quadrangular, and hailed from the Hellenic era. It was situated just a few steps from the sea.

'The frieze is Doric,' the Professor said.

'What about the base?' Mrs Lozzi asked, who was increasingly fond of that long walk along the coast and through the annals of history: perhaps she had a third itinerary in mind.

'The base,' the Professor replied, 'is a square piece of calcareous stone.'

There were Greek tombs which had been hollowed out of the rock everywhere, with the names of the deceased still faintly visible. There were also numerous shards of unlaboured – yet nevertheless stylised – rock that rose naked out of the sand.

Having retraced their steps and walked towards the interior, they reached the city's ancient gate with its imposing square pillars; the gate stood between 'nothing and nothing,' as Mrs Lozzi put it, sounding ever more knowledgeable. They even visited the ruins of two Christian basilicas and the ancient Roman forum.

At which point, the entire group's cheer picked up – as if they'd suddenly reawakened and, having chased tiredness away, all the fatigue caused by the heat and all those thoughts, which were headed in god knows what direction – and they descended to a lower level. There was a vast cistern underneath the old Roman forum, which resembled an underground city, 'it features twenty-one vaulted galleries,' the Professor elaborated, 'which are five metres tall, thirteen of which,' he added, 'are eighteen metres long and are lined up from east to west; while the others are situated on their sides, four one one and four on another, all eight of which are lined up from north to south and are fifty-two metres long. Inside the vaults, spaced out at regular intervals, are cylindrical openings which were used to air out the galleries as well as draw water…'

'The light!' Lambertini yelled.

The group had scattered childishly around the galleries, some were running, others were hiding, others still were talking in whispers: their excitement was at its peak, and all those lights and shadows seem to lie at the very heart of the drama's plot.

Suddenly, all heard Lambertini's booming voice yell from one of the galleries' cavernous interiors:

'Keep reading, Professor!'

The latter recited the following from memory: '*When the time for the prayer arrives, I perform a copious ablution and go to the place where I wish to pray. There I sit until my limbs are rested, then I stand up, the Kaaba straight in front of me, the carpet under my feet, Paradise on my right, Hell on my left, and the Angel of Death behind me; and I think that this prayer is my last.*'[1]

---

1 As-Sirāt, the bridge all Muslims must cross to reach Paradise.

8

MAIDAN AL MILH[li]

'A man can only save himself through solitude and he only loses himself within that solitude.'

'Why is that?' a lawyer who was sat at the same table asked in an amused tone. They were at a café on Piazza del Re, which was once Piazza del Sale, a desolate square where a mountain of salt had reigned supreme prior to the Italian colonization, and where the delightful, shady Municipal Gardens now stood, whose beautiful oleanders were now in bloom.

'Because only within solitude can a man fix the co-ordinates of conversation, whereas he would otherwise find himself trapped by the presence of the other. This is why marriages usually end in disasters,' Fontanarosa said, taking his wife's hand in his and planting a kiss on it, 'loyalty doesn't offend us, but following someone else's co-ordinates, at which point – and I have no idea as to why this happens, perhaps the act of living together wears out both parties – these co-ordinates become only more restrictive over time and in fact they stiffen. There are times when I feel as though I might as well bid my willpower goodbye

---

li Arabic: Salt Square: a square in Benghazi named after the salt-sellers who used to congregate there.

given that Anita has reduced me to an automaton. Conversations wear us out, whereas dreams nourish us, being solitary in nature.'

'My husband is rambling…' Mrs Fontanarosa, who was entirely unimpressed with her husband's conversation, said. 'He's been talking his whole life and he still hasn't taken a single step in the right direction…'

'But you also said that a man can lose himself within that solitude…' the lawyer observed. He was due to attend a hearing at the courthouse the following day in a case involving a couple, and he was wondering whether that officer might furnish him with some insights, if only to heighten the illusion, like at a theatre.

'Of course,' Fontanarosa said, his face growing sombre, 'all because in the absence of someone else's authority, the smallest mistake can swell to outrageous proportions and completely overwhelm one.'

'My co-ordinates are good for something then!' his wife interjected, wholly dispassionately.

'Any mathematician will tell you that the tiniest error in one's initial calculations can give rise to horrendous discrepancies.'

'But I'll be right there to fish you out of that mess,' Mrs Fontanarosa proclaimed, placing her hand on her husband's. She was wearing a blue crotchet blouse, which was softly wrapped around her figure in a spiral.

The lawyer leaned his disappointed frame back: all conjugal drama resembled themselves, and yet none ever overlapped. Perhaps the Fontanarosas had cheated on one another, like the couple waiting for him at the *courthouse*, instead of sitting there with him at that *café* – in the evening, under a starry sky.

Had the betrayal been caused by the boredom that had turned all to rot? Had it been caused by dreams? His wife was a woman he could put up with. *I know how to deal with it*, he calmly confessed. He was a wiry man who spoke in an easygoing manner. Whenever he noticed the possibility of a betrayal – of having an adventure, so to speak – he never hesitated. Out of boredom? Was he chasing a dream too? Not even close: knowing that he was an irremediably secondary character on the stage of life – life being a harsh school – if any opportunity whatsoever presented itself, he never had the time to think it through: his *a priori* assumption was that he could not miss out in it. 'I'll have all the time to think about it,' he would tell one of his colleagues, in whom he confided, 'later on, if only out of remorse.'

He appeared to be a man who was ready to sign a pact with the devil: in fact, his adventures with a few loose women had given him the illusion of the devil's presence, which had already altered his typically colourless complexion. The judges he worked with apparently hadn't even noticed his psychological turmoil – let alone felt sorry for him.

He envied those officers their uniforms, as though they were magical capes.

He was talking passionately with someone whose features were uniquely blessed: he wasn't intent on subjugating her mind, but rather her body – or at least figure out her secret price. Thus, he wasn't sitting there waiting for the devil to offer him a choice of prey, but that the devil would make him worthy of receiving such a prize. No kind of possession is diabolical, only the vainly awaited metaphor he was expecting was diabolical; thus, each new adventure left him feeling disappointed: once it had vanished, he found himself staring into a mirror exactly like he had before he'd embarked on that adventure.

'It's as if *he* was the one who wanted to be someone's prey,' the friend in whom he confided bitingly remarked, confiding in his own turn to a group of colleagues assembled in the courthouse's lively corridor, as they hurried from one hearing to the next.

9

SHARKS

One fine day, the nuns of the Sisters of Charity of the Immaculate Conception chased all the men out of their noble institute on the Corso Italia. While in previous years they had tolerated their presence up to the fifth grade, it had dawned on them that fatal liaisons could occur even at that age, and thus they had decided to come to the rescue, as a wit put it, 'Maybe they happened to read some books that, while not being necessarily harsher than the Bible, knew enough about sin to demonstrate that its influence could corrupt ages previously deemed too innocent; only the devil exists, alongside his trusted servant, free will, which serves to keep one fully informed of sin.'

It was still summer, and thus the 'sudden attack had been carried out in the absence of all the schoolchildren: maybe they were afraid the children would rise up in revolt.'

A tireless chatterer, he had been walking with a friend to Piazza XXVIII Ottobre,[lii] on which the Governor's severe palace abutted, with its oval garden that sloped down towards a pool, at the centre of which was an ochre-coloured obelisk made of porous stone. Like horses racing around a track, the two friends

---

lii XXVIII: 28th October 1922, the date of Mussolini's march on Rome.

walked around the oval garden despite the sun having reached its most blinding heights. At the top of the obelisk lay a bronze sculpture of a silphium[liii] plant, just like on the face of ancient coins, a plant that has since been engulfed by the shadows of time: according to the ancient Greeks, it was that distant province's chief source of wealth.

The ostracisation decreed by the nuns proved difficult on Gioacchino. His father was Commendatore Clemente Vanzi, who was both stern and generous. No charitable organization had ever knocked on his door in vain – and it was a well-known fact that the Sisters tirelessly offered their help to the needy. This ensured that Gioacchino was treated with some special regard. Not that the grades on his report cards had risen thanks to that situation, in fact sometimes he was given grades that felt like a slap in the face. Nevertheless, he was constantly surrounded by a patient and warm environment, as though he was a part of the convent's big family. Gioacchino had been enrolled at the establishment run by the Brothers of the Christian Schools,[liv] which had just moved to its new premises, which were a gleaming white, and militaresque.

He found congenial classmates there, and he quickly appeared to have been bitten by the conversational bug, despite being usually considered taciturn at home. Whenever his mother went to inquire after his educational performance at school, she would be surprised when the teachers told her that sure, he wasn't doing

---

liii A kind of fennel once used as a seasoning as well as for its medicinal purposes. It was one of Cyrene's most prized exports and particularly sought-after in Rome.

liv Also known as the De La Salle Brothers: Catholic religious teaching congregation.

badly at all, but he was an incorrigible chatterbox who constantly distracted all the other boys.

'Are you sure you're talking about my son?'

It seemed as if those who considered themselves to be religious thought that talking was their exclusive prerogative. Scolded by his mother for his behaviour, the boy burst out: 'They're the chatterboxes!'

Nevertheless, the incident was subsequently avoided, given that Gioacchino didn't appear to be too ill at ease there and his teachers didn't seem to treat him too harshly. As for his mother, she didn't agonise over the issue, given that maybe they were all chatterboxes.

Occasionally she wondered why Gioacchino was so taciturn at home and yet so *irrepressible* at school, as the headmaster had put it, a religious man lacking any charisma and who was so boring that even she didn't like him. She didn't mention anything to her husband, who didn't tolerate any problems in the family milieu and disdained any and all psychological difficulties.

'In any case, it seems that his initiation rite – his passage from feminine society to male society – didn't go as planned: the boy doesn't seem to want to accept the *Brothers* as models to aspire to.' His mother was at the hairdresser's for her usual hair straightening session and was talking to a friend of hers. 'I'm being careful not to annoy him too much: he'll be in middle school next year, and maybe he'll meet someone there who can shine a light on a plausible path for him in life.'

'What about his father?'

'My husband? Who would dare to want to be anything like him? One would need Hercules' strength and King David's boldness to match his heights… My husband would probably laugh the whole thing off, he's such an inimitable character. The secret behind a great businessman is his faith in his own irreplaceability,' she added, making a gesture with her hand that demanded obedience, just as when a singer put their hand on their breast at the opera. 'Men are obsessed by role models: some don't find any, like my son; others are simply hypnotised by themselves, and view themselves as incomparable paragons of excellence, just like my husband. Whereas we women have a carefree approach to life: the only role models we seek are in the pages of fashion magazines where models display the clothes they are wearing, and not their *world views*!'

Mrs Vanzi made a horrified gesture, as if an incandescent fireball were heading straight towards her: she felt she was dreaming.

Dull as a dish rag, and unable to move without affectations, the hairdresser smiled triumphantly as he observed himself in the mirror, while he kept those beautiful ladies prisoner with his curling irons.

'In the evenings, we take a stroll along the Corso. My husband thinks it's foolish to stay at home to entertain the children. The servants are there to keep an eye on them and the rest doesn't matter, in fact he can't even see what that 'rest' might be. Picture me involving him in the troubles between Gioacchino and the Brothers, do you think he ever asks about how his son is doing at school? Forget about him taking the time to go see the boy's teachers himself, that's out of the question! *He should stay on top of his duties* – that's all he says. I have been avoiding the explosion of this drama between Gioacchino, his father and the Brothers by staying silent: they are only allowed to communicate, fight or act through me. And I keep my mouth shut. The boy hasn't been put back a year and he occasionally gets good grades, which seems to indicate the presence of some intelligence *somewhere* in that head of his. If he wants to talk at school instead of at home, then he's probably got reasons of his own for doing so. It would be a lot worse if he was bald, or a cripple, don't you think?'

She appeared to have been bitten by the same conversation bug that had affected Gioacchino, maybe she was mocking him or was instead piously justifying him through imitation.

'During that evening promenade, we cross paths with everyone who lives in the city, but my husband, he's not interested in anyone, at most he'll cast a quick, bewildered glance at some good-looking woman, looking as if his eyes were busy chatting, but his mind is almost always somewhere else. If he's present during the promenade, he wonders whether the crowd is impressed by his presence, like the last Emperors of Rome. I, on the other hand, wish to make no impression on anybody, but I still want to seduce everyone, that's my way of talking, I'm loyal to my husband but I'm as greedy for tributes as a tyrant, a sweet tyrant, I like to make a guest appearance in other's dreams – just for fun!'

The hairdresser looked at her ecstatically but silently, yet his hands playfully carried on of their own accord.

By the time they had reached the end of the school year, nothing had seemingly changed, Gioacchino was still a chatterbox, his teachers always unhappy, and the boy usually read in class instead of listening to them as they rattled off useless notions – occasionally, he would keep a book on his lap during the Brothers' lessons, books like *The Vicomte of Bragelonne: Ten Years Later*[lv], which the teacher himself had imprudently recommended – his parents went out on their evening walks, the lights on the Corso remained many and bright, as though the city was a perpetual party, and thus drama had been avoided…

Yet it nevertheless finally arrived.

Truth be told, there had been nothing unusual about that Saturday. At the end of the lesson, one of the teachers, who appeared to exhibit a particular dislike for Gioacchino, suddenly became affable with the others – and, in an astonishing turn – was even kind to Gioacchino. He read out some names: yes, they had to stay behind after class. Gioacchino wondered what could have possibly happened, he felt that the teacher, who was also the deputy headmaster, was showing the kind of goodwill he'd never seen before – on either side – as he naïvely observed. So what was going on?

Once the others had left, there were five children left behind. Why them?

At that moment, the drama erupted in all its might. The school needed a games-room, which they would all benefit from, especially them, since despite the fact they would be leaving for middle school in a couple of years, their extra-curricular activities would still take place at the Brothers' institute, meaning that the games-room would stay open for them, etc., etc. – it seemed as if the teacher himself had been bitten by the chatting bug that day.

[lv] A sequel to Alexandre Dumas's *The Three Musketeers.*

Yet the entire drama was encapsulated by a single sentence, in fact by a single word:

'I'm speaking to all of you because you're the sons of this city's sharks: talk the matter over with your parents, and let them finance the project,' leaving Gioacchino, whose father was presumed to be the biggest shark in town, to feel the sting of that affectionate slap.

It was as if money had burst into his happy, innocent life for the first time in his life. He had also understood that he was the main character in that great theatre of the world!

Gioacchino remained silent, in fact from that day on he never talked in class again.

'Oh yes,' Gioacchino's mother said to her friend, while sitting under the hairdryer, who had now set up shop at the Officers' Club, the temple of the god of Strength, who was caught in a timeless struggle with Pluto, the god of Money, whose temple lay elsewhere, and perhaps even with the Church, whose vast cathedral rose out of the shore – they could see its cupolas which from that distance appeared to be floating upon the water, 'I finally heard his confession.'

She preferred to spend her time at the Officers' Club rather than the Merchants' Club. She looked upon military life as belonging to the world of infancy, where games are played according to strict rules that were both senseless and unchangeable, and it seemed like a happy extension of the uncontaminated bliss of childhood. Bourgeois life, however, lay in the realm of mediation and compromises, if not, everything is confused with its opposite, which swallows it up. 'I would have liked to marry the commander we met in the square,' she had confessed a week earlier, out of the blue.

'A marionette!'

The President of the Chamber of Commerce, who was a friend of her husband's, and who had been present at that confession, was parodying a soldier's pride without getting up from his rocking chair.

'An *actor*,' Gioacchino's mother corrected him, 'besides, children always dream of military uniforms, I never heard a boy say that he wanted to be a lawyer when he grew up. Soldierhood sublimates childhood and transports it to a world of heroism, idleness, elegance and incredibly dangerous games.'

However, this conversation took place before the most recent dramatic turn of events.

The two friends were sat on the shaded veranda. They had bowls of ice cream in front of them, whose colours were simply dazzling. Her friend smoked, with provocative delight.

'That word – shark – really upset him. Not because it was so indelicate – what can you expect a boy to know about that? It's because he has finally understood the power of money: the war between him and the Brothers – who were so different from the nuns – had come to an end and the enemy had given up: he had been entranced by the sight of all that gold. Anyway, as I was saying, the boy's rite of passage from the world of women to that of men, which failed to occur when he switched schools, thanks to the nuns' fears that the boys would soon be subject to woeful passions, has now become a reality: having learned the value of gold, the boy has finally entered the world of men. Now we'll see.'

10

THE DICTIONARY SAYS

'Faithfulness? It's something that's incredibly noble, strange and incomprehensible, even a little ridiculous too: despite what we generally assume, it lies outside our willpower's control – just like mysticism, you understand? Let's open the dictionary.'

The man pulled out a little dictionary from his greatcoat's pocket, which was partly unbound, its type was minuscule and nearly illegible; the dictionary never left his side. He used to say that the dictionary was an esoteric book, where all of creation was featured in the shape of words, meaning all that bears testament to the supreme mystification and supreme knowledge. His large fingers had something bestial to them as they ran alongside those minuscule words, which had almost been worn away by time.

'Here is the definition: *mysticism, noun, from the original Greek myeomai, "to be initiated", belief that union with or absorption into the Deity or the absolute* (I'm already confused here, where do you draw the line between them?) *or the spiritual apprehension of knowledge inaccessible to the intellect* (the parallel here is perfect: faithfulness is personal, in fact collective) *may be attained through contemplation and self-surrender.* (I've gotten confused again here, how can you attain something that lies beyond our world? Isn't it hypocritical not to assume that one would never exaggerate things at that point?)'

His face had a certain universality to it.

'Dear me! Dear me! Putting one's reason to use means bouncing from one mirror to the next and always winding up at the starting point, stuck…

'*A means to achieve direct experience of the divine* (I never thought it would be indirect, maybe this means without any intermediaries or rules – which I like) *and with the supernatural* (here I feel right at home: what's more natural than the supernatural, forgive the pun, what a breath of fresh air it blows into life, which is otherwise so cruel and stupid) *through irrational means* (I should think so!) *related to spiritual contact and one's own feelings* (but feelings are a subspecies of the soul).'

The sophism of his words contrasted against his fresh, healthy appearance, which concealed a repressed and chilling aggressiveness.

'Let's keep reading – we're still on *mysticism* here – *any philosophical doctrine which aims to achieve first-hand awareness of the divine, or various divinities*: well, of course I would hardly a philosophical doctrine to not be first-hand and instead meander around like poetry!

'But let's return to the subject of faithfulness, and let's put those other comparisons to the side, since they're so misleading.'

It was as though he had wanted to carefully dissuade anyone who might have been eavesdropping on them, lurking in the shadows. Yet it was a fake: within that shadow, which was a mirror, lay only yet another part of him.

'My stance before the idol of faithfulness is uncertain, as it is a most demanding idol. I am intellectually drawn to the idea because it is a definitive action: let's say that I'm in love with a woman, and all other *variations* don't interest me at all; it nevertheless feels like a kind of castration, contrary to nature and what is natural – faithfulness breaks the rules of metamorphosis, which is terrible.'

He would occasionally rise from his seat to respectfully greet a lady who was passing by, or make a slight gesture with his hand if he saw a fellow officer – as though he thought he had to explain himself to as many people as possible.

'Have I been loyal to my wife? Never. Not because I don't love her, god forbid! Even less because I'm more loyally in love with another woman, it would be ridiculous to break my faithfulness towards one woman only to give it to another and find myself again at the same *impasse*. Let's just say that these are events shaped by uncontrollable forces. Let me give you an example: you love sunny skies, don't you? But sometimes it rains, in fact a storm breaks out, as furious as a torrid love affair (one can always turn comparisons on their heads). Well, can you do anything about that? At most you can open an umbrella and shelter yourself from the rain. Whereas in our case: *we lie* – we keep the affair concealed from our wives not because we're afraid of them, but because it would be senseless – in fact, contemptible – to cause them any suffering. When it comes to sentimental relationships, lying is nothing but *finesse*.

'Or an umbrella, if you like – which doesn't really strike me as one of mankind's greatest discoveries. So, as we were saying – one always runs the risk of losing one's thread – faithfulness eludes our control just like the sky (I'm not making any allusions to our previous conversation about mysticism here; if you don't like the sky we can just as easily use the sea, which like the human heart, is also capable of being rocked by frightening storms).

'Can one redeem one's unfaithfulness through emotions? Not at all! Feelings nevertheless marvelously *embellish* our unfaithfulness. Let us make a learned comparison: unfaithfulness is the synopsis red on the palette of feelings (or masked feelings, since it's always carnival in one's heart and you never know the identity of the characters who reside in it).

'People want to separate the heart away from nature and enslave it to reason. Nature is metamorphosis, and unfaithfulness is an imitation of that metamorphosis. Shutting it up within faithfulness? Anything that is brought to a stop, nature allows to perish.

'Faithfulness means trying to stop time – which is also against nature: time takes its revenge by letting everything dry out (time and nature are in a perfect symbiosis). I have seen couples who are loyal to one another and resemble funereal status. Does unfaithfulness keep us fresh and young? I have no idea, but it gives us the illusion that it does, which is blissful. I don't understand the pleasures autumn brings? But nothing makes me think of autumn more than unfaithfulness: everything acquires the most unusual and varied colours – and all is already wrapped in the embrace of death, the hard winter.'

They were sat at the Zizzo pastry shop on Piazza Cagni.

'Would you ever dare to have this kind of conversation with your wife?' Gallini the surveyor asked him, being his interlocutor.

'There's no need,' the officer said irritatedly, putting the dictionary back into his pocket, 'to talk about anything with my wife. I'm not a dictionary and I therefore don't need to furnish any explanations for words, or in my case, to constantly provide explanations for my entire range of actions: life keeps going and runs over everything in its path. Besides, things never get better for dictionaries: languages evolve and change, as you know.'

The pastries – among which were sugary, almost lascivious Sicilian sweets – were excellent, if not the freshest. The officer was a glutton. He inhaled each bite so as to be able to speak.

'Everything that is alive also changes: and you would want a heart to stay loyal? Loyal to whom?'

He gulped down his soda – which looked like fog in the stuffy African climate.

'Our sovereign divinity, Time, is responsible for all unfaithfulness, since it forces everything to undergo a metamorphosis – and by so doing laughs in the face of Faithfulness, who is my accomplice and a model I aspire to.

'When dealing with occult forces, I employ the same kind of caution that my comrades reserve for everyday life and social events,' he added in a hushed tone, getting up.

He left, picking up his pace as though he was late for something.

'That bastard!' a roly-poly woman who was sat at the next table exclaimed. She hadn't touched a single pastry.

The surveyor also stood up in a hurry, and as if afraid of the woman at the next table, he sped into a nearby alley, even though he had no idea where it abutted.

As though it was Carnival time, the surveyor asked himself whoever could have been hiding behind that mask of fat – *which wasn't funny at all*, he observed with a shudder. He felt like Sganarello, when the Commendatore says yes to the grave and accepts Don Juan's challenge to a duel.

11

PURIFICATION

They were childhood friends. Each knew the other's story, but instead of simplifying things between them, it complicated them. Whenever they talked, they seemed unable to hold back, because both would respond to the various characters that the other had assumed over the years. 'It's a real headache,' Captain Cafiero facetiously remarked, being a man who concealed his true thoughts with humour, which occasionally produced a discordant effect.

Nevertheless, Pacella – a bank employee, as well as a poet who wrote in dialect – had already laid claim to the real discordance in that situation. Thanks to his lively exchange of ideas with his friend, he had been able to confess his abnormality to him: he was an anti-fascist. Captain Cafiero wasn't afraid to be seen in his company: Pacella, who hailed from a distinguished Milanese family, knew how to move about circumspectly, despite his free-spirited nature, being both prudent and slippery. In fact, given that he suspected the clique currently in power – the Fascists – of suspecting him, he had become the most careful of all when it came to trying to avoid getting caught in a trap, and he concealed his anti-fascism as though he belonged to some secret revolutionary cell – not that Captain Cafiero thought there wasn't much to that *cause.*

Nevertheless, it existed on paper.

He wrote poetry in the crepuscular mould, which his dialect brought colourful vivacity to, and so long as his political tirades didn't spoil everything, his verses scanned as banal but nonetheless fresh. Captain Cafiero had them read out to him, having had some difficulty reproducing the exact sounds despite the poet's excellent orthography. Born in Milan, his dialect was like the Navigli, absent from everyday life.[lvi] The poems were all unpublished since Pacella would never have consented to seeing them in official Fascist publications. On a few occasions, Captain Cafiero had suggested that he send off a few fragments – the ones where his political sympathies were completely absent – for publication, and each time Pacella had proudly replied that he would in fact go ahead and publish the most political of his poems.

And the conversation would end there.

However, the *movement* whose existence Captain Cafiero had doubted, burst upon the scene and in the most theatrical of manners. Pacella had founded a revolutionary cell, and was preparing some anarchist coup de main – perhaps the assassination of the colony's Governor, given that the Duce was on the other side of the sea? Was he therefore aiming to strike the Governor's Palace since Palazzo Venezia[lvii] wasn't *close to hand*? It

---

lvi The Navigli are a system of interconnected canals in Milan, Italy. They fell out of use in the late 19th century and are currently being revitalised.

lvii Palazzo Venezia: Palace in Rome where Benito Mussolini kept his offices.

was none of the above. An idealist, and as a direct consequence badly informed, Pacella had widened his topographical knowledge of the city, and having become a habitual frequenter of the cafés along the Corso, the Giuliana beach, and the only decent bookshop, which was also on the Corso, he had finally discovered that there was a Via Marina a little further along, past the old Turkish city, along the littoral. A lady belonging to the supercilious local bourgeoisie would never be caught dead walking along that ill-reputed street: it was where the city's two brothels were situated.

Whoever had led Pacella to that street, history does not say. Maybe he had stumbled onto it by chance, and at night, under those strange lights, he had a revelation. Stepping inside that brothel's entrance had unleashed a powerful feeling in him, as though he'd just infiltrated the crypt of power armed with explosives.

Naturally, a man always keeps explosives in his reserves. He had struck up with a woman on the first floor, who had big black eyes and was both a skeptic as well as a sentimentalist. Business was transacted.

From that day on, Captain Cafiero could barely recognise Pacella. Not that he was jealous of the prostitute for having stolen his friend away from him, nor did he envy her having supplanted his long-standing place as his confidant, yet because he could not understand on what scene Pacella was operating. He had lost all his earlier reserve, and the verses flowed out of him in a flood; they looked like the footprints left behind by a race, and they were all bad now, erratic and superficial.

Nevertheless, Pacella had finally discovered *the cause*.

In his solidarity with the fallen woman, which was a complete negation of Fascism's values of social respectability, he had found the ultimate expression of his anti-fascism, if only temporarily. Hand in hand, the poet banker and the prostitute with the big black eyes walked into the depths of the night, where the sun of the future lay hidden in wait.

Captain Cafiero listened to him, without either approving or disagreeing with him. Quite the contrary, the scene intrigued him. He couldn't understand how Pacella could have confused the nervous, trembling way one steps inside the brothel with finding himself in a public square, shooting, killing and turning the world upside down the way revolutionaries do. Pacella was taking it too far, he claimed that the Duce had subjugated the spirits of all Italians: in any case, who knew if everyone indeed had a soul, and the dictatorship was functioning efficiently without turning bloodthirsty. It was nevertheless strange that he found the symbol of Fascism's offenses in that prostitute, and her redemption would eventually trigger to Italy's own, which he had long yearned for. In the meanwhile, he negotiated that body, and paid for it: briefly put, in bed he was the Duce.

Maybe even worse than the other – who at least took some interest in the soul, if only to ensure its subjugation. Who knew if the prostitute truly loved Pacella, or laughed behind his back, or exploited him for her own ends, or if she had even noticed anything at all given that he was a customer like all the rest, and the fact that he was talkative wasn't unusual in those kinds of places?

How would it all turn out in the end? Captain Cafiero listened to his friend's *foucades*[lviii] with growing embarrassment. While

[lviii] French: 'caprices' or 'whims'.

his offended dignity as a citizen had earlier endowed him with a great deal of humanity – now his triumph as a man, which he'd been forced to pay for, made him seem increasingly mediocre, just like his poetry, filled with stifling verbiage and tired forms.

Their friendship slowly came undone.

12

OBLIVION

'One only removes a mask in order to replace it with another,' Captain Lambertini cockily said, as though he was replying to someone, either challenging him or accepting a challenge.

The assembled guests looked at one another with embarrassment, a sudden chill held them all back, as if everyone present wanted to shirk the suspicion that the phrase had been directed at them.

Lambertini looked as though he hadn't noticed anything and he carried on picking his chicken clean with great rigour.

His wife followed him with her eyes: she had spent eons trying to discover her husband's real expression, which was always ready to flee from sight into an endless escape.

A handful of harsh jokes had been swapped the previous night.

'You're always running away...' he had said, as though he'd meant to say: *you're a liar*, *you're guilty*.

'Am I running away from the past or the future?' Lambertini had mockingly replied.

He looked like a tempter who was operating on two different scenes: had the time come to shed light on the past, or was it about stipulating a contract for the future? The squabble ended there, in lieu of understanding the story of his life, as the opening sentence had led one to believe. They were in their bedroom, when time seemed to stretch into infinity until it was ready to dissolve. That night, Andreina's dreams were rather strange, but they had nothing to do with that squabble. Something bothered her that morning, in fact she was suspicious: that her husband was manipulating them to ensure that nobody would be able to follow his tracks. It was all a joke, he was making fun of her. That large, solidly-built man, who was devoid of any elegance and more than happy not to have any (either due to mysterious theatrical necessities or out of sheer arrogance), believed himself one of the world's finest gentlemen (or so his maliciously-tongued friends said of him), but that he had a *secret*, and that he wasn't afraid of anyone, not even his wife.

'My secret?' Lambertini icily asked when the rumours reached him. 'But it's simply about always keeping a mask on, and taking care of them, changing them as and when needed, just like actors can take on roles that have nothing to do with them, but which only they can play convincingly. It would be misleading to think that I want to hide something. Masks prevent direct communication because it's simply impossible. You should read Immanuel Kant: every kind of communication is… subject to conditions, or at least that's the impression I got when I studied this in secondary school, who knows… I'm about as interested in him as he is in me. Other people go ahead and mislead others, I won't be one of them: by showing their open faces they… it's all useless. The deception lies in the way the weak pretend to be sincere and direct. One can either bring the theatre into their life, or else live and sleep in prison.'

'This is my husband's poetics, do you see?' Andreina, who was present but bored, said. 'He *writes* his own orations, right here on the spot.'

The day went calmly by, despite the fact it was a Sunday and that they therefore had to spend the whole day together. Now they were sat having dinner with their friends in the breezy African night. The *chalet* had been painted blue. Ahead of them lay the boundless sea, and the lights only stretched as far as the water's sandy edge. The conversation didn't manage to stray beyond conventional subjects, but it flowed so quickly and effortlessly that the phrases being spoken coalesced into a kind of collective dance, where phrases replaced moves and steps, and everything expressed both joy and harmony. Nobody seemed to want for anything more, or look at anything – a secret music kept everything in concert. Why had Lambertini therefore introduced the misleading detail of the masks? It seemed as though the others – and not him – had tripped on some invisible thing and were now keeping quiet.

At that moment, the army doctor arrived, a certain Marinelli, accompanied by his wife, who was a foreigner. He was a very thin man, yet one whose thinness had nothing dry or stiff to it: he looked like a shadow, a strangely elegant one. He hadn't been in the colony for long. Discreet and reserved, he had made no effort to create a circle of acquaintances. It was as if he still lived elsewhere, and that only his shadow had arrived in Africa, having been somehow secretly projected down there by a secret light. Lambertini had been the one to suggest that image, which hadn't been admired, although it was ironic and suited to his mocking brilliance. He was nevertheless the only one to exhibit any interest in that newcomer and that female double of his who followed him everywhere. It was as if her different mother tongue was a disqualification which disbarred her from talking. Actually she did speak, but only in little bursts, and in a low voice, as if she wanted to speak and let the trail of her words dissolve in her interlocutors' minds.

Andreina found the friendship between the two Captains utterly ridiculous.

'You appear to be stuck in the formulaic phrases strangers use after being introduced to one another: all you do is swap stock phrases.'

'You're mistaken,' Lambertini replied, 'our ideas couldn't be any more different when it comes to Chopin's powers of interpretation.'

Marinelli, who played the piano with his bony, almost transparent hands, was in favour of a Polish interpretation – or so his friend would put it, with a flourishing gesture of his hand – as if to say both passionate and romantic, while Lambertini, who was incurably tone-deaf and whose large brutish hand could barely play a few notes on the piano, was instead in favour of an orthodox interpretation that was both perfectionist and white, a view that seemed on the ascendancy in Europe's distant concert halls. They had shown themselves capable of fighting over the issue, duelling over it 'according to how the winds were blowing,' as Lambertini said, 'or the whim of the moment.'

Yet Marinelli was the only one to play the baby grand piano in the ballroom of the Officers' Club – a bizarrely shaped, single-floor building – since Lambertini would have never dared to place his ugly paws on the piano in the former's presence.

The duel symbolically unfolded over the course of infinite diatribes, and its outcome always remained a mystery to others.

Even though, as Andreina put it, all they did was exchange hackneyed phrases.

It was said that even Marinelli had complained of this in his allusive, evasive way.

Now that the medical officer's arrival had revealed the identity of the person whom the joke had been addressed to, if Lambertini had said that he only removed one mask in order to replace it with another, it was to let his friend know that he had chosen banality as a mask, but that it would be unwise to stop there. Whether it was a warning or an excuse, he had finally opened up.

Andreina noticed that the medical officer's arrival had suddenly warmed the room: once the letter's secret addressee, the phrase which appeared to necessitate the assistance of a mask, every other person seated at that table overcame their awkwardness and resumed their conversations. Some of them had even started to laugh, as though they'd just looked over their shoulders and were surprised by the silence into which they had fallen, as though it had been some sort of trap.

The newly arrived couple sat at the table, far from the Lambertinis, whom they greeted with a wave of the hand.

The tear in their relationship appeared to have been repaired, nothing had happened.

Only Lambertini was looking at the starry sky, and he was asking himself, just like Andreina had done, why he should nurse such an intense curiosity for the army physician who'd only just arrived in the colony, but who had already earned himself some public esteem for the probity with which he exercised his profession, but whom nobody seemed to care about, that is apart from him.

Now that he had asked himself that question, he no longer wore the ironic smile with which he'd greeted Andreina's own question. In fact that smile had been replaced by a painful expression. Andreina was looking at him. She knew that her husband – who was always vague, theatrical, blustering and standoffish with others – was only serious whenever he answered his own questions. What kind of question was he trying to answer?

She stretched her arm out towards her husband's plate, which was right in front of him, and she stole a carrot which Lambertini had left to the side – he was very fond of carrots and had been saving that special morsel for last. Lambertini immediately came back to his senses, as if someone else had travelled into the realm of shadows.

Andreina hurled the carrot into the sea, which lay behind her, and her gesture unfolded so rapidly that it seemed mechanical. Everybody laughed, even though they didn't know why.

However, Andreina noticed that the army physician was looking at her with jealousy in his eyes. He was a very courteous man: it seemed as though all his words and gestures had already been written down on a piece of paper and he were merely playing his part by reading them out loud.

Was he jealous due to some rude or silly gesture?

Andreina and the army physician lingered observing one another, each lost in their own dream. Which were both about the same man: Lambertini – whom had already made some witty remark about the carrot to a lady who was sat beside him.

The latter put one of her own carrots on his plate. She had a soft spot for that strapping, authoritarian man who was devoid of all grace and elegance. It was as though she'd slipped into his bed.

They laughed, as though embracing.

Time flowed either quickly or lazily, yet its artificial subdivisions, as organised by clocks and calendars, was nothing – to parrot the Captain's words – was nothing but a mask. Thus it manages to fool the simple, or manages to console those scared of change, 'or acts in concert with its accomplices, meaning those who understand that the game is determined by other rules,' Lambertini explained, 'maybe time deceives itself in exactly the way it deceives all men, and so, exhausted and worn out, it searches for peace within rules.'

In the mouth of such a self-assured, haughty man, the word *peace* sounded like a wink.

Nevertheless – and without ignoring his question, as to why that man seemed so reserved and insignificant to others outside of his professional capacity actually felt like *somebody* to him – time was doing nothing to come to their aid. It felt like time was in no hurry to unroll the papyrus where their story – or rather that 'of the two-faced Captain,' as Lambertini put it – had been written.

There was a reproduction of one of Bellucci's canvases hanging in front of his bed, which depicted a very ancient man, who was in fact Time himself, as he discovers a Sibyl, a curvy, bare-breasted woman. Well, the epiphany still hadn't materialised, *as is often the case*, the Captain commended, both amused and disappointed.

It arrived nonetheless, when they least expected it.

One day, they were sat at the Café Italia on the Corso (gentle music meandered through the trees of the garden where one could see a four-piece orchestra on the stage, and all the seats at the tables filled, all covered by the patina of elegance 'and the absurd,' as Lambertini said, of colonial society, which lagged behind all the advances made on the European mainland, which was in fact a remnant of the extreme indulgences favoured in the eighteenth century, when conversation flowed effortlessly along without going off the deep end) and Marinelli suddenly made a vague allusion to one of his stays at a sanatorium just a year earlier.

Lambertini jumped up with a start, horrified.

Naturally, he was horrified with himself. He had made an atrocious gaffe the previous evening, when he'd discovered that that skinny man, who was almost the shadow of a man, but who was as tall as he was and around the same age, weighed sixty kilograms, while he – who had 'bones made out of solid steel,' as though mocking Fascism's vocabulary – weighed an extra thirty kilograms. 'How is that even possible?' he had incredulously exclaimed, being full of envy, before bursting in a laugh. It was as though he had discovered that he was a monster, or that the other was a ghost.

Simply put, he had made fun of his friend's illness.

Yet at the same time, the truth – or better yet, the Sibyl – had been discovered. If he had any curiosity for that man, it was directed towards one of his secret traits, his illness, which the others had been unable to see. Illness as a *metaphor*: of what exactly? He asked himself while sitting back down, not embarrassed at all by the shock stamped on the faces of his friends who were sat at the same table. He started talking again, as if he hadn't heard anything in the first place and as if time always held his cards in its hands.

However, those thirty kilograms between them, despite seeming like an unbridgeable distance (that man was sick, *voilà tout*), were actually bringing them dangerously close together: because only he was the only man in Africa, he commented sarcastically, who had immediately detected that bottomless pit and had remained somewhat subjugated by it. Yet those sensual, nocturnal notes of Chopin's, to borrow a trite cliché, had pointed to a path: there was nothing left to do but listen. 'And I listened!' he loudly exclaimed.

'Who did you listen to?' Andreina asked.

Lambertini pointed his index finger to the garden where the orchestra's music meandered.

Lies are in keeping with his character, Andreina thought. And she finally turned her attention to the elegant chatter of a young Lieutenant who was trying to ensnare her: women were rare in colonial society, and every single one of them had a litany of tireless admirers, who were often young and interchangeable, as the uniform indicated.

At that exact moment, the pianist, a red-headed woman, whose décolletage was as ample as the Sybil's, and who was wearing a lilac dress, and had shiny arms, launched into a solo and attacked the brilliant *arrangement* of one of Chopin's melodies. It wasn't until much later that it was learned that the army physician had put in a request for that specific melody, given that the pianist was one of his patients.

On one occasion, Lambertini made a reference to the man's intuition – yes, there was something special about that man – in the presence of Major Carloni, who was ill-disposed towards the doctor.

'Why should illness indicate anything special?' the Major asked, irritatedly, 'please explain.'

'But nature only becomes interesting where it makes a mistake, since rules are commonplace and don't therefore fuel any curiosity, just like mass-produced goods in a marketplace,' Lambertini replied. 'Where nature makes a mistake, however, it's as if the divine has pierced through the cracks – or maybe the infernal, who knows, but the hand that governs it is alien, *it comes from an otherworldly place*. Pain is sacred; even religion teaches us that.'

'My husband is getting pain and evil a little mixed up,' Andreina confided in a low voice to a friend who was sat next to her. 'He's either trying to justify his wickedness or his ignorance, I really can't tell.'

'Does he cheat on you?' the other whispered.

'It's difficult to know when a man is cheating on you if he always wears a mask on his face, as if he confused life with a carnival. One would have to know whether the betrayal occurred in the first or in the second instance. This confusion is the source of his wickedness. Doubt is the *péché abominable*[lix] of any intimate relationship. I'll say my piece on the Day of Judgement – but not now,' she added with a smile.

'Is it the source of his *péché abominable* or his inexhaustible grace?' her friend asked, laying her arm down on the divan: she looked like she was waiting up in bed, alone.

[lix] French: 'abominable sin'.

'You chase away those you hate, but you kill those you love,' the handsome officer said to the lady next to him the following morning, the same woman whom Andreina had confided in the previous night, while the army band marched along the Corso.

The woman wasn't even listening to the officer, instead she was looking into his eyes, which were clear and *introuvables*,[lx] as she put it – or perhaps she'd meant that they were peerless, or that like Andreina she was now accusing them of lying, being the accomplices of a soul that wore its secrets like a uniform. She stared intently into those eyes, as if aiming to shoot. Lambertini noticed this and smiled, as though bestowing his blessing. To be killed or to be loved? That's up to you, he thought to himself, distracted by all that sound which seemed to be erupting out of everywhere, like when a theatre is drowned by the sonorous deluge rising from the orchestra pit.

The military parade had bewitched him, like a kind of travelling theatre, it excited him, as if he was a simple conscript marching for the first time alongside two thousand comrades-in-arms, all wearing the same uniform, which was either a magical cape or a funerary shroud. He said that that musical discourse, which was so aggressive and well-known, so brilliant and so seductive, and which spoke of virile solidarity, mimicked both movement and time, just like when one is attending a ball or drinking in a dive, sipping champagne or guzzling cheap wine, people at a parade equally find themselves swept along by sounds, all at the same time, as if everyone were holding hands. 'Military parades inspire a multitude of paths, not all of them are smooth, of course, but it's the magic city. Do you know what the

lx French: 'unobtainable'.

savages say? *Death is a beautiful woman, who lacks for nothing except a heart!*'

The woman next to him was happy that the warm word – *heart* – had been finally dropped into the conversation, if only in a serious context. Even she was now excited by the parade. She would have liked that strapping man to step onto the street with the band, so she could look at him as a prince – *my lord and master* – who was headed her way.

The music had made her forget all about her friend, Mrs Lambertini, who was standing next to her, wearing a large black straw hat which brought her tiny face into sharp relief. The latter elbowed her slightly. Was she jealous?

Can one really be jealous of an image? Because that's all there really was lying between her and her husband: the image of that Captain which dwelled in his mind. They fornicated via music, and didn't do so in a bed. The lady's excitement grew.

'Are you personally acquainted with any savages?' she asked the Captain in a malicious tone.

'Are you kidding? The anecdote is quoted by Chateaubriand.'[lxi]

'I never know where I am with you: I thought we were deep in the savannah, but now I see we're just in a Restoration salon.'

The music was hot on their heels.

That evening, at the Officers' Club, the army doctor played Chopin in a 'pseudo-military manner,' as Lambertini had mockingly put it.

The doctor's foreign wife was standing next to the piano, *like Cassandra speechlessly stalking the scene in Agamemnon,*

[lxi] François-René de Chateaubriand, (1768–1848): a French writer, politician, diplomat and historian.

Lambertini thought, but this time his ironic tone was absent: he was looking at that mute woman and feeling the weight of Agamemnon's furious destiny on his shoulders: *will I too be killed in a bath?* he asked himself, suddenly regaining his strength.

'*First of all, it is right to salute Argos and the gods of the country, joint authors of my return, and the redress which I exacted from the city of Priam; for the gods hearing suits…*'[lxii] Lambertini declaimed.

However, nobody paid him any heed, because the declaration had taken place in his mind.

Only the army doctor seemed to keep up with him, or rather foreshadow his every move on the piano, just as two embraced figures chase one another endlessly in a dance.

The mute wife diligently turned the pages, like a clock keeping time.

The Club was very animated, people were chatting, laughing, people were observing and admiring, there were those who looked for someone, and those who avoided encountering others.

From the window one could admire the tall, slender palms, which looked like additional characters wandering through the transparent night, occupying a third plane beyond that of the colonial society and the music's shrill, desperate notes.

Standing amidst a group of friends, the woman who'd received Lambertini's confidences in regards to the savages and Chateaubriand was praising the Captain's erudition. 'He can quote Chateaubriand by heart,' she affirmed, ecstatically.

The story reached Andreina's ears, who went over to her, intensely annoyed.

[lxii] Anonymous. *The Agamemnon of Aeschylus* (Oxford: James Thornton, 1880), p.24.

'You should know that Professor Rovetta was the one who quoted that line during one of the lunches in the beach *chalets*. My husband never wastes his time reading books, he's basically relapsed into illiteracy.'

Someone – there were no secrets in that small colonial society, which was just like a royal court, where words travelled and performed actions like characters – referred his wife's comment to Lambertini, who bowed obsequiously, as though standing before a judge:

'I'm busy reading the book of my life, the book of my destiny: as such, I lack the time for any other books. If anything, just like an author, one can read me and learn my lines by heart. But my wife only knows how to read writing: she lacks all intuition. In such a situation, blindness fatally appears out of nowhere. Illiteracy, as if!'

The last sentence sounded like a hiss.

An old lady crossed herself. 'I can smell sulphur…' she confided to a woman next to her, who didn't understand what they were supposedly talking about. 'That man's already got one foot in hell…'

'What about the other foot?' the young lady asked her, frightened.

The two captains separated by thirty kilograms of weight – meaning, in other words, a radically different destiny – seldom saw one another now – one of them had only recently been discharged from the sanatorium – and nobody seemed to know why he had consented to be dispatched to the furnace of Africa – while the other recounted the exhilarating anecdote of having been visited by an illustrious physician, a stern man of few words, it had been a painstaking and long-winded visit…

'And by the time he was finished, I was lying naked on the examination table, he drew aside and turned his back on me, looking as though he was trying to find the right words, by which point I already felt like a goner, when finally, and very sternly – as though he wanted to banish an infernal image from his eyes, or was pleased by the work of nature – he gravely uttered the following words: *You are a perfect exemplar of a man... Well, thanks, Professor,* I exclaimed, with bestial hilarity, jumping to my feet: this is definitely a piece of good news! I was so happy that I could have run naked up and down all the streets.'

Lambertini's arms were animated, he was sitting down to a meal with friends under an arbor: he looked like a wandering merchant trying to attract his potential customers' attentions.

Andreina's gaze was elsewhere.

The two couples had decided to go to the river Lethe, a few miles away from the city, where at the bottom of a horrendously steep ravine laid a majestically large subterranean cavern where a pool formed the beginnings of a subterranean river. From where the water came, nobody knew. The colonial government was responsible for re-baptizing that river with that August name from antiquity, having diligently set itself to the task of extending a veil of familiarity over that obliterated, monotonous land which belonged to others. The name was like a tomb that testified to their control in a bygone era, thus legitimizing their return. No investiture is more sacred than a myth.

Starting from the first grotto, which was ample as a theatre hall, one could progress to the second, and from thence to a third. In order to pass from one to the other, one had to lie flat at the bottom of the boat, since the wet rock was almost level with the water.

Attentive to ensure the gaiety of its colonists and officers, the government had built a lodge right at the top of the ravine, a place where one could take pleasure in innocent delights before slipping down the river of oblivion.

It was crowded on a Sunday. There were those who went there in a carriage, while others drove there, as if the present had one foot in one era and one in another.

The ravine was silent and rocky, the few scattered clumps of brushwood seemed to depict the damned – those to whom oblivion had not been granted, and who now desperately called out for it, perhaps had been doing so for centuries, that place had been included in the old Greek Pentapolis. In fact, it was said that the vegetable gardens not far away – situated in sudden depressions of the ground, were the famous gardens of Hesperides, which exist outside of the verses of famous poets, unlike what some incredulous people believe.

Having reached the bottom, one entered a black cave. A little farther lay an immense grotto, where the water stretched like an immobile mirror. There was a minuscule jetty, which looked almost unreal in its context, to which a boat had been moored. Strange whitish crustaceans, spectral-looking, and not much bigger than a finger, walked along the bottom. From that jetty, one could progress to the other grottoes, which the colonial government had illuminated in various different colours.

The day-trippers were squashed into a Fiat that was green and black. The men were seated up front, while the ladies were in the back, the dust on the road, the immaculate sky of the plain above them.

The women, who didn't like one another much, put their faith in punctual courtesies. *It's as if we both thought the other was laying eyes on our husbands*, Andreina thought benevolently, *go figure that the war should break out elsewhere…*

As for the men, they actually liked one another a great deal. For this precise reason, instead of courtesy, there was a cold distance between them, punctuated by embarrassed silences. Only music seemed to bring them closer together, but music is *dumb*, or rather it can't carry on a conversation. 'My husband is trying to wrap up all his loose ends in a hurry by saying he doesn't like simplifications, that masks are a substitute for music,' Andreina explained.

Once they had reached the lodge – a white dot lost in the boundless barren expanse of the moors – they left the car with a sigh of relief. The drive had excited both couples (even the doctor's foreign wife was smiling now), and they stepped inside the lodge's entrance making as much commotion as though they'd burst in dancing.

At that moment, however, the army doctor said:

'I can't for the life of me understand why you always choose to talk to me with such banal phrases…'

'That's right, because I, unlike you, do not know how to play the piano!' Lambertini exclaimed, aggressively. 'It's far too easy, my dear doctor, far too easy to just lay one's hands on the keyboard and communicate. In fact it's vile – did I say that right, dear?' he added, turning to his wife, having recalled her observation.

'But my husband is utterly banal,' the latter exclaimed, 'only his shell has some theatrical relief to it. Don't smile and look so pleased with yourself,' she added, disdainfully, 'if I were the director, I'd give you a role…'

But she interrupted herself.

'There are those who simply radiate grace and those who seek it,' the Captain retorted, 'whoever seeks grace often brings the weight of a fatal destiny upon himself and those around him.'

'Watch out, that's just his take on the character of Don Juan,' Andreina said irritatedly to Marinelli.

'So what?' Lambertini snapped back, provocatively.

But at that moment, the army doctor nodded his head slightly, and maybe because he wasn't paying him any attention anymore, Lambertini perceived it as a condemnation. He laughed, naturally at times there are horrifying shadows. But they are only shadows.

'Allow me to invite you to lunch, Captain,' he boomed, smugly.

The statue that was the army doctor replied once again with a nod of his head, mute.

The subterranean jaunt inside the grottoes of the river Lethe instead unfolded in the greatest gaiety and serenity, as if the ménage à quatre had taken a step back, having rewound to the opening scenes of a distant first act, where life flowed smoothly without any bumps and where one still had all of one's cards to play.

'My dear friends, I give you oblivion!' Lambertini said in his irremediably theatrical tone. 'We have now been offered what will happen: we have been freed from all forebodings. What do you say to that, Captain?' he asked his comrade-in-arms, who was as wan-faced as the crustaceans who were trailing their boat.

Marinelli smiled. He had no trouble admitting that he liked Lambertini. That paper hero was nevertheless a pentameter hero: one with its own musical reality to it, even if his enormous hands lingered inert and hampered on the keyboard.

'Whoever told you have any forebodings, that I have some kind of message?' he exclaimed, raising his voice, 'Music teaches us to read everything, even when it comes to our everyday lives, with mathematical precision – and at the same time with extreme indeterminacy: for instance, could you tell me what this or that prelude by Chopin really mean?'

'That depends on who is playing…' Lambertini gloomily half-retorted.

'We're still here, you know,' Andreina said, pointing to her friend; the gesture was ambiguous and allusive.

Water dripped down from the grotto's walls, in the way it had for thousands of years before the colonization of Africa had begun, meaning the colonization carried out by the Greeks – sublime vestiges of which they had witnessed on the high plains – as well as by the Kingdom of Italy. History, the apogee of *grand opéra*, doesn't compare well with nature.

So Lambertini went ahead in his explanation as he lit a cigarette and appeared to be daydreaming on his own on his couch at home. When they returned to the light, they joined some friends who were taking their coffee out on the lodge's verandah and they mingled effortlessly. Conversation flowed quickly along, there were no obstacles or seductive stops. Yet above all there was no pretentiousness whatsoever, as if on leaving the grotto the actors had left behind their costumes and forgotten all their lines, and were now losing themselves in the crowd amongst the spectators.

The black and green Fiat brought them back to the city, sputtering along, as though taking part in the new-found serenity and the easy-going conversation, which flowed so freely since the river of oblivion had freed both couples from their forebodings, or *from the future*, as Lambertini had said.

The only moment of panic occurred at the gates of the city, when a camel nearly barred their path, having run out from behind a crumbling wall as though it had been leaving its own front door. Lambertini managed to retain control of the vehicle, which finally earned him some praise from his wife.

'Darling,' he said, 'we saved ourselves.'

They looked as though they'd forgotten all about the other couple, who were sat in the back, speechless, a little squashed together, despite the army doctor being an exceedingly thin man – thus a load that was pretty much imaginary.

'A dream is solitude, a jealous woman who wants you all to herself,' Captain Lambertini said, undressing.

He was in the army doctor's bathroom, he had been having some trouble with his leg over the past few days, with sharp pangs of pain and a nasty bruise.

He couldn't keep his mouth shut for a single moment for the entire visit.

In fact, he interrogated Marinelli, and amused himself by provoking him, casting filthy aspersions on the purity of Chopin's character, making up malicious interpretations for all his sweetness, grace and digressiveness, that perpetual flight. It was as if he was jealous of the amateur pianist's love for the Polish exile and was trying to persuade him to study other composers.

'And I do,' Marinelli said, 'I go through all the scales, all the *Gradus ad Parnassum*,[lxiii] as well as other transcendental exercises. In traditional societies, the climax of the initiation rite gave way to sacred dances: but I play Chopin.' And he let his fingers run in the void, but the gesture wasn't playful or reassuring, it was like an exorcism that wanted to draw demons in instead of banishing them. 'Do you see how easily I can imitate your kind of conversation, Captain?'

'You can see how naked I stand before you. I can't understand how you've failed to grasp *que j'ai mon coeur mis à nus*,[lxiv] just like Chopin in his *Preludes*, to borrow a phrase from god knows who.'

'For that matter, the quote belongs to Baudelaire.'

'What does it matter?' Lambertini bitterly asked. 'The philological roots of that statement don't interest me. Look at my body: I want you to analyze my body, and not my soul, or my language or my choice of vocabulary.'

'You can't really think that your body is a keyboard, do you?' the army doctor replied, who suddenly seemed to gain confidence, parodying the Captain, who now felt ill at ease.

'Without the musical staff in sight you seem at a loss,' Lambertini said, with some bother. With every step he took he felt he was losing ground, their relationship had been turned on its head, and while the army doctor had earlier seemed excessively taken with his sentences, he now appeared intent on breaking them down… *into what*? Lambertini ironically asked himself with a start, albeit the fact he was also troubled.

---

lxiii Latin: 'Steps to Parnassus'.

lxiv French: 'I've laid my heart bare.' Name of a journal written by the poet Charles Baudelaire.

The light, in the doctor's examination room, was blinding.

'Are you done?' Lambertini asked impatiently.

'I'll tell you when I'm done,' the latter sternly replied.

Lambertini felt as though he had taken another step back. But he wasn't seized by panic, in fact he was immobile. *Just like Don Juan...* he thought, in an attempt to recover some of his earlier bravado. The army doctor wasn't the Commendatore, after all! It was true: by laughing he had evoked that fatal figure during the trip to the boundless plain where a ravine opened up to lead one down to the river of oblivion – *and I even invited him to dinner! Is this the dinner? Why is this usually courteous man now making me restless? What does he want?*

'I've often asked myself why you came to Africa,' he said, as if dreaming.

He laughed.

'Now I'm ranting and raving,' he observed, as if talking to himself.

The other paid him no heed. When he noticed this was the case, Lambertini tried to pull himself up on the examination table, but Marinelli's hand pressed against his chest. 'Stay still,' he ordered him.

That usually ceremonious man was giving him orders! Who was he then?

Lambertini would have wanted to jump off the table, *now I'll grab my sword and defend myself,* he thought, he formulated his inner dialogue with the same deceitful care with which he formulated his actual words.

'Give me your hand,' the other said.

Lambertini felt a brief upsurge of excitement, but an imperious statue of a man stood before him and so he tendered his hand.

The other waited for a moment, which Lambertini felt lasted for an eternity.

'You're not doing too well,' he said.

The following evening, at the club, the army doctor danced and Lambertini observed his movements. Truth be told, he wasn't moving much. He hinted at steps instead of actually taking them, it was as if he was talking about them. He wore a short beard. It was the rocking flow of a dreamlike image more than a soldier dancing.

'Has his dancing hypnotised you?' Andreina asked.

'*C'est la danse macabre…*'[lxv] Lambertini retorted.

The officer towards whom he felt an unjustifiable attraction, and with whom – the realm of music aside, where the conversation taking place between them was concealed to both – he exchanged a few ironic banalities, even though he never failed to imitate an actor, who carries a sacred script in his mind, well… the other was his double, his death in other words, as the latter had in fact revealed to him by *saying you're not doing too well.* The thirty kilograms between them were a playful and mocking metaphor that death employed to better mask itself and deceive him, by talking, which was exactly what he enjoyed the most. Beneath that uniform lay a skeleton – *how could I have failed to spot it right away?*

He had been shocked when Marinelli had revealed that he hadn't been discharged from the sanitarium for that long, and he had reproached himself over his gaffe, because he'd poked fun at his friend's weight loss. He had listened to the music of Chopin, *a kind of celebration of the ephemeral, behind which lies*

[lxv] A line from Baudelaire's *Les Fleurs du mal.*

the gaunt face of death, he had explained to the female friend who'd stood beside him at the parade. Now that the other had finally removed his mask and he had made it clear *death will come for me, and not him!* Lambertini thought, as he jumped to his feet with such a dramatic surge that the people around him eyed both reproachfully and interrogatively. Nobody ever knew who that man was really talking to, or whom he was replying to.

Indeed, the only immeasurable secret each one of us conceals is our own death! he thought, referring to his own secret, which he was already using as a source for vain confabulations.

Yet he quickly recovered himself and, while still standing, muttered some nonsense to the people sitting at the neighbouring table who never even noticed that he was fooling around with them, despite being annoyed.

This was not the case for Mary, who was looking elsewhere, staring at a fixed point, known only to her alone: whether unscrupulous or tormented, Cassandra was aware of the deception, but silence had been imposed on her, and she was a prisoner of her own foreignness. Only that while Agamemnon had kidnapped that woman from Troy as it went up in flames, Marinelli's wife had made her first appearance in colonial society before a single shot had been fired at the British army, which ruled over Egypt. It felt like the director mockingly confusing the order of events in order to give them a fresh spin.

Death *roams outside* of time, which it shapes and manipulates as it likes, and the chronological sequence becomes the embodiment of everything – the totality – *and is the mocking mirror of the Last Judgement*, Lambertini thought, *rien que ça!*[lxvi]

[lxvi] French: 'that's all'.

In the middle of the hall – which was now empty, where the light was more intense, as though a great chasm had opened up before it – was nothing but death, which was swinging instead of dancing.

The female friend from the parade placed her hand in his, brought him back to his seat, and looked as though she was pulling him up into her bed, telling him in a hushed voice, now that they were on a first-name basis: *tu es beau et tu le sais,*[lxvii] as though that secret language had finally legitimised their desire.

[lxvii] French: 'you are handsome and you know it'.

BOOK TWO

13

LOVE, DOUBT AND EACH WICKED HOPE[lxviii]

A thick curtain, similar to a theatre's drop curtain, in front of which two people are sat.

The wind is blowing furiously, but it remains off-stage. Gambarotta, the Colonel from the Civil Engineering Department, is in dress uniform.

A couple is on its way back from a military parade to mark the anniversary of the Charter.

Isabella's black hat lies atop a chair.

A grey cat warily moseys around while the Colonel speaks in a hushed monotone.

Isabella is motionless, as though posing for a portrait: in fact, as though she was a portrait, her destiny having already been fulfilled.

[lxviii] From the opening lines of Vittorio Alfieri's play, *Philip*: *'Desio, timor, dubbia ed iniqua speme,/Fuor del mio petto ormai'* or 'Love, apprehension and each wicked hope,/Leave ye my breast.' Source: Edgar Alfred Bowring (ed.), *The Tragedies of Vittorio Alfieri: Philip. Polynices. Antigone. Virginia. Agamemnon. Orestes. Rosmunda. Octavia. Timoleon. Merope. Mary Stuart* (London: Greenwood Press, 1876), p.5.

The cat sniffs at her purse.

'*Has my behaviour really been so nasty and shameful? Why? Coupled with the certainty of my guilt, I wanted there to be witnesses. A cautious course of action: now I have all the papers in order and I'm pressing ahead. You wanted to betray me... with my son. Does passion legitimise deceit? Not in the slightest as far as I'm concerned, and not simply because I was the victim: Deceit sullies everything, without requiring any additional legitimization. Did you hope you could betray me in secret? You were wrong, I saw you when you met for the first time: there were four of you because there were two witnesses at the far end of the garden... with my own eyes.*'

The cat left Isabella's purse behind and in a leap he went to stroke itself against the officer's legs, who petted it without looking at it.

'*I allowed your passion to grow because I wanted to ensure your guilt as you stood before me... I handpicked the witnesses with great care, they are solemn and obedient. They will speak if I ask them to speak and they will refuse to talk if I do... If you think that the crime has been made all the more irrevocable due to their presence, you're wrong: the real scandal now lies in the poison stored in that phial, to be used at my discretion...*'

The Colonel stood up: he paced back and forth.

Having wound up underneath the table, the cat eyed him suspiciously.

'*My ploy, which I had planned for some time, was to find proof of your guilt while still preventing you from making that mistake: my honour hasn't been offended anywhere outside of the tiny theatre in your mind, which nobody cares about. It's up to me to decide how the affair unfolds from hereon in, and it'll be to my advantage, not yours. Pessimism, clairvoyance… all they're good for is staying one step ahead of the others: it's an important quality for a soldier, which is a difficult profession.'*

'*Running away with Carlo… But he's a weakling, who would never have the courage to kidnap me from you: my figure, which he keeps close to his heart, keeps him away. You don't love him, but rather the distance which separates us. He's sentimental… delicate… – he's like a shadow which instead of repeating your movements, does the opposite.'*

The Colonel stopped pacing.

'*You feel oppressed, here in my house. But if you had ran away, you would have had a weak flame by your side which would neither have warmed you nor brought you any light: that son of mine disappointed me before he did anyone else. You would therefore send him back to me after a brief… – that is provided he learns how to overcome his pride and so long as he wishes to break that wicked oath of loyalty in the way that you broke the one you swore at the altar. It isn't true that fate has been cruel towards me, assigning me my own son as my rival: instead it favoured me by selecting an individual of little worth, even though my blood runs through his veins. Fate hasn't steered me towards a duel: it plagues me with a filthy dream.*

'*It must cause you great bitterness to know that that boy is still your heir, one day I won't be there anymore and someone dull will take my place, not in your heart, but in the great theatre of the world: time has set an inescapable trap for the Gambarotta family.'*

The cat stopped looking at the Colonel and directed its bright, questioning eyes towards Isabella: why was she silent?

'I listened to all your delirious monologues. I know that the black role was set aside for me: there you were, in front of me, dressed in white. All of a sudden there were two people. Carlo wore himself out with too much self-love... he intuited his stepmother's escape... and even on the stage of my mind one figure becomes two, but I'm there too and I'm the one who should be in the director's seat – I alone am destiny.'

The Colonel stood up again and looked outside the window.

'I watched you exhaust yourselves in the midst of your agitation... – and in the end you gave in. From your very first meeting, you knew I was hot on your trail. The surprise... when you found there were four of you at the agreed meeting place, it wasn't the way it was supposed to be: by splitting up the scene like that, with a black side and a white couple, you were demanding my presence there. But you wanted it to be implicit, your intent was to defile our double bond... Hello, Hello.'

The telephone had started to ring impatiently and the Colonel picked up the receiver.

He lingered while listening.

'But no,' he said, 'I already explained to you that this stretch of road needs a bed and gravel layer approximately five miles long. As it stands, the Public Works Department has completed the section leading to the eastern gate. As for the wells, they were dug by the Civil Engineering Department, who left a carriage-boiler that can be moved from well to well, and which, thanks to some pumps and a cloth tube, can shift the water around from well to well – do you understand? Pipes that are 145 mm in diameter channel the water from the reservoir to the city, storing it in the two tanks that were built at the top of Giuliana beach, which rise thirty-six feet from the ground. A few additional side-pipelines here and there will convey water to the various barracks and military hospitals. So, bluntly put, I don't understand your question. Go to the place and check on the situation yourself.'

Relaxed, the cat stretched out – this was its everyday life. It was useless to pay any attention. It closed its eyes.

It didn't notice that the Colonel had already replaced the receiver and with his back turned to the window, he resumed his monologue:

'*Anyone who seeks to play the role of the victim can't deny the executioner anything – it's always the same old story! The executioner was right there, in the shape of the two men. If I let you get all the way to a rendezvous it was to lay your dreams bare. Carlo is far away by now… it's unlikely that he would dare to come back. He'll try to write… I'll intercept the letters. I keep as tight a rein on the colony as if it were a piece of paper, there's a reason why I work in the Civil Engineering Department.*'

The cat was dreaming, as though it too was in the midst of a secret monologue. It tried to chase something away with its paw, without opening its eyes.

'*Only passion could give you an escape path and yet you chose to exalt yourselves with the desire born of sacrifice: I'll limit myself to preventing you from carrying that out, I no longer require the love of my wife and child. Carlo is afraid: I shouldn't add to that fear, given that it seems that I gave him enough of it simply by creating him. He wore himself out in the attempt to bring some order to his emotions and to forge a real connection with the world: he wanted to exclude me from that world and now he sees that I am the world.*'

The world woke the cat, as if it had understood the idea. It stretches again, it wishes to recover its strength and control over itself. The duel begins and one must show oneself to be astute: his whiskers are stiff and white.

'*Regardless of where he runs or flees, he will find me there. His fear is a sure-fire guarantee. I only gave you a rival to humiliate you.*'

The cat began to run, but all the doors were shut. It didn't lose its verve. It remained sat down, waiting, as if it was a sacred simulacrum.

'*I only gave you a rival to humiliate you*,' Colonel Gambarotta repeated. Then he stayed quiet.

Yet he promptly picked up his monologue again:

'*The desire to compromise yourself seemed to you like a way out, something that could resolve the situation, if in a ruinous manner. But I won't let anyone dictate the chronology of events, it's the first rule of the military arts, which is based on being able to divine the future at any given moment: I stopped the act in its tracks, you were put on hold halfway through. The desire to break with me made you choose a rival who was in my own house, but you didn't notice that he was someone who was already predisposed to being a rival: you are running away with a man who is worth about as much as one of my fingers! When you see that he won't dare to take you away with him, and that even if you do run away, not even the whole desert will give you enough space to hide in, and I will get a hold on him again, and all desires will be extinguished. I can choose to humiliate him before his beloved – who is also my wife and his stepmother – whenever I wish. The memory of your crime, which was sought but not carried out, is my loyal and most punctual servant.*'

The first witness entered, out of breath. His modest attire stands in stark contrast against the officer's high dress uniform.

'*Carlo has come back!*'

He leaves in a hurry, followed by Gambarotta. Carlo enters and takes Isabella away. The cat doesn't budge, but observes everything.

The second witness enters, but doesn't find anybody, and sorrowfully spreads his arms. He's also badly dressed, he looks as though he's forgotten he's an actor and he's just wandered onto the stage by accident.

He yells:

'*Isabella has killed herself, Carlo has killed himself.*'

The first witness enters again.

The witnesses stare straight ahead and say:

'*We can attest to that.*'

Lights.

'The cat just stayed there, he obviously didn't understand what happened in the big finale,' Mrs Brignole said.

'Gambarotta didn't give the cat any lines, that cat just wandered over from the Club and wrote his own part: nobody will ever know the dramas he's lived through!'

'Honestly, so the cat didn't really get what the whole drama between Filippo, Carlo and Isabella was really about, and we didn't understand him?'

'That's right,' Lieutenant Giovannini said.

'Lieutenant Rossi didn't have a hard role to play, as the young pretender he barely stepped on the scene.'

'But he's always there, that is in Mrs Leoni's mind – meaning Isabella. She dreamt him up, didn't you notice that?'

'All in all the play was a little gloomy. I wouldn't like a husband like that.'

'So if you did you would betray him?'

'That would depend,' Mrs Brignole said, 'that would depend,' she repeated.

The Club was packed and the audience was complimenting Gambarotta on the play he'd written and performed in. Mrs Leoni, who had performed the rather difficult role of Isabella, was also being praised.

'It sure looked difficult,' Major Tanzi drily exclaimed, 'can you imagine, she didn't even say a single word!'

The Officers' Club on the Corso had been bitten by the theatre bug, it was the ultimate game they could play to counteract the reality of the place they were in – 'without even realizing' Major Galì said in a disenchanted manner, 'that the artificiality of the colony's situation makes theatre as *effortless* as everyday life, and allows the two to get mixed up. We think we're avoiding reality on the stage but it is actually the stage itself which shapes our day to day lives: there's nothing necessary about this society, just the mere fact that we the military – unproductive actors – are in charge here instead of society's actually productive members is a testament to that. The stage isn't an alternative to reality, it's a distillation of that reality, which gathers all its essential rare liquids. The theatre is the temple where facts of everyday life are celebrated as a vision of the world: even we in the audience are actors are woe onto us should we ever forget that.'

'But what are you saying?' Mrs Brignole asked, a tiny, *peppery* lady, as people used to say. 'Are we privileged – or are we condemned given that we don't know the end is near?'

She seemed amused by the riddle.

The Major shook his head.

'Actors don't judge the roles they play,' he replied.

In another corner of the beautiful hall, where the stuccoes appeared less decorative and more artfully arranged – to put everything in doubt, even the static, colours, shapes, the entire order of the world, taking advantage of the interval between one play and the other – the Club's other guests were talking as if they were strolling along an imaginary *foyer*.

'In a permissive era,' Captain Lonardi, the tall figure leaning against the French door that opened out onto a limpid sky, was saying, 'every deception is a game, and not an insult. Opposites don't meet and neither do they guarantee one another: in fact they are interchangeable.'

'Oh yes?' asked one of the ladies next to him, who wasn't paying much attention to what he was saying, but who wanted him to keep *speaking*, since she felt as though she was being caressed by the sound of his voice. Her husband was on a mission deep in the desert, far, so far away… whereas there they were cradled, suspended even, in the seashore's seductive freshness.

'There's no longer a single endless path that one must necessarily read: one can now take various paths – which are brief, ephemeral, which lead you nowhere specific, or even take you back to the very place you had left.'

'We never know where we stand when you speak,' the lady said, craning her chin into her neck, as if contracting in a sudden twitch. 'The ephemeral road…' she mouthed, the only words which had remained impressed in her mind.

'Do you mean to say that wisdom is impossible because that *place* no longer exists?' Colonel Gambarotta asked.

Yet one couldn't be sure whether he was playing the role of Filippo II or whether he was speaking as himself. After all, hadn't he written the play?

'Just like the opposite *place* doesn't exist,' the Captain replied, 'Hypocrisy is the theatrical restoration of values, distances, fictive itineraries, it makes life eventful. It serves the same function as perspective does in the art of painting: *trompe-l'oeil*.'

'Should I therefore abandon myself to hypocrisy? Mrs Cecchetto asked, alarmed. 'And who with?' she added, insinuatingly. The figures of her husband and her lover appeared to be vying with one another over something, between the desert and the sea.

'I also wanted to write a play using the character of Don Juan…'

'They've already done that,' the lady said, finally feeling self-assured, 'it's already been written.'

'Well, let's try to live it out then, not on the stage, but in our mental theatres, the real source of all our wickedness,' Captain Lonardi said.

Mrs Cecchetto was surprised to learn that that's exactly where she wanted to go, the mental theatre.

'That Don Juan story is so out of date, it's a story that belongs to a time when one tried to stimulate one's appetites and not repress them. Society doesn't abhor Don Juan, they praise him. He was a demonic and aristocratic figure: even mediocre people who are nothing but afraid now fool themselves into thinking they are rebels and free spirits thanks to the great power of cinema, which shows everything and thus legitimises it.'

At that moment, the Prefect passed by the table and Captain Lonardi promptly shut his mouth. He even gave him a nod of the head.

'In that famous play, Don Juan doesn't premeditate his acts to illustrate his blasphemous intentions, but instead he simply chases his appetites, which others still interpret as demonic.'

'What about you? What kind of appetites do you have?' the lady whose husband was in the desert cheerfully asked.

'Those who got offended slandered Don Juan. Frustration arises when one's appetites are repressed: it satisfies a weak-willed person's quest for personal identity.'

Gambarotta looked at him. 'Get to the point.'

'Never!' the Captain exclaimed in a fit of passion, 'Irony is the last paradise, a postscript to history rather than an introduction to it – it's the only escape out of mediocrity. Irony marks the triumph of the mental theatre on everything: if the path itself is mediocre, the mind provides its own stage. This is why the idea of writing plays for soldiers appeals to me.'

'So why haven't you written one yet?'

'But it's the one I'm reciting right now: according to my genius – *selon mon* génie – I am both on the stage and on the street… Theatre life is like religious life, which never takes place in a specific place bur rather unfolds in the wider world and the mind. After all, secrets are the final refuge of those who want to bend the will of others to their destiny.'

'Such eloquence!' Mrs Cecchetto exclaimed.

'Deception is escapism,' Gambarotta disdainfully remarked.

'Escapism is the preferential order of our times.'

'We are fleeing from something, towards something else,' said an officer who had been silent up until that point.

'Even war?' Mrs Cecchetto asked, stunned.

'Actions, feelings, thoughts… these are nothing but stories of detachment,' Captain Lonardi said, 'If only one could flee *towards* something… Escapism doesn't leave a blueprint behind. It leaves a thousand: the doodles of a complete maniac.'

'In conclusion,' Mrs Cecchetto said, leaving the entire circle around her stunned, 'you, Captain Lonardi, have proclaimed yourself to be Don Juan. Why, the nerve!' she added, conspiratorially.

'Who doesn't think of themselves as Don Juan these days?' said the officer who'd previously been silent.

'Well, me,' Captain Lonardi said.

'Really?' the lady asked.

As far as she was concerned, Captain Lonardi was playing along.

'Those who rid themselves of laws march towards the inevitable finishing line placed before them: solitude.'

'No woman will ever come and ask me about the master, no knight will ever want to avenge his promised bride, Donna Elvira won't follow him over mountains and the Commendatore won't come to dinner?' the officer agitatedly asked, as if fishing for a role, perhaps that of Siganarello.[lxix]

'I am the invincible seducer of women.'

Mrs Cecchetto's heart skipped a beat.

'The character of Don Giovanni legitimises himself as the metaphor of one's will to make the whole of reality as real as possible. A demonic amplification in which the others, who are

---

[lxix] References to characters in *Don Giovanni.*

made ignorant by the poverty of the lawful, are bound to lose themselves in: the proliferation of the real frightens them. The law demarcates the confines between the real and the possible, and separates them. It's the government of the possible which has been reduced to a handful of clear paths: it claims that this is reality and claims it as *lawful.* In the face of such a disappointing equivalence, Don Giovanni comes into subvert that equivalency between what is real and what is possible.'

'What about the role itself?'

'The equivalency of what is real and possible as a mental fact. Not as an example or a scandal.'

'It's a little complicated,' the lady hazarded, feeling the ground slip beneath her feet.

'Is it no longer worthwhile to defy the law?'

'A perspicacious observer could find the mental character of the operation scandalous.'

'But what an entertaining play!' Mrs Cecchetto exclaimed, unhappily, unable to find any further *points de repère.*[lxx]

'And what if Don Giovanni went too far by remaining a prisoner of his own career? What if instead of scandalously converting the possible into reality, he was in actual fact a prisoner of the possible, which prevented him from forging a true connection with reality?'

'Why don't you ask him?' Captain Lonardi said, shrugging his shoulders, 'I don't know how the story proceeds. After all, I didn't write the play and maybe it's acephalous.'

The woman looked at him without knowing whether she should feel reassured or disappointed. Was it up to her to come up with a sequel to that story?

[lxx] French: 'points of reference'.

'What irredeemable distance did it consume?' Gambarotta asked.

'Those who desire my salvation don't know how to give up claiming my guilt: you are characters who have been feeding off my sins now for over four centuries.' Captain Lonardi stressed, 'Running away from one's mistakes isn't enough, you want others to make that mistake: the devil is a martyr.'

'Would you hear that!' Mrs Cecchetto exclaimed, highly interested.

'Someone once said that humanity can be divided into fallen angels and evolving monkeys. As far as I'm concerned…' Captain Lonardi paused, 'the place where they're running to doesn't coincide with the place that we lost.'

'That's enough now, Captain,' Gambarotta sternly remarked.

Mrs Cecchetto hurriedly adopted a detached – in fact *distinguished* – attitude.

Yet the second play was already underway by then, and the performance had been entirely written and performed by Captain Valentini, a reserved man, who had shocked everyone when he'd announced that he would be taking part in the *matinée* in the Club's salon.

There was a person on the stage who played the role of the director as well as four young men who worked as stagehands: they carried on shifting around a few objects, stepping on and off the stage, causing confusion. Nobody knew if the play was about to start or if it had already begun: but if that was the case why weren't they talking? 'Could the play already be over?' one of the ladies asked, frightened.

Valentini was on the stage, but he was waiting for the others to finish their work. Nobody knew what that work involved because their gestures all mirrored one another as objects were moved only to be put back in their original place.

Finally, everything came to a halt.

Valentini sat down at the table. The director and the stagehands stepped aside.

Silence.

Valentini's head was leaning against the back of his hand.

He exclaimed:

'*God! God! God! If only I could see him! If only I could hear him! Where is this God?*'

The director and the stagehands who were lingering on the side of the stage began to clap, as they were the only ones who'd understood that the play was already over.

And they immediately resumed moving around the objects on the stage in a circular motion.

14

THE LIBRARY

'Culture? But it's nothing but blackmail! Do you know how we usually spend our Sundays? Reading. My husband sits in front of me with a book in his hand, distant, absent. To tell you the truth: I wish he'd run off with some woman instead, at least I'd know where to go find him. But in books!' she concluded, dismayed, making a wide gesture with her right hand.

She was wearing a white cotton dress, trimmed at the bottom by a *volant* of fan-shaped pleats.

'Why don't you burn them all?' her friend, Major Mari's wife, asked.

'*A vast undertaking*! Only the barbarians managed to do that and that was a thousand years ago. And then: what about his memory? Those dull notebooks in which he confides? I never quite figured out where he hides them.'

'You have to figure out where they are and then… we'll burn them all! I'll help you do it.'

'Then his mind would get all blistered, or castrated even: what use would I have for such a deformed, impotent being?'

She continued to scrape the fingers of her right hand against the palm of her left, as if wanting to scrub some sand or dust off them, regardless of whether it was real or metaphorical.

'What kind of books does he read?'

'*Des bêtises.*'

'But I've never heard him recall a book or refer to it.'

'The Captain,' the General, who was sat on the *chaise-longue* beside the two ladies on the interminably long deserted seashore, remarked in an annoyed tone, 'never mentions any books out of respect for superstition, in the same manner as the priest of an esoteric cult doesn't reveal the content of the sacred books, whose secrets are known only to a select few. Folly is subject to far steelier rules than reason. However…'

'However?' Mrs Mari asked in a malicious tone.

'The way he talks is so complex, or if you like, so simple and clear, that culture appears to have been its obvious – nay, inescapable and fatal – foundations: one realises this after chatting to him just a little. The coordination of his conversation is regulated by a system of references that is difficult to circumscribe, where every door leads to another. He's the only one who's been able to understand that only in a library may one find the kind of space to balance against one's presence in Africa – and thus he's the only one who manages to live here effortlessly, in a legitimate fashion.'

'It's easy to relish all that chatter,' the Captain's wife replied, bitterly, 'but do you know what it feels like to talk to a library? At times I feel as though I were stuck in a carnival, chasing countless masks around because my husband lies beneath one of them.'

'You're wrong there: your husband lies behind each and every one of them. This is the reader's imagination. The individual –

meaning a specific identity and a single face – dies in the midst of reading. You talk disdainfully of feeling like you're in a carnival. As for me, your husband's discussions are like a labyrinth. Don't forget we are here in the colony to bring civilization. What image has civilization produced that is as genuine as a labyrinth?' the General asked, who appeared to have overcome his proverbial coldness. 'Truth be told, your husband is the only credible colonist around here: he has picked up a sword but inside his head lies a library, which is a divine attribute. It's beautiful to watch a mind summarise the history of the world: the seductiveness of a mind is an all-conquering force.'

'Arthur insists on seeing everything through a magnifying glass, reading distorts everything: it's the sign of a sick mind.'

'It doesn't distort reality, it lays it bare.'

'You seem fond of your Captain, mon *Générale*.'

'Obeying the rules is enough for me, and the Captain is highly unyielding in this respect. In a world that grows ever more empty, rules have replaced destiny, which has orphaned us. Obeying rules makes life as fatal as destiny: all the rest is a dream, and reason is the restless shadow of that dream.'

'Maybe you're the one who's looking at my husband through a magnifying glass.'

'You must understand that without any lenses everything becomes insignificant and there's no rhyme nor reason to it, as well as any of its *artistic* derivatives: feelings, fear, desire, ambition – or shadows: disloyalty, betrayal, dreams. Time is setting and reading colours everything in so wonderfully well… Besides… believe me… none of us express ourselves better than when we talk either to ourselves or silently to others.' At which point, as if giving an order, he added: 'Obviously, the only other means, par excellence, is via a book.'

'Maybe *Arturo the coloniser* has confused me and his wife with the natives,' the Captain's wife bitterly commented.

'I must disappoint you there: in order to be a true native, at least according to the colonizer's conventional stereotype, you'd have to have a quality that you do not possess – and which would balance out the Captain's erudition – *naivety*. That's why all your conversations are dry and stiff.'

It appeared to signify that the audience had been brought to an end.

15

THE COMEDIANS

‘… all right, I’ll tell you a funny story, about a doctor who’s just left, the hospital’s head physician, Doctor Emo, told me: he’s a man who knows this city’s secrets better than its priests and in any case (relying on the strength of his good heart, which appears to absolve him from any of prejudice’s malice) he never has secrets of his own. He devotes his attention to the human body and doesn’t give a fig for sentimental matters. He occasionally uses human bodies to carry out investigations, just like he did with the case of those three people whom he cured of syphilis without any of the three knowing he was treating the others. He kept their names quiet, thus ensuring the invention of a new game or eccentric pastime in town: hunting after the identities of the people in that love triangle.

‘But the story I wish to tell you is a publicly known triangle, and the tight-lipped doctor who just left is the opaque tip of that triangle. Just think that he was always in a good mood, tolerant, easy-going: some said he wasn’t too bright, while others smiled and said he was kindly. He had a beautiful wife and his open character appeared to be a reflection of that possession… which was excessive.

'As is typical of the colonies, the imbalance between men and women is remarkable, and so we're left to fight over the same muses, so you can well imagine what envy that meek man with the beautiful wife inspired among the others! People rushed to see her as if they were lining up at the museum to see Venus lying naked on the grass in the shade. But this Venus was chaste: she merely smiled at the collective homage to her as though it had been directed to her portrait. As for her husband, well… he turned a blind eye to the whole thing, pleased by the festiveness of it, as if each new trembling suitor added to the precious wealth of his marital chest. I'm sure that during the golden hours of that nocturnal possession he kept all those faces in mind – who formulated his desire into a howling orchestra which he alone could satisfy. He was like a boss trying to make a speech to a delirious crowd: but instead of words there was the body of a woman.

'All this was related to me by Doctor Emo, but it was the city which either tormented itself over the enigma or laughed about it: the Little Doctor's Beauty. The Doctor used to be a chatterbox and not the silent man who now seems to want to avoid the rest of the world, and has turned a deaf ear to everything, as if he was the patient in this clinic – and not me, with my broken leg.

'Venus may have been chaste, but devoid of a classical education, the Doctor had ignored the fact that Mars conquered her heart by secretly undermining Vulcan. It was true that there were already some soldiers among the Proci[lxxi] and that some were insistent, but only one of them won the game: let's call him *Captain Mars.*

[lxxi] Penelope's suitors in *The Odyssey.*

'Don't ask me to pass judgment on him. I'll merely say that he wasn't loyal to any of the lovers whom were rightly or wrongly attributed to him, and that he was a reserved man, although he talked a great deal, and often disappeared only to reappear, as if he had a great gift for ubiquitousness in conversations just as much as he did in bed – occasionally you would ask yourself: *just what is he talking about?* One often saw him around, a triangle with a golden tip. If the Doctor had previously bragged about having one of the most beautiful women in town as his wife, he subsequently began to brag about having a *hero of love* as one of his rivals. In the colonial city, which was as tightly-knit as a royal court, the constant chatter and gossip encircled the passage of the trio with a halo of sound. But then the image began to embed itself in everyday life without any talk attached to it: after all, as someone put it, *so long as they're happy… In fact*, he had added, *I don't envy the little doctor: by cuckolding him it's as if that officer avenged us all!*

'But the cuckold was blessedly happy. Perhaps I'm exaggerating and you're growing suspicious: regardless, the presence of that third wheel didn't seem to put the Doctor out at all, and that's a fact.'

'As nature teaches us, everything is in a constant state of metamorphosis, and nothing remains as it once was – our eyes deceive us. However, it was later learned that: the Captain, not content with having cuckolded the Doctor, was now cheating on his new lover, barely after that beauty had managed to tame his ubiquitousness. Of a far less easy going character than her husband, when the lady found out, she caused a scene, and there are those who swear that she grabbed the Captain's pistol. However, Doctor

Emo, who knows the story better than anyone, claims that it was a hunting rifle she had stolen from her husband. But when Emo wants to tell you a story, he doesn't just want to laugh at the actors involved, he also wants to laugh at the listener, meaning you: sometimes revelations are pulled out of thin air merely to phagocytise some reality that you're comfortable with into an unreal situation.

'The relationship was ended. There were even those who said they had detected a trace of melancholy in the husband. Yet there were those who explained with the way that beautiful lady had grown embittered: betrayed by her lover, she wanted her husband. So the world goes, as it cruelly tramples upon the weak. Whenever they went out onto the street for their evening stroll, everyone would look at them, as though asking themselves, *where's the third one gone?*

'Finally, the Captain was transferred to an outpost at the border, where he could only pay court to numerous, slender palm trees that poked out of the dunes. There were those who said that the General envied his good fortune; there were those who instead said that the conspiracy had involved everybody. Given that the pretty lady had surrendered herself, there had been a need to remove the chosen one and try to take his copulative functions away. Perhaps, now that the officer had been sent far away, the husband had also lost all his rights, and this explained the origins of the black humour impressed upon his face. It was as if his bed had been kidnapped and dumped out in the desert: the beautiful lady was under the power of a spell which nobody – not even her lawful husband – could break.

'Then the entire affair faded into the background, it was as if the woman had just disappeared, and one could only see her image out on the Corso. There were some newcomers who, *believing they'd just discovered America*, as a friend put it, *tried* – as they say, rudely – *to chat her up*, but there was no chatter to be had.'

'One day, however, it was learned that the beautiful lady had been taken ill – gravely ill. There were those who suspected her husband of having poisoned her. He had become serious in that way, that's for sure, in some sinister way – and, I don't know why, he'd even grown uglier.

'You're already picturing how the story ends: the lady died not long thereafter.

'But at this point Doctor Emo jumped out with his revelations.

'He says he's only confided these revelations to me, because we're from the same village, on the Brenta. As for me, I haven't shared the story with anyone else; I'm making an exception for you because you're just passing through – despite your forced stay in this hospital, where we have been plunged once again into the idleness of childhood, where stories have replaced… the games of our youths. Your intestinal troubles are certainly strange my dear accountant, nobody else here is affected by them. We don't get the kind of infectious diseases here that you do in other viler parts of Africa. Everyone here *dies of love*, just like at the theatre.

'And I'll show you how.'

'The beautiful lady was therefore stretched out on the bed, which had reappeared from the desert only to host death, and not love. Our Doctor – not Emo, but the husband – you follow? – sat there stunned, *as if he'd just gone bankrupt*, as my merciless friend put it, after having visited him. His luck had all been used up. Her agony was both quick and slow, we're at her final days here, but for many days the lady never poked her head out in the street.

'Finally, one morning, when Emo was there – this is what he said, I have my doubts, maybe he got all his details from the cheerful, roly-poly servant in their employ – Captain Mars was seen heading towards the house and then he came to knock on its door. Who warned the husband, who was in the bedroom, nobody knows. But he leaped up as if he was twice as tall as he actually was, perhaps he'd recognised the specific kind of ring, conjugal and unique, perhaps he'd seen his wife's eyes brighten up since she would have recognised the sound even better than him, and he dashed to the door, quick as lightning.

'He seemed like a different person: his eyes were aflame with rage.

'The Captain didn't flinch. He gave him a military salute, either mockingly or obsequiously, who knows.

'Not a word.

'Even the husband was reining in his anger, but he really did seem like somebody else. There are those who say – yet again! – that he was holding a gun at the time. Emo said that his anger had transfigured him and that he did not need a gun.

'Now I hope you'll remember that a gun had already been mentioned when the pretty lady had discovered that Captain Mars was cheating on her. And now it reappeared. The bed was a part of the scene, as was Mother Death, in addition to Doctor Emo and the maid. As a rule, the final scene in a play is usually crowded. The allotted time was very brief and they had to resolve the matter quickly, *but it wasn't easy*, Emo remarked. What would you have done, my dear accountant? Would you have run away? It's like I said: it seems the husband had morphed into something terrible, he too had finally become a god, just like Mars and Venus, gun or *no gun*. Would you have sought shelter behind Doctor Emo, who's so big and tall that he could hide two people behind him? Would you have asked the maid in her long frock to help you?

'The handsome Captain didn't budge from his spot. His face was serene, but closed. He wasn't menacing – as if! – but neither was he scared. There was no room for him there, the husband's rage told him. Which was right. But if there wasn't room for a person there, would there also not be any room for mere words?

'*I only came here to tell Lina that she was the only woman I ever loved.*

'Doctor Emo said he'd seen them all, but that this was certainly new!

'That proud man bowed deeply and added:

'*If you would be so kind as to tell her yourself? I owe it to her and I would never forgive myself if I kept my mouth shut out of cowardice.*

'*Can you believe it?* Elmo told me, *I've been around the block, but…*

'Why be so formal among friends?

'But now the Captain was on his knees, begging him – this represented the metaphorical transformation from informality to formality.

'Her husband wasn't an insensitive man: he had always loved Lina.

'He would have done anything in his powers to save her from death, despite the fact she had betrayed him: but death was already there. The only thing he could do now was to not prevent the latter from playing his last card.

'He threw open the bedroom door.

'Captain Mars stepped in.

'He said what he had come to say.

At that exact moment, the beautiful lady shut her eyes forever.'

'Excuse me,' said the man who was lying on one of the beds next to that of the functionary of the colonial government, and turning on his side, he asked: 'What's so funny about that story?'

'But, my dear accountant, we're the comedians!' the functionary exclaimed, 'we chased away the melodramas of everyday life, the symbols and rituals, the excess of the theatre where life remains warm at heart. If everyone had known in advance how the final scene would unfold, they would laugh at the story as it was a bad libretto, but they don't hear the music that redeems it! The entire city turned out for her funeral. Here is what that friend who sullies everything with jokes said: *there you have it*, he said, *while the archaeologists are busy unearthing the ruins of those ancient temples devoted to the immortal Venus, here we are burying a lusted after image of that Venus, who will be ash by tomorrow evening at eight.* Ever since the art of opera was invented, the history of the West (meaning an esoteric history, the rest is noise, vanity, and daily brutalities) has unfolded there. History as a *mythological system*, you understand? The creation of gods as gigantic shadows of everyday life. Look: the heroes of melodramas, the only *people* one could compare to the gods of Homer and Olympus, can only be seen at the Scala – and nowhere else. These are our substitutes for the Greek gods of old. They dwell in the invisible, which is sound.

'Dear me, how I love those who know how to bring a spark of light to this sombre world and chase the darkness from the path of everyday life.

'If I asked to be reassigned to the colony, a provisional, burlesque world, even though it abounds in metaphorical riches, it's because it's a parody of opera of all its excesses: it is triumphant and upsetting, and always an inch away from the ridiculous. It's the same impulse which had led me to passively accept the coming war, the last melodrama that is still performed out on the streets, an atrocious drama filled with sounds, ruins, blood and victories. War is a fact of life that we shall have to endure, and yet it unravels destinies enough to put any libretto to shame.'

A pause. Silence.

'Do you understand why I said that we were the comedians? What isn't comical about our potential and inadequacy, which debases everything? What isn't comic about our smiles, which accompany all our actions and sully all in sight? Comedians no longer stand on the stage, they sit right in the audience, they are a *choir*, which was once a custodian of our highest values, in short, *we are the comedians* my dear accountant.'

'Just keep your leg still!' the clinic's orthopedic surgeon exclaimed irately as he entered the room and saw Colla the functionary in such an animated state. 'What's come over you?'

The functionary turned over on his other side and immediately fell asleep.

16

ANABASIS ARTICULATA

'The *anabasis articulata* is a leafless plant with fleshy stems that comes in two varieties: one whose branches bear flowers and one whose branches don't,' the colonial functionary said as he displayed the images he'd printed on a milky background in the dark room. 'This instead is the *neurada procumbens*, and a tiny thread of tissue always survives in the rootstock. Please magnify this, go ahead and look, here we have: *lotus creticus*, a copiously-branched perennial with whitish leaves and golden-yellow flowers.'

Captain Valentini showed no emotion. Yet his patience appeared inexhaustible, as though he were carrying out an important duty. *Like what?* the functionary circumspectly asked himself.

Owing to the crystal-clear photography, those examples of flora had acquired the appearance of Japanese calligraphy and its thin, elegant brushstrokes. They looked less like pictures of African flora and more like the enigmatic, imaginative doodling of a pen.

'This one on the other hand is *vicia pseudocracca*.'

The Captain picked up the shiny sheet. Everything was growing ever more immaterial, as if the artist had melancholically internalised his visions.

'*Pituranthos tortuosus*, an endemic and aromatic plant with whitish flowers. *Erodium hirtum*, *haplophyllum vermiculare*, *statice thouini*...'

The functionary sighed.

'Perhaps I'm boring you, Captain?'

The officer nodded slightly, like a tree top signalling the direction of the wind. He seemed to be aphasic. They had spent the past four hours together and he had merely uttered a dozen words, save for the customary phrases one employed when they shared a drink or to ask a question about which path to take. They had driven their jeep in the boundless brush in search of flora, and now, sitting in the functionary's office, they were *reading* the photographs the latter had taken in his patient and diabolical quest to catalogue everything. The distinguished officer's aphasia didn't bother the scholar, as far as he was concerned he had the kind of nature that meant *he only spoke in the heat of the fire*, and he was pleased with this turn of phrase.

Commissioned by the government, this scientific enterprise didn't interest anyone in the slightest, but having planned for a book on the colony to be published before the end of the year – which would include all aspects of life there: landscapes, industries, the artistic and the political – the colonial administration had deemed it worthwhile to include painstakingly detailed information and illustrations on the local flora. They wanted to show that the boundless African lands which had been conquered were even more precious than previously thought – and alive, not buried under piles of sand.

The scholar occasionally felt that rather than studying the flora of the area, he was actually examining its past, that he was travelling on a path parallel to that of an archaeologist's: thus not along nature's eternal and vital cycle, which constantly goes round in a circle, but on the linear road of history which is destined to end in nothingness – as proven by the superb ruins of the old Greek colonies on the high plains, with its deserted temples and abandoned theatres.

If he ever spoke about his research to his colleagues in the government, they would sooner or later interrupt him with the same question: 'Oh yes?' which expressed both their tedium and distractedness.

He therefore remained speechless, as if locked away in a prison cell. He was like a madman, the umpteenth adventurer in his timeless attempt to achieve the fabrication of gold.

'But nature is the real gold.'

He hadn't been able to find anyone who, like Valentini with his silence, expressed any respect at all for his research. There wasn't a single corner of the exterminated province which they hadn't covered. It was as if Lieutenant Rossi had mockingly said that he'd 'gotten smaller thanks to all that running around.' He was pale, wore spectacles, and had a face which looked like nature had doodled it off in a hurry in a moment of uninspired apathy, 'leaving the job half-done,' as Rossi had concluded. The functionary, for his part, did nothing except redouble his zeal: not to capture the attention of the colonists, but instead to run away from them.

One day, however, under the heat of that implacable sun, amidst the desolate silence of everything, while he was trying to rip a sapling from its cradle between two black-grey rocks in Tocra, at the foot of the plateau, he had found Valentini's eyes pinned on him. He had felt his heart jump, it was as if he belonged to some animal species, maybe even a dangerous one, but he had quickly recovered: 'I'm stealing…' he said, pleased by the attention of others.

Not that this had led to them striking up a friendship, but those cold eyes appeared to be alert. He suggested a run for the following Sunday, out onto the boundless plain whose scattered flora he was better acquainted with than anyone else: the sheer scale of space seemed to overwhelm everything and thus it made any vegetation seem even tinier than it was.

The functionary was sweating in his well-ordered office, while Valentini was fresh as a rose, in fact, as fresh as a statue, absent and immobile. The functionary experienced a moment of unease. How would it all turn out in the end?

'*Tamaris articulata, moricandia suffricotosa, acacia tortilis…*'

An interminable litany as the photographs were passed from one person's hands to the other's, in a quasi-mechanical fashion, as if their hands functioned like automatic springs.

All of a sudden, the zealous functionary put his cards on the table. 'My dear Captain,' he said, 'nature is a book that knows no end: it's sorcery,' at which point he shut his briefcase with a stern gesture, leaving his palm resting upon it.

'Very interesting,' the Captain said.

The light in the room was scarce, except for around the table, where there was a lamp with a screen of crumpled yellow silk.

Finally, the Captain recovered his speech. He employed courteous, frugal phrases to express his gratitude, adding that he was sorry that he'd wasted his time – 'a whole afternoon,' to be precise.

The functionary was ready to make his rebuttal…

But the Captain had already left.

'As though he'd just left a shop,' the functionary muttered, once on his own.

'*Rhus oxycantha, Erodium hirtum…*' as though he was reading the name out at roll call.

But the window gave out on the vast, empty sea.

'Well, that was interesting,' he concluded.

The doorbell began to ring.

It was the officer, who loquaciously excused himself right away for having forgotten one of the functionary's pencil sharpeners in his pocket, after having borrowed it during the long ride out of the city.

Once he'd taken a left and walked to the end of a little alley strewn with the kind of oleanders that grew in Africa and which were so fragrant, Valentini reached the white seafront promenade. He hadn't noticed that the functionary was at the window watching his every move like a shadow.

So it's over then, he thought.

For a few months, he had been the talk of the town: a reserved officer who loved solitude, who always walked along the seashore or the Corso on his own, had fallen in love with a girl much younger than him, who loved him in return. Now one would see them on the Corso together, but never, as Lieutenant Rossi pointed out, in the same direction: he would go up and she would go down, he would go left and she would go right, these are the workings of a mechanism whose function is unknown to us. 'Eros… is younger than me, a boy really, and his vile, celestial science can come up with an endless series of games, many of which are often incomprehensible.'

Valentini came to a halt at the quay.

It was winter: the brief, inhospitable, wet, windy winter typical to that distant shore, when Africa appeared anguished and menacing.

Tall as she was, and with a lively gait, the girl loved reveries and daydreams, it was as if reality's role was merely to provide inspiration for the romantic novel in her mind, where space was infinite and time enigmatic. This was why one always had to struggle with her: not because her heart couldn't make room for anyone, but because it couldn't accommodate reality. But why hold it against her? Reveries were nothing but the flip side of solitude, which was dear to him, and thus they were cut from the same cloth: '*nous sommes faits du même bois*'[lxxii] as she would say.

It was all over, and the speed with which it had happened had left him feeling offended: *who did I fall in love with?* he kept asking himself without ever finding an answer. Had he really been dumped? Had nothing touched that heart except his shadow? Where had they spent their time together? In the real world or the imaginary one? Francesca, whom he occasionally saw at the Club, or on the street, the beach, at church during mass, or chatting cheerfully to people her own age, seemed to have forgotten all about him, and whenever they crossed paths, her eyes always had a jeering expression in them.

[lxxii] French: 'we are made of the same wood', metaphor, similar to 'cut from the same cloth'.

'Listen, when you talk by Via Generale Briccola don't bother to look up, I don't live there anymore,' she'd mockingly told him.

How far removed she seemed from the first image he'd had of that fleeting, elusive soul. The image was now crying because it had discovered that it did not have a life of its own: it wasn't that Francesca had disappointed him, but that reality had disappointed his image, repudiating it: the entire drama had never even left the realm of his imagination.

The sea now seemed like a mirror where that man contemplated either his own reflection of that of his demonic double. A chilling breeze was on the rise, as though it wasn't brushing against Africa, but the Night itself.

He coughed.

He appeared to be confiding in someone, in the shadows. In fact, it looked as if he was being confided in: it was his *self from yesterday* who needed to justify his actions. The two men were two black figures, and one could barely tell them apart at that late hour.

Marionettiste amoreux, je me promène avec ton image…[lxxiii]

It's not that I'm disappointed by reality, the other said, *but the image is, that golden shadow, look at the body that deludedly casts it aside: as if it had been profaned. It's she who suffers, the image! And where? In my heart: the only place it exists.*

He looked around himself as though afraid someone were eavesdropping.

[lxxiii] French: 'Loving puppeteer, I walk alongside your image…'

He was a reserved officer: 'a lights out kind of guy,' as Lieutenant Rossi said.

Ever since Francesca had left him, he felt as though everyone around him could perceive the void that accompanied his each step.

The botanist had left the house, where he had felt ill at ease after his guest fled, and he headed towards the seashore, as though looking for him. He found him standing still and absent-minded on the quay. *What was he doing? Or better yet*, he playfully corrected himself, *what was he thinking?*

He stopped at a reasonable distance, *after all I'm only a little guy*, he bitterly conceded, and searching for refuge in irony, he added, *I can blend in easily*.

One could hear the beating of the waves on the cement shore, a solitary, obstinate beat which sounded like a clock's ticking. Not the solemn tick-tock of nature, but that of a tormented heart, unable to find any peace. Yet he was wrong: Valentini was a surface that didn't retain anything, just like how bronze statues are hollow on the inside. It was all the more striking now that the sun was setting and Valentini's immobility appeared to be definitive.

'He looks like a monument,' the colonial functionary muttered in a single breath. He was no longer thinking about African flora, but was instead ensnared by an indecipherable image that was both human and inhuman.

Yes, Valentini's black silhouette looked like the monument to an Italian officer who had been forgotten *by history* on the quay – just like how up on the high plains, in the places considered sacred by the Greek colonisers in Cyrene, or in the ancient ports along the sandy seashores in Teuchira, Apollonia and Ptolemais, one only needed to dig a little, *and until very recently*, one could still unearth statues, most of which were mutilated, but whose faces had not been impressed with the wounds and the expressions of pain and horror that characterised their end. *This is why statues are superior to people*, he thought, *their soul is disconnected from the miserable vicissitudes of matter*.

He knew nothing of Captain Valentini's love affairs, given that he'd only known him for a week. Yet amidst the darkness of that heart he could not recognise Francesca's silhouette. It felt to him like a darkness unto itself, inviolable. And this was the Captain's great mystery. He appeared to be out of step with time – indeed, just like statues, the functionary cheerfully thought to himself, pleased with his razor-sharp wit.

Major Carloni was headed in their direction.

'Where are you going looking so pensive?' he asked, despite the fact Captain Valentini had remained perfectly still. 'I saw you with our most learned, pedantic botanist. Has he fallen in love with a flower yet?'

'No,' Captain Valentini said in a distracted tone, 'nature wouldn't know what to make of our feelings: one must be careful of that.'

And all of a sudden, without saluting his comrade-in-arms, he went on his way.

The zealous functionary had kept his ears pricked, but had been unable to pick up any of that conversation. The clock-like splash of the waves on the whitish cement had grown louder, it was the sound of a thousand year old shadow that was advancing to obliterate everything in its path.

17

THE MOTHER

Under a scalding sun that reached into every nook and cranny – like a stream captures all objects in its wake – the funerary procession wound its way through the city until it reached the cemetery, situated along the arc of the lagoon where the tracks for the train that brought people to the Giuliana's golden beaches were situated.

The blessing of the body was carried out quickly: nobody would have expected more, the heat was stultifying.

The pleasantries and formulas exchanged between the bystanders were also brief: having been an invalid for so long, the boy had chosen a terrible moment to leave this world. The plants in the cemetery, parched and yellow, looked to be crying out for help.

It was with great relief that everybody reached the beach. Almost naked, they jumped into the sea as though performing a collective purification ritual. Bright and fresh, the water was in constant flux. It was the middle of the summer, when all life resided in the sea, and not on the flat, arid land, or in the colonial city's dusty labyrinth.

Two people had carried on along the road, until they reached the Monument to the Fallen,[lxxiv] which springs out of the extreme tip of the Giuliana beach, where many years earlier General Caneva, the obscure chief who had mimicked Napoleon's Egyptian proclamations, had landed his expeditionary corps. Atop a short series of steps was a kind of obelisk, at the top of which lay a statue depicting Italy, with a sword in her hand. Inside the obelisk lay the ossuary.

On the rocky promontory, by the monument's shade, the sea breeze blew and slowly rocked all in sight: everything in the vicinity was dry and strewn with porous stones but breathing was easy, as if one's head 'was elsewhere' as Bedendo the pharmacist cheerfully said.

'Death is a cessation of the impressions through the senses, and of the pulling of the strings which move the appetites, and of the discursive movements of the thoughts, and of the service to the flesh.'[lxxv] Doctor Risi declaimed, resting his back against one of the steps leading up to the monument, and then he lingered quietly. It seemed like he was using Marcus Aurelius's words like a sexton or choirboy rang bells to announce to the faithful that the religious ceremony had begun, a re-evocation of a sacred agony: he wanted to narrate the last days of the young man whose body had been buried in a distant land.

One could see the ships in the port, and a little activity on the distant quays, as well as the peaceful white city in the distance. Yet like some paintings which employ a particular perspective,

[lxxiv] Monument to the Fallen: monument built by the Italian colonial government to commemorate the dead soldiers who fell during the war of 1911.

[lxxv] Marcus Aurelius, George Long (tr.), *The Meditations, Book Six.*

almost the entire line of sight was dominated by the sky, which was clear and devoid of movement.

When I got to the little square it was an intensely foggy morning where one stumbled around blind, and Riccardo was stretched out on his bed, with his head tilting down and his eyes closed. The light in the room was still on and the stillness of everything induced a great silence.

He had been found unconscious at the foot of his bed.

Two hours later, I was about forty miles south of the city, on the outskirts of Al-Abiar, where the mother's farm was situated. She lived with a man I did not know.

What happened?

He tidied up his hair, which was fine and red, and seemed to be hiding his emotions. We were under the villa's portico, which had been built unusually well. The windows had double panes of glass, the only ones of the kind I'd ever seen in Africa; but they did nothing to shield one from the cold, although they did keep out the heat and maybe even the sand, which the winds hurled with such fury against the flat land.

I once visited a funerary monument not far from the villa in a deserted landscape; although its traces couldn't be detected at the surface, one is able to go descend down an invisible staircase for a few feet. On the walls of one of these two subterranean rooms is a fresco depicting the death of Polyxena, King Priam's youngest daughter, whom a triumphant, implacable Pyrrhus sacrificed to the flames. Considered against the poverty of its surrounding landscape, it was like a sad dream.

I told her that I had come to fetch her. She moved strangely, as if dancing, but she didn't reply. Then she spoke again: *give me a moment and I'll come with you.*

We climbed into the car. The road from Al-Abiar is tight and dusty, and it felt like I was driving blind.

We entered the city through Berca.[lxxvi] We took the straight road that takes you to Piazza Cagni. That was where Ettore's house was, but his window shutters were closed. Tragedy never knocks on everyone's door at the same time. Then we went along the Corso and up the narrow Via Torino. Finally we entered Riccardo's house, next to the new fish market.

On stepping inside the bedroom, his mother hesitated, and once again she started swaying in that dance-like way which seemed like a substitute for words or tears. Riccardo's eyes were closed. The light barely filtered through the windows. I touched her elbow, but she appeared to be unresponsive. She swayed her arms here and there. But she said nothing. Her bright red hair was the only spark of liveliness in the midst of that gloomy morning.

Did that woman have something immature about her? Maybe her husband's early death, as well as that of her first son had left her feeling youthful: ever since then, she had decided not to see anything, an absence that blessed her with youth. It seems she had wound up at the farm in the way others wind up in primary school. She didn't exercise any control over her son. She never reproached him over anything, maybe out of indifference or desperation, and she knew that he would soon take the descending staircase that others had taken before him. Maybe she noticed that I was observing her. She placed a hand

---

[lxxvi] Berca: now called Sidi Daoud. Southern suburb of Benghazi.

before her eyes, which were a little dilated, just like Riccardo's used to when he was melancholy. Did she fear being reproached? But what did the others know! She looked at her son and tried to stroke his black hair, which she even planted a light kiss on, either out of tenderness or fear.

Riccardo was twenty-three years old. He worked as an accountant in a business firm. The hot-tempered entrepreneur who owned the firm trusted him, but often told him that he took to his work dispassionately. *Sure, sure, I know*, he would say, *he's a little sickly: but that's not enough.* Not that he ever explained what wasn't enough, nor did anyone ask him, not even when he mistreated the pale young man. It was as if he was trying to find where the boy's willpower could have hidden itself inside that weak, frail body.

The fog blurred the contours of things: the windows, the palm trees, the white terraces, and the sky. The mother stood up and went to the window. The same tremor that had affected Riccardo's hands was visible on her hands.

At that exact moment, Riccardo woke up. He curled his fingers into a fist.

How are you?

The tone was very exacting, neither worried nor cold, it didn't seem natural at all. His mother's face was close to him.

Don't cry.

I hadn't seen any tears. But they appeared to understand one another in their own way, and could see things in the other that were invisible to the rest of us. The mother made a gesture, as if she was wiping away a tear. And she asked him again: *How are you?*

Riccardo looked outside the window for a moment. It had just stopped raining. Yet the morning felt heavy. He shut his eyes.

The mother stood and left the room, gesturing me to follow, and so I did.

It's like he's lost all will to live, isn't it? She looked outside the window, as if she was alone. Maybe the likelihood of her son's death felt impossible to her, or perhaps she'd always envisioned it. What runs through other people's minds is also hidden underground, just like that painting of *Polyxène égorgée*.

Riccardo had always been sick, that's true, but he was happy and that's why it's strange that now… This is why I never looked after him much.

She said that she felt estranged from Riccardo, that she didn't know anything about him. Or perhaps she was worried that she would be told everything about him all at once on the spot. This was how she behaved over the course of the following days: she would be on the alert, as if wanting to be told something, and she would always be distracted, as if she never really heard what she was told. It was a drama that had gone on forever. Her husband, an officer in the navy, had died when he was still in his prime, and her first son had died in his infancy. The little vegetable patch of life had been tended to in the valley of death! They were delicate flowers, with tender colours, who had fled into cemeteries.

Then Matilde, the hot-tempered entrepreneur's daughter, came to visit. Four days had already gone by. Riccardo looked like he was sleeping. The mother was next to the bed and her eyes were pinned on him. Yet the light within them was still seductive. She'd been there like that for an hour, or maybe for all eternity, as if Riccardo had always lain in that bed and she had always been there to watch over him.

Matilde entered the room without making a sound. The mother stood up. Matilde said something confusedly in a hurry and then looked at Riccardo. She sat down next to him, carefully. She was behaving as though she wanted to impress every detail in her memory. Maybe it was a distraction, so as to overcome her emotions. Nobody spoke because nobody had anything to say. Matilde took Riccardo's hand in hers. Her lips trembled as she hesitated for a long while before loosening her hand out of his. A pitiful silence delicately settled over everything.

She went out into the corridor, where I followed her.

Four days ago he came home really late. In the morning…

She interrupted me: *Where had he been?*

The mother was standing there on the threshold. She raised her head, upset by the sound of that question, and went back inside the bedroom. I thought I saw her smiling at Riccardo, as if they shared secrets that nobody else would ever shed light on.

Did you ask anybody?

No.

The mother reappeared on the threshold, I don't know whether she was being serious or ironic. We were standing in silence.

Besides, it wouldn't do any good to find out where he was: it wouldn't change anything.

The mother smiled and made a gesture with her hand. Didn't I tell you? It was as if the conventicle in the corridor had been a tribunal that had just dismissed all charges against her. You reached this conclusion a long time ago: there was nothing to look for and nothing to find. It was all right there in front of us: it's easy to see that now. It was as if she'd said, finally!

That's true… Matilde said, *all that happened didn't matter in the end.*

What do you mean, Doctor? the mother asked, as if she'd just woken up or was mocking the whole scene. And without waiting for an answer, she headed off to the kitchen, her hands suspended in the air.

The weather outside looked like it was starting to clear up. Here and there, the fog appeared to be dissolving into a swirling whirlpool that revealed a brighter blue up above. Riccardo moaned in his sleep. I met her gaze. I tried to smile, Matilde looked away. As if his name had been called out, Riccardo woke up.

And then?

Riccardo took her hand: but it was a mechanical gesture.

I said: *And then?*

Matilde was sat on a stool. She placed her hand upon his brow. The mother was watching those banal quotidian gestures with great astonishment, and they must have seemed inconvenient or useless to her. Her left hand was making a strange and repetitive gesture, it was as if her fingers were playing with invisible strings.

How are you? Riccardo asked.

Fine. I'll be better when you've recovered, Matilde said, pointing one of her fingers at him.

Do you love me? I can't see very far ahead. It means I'm not doing well, isn't it?

The mother went to sit by the foot of the bed and in a clear voice she said:

No.

Instead, Riccardo nodded yes several times with his head.

We stayed sitting next to him, his mother and me.

One day, she approached me in the corridor and said: 'It's strange, I was always afraid of making a mistake, of hurting anyone. But who? In the meanwhile, the only person I've hurt is me and even here next to him I feel like a stranger. She interrupted herself. She seemed bothered by the fact she had allowed herself to confide in someone like that.

Do you want some cognac?

I smiled. I told her: *Riccardo likes cognac too.*

We resemble one another, he and I. Even if it bothers us to see it. We live out our feelings furiously on the inside, and this is why we hide them. And then he was so happy, he…

Suddenly, she added: Isn't it true?

At which I replied: Yes, of course.

The last thing on my mind was to heap reproaches on that woman after she had come blindfolded to be put to this latest test.

He was happy, whenever he came to see me…

She made a few incomprehensible gestures. *Riccardo didn't need me. Or maybe he pretended not to. And I had to pretend to believe him. Do you understand?*

I nodded that I did.

Even now he pretends to be calm. As if dying didn't matter to him. Maybe he does so out of pity for me: I've already seen two of them die.

But who knew if Riccardo was pretending. He had reached the end, where the line between wakefulness and sleep grew blurry.

Maybe he had even forgotten about Ettore, given that he didn't ask after him. There was no longer any hope of saving him. Seven days had gone by since the last time he had managed to leave the house.

It was already evening by then. I heard a knock at the door. I went to open it: it was Ettore.

The mother looked at him and then she looked at me. But she didn't seem to know how to ask who it was. Maybe she was afraid that I already knew. She had started to move around her son's room confidently.

Riccardo was unconscious.

The mother was sat on the armchair. Her hands often communicated something, but to whom?

My eyes met Ettore's. Riccardo's breaths were almost unperceivable.

Ettore put his hand to his face. He was making no effort to play a part. He looked at the mother, who looked like she wasn't really there. It was a beautiful evening and there was a sweet warmth to the air.

It was late in the evening at that point. The last evening. No sounds could be heard. The window was shut. It was as if it was suspended outside of time and space.

How is he? Ettore asked.

The mother looked at him, the light in her eyes intact. Ettore noticed that she wasn't paying him any attention. Some time passed. Ettore took Riccardo's hand gently in his and having brought it to his lips, he kissed it: he too now had finally forgotten about us.

But neither one nor the other expressed any grief or pain. I felt as ill at ease there as if I'd intruded on the scene. I stood, noisily scraping the chair along the floor despite myself. I looked at Riccardo, but he could no longer hear anything. I looked at the mother, I looked at Ettore.

As though at a parade, Ettore jumped to his feet. He didn't look awkward at all, in fact he was smiling. There was that sphinx's smile, which Riccardo had so dearly loved. He looked at Riccardo. Then he left, without a word. That silence was as difficult to bear as tears, it was his way of crying.

I went to stand by the window and I saw him walking down the illuminated street. His pace was normal. He headed down a little alley which was always deserted at that hour. He hugged the walls as he walked, occasionally letting his fingers scrape along the stone. An infantile gesture reserved for moments when he felt loose. He never turned around, not a single time. I followed him with my eyes for a long stretch. His pace remained steady and normal throughout.

Outside, it was just like any other evening, since the plants and the stones had already seen everything there was to see: which was why they stopped being sensitive to sadness.

The following day, at two o'clock, Riccardo died.

His wasn't a face, but rather the effigy of a face, like in those funerary monuments. His eyes were open, even though the light which he'd inherited from his mother's eyes had now flitted away.

18

WORDS

He was writing to a reserved, austere person, whom he hadn't met, but whom he'd heard a great deal about, chiefly owing to his inviolable enigmatic nature. He had occasionally spotted him at the cathedral, looking tall and sturdy and strangely respectable at that eleven o'clock mass, where even the colony's Governor sometimes made an appearance alongside his officers, all of whom lined up in a row and positioned themselves on the right side of the aisle. One of the stranger's gestures had always struck him, since it reminded him of his father, whose job it was to take him to church (after he'd been *endimanché*'[lxxvii] by his mother, who instead attended the gloomy early morning service); his father would hold him by the hand, but he wouldn't utter a single word on the entire journey there. He hadn't felt close to his father, who had frightened him instead of making him feel safe.

Well, the stranger, just like his father, had stepped inside the church, stopped, and without even dipping his hand in the stoup, he had crossed himself while bowing his head in humility. While entering the church with his father, he had raised his gaze, and

---

[lxxvii] French: 'put on his Sunday best'.

that gesture turned the world upside down, light and darkness, just like how music reshapes it in its own manner. The father hadn't taken any notice of the boy that was spying on him, just like when the saints, up on their colourful altars, appeared to ignore the human shadows at their feet. In that moment, while he bowed his head, a chain seemed to be emerging out of the shadows, linking God to his father and his father to him through the hand that was clenched in his.

The stranger recalled his father's image: it was for this reason, even though he had never spoken to him, that he was now writing to him. He was asking him if one's faith in God could ever be substituted by the desire for God, to see Him in all His glory, and at the same time to be judged by Him so that one could know, having reached the end of one's path, what direction it had taken. If life was chaos, he wrote, at least one could find the *catalogue* (he chose this word specifically in an upsurge of modesty) of order intact in that supreme Judge.

He had wanted to add that maybe the catalogue was a fixed point concealed in the vast unknown of the universe, but suddenly feeling startled he had stopped: rhetorical figures were deceptive, and his father's stern shadow fell across his writing desk, enveloping it entirely.

It was the first Monday of May, and it was muggy, the lands of Africa were inhospitable. There was constant, blinding waste of light, which instead of making the place look festive, instead seemed to menacingly reveal its true poverty. In the courtyard of the nearby barracks, the military band was playing a march, defying silence in a collective dream, a silence which was as old as the stones themselves, the magical embodiment of time. It was rehearsing its repertory for the annual march to mark the anniversary of the Charter.

The writing desk was pushed up against the window.

Lieutenant Valenzi signed the letter, slipped the sheet into the envelope, licked it shut, left his house – he lived on the narrow and lively Via Zuara – made a pit stop at the tobacconist's, then headed for the mail slot where he slipped the envelope into a red iron box bearing the shield of arms of the Savoy dynasty, turned and lingered for a moment, rapt, as if more words had come to him.

He shook his head and quickly retraced his steps.

He felt as though he himself was an envelope, *without a recipient*, he added, disappointed. The stranger would never answer his letter. Or maybe, he hazarded, the following Sunday the man might bow his head in a slightly different way, in order to signify God knows what, perhaps to please on his behalf or take him by the hand. He intended to keep his eyes on him as he mingled with the other officers, confusing himself amidst that throng of soldiers who had been made almost indistinguishable by the elegant, repetitive game of the uniforms. In the same way that the white marble – which had been lavishly heaped onto the walls, and which had such dark and subtle veins – functioned like a fleeting kind of decoration when repeated across several successive slabs. Maybe he could even remain close to him, since they weren't acquainted. Perhaps, in that holy place, a voice would whisper a warning to the stranger that he would watch out for the man beside him, who wanted to make him his *interpreter*.

It was one of the thousand and one days of limpid skies in Africa, and there wasn't a cloud in sight. Lieutenant Valenzi looked at the sea, which was as restless as life itself, and had a dark hue to it, all the more so in contrast with the spotlessly still blue above. At that moment, in the midst of this pause – from what? – he felt as though he'd been abandoned in Africa. However, there was still the stranger, wherever he was. Maybe he would cross paths with him along the seashore, which he was staring at now as though it were a page; or at the harbour where two columns held the bronze statues of Rome's she-wolf and St. Mark's winged lion (the symbols of colonial power) aloft. Yet he wasn't concerned with history on that day; he felt as though the sea's restlessness was far more eloquent than the city's, which was anonymous and ill-defined. He walked along the white stones that marked the extreme limits of the earth, a path typically favoured by children, who preferred it to the slick asphalt and the cobbled pavements – as though he wanted to make himself invisible by not running into anyone.

Beyond the well squared-off stones lay irregular masses half-submerged in the water, they had been put there to shield the coast from foam-crested breakers. On stormy days, the spectacle would assume epic proportions, leaving onlookers unsure as to whether the sight was terrifying or liberating.

Whenever coastal storms were in sight, the lifeguards on the Giuliana beach would raise their red flags to warn others of danger, as if the town had been besieged by masked forces. The custom of warning bathers had been imported from the motherland, and he knew that, but he nevertheless thought that they gave off a sinister effect, as if those flags weren't regulation signals but rather the flags of other armies and other conquerors, who had come to partition Africa and dislodge His Majesty's army from that boundless continent. Nature had allied itself with the forces of the invisible, and those forces didn't seem to be benign at all. The sight of the bathers fleeing the beach to avoid the storm assumed a comical and sinister aspect of parody, almost as if a carnival were about to begin, yet one from which they – or joy itself – had been excluded.

He was occasionally overcome by a headache, especially if the winds rose from the south, as if the sea were intent on pushing back the earth, and thus detaching the colony from the motherland forever. As a little boy, he'd been unable to sleep when the wind seemed to want to burst through the windows to carry everything away. But he always remained silent and never called out for anyone. Besides, his father never put up with his son's fears, as though the mere act of being afraid meant that he'd been disobeyed: fear had been banished from his robustly ordered world. Perhaps he had tried to please his father by opting for a life in the military – but everything carries a shadow with it, and it is useless to try and detach oneself from it. This was why the secret ceremony in the church, when his father bowed his head, had left such an impression on him: at that moment, even his father would admit that nobody was in control of anything, that we were ruled by a higher power, and that man can never know the real direction of the path he has taken. The game was up for grabs and the game was being determined by other hands, perhaps the Higher Hand itself. Not that these were the precise thoughts that had run through that boy's mind, but life flows like an interminable voiceover on the *enigmatic experiences* of youth. Albeit consecrated to action, the military life allowed one far more hours of idleness than any other profession, just like how hunters can remain crouched down in a forest for long stretches at a time, lurking in wait for the moment to act, which is then lightning-quick.

For the past few months, the winds of war had been blowing, announcing the time when the enemy would drop his mask and materialise before you. Who knew who would send them? That it was pointless – grotesque even – to try and impose extravagant meanings on facts determined by the endless competition among nations was obvious to him, but merely *knowing* this was useless to him. Life unfolded on multiple planes, and what is obvious on one plane can be confusing – or even meaningless – on another. He would keep fighting forever in that endless splitting of personality that he felt was occurring within him as he walked along the seashore, which was almost deserted during those dog days of summer, before growing lively in the evening, when the colonists and the soldiers went out for their ritual strolls. Was he afraid of war? Or was he lusting after it? Fear is a confusing force, you never know whether you're scared or what you're running away from in the present, or whether you're afraid of the future that you're running towards, which looms dramatically into sight.

He was growing impatient with his 'cosmic ignorance' (as he put it, cautiously indulging himself in mystification). He wasn't acquainted with the cosmography of the stars, which could always be seen in Africa and were thus easy to recognise. A sky with fixed stars was as enigmatic as the sea, which unlike the former is shaky and restless, ceaselessly advancing and retreating, as though it was unable to bring the conversation – or *its letter* – to an end. Maybe the sea had been questioning the stars in the sky for thousands of years and hadn't managed to get a single word out of them: this was why he had witnessed sudden outbursts of anger, in the same way that he was tormented by images and powerful forces in his sleep. He occasionally looked at the sea as if it was his mother's lap. Why was that? *Perhaps because it separates me from the motherland*, he thought, *and what keeps us apart obviously also brings us closer together. Re-immersing oneself in the sea in order to rediscover the motherland, in the sense of rediscovering my ancestral home and not some so-called Great Power, which are words that are bandied around all too easily in these troubled times. Yet doesn't plunging into my mother's lap not also mean abandoning life itself: in other words, suicide? Maybe dying, or going into the great beyond, means no longer casting a shadow, thus allowing everything – thoughts, actions and feelings – to recover an unequivocal meaning.*

From the shore, one could spot the cathedral's imposing bulk and its two cupolas: the pride and joy of the colonial government. It was a lousy example of contemporary architecture, he thought, exemplifying an era unable to find happiness in art. Yet the familiar sound of bells, a kind of pleasant wave, appeared to blot out all criticism of the building's quality, which (as that sombre, celestial sound implied) didn't serve an aesthetic purpose.

Sometimes he went out late at night and roamed without a destination in mind. It was his way of giving way to dreams. Occasionally, if he crossed paths with someone, he was asked whether he was on his way back from some secret, amorous meeting. Lieutenant Valenzi would always reply in the affirmative, without the slightest trace of shame, even though he never had a clue as to where he might have supposedly been, just like when dreams vanish into nothingness upon waking up.

His predictions turned out to be incorrect, perhaps he'd made a mistake in never asking his father any questions, feeling crushed by his silence, which it was up to him to uncork. The stranger's reply arrived only a short while later. It was a Thursday, and the day had gone by just like any other, with him giving and receiving orders, the barracks he lived in being almost like a gargantuan projection of a chessboard where a boring game was being played.

On a little piece of paper, the stranger had written out the following verses, which embodied the happy song of one's soul:

Upon a darkened night
on fire with all love's longing
– O joyful flight! –
I left, none noticing,
my house, in silence, resting.

Secure, devoid of light,
by secret stairway, stealing
– O joyful flight! –
in darkness self-concealing,
my house, in silence, resting.

In the joy of night,
in secret so none saw me,
no object in my sight
no other light to guide me,
but what burned here inside me.[lxxviii]

---

lxxviii Opening lines of 'Dark Night of the Soul' or 'La noche oscura del alma' by San Juan de la Cruz, or Saint John of the Cross (1542–1591) a Spanish mystic and poet. Translated by A. S. Kline.

Having finished its daily routines, the military band was marching back to the barracks along Via Regina Elena while carrying their mute instruments under their arms.

19

IMAGES

He had greatly profited from his studies at the Academy of Fine Arts on the historic Via Brera, where he had so distinguished himself by dint of his technical expertise that it had allowed him, once he'd graduated, to scrape a living making copies of various famous paintings at the museum, which kind of took after the Florentine school, and which turned out better than the ones the Venetians produced, owing to his natural predisposition towards clean straight lines in his drawings.

In cahoots with some coevals of his who were annoyed by the innovative ferment of their times, as soon as the horridness of war had evaporated, he had tried to create his own original paintings. *Yet even when he creates his own paintings*, a friend of his mockingly put it, *Amilcare looks like he's copying someone else's, and someone's ugly painting to boot!*

Another comrade said that while technical skill was uncommon, it allowed a patina of coldness to extend over everything, a*nd not in the way Ingres reworked Raphael's paintings injecting them with even more elegance and sensuality – in fact*, he pedantically added – *his paintings look as if someone was* *imitating Ingres's reworkings of Raphael; to put it bluntly, Amilcare is as bad at copying as Ingres was good at teaching.*[lxxix]

As soon as he'd left the academy, he had been quickly forgotten by his coevals, as though he'd taken up a new profession entirely.

Thus, he had wound up in the colony, the well-established refuge for those seeking a fresh start.

He quickly built up a bourgeois clientele who gave him photographs from which he was expected to extract prestigious-looking oil portraits. Almost against his own will, he had become a consummate master of the form. His use of colour (which he couldn't inject with the *luminous spark* of life, as the director of the municipal marching band put it, who painted Orientalist scenes in his spare time, and who only had a few mean customers from the lowest rungs of society and who therefore envied his rival's more distinguished customers) was deemed of secondary importance. What really mattered was that the painting was an exact replica of the photograph, and that its perfect resemblance with the subject was emphasised. To put it briefly, one had to merely replace a photograph's shiny, yellowish back with the nobility of a large piece of canvas and shiny oil-based paints. The backdrop was always generic and the objects, if any were depicted at all, were usually reduced to the back of a chair, or a book, or a walking cane with an ivory knob.

As one would expect, the paintings were always of dead people.

[lxxix] Jean-Auguste-Dominique Ingres (1780–1867): French Neoclassical painter.

'He paints the heirs of wealthy people,' the pastry-maker on Piazza Ammiraglio Cagni said; the young man was one of his usual customers, who always came in alone and at odd hours, while everyone else was busy slaving away in their offices and shops. Just like at the Academy, the unhappy painter seemed like he was always being chased around by a shadow which concealed a mocking demon within it. 'I am the one who projects it,' he had said in an aggravated, bitter tone in front of a Captain who never said anything about his paintings. He occasionally exhibited his work in a photographer's studio, not far from the Piazza. The officer's silence – he lived right in front of the photographer – wound up thrilling the painter, so much so that one day, after seeing him standing still in front of the studio's window, he told him that he would not charge him anything should the officer ever find himself in need of his services.

Captain Valentini pulled a grimace, almost as if it was a nervous tick. Perhaps the mention of money hadn't found any place in that reserved man's plans. The painter was so disheartened by the outcome that he avoided the Captain from that day on. Even though he had invited him into his studio only a week earlier to show him some work in progress.

Why – aside from those portraits, to which he occasionally added a shiny brass plaque bearing the deceased's name and titles at the bottom – wasn't there anyone who wasn't a *cavaliere*?[lxxx] There wasn't a single gallery in the colony, and so he was forced to work from photographs even when copying very famous paintings. The most requested image was that of the Virgin Mary (in the style of Carlo Dolci, Guido Reni or Bartolomé Esteban

[lxxx] Italian for 'knight'; similar to OBE.

Murillo...[lxxxi]), which would be hung above one's bed to keep the evil spirits away. His Virgin Marys were always young and modestly dressed, although they would have easily looked like ladies of the court were it not for the priggish veils over their heads, which added a touch of peasant grace to their expressions.

Those portraits renounced all claims to drama and psychology: *they don't keep me company*, he would say, annoyed.

He often worked from black and white reproduction, leaving him to be inventive with his use of colour (he would use blue instead of the original's pink, or white instead of yellow); easily satisfied, his clientele never even suspected that taking such liberties was so blasphemous, *in primis*[lxxxii] from an artistic point of view (the bearded professor of Classics at the local secondary school who had edited an edition of Ovid's *Metamorphoses* with a verse translation en face commented). Our painter would sometimes think of the visitors who came to Via Brera to look over his shoulders to see whether he was copying out his work diligently; he didn't even know whom he liked best: that new colonial aristocracy or the old couples whose final stages of the journey would only be accompanied by boredom.

Despite the modesty of the way he practiced his art, his preferences were for the great masters of the past, a predilection that was occasionally exclusive and almost paralyzed amidst the subjects of tradition, until in the end he began to take to his work reluctantly, producing poor results especially when his preferences weren't taken into account. Aside from his portraits, where he appeared to be remoulding himself in his dreams (he

---

[lxxxi] Painters.

[lxxxii] Latin: 'first of all'.

was a short, fat, ugly little man with bewildered features, and if in his paintings he tended towards oleography, his face was the complete negation of that style, being shabby and slovenly, 'a wreck' as someone put it) and the paintings of the Virgin Mary which he considered himself a virtuoso of, he loved Mary herself, but only during the most solemn moments of her pure life: from the Annunciation, with the angel bowing before her, to The Entombment of Christ[lxxxiii] (another name for the moment more commonly and traditionally known as the *Pietà*, where the Virgin Mary cradles Christ's dead body).

The city's bourgeois ladies looked at him astonished whenever he explained to them that those were the only moments that inspired him. 'The rest all belonged to Jesus,' he would add, enigmatically.

One of the ladies would usually cross herself, either out of suspiciousness or worry.

As for his favourite artists, his taste had settled on the great Sebastiano del Piombo. Perhaps because the latter employed dull colours, Amilcare's copies of del Piombo's canvases usually turned out very well. In any case, this was the explanation volunteered by some busybody. 'Everything speaks in the dark,' he'd concluded.

He had never laid eyes on the gigantic *Pietà* of Viterbo (which he stubbornly insisted on calling the '*Pietà* of Orvieto Cathedral,' although god knows why that was) with its perfectly limpid sky, where the departing sun has left a reddish afterglow in the background while the moon rises into sight; the Mother, whose pain seems to lack all meaning, is sat with an empty lap.

[lxxxiii] Names of paintings by Caravaggio.

Christ has been left naked on the floor next to her. A photograph he had treacherously ripped out of a book from the Municipal Library, he had settled on copying out the altarpiece behind the Virgin Mary, keeping true to its impressive original dimensions, only to decide shortly afterwards that he would keep the painting for himself. He therefore had a vast piece of canvas shipped to him from the motherland, and once he'd nailed it to the frame, he took to his work. His customers were irked, the photographs of those cavalieri, those respected and well-to-do ancestors, were lying dormant in his drawers. Whenever questioned over the delays, the painter would distractedly excuse himself. On one occasion, one of these clients had slammed the door on their way out. 'He really does fancy himself an artist, doesn't he?!' a construction wholesaler exclaimed.

A few had already jealously reclaimed the photographs of their fathers or grandfathers (female subjects were rare: it seemed that families, like Nations, only consigned the image of their rulers to history, and not their consorts).

Nobody appeared to pay any attention to the large canvas on which the man had been working, as though it had been confused with the wall.

The photographic reproduction was ridiculously small, it looked like a fly in comparison to the vastness of the canvas, and it was incredibly difficult to discern its secrets. Yet the sky had already been painted and the Mother stood out tragically against that void, which is *as deep as the abyss itself* (or so its maker thought).

All that was left to do was to paint the figure of the dead Christ, but the painter was hesitating.

One day he was overcome by the wretched idea to share the difficulties he'd had with a dressmaker who worked on Corso Italia, who had asked him why nobody had seen him around in a while. By the following day, everyone in town knew that Christ had refused to appear before that second-rate house painter. The rumour eventually made its way to him and it wounded him, making his artist's block even more difficult to bear. He no longer felt like staying shut in his studio all the time, but neither did he feel like going into the city: this explained why the odd wayfarer would occasionally spot a short man walking along the boundless plain with no particular aim in sight.

Sure, he also owned a reproduction of that painting, but it was indecipherable, not the kind of blueprint he utilised for his portraits of the dead *cavalieri*.

One day when he'd gone out to buy some paints, he bumped into the Captain, who greeted him with a nod of the head. The painter went up to him, and talking about this and the other, he gave in to his weakness and explained his hesitation. 'Of course, the way the subject has been positioned,' the painter elaborated, 'is altogether indecipherable, and that much is clear even when looking at a poor reproduction like this,' and since he was carrying it in his pocket, he showed it to him, 'there are a thousand details to this body… forgive me, to this *soul*, that I simply can't see them all and don't know how to capture them with my paints. How could I then possibly reproduce these paintings? Could you explain to me how I could do that? Please forgive me, I don't have much of a way with words, but if I had a model like Sebastiano did then at least I could copy…'

All of a sudden, he yelled:

'And by copying I will finally be able to understand!'

He shook his head, atop which lay a threadbare cap, and then he went on his way.

One would see him frequently out in town after that, sullenly idling about, even uglier than before, looking like he didn't know what do with his talent now that it had been definitively defeated – or with himself for that matter.

He dwelled in a modest house along the lagoon, on the outskirts of the colonial city, where the sun seemed to beat more ardently and where the dust, whenever the desert's furious winds picked up, was blinding. He always kept the door open on the off-chance the sea breeze would reach him there.

One day, Captain Valentini appeared on his threshold.

He headed straight towards the large canvas, which he stood observing for a long while, as though searching for his place in it. The black and blue sky had been painted, as had the aggrieved Mother who was clenching her hands together in agony, twisting her torso as she cast her glassy gaze into the distance.

The painter observed his strange visitor, as though he hadn't recognised him. So it went for a few minutes. Then more minutes went by and then some more after that. Until one lost count. It seemed as though the Captain had encountered the same difficulties that the painter had faced, something didn't quite add up. In the end, he hung his head. Just as the painter had told him in a moment of confessional catharsis, only by copying would he be able to understand.

But what? he asked himself.

But he was only talking to himself.

Then he overcame every reserve.

Slowly and meticulously, as though carrying out a duty, the Captain undressed himself until he was naked and then lay flat upon the ground, lying perfectly still, looking forlorn and abandoned, his head leaning against a cardboard box.

Lo and behold, the painter now had his model.

He threw a rag soaked in various colours at the model's hips, according to an old painterly tradition. He picked up his palette and began to prepare his brushes.

His *Pietà* would finally be completed.

20

THE DIARY

The story was well known and it fuelled a great deal of curiosity: a respected industrialist had kept a diary while in the colony. The interest was fed by indiscretions: there were those who said the diary was as long as the Nile, and that the police, who were aware of its existence, were greatly alarmed by it. What would its revelations give rise to? Thanks to his good fortune and versatile profession, which had placed him in contact with every rung of society, what information had the industrialist collected that might – even theoretically – jeopardise the security of the state? What had he written about *in particular*? If nothing appeared menacing about the present – the city was peaceful and beaming with optimism – could its past be considered as such? Had he slandered the good name of Fascism? In any case, that man had tried to capture time, in other words he had left behind an account. It thus posed no danger to the security of the State, but rather it jeopardised the Regime's image in the annals of History, it operated in the realm of the future, which it bent to its will.

The industrialist had lived in an isolated villa on the outskirts of the city, which had lent greater mystery to the entire affair; in his forties, the industrialist was still a bachelor, which contributed to people's inability to categorise him.

Not many had shown themselves willing to read the entirety of the long diary, but there were a great many who were eagerly waiting for the story to take a dramatic turn: for instance the police bursting their way into the man's isolated villa to reveal his hidden face, or learning that the man had run away with some kind of treasure, perhaps absconding in a ship, sailing away under cover of night. They were even prepared to ask the police to intervene and together to let the man go in his way – in other words, they were anxious for the affair to turn into a novel so it could break the sleepy monotony of their everyday lives.

'Diaries are made to be written in, and not to be read,' an aspiring writer declared one day. He was at a café with his friends, the industrious city ground to a halt at seven o'clock in the evening, at which time everyone treated themselves to a stroll along the Corso, or to a cup of coffee at a café, where a little orchestra playfully missed a few notes here and there. A breeze rose from the sea, making everything feel light and removing all meaning from conversations, acting like an agent of time, which swallows everything up. He was explaining that the diary's value lay in the here and now, for the road it covered in the present, for the desire for clarifications that it expressed, for its escape from all that was already known, as well as reflections, games…' whatever you like, but they become real the moment you write them down. Re-reading them is a dangerous adventure even for the author himself. Where once there was life, now there's pointless minutiae. It's a mistake to think that someone writes in order to keep the memory of the present alive – we write in order to give the present a face; but I burn all my stuff right away.'

There was a functionary from the police department with his regulation stiff, black moustache. Having picked up a bit of the conversation, he was irked by the way he felt they had undervalued the police's raid on the gnome's hiding hole: there was nothing but ash – the writing had magically vanished when it had been brought into the light, or rather the present. Yet what value could that manuscript have, which the author had destroyed as if the present and the past, or the present and the future were irreconcilable, and devoid of a common language? Why should the police be frightened by the solitary grimaces of a man staring into a mirror, even if they did occasionally mock the State?

Tarenzi, the industrialist, who had at one time confessed (this was all written down in the file bearing his name at police headquarters) that he loved *abstract conversations*, and had urged his friends to avoid him, out of laziness perhaps – now he was exalting his memoirs, a literary genre which presumes that the text will be read, whereas diaries do not care for their readers. The diligent functionary felt like he was being mocked: first he claimed in public that he'd written a social diary, outside of anyone's control; then he said that the police raid would be too late because the diary was designed to fall apart before anyone could lay their eyes on it. However, then he also added that in the act of vanishing, the diary generates a river of words – and memories – some of which were destined for posterity, while others, the mocking ones, were destined to be confiscated by the police. B*ut will they be reliable memories?* the functionary asked himself, *or will they have been written especially for us, in order to pervert the course of justice?* Not only had the diary been destroyed, but a text was being put together to act as a trap, to throw the authorities off their tracks. The functionary looked as though he was already writing his arrest report, as though he was about to set off to find the fugitive with a spring in his step.

Yet the latter paid him no heed and kept talking and talking: it was as though he was trying to hypnotise the woman beside him, a silly ugly woman. The functionary wondered whether the man hadn't repressed his instinct to mock the woman by instead pretending to turn to that lady as *a figure of authority*. Instead of anger, however, he experienced an unexpected feeling: he too wanted to be like that rich, confident man and worry only about keeping an eye on himself rather than on other people. There we have it: this is the diarist's gold mine: the profligacy of carrying on a conversation with oneself. Yet instead of waning, his mood soured further: envy had forced its way into the mix. That man wasn't jeopardizing the security of the State, he was ignoring it altogether. As for himself, outside of his wretched job, which left behind the disagreeable stench of all the people he controlled – all of whom had broken the law in some form, for one reason or another – what was left for him *outside of the State*?

To be sure, nobody had forbidden him to keep a diary. And he knew so much more about that city, thanks to his ancient profession, than that industrialist and all his specious self-regard.

'A diary exists in a constant state of metamorphosis: I transcribe, make additions…' the industrialist told the roly-poly woman, who had tiny feet, just like in caricatures, which feed off visual contradictions.

If everything constantly changes, how does one choose the right moment to intervene? the functionary dutifully asked himself. Perhaps the fatal page hadn't been written yet, or maybe it had been torn out. The policeman's job was difficult, the relationship with the criminal they're after can often be as complex as their relationship with their lovers. The slightest inaccuracy can lead to fatal consequences, and the cards on the table change entirely.

Now he felt as though he was a hunter in his hiding spot waiting to surprise his prey at the right moment. The image was gratifying and he retained it. He was slightly excited, as though he had reached the end of a long private drama, and wasn't just merely carrying out his duties. He looked at the Corso, which was busy at that hour. It looked like a forest where there were people instead of plants, and that they were moving around of their own volition. Before going out on their evening stroll, people had straightened out their appearance, which endowed the portrait with an unusual elegance.

'Diaries,' the man explained, brandishing his beer mug with an airy gesture (there was always something parodic to his gestures and conversation, which his unusual height accentuated), 'are made up of… personal accounts of one's readings, confessions, echoes of emotional events, amusing anecdotes, scrupulous accounts of various states of mind, hopes and disappointments, reflections and conjectures: diaries must always follow the same rules, just like how rivers flow downwards and incise their beds. The day we'll see a river climb a mountain without keeping to a distinct path will be the day we see a diary that resembles no other.

'Almost the entirety of our lives goes by atrociously slowly. A novel is the work of the devil because it condenses the complex adventures of the Karamazov brothers in merely eight hundred pages. And memories – and this is the point I wanted to make, my dear friend – *are* the stuff of novels: the devil erased hundreds of the diary's pages in which, Ivan's days – all of which were identical – had been narrated with the slowness of destiny. The fluvial Dostoyevsky was in fact rather brusque in the end: these are the tricks of the trade (or, to those who prefer it, the deal one strikes with the devil, where one offers a sacrifice to a mendacious god). Why did I rip up the diary? All of life's exasperating slowness lay within it, not the deceitful pace one finds in novels, which memoirs instead manage to recover.'

To recap, the functionary said, slamming his blue pack of cigarettes down on the coffee table. *This man would have me believe that the diary has been destroyed, as if he'd neatly predicted that I'd want to advise my superiors to order an investigation into the matter: why give me such news if not to deflect suspicion away from yourself? Nevertheless, you've also confessed to writing your own memoirs. And what if reading them turned out to be a labyrinthine enterprise, and what if, having reached the end of that labyrinth, I had learned nothing more about the fat woman hanging on your every word right now, what then?* That man who was keeping a diary, as though he'd wanted to metaphorically confess of having a doppelgänger. That the only liveable reality lay in the imagination, because only in memoirs – and not in diaries, which capture the slowness of life – can one find the same captivating pace of novels, where the immense mess of the Karamazov brothers fit, *barely*, into eight hundred pages. He knew all there was to know about the Karamazov brothers, he had seen a film adaptation just a month earlier where the vast cast had played their roles well…

Because only in the imagination does the poison of life disappear, which is its slowness, its repetitiveness, its near-absence, really…

Maybe by exposing himself to scrutiny, perhaps even to criminal charges, he had wanted to reveal his need for such an imagination, he practiced the art of escapism in order to give his life some respite.

But what did he reveal in the end?

The secret functionary seemed as cocky as a musketeer.

To be a spy, which is a task I've bitterly come to terms with, is the concrete figuration of his dream: I too live in the imagination. Although it is equally true that it is someone else's imagination…

At this point the roly-poly woman rushed to his aid: 'Why are you telling me all this?' she asked. She was wearing a low-necked dress, exposing what was still fresh in her: her ample, candid bosoms.

The functionary pricked up his ears, as though he was at a concert.

'Am I not the protagonist, after all?' she picked up again, not impolitely, as if wanting to hint at something: desire for attention, or perhaps desire itself. 'You look so melancholy…' she added, expertly changing the tone of her voice accordingly.

'Distant,' the man suddenly said, as though he'd just fired a gun.

'Oh,' the lady said, saddened, 'you're a real master at the art of paying someone compliments!'

At that moment, the roly-poly woman's husband appeared, Colonel Nucci.

The diarist jumped to his feet.

'Where have you been?' the lady impatiently asked, even though, the steadfastly diligent functionary thought to himself – she was probably only upset by the fact he'd returned.

'I went for a walk.'

'To mull over what?' she asked him, distractedly.

'The past.'

'That means you must have just stepped out of his diary,' and he pointed the man out.

Who bowed.

The functionary was thinking that he would have liked to live in that diary: maybe his life there would be less wretched and dreary than the one reality had dealt him.

He picked up his cigarettes and walked off in a hurry.

21

THE PALACE OF DEATH

Major Laurenzi had *run aground* in the dusty road on the highlands – as he later humorously told the story sometime after the incident – and his jeep had refused to move in any direction. It was the most fertile sector in the province, lushly verdant and pleasantly wavy; Barca, the historic county seat, was already far behind him, and the valley appeared uninhabited, in fact it looked as if it was unknown to anyone, as if it had been added to the landscape just a moment earlier.

'Do you know why the jeep refused to budge?' he asked, cockily jumping out of the car. 'It caught a sight of the palace of death and it refused to go any further.'

'And where would this *palace* be?' Lieutenant Nerino asked in an alarmed tone, trying to give his question a twist of irony.

They were alone in that place, and the jeep's wheels were as firmly stuck as a dog's legs when it has picked up the scent of danger. Sunset was drawing near: this meant that night was on its way. How could they possibly keep calm when this *palace* was their journey's destination? 'Wouldn't it be better for us to retrace our steps on foot and go back?' he asked, frightened.

There was no hope that anyone would show up on that rugged road. 'That said,' Major Laurenzi humorously said, 'it's quite common in this uninhabited land to wander around like Adam, thinking you're all alone in the world, until you suddenly find yourself face to face with – well, not so much Eve, *alas*, but a nomad, say, maybe even a very old one, who looks like God the Father Himself, who nevertheless fails to tell why he's showed up and what he wants from you; in fact,' he added, 'you don't even know if he wants you to see him or if he wants to pass by incognito, having perhaps grown *weary* of man's stupidity.'

Lieutenant Nerino couldn't decide whether he wanted such a nomad to appear to free him from the Major, or whether it would be better to keep close to the Major, out of fear for the eccentric wanderer who felt annoyed by the very human race which he had created. He was angry with himself for having naïvely volunteered to accompany his superior officer. The latter had hesitated at the time, which in retrospect now seemed perfectly clear: Major Laurenzi already knew that the palace which had terrorised their jeep lay at the bottom of that road. In a sudden burst of good cheer, which proved brief and of little comfort, Lieutenant Nerino asked himself if he too, like the jeep, would fix his legs firmly and refuse to budge further, having picked up the scent of death not far from there.

'We could certainly,' the Major said, 'go back to Barca on foot, despite the fact we can't see anything out here, but we're not so far after all, and there's a colonist's house about halfway back to the town, we'll borrow a bicycle so we can flee f*rom Vesuvius as it erupts*. But this is also exactly why we have all the time we need to reach that palace, take a look at it, and contemplate *le magnifique* *témoignage de notre néant,*[lxxxiv] as the preachers of old used to say. It would really be unforgivable for us to have come all this way and not to take the last thousand steps to the temple – which reminds us of our former greatness, the monument is over two thousand years old, and it also reminds us how insignificant we are, because it's a tomb. War is brewing now and there'll be untold bloodshed: and alas, none of us will be given a glorious burial. Despite the heroism we might collectively display, we may well even lose this boundless land where we wound up some thirty-odd years ago. I don't think we'll find shelter or burial even in the works of poets, like unlucky Hector did, that's how Monti[lxxxv] called him, or Tasso's[lxxxvi] heroes, on both sides of the Crusades, who found so much gloomy sweetness in their eloquence: in the future, poets will mock militarism, they'll sing loudly of pacifism and a universal harmony where the hero has been marginalised. If the Creator has grown weary of humankind, the Muses are equally tired of the cults espoused by today's scribblers: they too emigrated, but not to Africa, (an exterminated space), like we did, but to crammed, dusty libraries.'

Lieutenant Nerino was anxious: he wanted to run away to Barca, abandoning the Major who insisted on proceeding on foot and the jeep which had been immobilised by terror – in order to find some proper shelter before darkness extended itself over the

---

lxxxiv Author's note: French: '*The magnificent account of our nothingness*'. Source: *Jacques Bénigne Bossuet, Oraisons funèbre de Louis de Bourbon*, (Oxford: Oxford University Press, 1851). p.270.

lxxxv Vincenzo Monti (1754–1828) an Italian playwright and poet who translated Homer's *Iliad* into Italian.

lxxxvi Torquato Tasso (1544–1595): one of the greatest poets of the Italian renaissance.

plateau. Major Laurenzi had dragged him along as though he'd hypnotised him with his chatter. That's what authority was: the power to make others walk along dangerous roads! It was merely the reality which the knightly epics had once described, even though he only nursed a vague recollection of them, he hadn't opened a book since he'd left school behind, and he had never imagined that he would himself be a teacher – or an enchanter, or the devil himself – in the garb of a superior officer in the silent lands of Africa where there wasn't a trace of paper in sight. Just like in those long epics, his will lay bound on chains, and nobody would come to free it. Nothing was headed his way except for the night, which was limitless in Africa, where not only the sky turns pitch black, but also the pain, the vast expanse where terrifying knights might make an incursion.

'Can't we postpone the visit to another day?' Lieutenant Nerino jokingly asked, his military dignity preventing him from showing any fear: least of all to a superior officer! The jeep belonged to a mechanical world, which, like the animal one, could plunge into the depth of cowardice (and leave them stranded in that deserted land!); but a man, a soldier, had his duties: he had to be heroic, defying both death and its palace – otherwise, what was the point of wearing a uniform like his?

'Look!' Major Laurenzi exclaimed, and in an instinctively defensive gesture he barred the young man's path with his arm.

Lieutenant Nerino raised his eyes and for an instant, perhaps having succumbed to cowardice, he saw nothing at all, there was only a brownish mound. However, *mirabile dictum,*[lxxxvii] right at the foot of the mound, almost carved into the rock, one could

---

[lxxxvii] Latin: 'remarkable to say'.

see *the palace*, which was a tomb on two levels 'from the Hellenic era,' the Major explained, 'or at least,' he added, as if wanting to throw a veil of reassuring uncertainty over his words, 'that's what Professor Berioli told me. Come on, let's go up.'

Although no longer in his prime, that man quickly clambered up the mound and stood facing the tomb. As the light began to fade, he appeared to grow more impatient, or at least that was Lieutenant Nerino's impression, who had in the meanwhile regressed to a state of infancy.

He once again experienced the temptation to flee, but he couldn't budge: he too had *run aground*.

'What are you waiting for?' the Major asked.

Frightened, Lieutenant Nerino clambered up the mount after the Major, as if he was the latter's ghostly child, and poking his head through the aperture between the two Doric columns, he stepped inside the atrium, where there were three stone triclinia lying next to the walls; through a door at the far end one could enter the sepulchral section of the monument, where the sarcophagus containing the body was located, inside a niche. Major Laurenzi – with his creased field uniform, his bristly beard, and his marked features which were suddenly muted – seemed to have stepped out of that tomb at that moment in order to greet a visitor. Caught between his split personalities as a boy and a young officer, Lieutenant Nerino was as frightened as if he'd been called up for an initiation rite to mark his passage from adolescence to adulthood and virility, so he tried to strengthen his resolve and kept quiet (or rather he tried to make some ironic remarks), but it was useless. The Major was altogether elsewhere by then; the present was still, but the past had begun to move, and the past is a night without end, as inscrutable as the dark sky.

It was up to Lieutenant Nerino now to prompt the Major to speak, the silence felt like the other side of the night. The Lieutenant remembered that divinities are always authoritarian and mute, as though they are forbidden to speak.

But these were nothing but idle fantasies. Finally, the Major said:

'Let's go upstairs.'

They found themselves on the loggia, between the three Ionic pillars, side by side once again, as night proceeded to fall, having turned silent and gloomy now too, struggling to spread itself fully over that vast, deserted continent.

The loggia was empty.

'Lean against the Doric columns on the first floor,' the Major explained, looking as though he'd just returned from a trip and was once again cheerfully chatty, 'they're quite stocky,' he added, as though exhibiting the structure to a group of assembled scholars.

Lieutenant Nerino couldn't free himself from the Major's mental grip – which meant lingering in a deserted loggia on the upper floor of a palace carved into the rock, 'towards the end of the sixth century,' as the Major had declared, all the way out there in a place where they hadn't seen a single house, aside from the sepulchral abode they had holed up in. He felt as though he were standing in a field facing an enemy who had challenged him to a duel – and his enemy wore the Major's face, which was nevertheless a mask.

Is this what the colony is really like? he asked himself, frightened.

A couple of hours later, they reached a white farmstead, where farmers from the Veneto, who had emigrated to Africa the previous year (having taken advantage of the government's grandiose scheme for reclaiming and then freeing up the land which they'd purchased at such a dear cost), welcomed them with warm obsequiousness and surprise: wanderers never came around their parts, especially at that late hour of the night. 'Africa is empty,' they said. 'A Major! A Lieutenant!' They wanted to run off and help them un-beach their jeep, but the Major, assuming a fatherly tone and demeanor, cheerfully calmed them down: 'You can't very well carry the jeep on your shoulders, and anyway, by the time you brought it back here, we would have easily reached…' and he made a gesture, shaking his hand in vague manner to indicate wherever Barca was, 'and so we should be off.'

Nevertheless, the old man of the house declared that he wouldn't allow them to leave, under any circumstances. He said that he would send his son on his bicycle to Headquarters to let them know that they were 'safe'.

And he showed them the modest, but clean and tidy bedroom where they could sleep.

The Major accepted without any hesitation, which took Lieutenant Nerino aback. It was as though he was in no hurry to get back to the present, to his ordinary life. Having left his heroic, knightly poems behind, he now appeared to find mental shelter in the realm of pastoral fables. He would have wanted to tell him so, but he was scared of his superior officer's skill with irony.

He struck up a conversation with one of the farmer's boys, who was his age, and it felt reassuring to hear the Venetian dialect, which made Africa's boundless spaces feel far more tame and gentle.

Over dinner, out in the courtyard, the Major remained in high spirits, and didn't appear to be ill at ease among those simple folk.

To whom he told a colonial fable.

'Once upon a time there was a deep-sea diver...' Major Laurenzi began, apparently winking at Lieutenant Nerino, yet when the latter reciprocated with a complicit smile, the Major's face bore no expression at all.

Lieutenant Nerino's cheeks reddened: he hadn't winked at him, but at his peasant audience who saw nothing unusual in him using the age-old opening formula of all fables. 'The ship had been at sea for over a month, in the gulf of Sirte, where rich beds of sponges lay at the bottom of the seabed, which were difficult to get to. The diver never risked those waters without his suit, in the way ancient warriors never faced their enemies without their shining armour. The knightly ceremony has found refuge in secret places, often out of sight, and are only usually practiced within the solitude of the mind, which the marine seabed is a metaphor of: the invisible is the safe-haven of the adventurous.'

The Major's complex eloquence seemed to Lieutenant Nerino to be an ironic allusion to the difficulties of rhyme which had been virtuosically overcome by the old epic poets: telling a story is an art form, and it shuns all obviousness, even what's natural. The simple folk, he thought to himself, were well versed in *the art of listening*, which doesn't know what do with the pretense of wanting to know everything about everything, as if everything were intelligible to man. Within the audience's patience lay wisdom, reality also comprises what is incomprehensible or ineffable, without which, perhaps, even what we do know would lose all meaning, or might only retain a miserably thin patina of opaque meaning.

He experienced a moment of irritation because the thoughts which the Major had *passed off* as his own were merely the scraps of a conversation he'd had with the Major a few weeks earlier at the officers' mess hall.

'Having gone ashore on the docks of the port, the deep-sea diver kept his eyes peeled and looked around himself, looked at the long road that opened up before him, and the three alleys that spilled into the piazza. He pushed his gaze further running along the port's half-moon, then lifted it towards the sky, looked at the piazza again, then fixed it on the ground.'

It was as if the story had just ended there, because the Major had stopped speaking.

However, the audience was in no hurry, they were used to the narrator's slow rhythm, which *maybe is as slow as the seasons*, Lieutenant Nerino thought to himself, trying to flee into his own wit.

'The diver's movements were lazy and calm, he kept to the slowness that would be forced on him by the water's resistance once he was submerged in the sea and descended to the bottom. The same slowness affected his thoughts. He looked gigantic. The slowness of mind was matched by a surprising determination in his actions. Always usually impermeable to the events taking place around him, and plunged in a kind of torpor, he mulled on his impressions for a long time, and they re-emerged only when he would have thought they'd been forgotten, and having baked in the depths of his mind, his thoughts were incomprehensible to everyone else.'

Lieutenant Nerino asked himself if those simple folk were really managing to keep up with the Major's story, and as if answering his own question, he felt a surge of satisfaction: whether Major Laurenzi had taken any notice of it or not, he was clearly the *most capable* listener in the audience. Yet those simple folk might have naïvely formed their own images in their heads in order to better illustrate the story – in fact they might have given the main character some definition, because there wasn't much of a story at that point. He felt a kind of envy and longing for when the Major, over the course of that long afternoon, had spoken to him and him alone: *that is unless he was really talking to himself then too*, he thought to himself, irresolutely.

'It was two in the afternoon, and the city had been forced back to sleep by the scalding sun: it crept into every nook and crevice, as if it was water trickling down. Roughly cut stones paved the square, with wide cracks between them, while dry, dusty plants, with little lymph left in them, lingered immobile, as though they'd been suspended along the way.

'There had to be some cool places, a little restaurant with a shady arbor, rooms filled with a light, breezy air.

'His companions had quickly found a street to walk down on and had vanished. Instead, he had just lingered there, patiently and calmly – as if he had found, in the abstract serenity of the sky, clear of the clouds which had marred it over the previous days, in that port where the size and magnitude of the waves appeared to have been arithmetically fixed, in the heavy silence overhanging the piazza, or the alleys, or the low, white houses – a kind of compliance: in the same way that while marine seabeds have to be explored slowly, and everything does indeed move about, nothing actually escapes, because all available space has been taken up.

'He wore faded blue trousers and an open white shirt which revealed his taurine neck, whose veins, thick as rope, slightly protruded out of his skin.

'Right at the end of the avenue which began at the piazza, lay a house on a corner which had collapsed years earlier after being shaken by an earthquake whose epicentre lay far away, in one of the islands of the Aegean. Instead of falling into itself, the edifice had given way in only a single place and it had been turned into a pile of rubble. He remembered that night: it was a full moon, and the stones appeared to have been dematerialised, made somehow lighter. Two nearby palm trees, which had been struck by rocks that had been hurled farther, and by the pieces of broken plaster which had filled the sky like confetti – had acquired a carnivalesque shape, with branches that hung off the top of the trees like sleeves. The night was limpid, in the calm after the sudden upheaval, arcane and thick – just like the seafloor.'

The Major had begun his story calmly composed, his hands resting on his knees, whereas he now appeared to want to physically illustrate the story, leading his hands to fly here and there, telling the same story, but not in synchronicity with his words. They were simple gestures, while his words had been carefully chosen, as though they were *destined to wind up on a page*, Lieutenant Nerino thought, who was once again trying to flee the situation through the door of irony.

Perhaps he had smiled: an old woman had glared at him sternly, as though she'd caught him being distracted during prayer.

'There was an inn in front of the house, and all the sailors knew of it. Even he preferred it to all the others, and at one point he had even been the innkeeper's lover.'

The narrator paused.

'I knew her too.'

Lieutenant Nerino was shocked: was he telling a story or accounting for actual events? Was he looking to increase the story's plausibility by giving it a touch of reality? He was disappointed to notice he was the only person in the room who seemed interested in that question. The audience was quiet and patiently awaited the narrator to resume his story: it seemed that as far as they were concerned, the narrator himself was a character in that story, and the various planes of reality blended in with one another, intertwining. Irony was of no help in these situations, just like in tragic situations. Was this a tragic situation? Not at all, they were safely sheltered inside the farmhouse, and had been welcomed with obsequiousness and human warmth by that family and its sing-song accent. *What constituted a tragic situation?* he asked himself. *Was it doubt? Was it the advent of the invisible? When we're pursued by death? Or are we still inside that palace, where I stumbled and fell on the floor inside that upper room, am I just dreaming up the Major's story and everything he's been saying?*

'She too had vanished,' the Major carried on, 'She had either fled or died – the inn by then was frequented by sailors who knew little of the city's stories, which were so long. She had liked to joke, the innkeeper, once upon a time – when she used to make fun of his colossal frame, when she would see him crouch as he climbed up the stairs in order not to hit his head on the steps of the staircase above his head, when it looked like he was swimming his way up the stairs.

'That staircase must have still been there, somewhere in that city, but getting there would have meant navigating such a maze of little alleyways that he wouldn't have been able to reach it. And what would it matter if he found it anyway? After all, the innkeeper would no longer be there waiting for him, to accompany him up the stairs while he bent his back so as not to hit his head – stairs which she could climb while keeping straight, while flapping her arms about to show him that she could barely touch the overhanging staircase above them with her outstretched arms, like a bird mocking a fish who while being able to slice through water, can't rise an inch above its surface.

'The innkeeper's skin was a ravishing white, and under the perennial shade cast by that staircase, she looked like a child of the moon.

'The game of flapping her arms about pleased her inordinately, and she never tired of it, it was a trait of the uncorrupted childishness that still dwelled within her. Yet the deep-sea diver also enjoyed that game, and he would pretend to bang his head in order to hear her laugh. The silvery peals of her giggles seemed to pour through the cracks of an invisible world.'

The Major is the deep-sea diver! Lieutenant Nerino suddenly thought, as intently as though he'd just shouted it out, and such was the passion within him that he felt he was being lifted up in the air, the spell having been broken. Nobody paid him any mind: only the old woman noticed the blush on his cheeks, and slowly, wearing a sad, maternal expression, she stood up and poured him some wine, which the Lieutenant proceeded to gulp down, as if he'd just been offered a magic potion: freedom and oblivion.

'On the day the house on the corner had collapsed, the innkeeper had made a few desperate scenes because a man was moaning in his bed, and nobody had managed to reach him so as to help him, he's done for, the doctor had said, passing sentence, and his relatives had just stood there looking miserable and dejected, only she had kept screaming.

'Life occasionally places certain situations in our path,' the Major said to the Lieutenant, as if they were now sat at a café in the city and the peasants from the Veneto had just disappeared, 'where any reaction you may choose will prove ultimately inadequate. The man's relatives were on the side of reason, but songs know no reason: that woman was singing a sorrowful melody, and since our ears distort sound, it was said that her scream had sounded like the yell of a wild beast. When pain and pity are deep enough, sound is indecipherable – *don't you think*?' he added, with a tone of banality that debased the entire conversation.

Lieutenant Nerino cheered himself up: he hadn't been the one who'd fallen asleep and had started dreaming, instead it had been the Major – who was talking to himself, this was why his speech was so ornate, just like the kind employed by heroes in tragedies, or by their visible shadows – the actors – as they recite endless monologues.

'Perhaps the innkeeper had wanted to flee – from the world, naturally,' he added, turning once again to face Lieutenant Nerino, with a sharp tone in his voice, devoid of any emotions, 'she was screaming like someone who had started to run, but misfortune hounds us at every step, and at some point it overwhelms us, only to one day turn around and embrace us: it's death, our death.'

The Major performed a strange gesture with his arms, as though he'd wanted to stand up but hadn't managed to.

'Much has changed in the time since these events transpired. The colonial government has devoted a great deal of attention to that part of the city behind the docks: buildings were torn down, land was reclaimed, the ground was swampy, and right where Piazza del Re is now, with its festive-looking Hotel Italia and its shady gardens, there was once a sinister kind of square called Piazza del Sale.'

It was as though the Major's only real preoccupation was to give his Lieutenant updates on how the city had evolved, given that Nerino had barely been in the colony for a couple of months.

'Everything is indirect and allusive, luckily we've been blindfolded and we soldier on with the certainty of sleepwalkers.'

A pause.

'And woe onto us should we ever wake up – *what do you think?*'

Every time that he had been called onto the stage by his superior officer, it startled Lieutenant Nerino as if someone had just shoved him.

'The deep-sea diver, whom we'd lost sight of, despite him being so big, thanks to thoughts inspired by the innkeeper's skirt,' the Major remarked with a cold smile on his lips, 'was standing still on the clearing in front of the jetty, understood that awful events that shouldn't have happened anyway… – a child who had died because of a simple chill, or that hunchback whom everyone in the city had talked about, who was miserable because he was a hunchback and who had become a murderer because he was a hunchback, having proved incapable, at fifty years of age, to take the step that would have inevitably saved him, that of coming to terms with being a hunchback…

'The child had died because he'd caught a chill: all that was left to do was explain *how* that had happened, and *why* that had happened, was it a quirk of fate or a Heavenly design – or had it actually been a case of murder, like people insisted.

'Everyone knew the deep-sea diver in that city because he had saved the life of a man at sea, when the current had dragged him far away from the shore, and nobody apart from him had had the courage to jump into the water and rush to stare certain death in the face. Instead, he had reappeared carrying the saved man in his arms. People always asked him *how it had all happened* meaning to whom or what had he placed his trust in before jumping into the sea: in his own strength, in his own courage. God?

'That instance of heroism had left him feeling utterly indifferent, as though the moment belonged to the nearly-drowned man rather than to him, who had just randomly happened to be nearby.

'The boy who had died from a chill was the child he'd had with one of his cousins a decade earlier. In that distant village of his, people said that the woman had rid herself of the child because she didn't want to be with her cousin anymore: he scared her. She didn't think of him as gentle, but rather as intensely wrathful. She had given in to him out of fear, and she'd ended up having his child.

Then she'd gotten rid of that child and had run away before he could come back. She wasn't scared of the man's cruelty, but by his silence: she feared his silence the way little girls feared the dark. The cruelty of that murder could never be explained without the mention of that old fear, which the deep-sea diver's presence had reawakened. That monster belonged to the night, and nobody has ever been able to contemplate the entire expanse that it unfolds over.

'It seems that the rumours regarding that murder were credible…

'Perhaps the deep-sea diver felt no nostalgia for dry land because he didn't have anyone there, no emotional bond tied him to his distant country and to ports like ours.'

One doesn't suddenly stumble upon death, rather it grows silently within us: while we cautiously peek at the future, it has already gained possession of what we're trying to cheat from it, meaning almost everything. Having slowly emerged amidst his memories, this thought insinuated itself into the story.

'He had reached the end of his destiny, the only certain path before us.

'A stranger, he looked around himself: here was a shore similar to many others – new and empty. Which explained why he hadn't disappeared down an alleyway along with the other sailors as they chased after their desires, but had lingered immobile in the middle of the square, like an enormous animal who'd been ripped from the water, rather than had walked out of it of its own volition.

'Once they'd returned aboard their ship late at night, worn out, looking rougher than ever, his comrades found him immersed in a kind of torpor.

'Someone tried to mock him, but to no avail, given that there also hadn't been much conviction behind the jest.

'They fell asleep with the bothersome image of the comrade who hadn't walked into town with them, an image they could not for the life of them decipher, but which had nevertheless been etched into their memories, clouding over the entire night's events: the dives, the wine, the girls, the smoke, the bitter and comical fistfights.'

On the other end of the room, a little boy began humming a nursery rhyme from the Veneto, it sang of innocence, of a springtime that followed the story's winter.

Lieutenant Nerino felt like an acrobat walking a tightrope.

At that exact moment, the door noisily burst open and the messenger who had been dispatched on his bicycle came in, holding the bicycle by its shiny handlebars. It was a dusty *Bianchi*[lxxxviii] of which he was inordinately proud: he announced that Headquarters in Barca had been notified – *and that everything was all right.*

lxxxviii Make of bicycle.

22

LITURGY

The first reaction had been panic, which had been intensified further by the surprise and incredulity attached to it. While the faithful were keeping their gazes fixed on the altar, an abyss opened up in the ground, as though Beelzebub himself was about to emerge, and all eyes turned towards the portal. The Bishop presiding over the solemn ceremony, who was a pious man – and whose name, Candido Moro,[lxxxix] was in fact a complete oxymoron – stopped dead in his tracks, astonished. Why had everyone turned their heads in the way the wind bends an entire forest's branches to its will in a storm – why were the faithful parting to make way for someone, *who was coming?*

Although everyone looked at him, the man wasn't looking at anyone. He strode forward with certain steps, which in itself

---

lxxxix Translator's Note: Spina's choice of names for his characters throughout his stories, particularly in this middle section of *The Confines of the Shadow*, borders on the mocking. Candido, the Bishop's first name, can be interpreted as either 'candid' or 'white,' meaning that when coupled with his surname, Moro, can mean 'White Moor'. There are a few other notable instances throughout, for instance General Occhipinti whose name literally means General 'Painted-Eyes,' which is appropriate given his theatrical inclinations.

made quite an impression. What was the Bishop waiting for, why wasn't he ordering someone to do something? But who would he order – and to do what exactly? Could he call the police and ask them to intervene? If he placed his faith in the forces of law and order, what would become of his religious authority or the sacredness of the setting? Had anyone ever heard of the police arresting Beelzebub or one of his minions? Could the police manage to get all the way down there? And who would take them there, who would act as their guide? In fact, who would save them? And what about the organist! Why was he still playing as if nothing at all had happened? Yet while the entire scene had been turned on its head, the organist hadn't stopped playing his devoted, strident notes – hadn't he understood that tragedy had just stepped onto the scene? The organ was like a star, like the sun or the moon, which allowed its light to fall onto the earth, indifferent to the dramas of human affairs down below.

The first part of the tragedy had unfolded in public. One of the city's wealthiest men (and one of its haughtiest too, even though he was also a philanthropist) – 'who was arrogant with the arrogant and humble with the humble,' as his friend the Bishop put it – had been the victim of an incident which had ridiculed him. His wife had betrayed him with their handsome doorman, a tall blonde man who kept to himself, 'the kind of guy who looked like he should be a forest ranger,' or at least that's what someone had said – even though it wasn't clear as to why forest guards had to be tall and blonde, and why if that was so, had he come all the way to Africa which was devoid of all forests and was nothing but dry and dusty? What would he protect these non-existent forests from anyway? The sky was devoid of clouds the whole year through.

An affair was both extraordinary and banal, and it never managed to slip out of that perverse entanglement. What stood out about this instance was that victim didn't have a jealous nature: it had never even occurred to the man that someone might dare to challenge him, especially challenge his place in his wife's heart (a buxom redhead, who was nevertheless rather dull). He was fond of his forest ranger, and even thought of the forest ranger's son as his nephew. He could come into his rooms whenever he liked, and he'd been more indulgent towards that brat than he ever was towards his own children, his numerous dependents or his fawning friends.

His arrogance was served by his reputation. While he wasn't afraid that his wife would cheat on him, everyone knew that he wasn't a faithful husband, since the success he'd had with other men's wives was well known. To put it briefly, he was an envied man, at least he was envied by many, and public curiosity, when news of the affair broke, was mixed with a certain schadenfreude: a rich man who takes a tumble 'is as funny as a clown,' the same man as earlier had said.

How had the lovers been discovered? The blonde, tall, solidly built forest ranger was a man of 'stony discretion' (we'll continue to call upon the aforementioned reporter, whom for the purpose of briefness and according to tradition, we shall refer to as *Anonymous*). His wife had been the only one who'd revealed the affair. To her friends? Not at all! In a fit of folly – 'amorous folly' Anonymous pointed out – perhaps because she'd been neglected or rejected, or maybe just to shatter the silence of that man, her lover, who always seemed to be as silent as a mute (it seems he acted without ever expressing any desire or tenderness), she had gripped a pistol in her hand and had fired it. During the scuffle (the details were still vague, the incident having occurred only a few days earlier, and the interrogations were still ongoing), a shot had been fired and the woman had been wounded. Repudiating her fit of folly, the woman was now vilely claiming that it had been the forest ranger – a good for nothing who kept harassing her – who had fired the gun.

The young man had been arrested.

He remained silent, always: he never accused her and never defended himself. Yet he was also careful not to confess to anything. Perhaps he 'had acted in legitimate self-defense' (as Anonymous suggested). Even the arrogant man was staying silent: having been questioned by the police over the incident, he had behaved in an irritated manner, as if he'd been nothing more than a casual witness.

Now (as the drama continues to unfold) faced with her husband's silence, the wife, who found silence 'nothing short of upsetting' (again, Anonymous's words), and this despite the fact her husband hadn't thrown her out of the house or slapped her around, experienced yet another fit of folly – human events always follow the old plots of plays in puppet theatres, it's always the same old song – and thrown herself out of the window. Everyone asked himself whether her husband had been the one to push her. Nevertheless, his alibi turned out to be unassailable: he had been taking care of business at the Banco di Roma when the fatal hour had struck, and had been sitting in the bank manager's office, where two secretaries were also present, although one of them (the elder of the two) had pointed out during her deposition that the man (and this had left a sinister impression on her) 'was already dressed in black.'

Nobody had paid any attention to the fact that during the ceremony in the cathedral, among the many assembled children waiting to be confirmed was none other than the forest ranger's son, who was a chip off his father's block – also blonde, tall for his age, like the rough sketches a sculptor produces before the monument is actually commissioned.

The cathedral was teeming with the faithful and the curious, and the ceremony was solemn. Of a slight build, the ancient bishop's vestments were white and azure.

Maybe no one had taken any notice of the boy because people were interested in the drama involving the family in question (Anonymous again here) rather than the forest ranger's actual family, which merely plays an ancillary purpose in the drama. As for the boy's mother, she had concealed herself in the crowd: How could she present herself publicly at that ceremony only a few short days after the tragic incident which had shunted her to one side, as if her husband had been the doorman of the building across the street?

According to the liturgical canon, the boy had a godfather, just like all the other boys. A friend of the jailed forest ranger, the simple man now experienced a great deal of pity for the boy, who seemed like an orphan now, having been humiliated by an incident that he understood even less than the baffled police investigator, who was standing there now with his hands in his pocket, and it seemed that nobody was able to impress upon him the fact that one couldn't stand in church with one's hands in one's pockets. Nevertheless, he didn't seem to be understanding anything at that moment. He felt hurt 'and contaminated by his father's silence, which made them look even more similar to one another' (Anonymous, as ever).

The *place* of the father figure in the boy's mind was actually taken up by two people, and this felt so natural that he had no idea of what an anomaly this was: could he have ever imagined that they would come into conflict, that one of the two adults would wind up in prison, having been thrown into it by the other – who was nevertheless still the victim? Whose accomplice was he then? How could he forgive one for having offended the other, and how could he forgive the other, who'd been indefatigably indulgent towards him, but had nevertheless punished the offending party, who was nevertheless his father? The world had been broken, just like when a ball is punctured and you can't play with it anymore. Needless to say, no one asked him anything – but there was nothing left to ask.

The priest who was preparing him to receive his holy sacrament had told him that he needed to believe in God, who was his real father. But the boy now seemed to fear even that distant – in fact, invisible – father. Employing a smile that was meant to be reassuring, but which was chiefly inspired by pity and indulgence, the priest was explaining that God… was the summation of both his fathers. The boy stood there glassy-eyed, as though he hadn't been listening at all, or was instead hearing terrifying voices.

The threshold of the master's house, which lay on the other side of the courtyard a threshold that existed for others, but not for him ('like a kind of wind-up carillon that keeps going forever, playfully and magically,' Anonymous pointed out, 'the boy crossed the threshold in whichever direction he liked, whenever he liked, since elves laugh in the face of rules!') – had now been barred to him, just like it had always been to all postulants and the multitude of pestering salesmen: the house in front of his no longer existed, and neither did his father's, while he was in prison waiting on the pending the investigation. *Pending the investigation*: that mysterious formula had shattered the world he had lived in up to that point, and while still very young (or so Anonymous said), the boy already had a past which had fallen into irretrievable depths, 'just like the old,' Anonymous had added. The curve of his life had already reached its peak and was descending towards its inevitable precipice. Yet where was that supposed to be, exactly?

The priest had told him that if the master's house was now off-limits to him, the house of God had now opened its doors to him, and that's what the holy sacrament truly meant, that he had been welcomed into the house of the master of the whole universe: after all, why would they have called the ceremony a *confirmation*? There was nothing in the boy's eyes, as if he was cut off from everyone else, from himself too. Not even in the house of the Celestial Father was there room enough for both his earthly fathers, who had fought a mortal duel: nothing now would contain them, no space would be big enough, an irretrievable 'organic duality'[xc](Anonymous).

For what reason had they fought that duel?

The object of the drama, the mistress who was always a little distracted – who had welcomed him with a smile, who had

---

xc Most likely a reference to Goethe's 'dualism in nature,' whereby nature was a manifestation of the divine, 'Gott-Natur'.

played with him, chattering endlessly, but in whose heart lay two different men – the object of the drama had vanished into a hole and the entire city, eager for a spectacle, had turned out for the funerals. He had run out of the house in time to follow the funeral procession, although he lingered on its fringes, out of fear that he would be recognised. The master was leading the way, ahead of everyone else, even both his sons were in the second row, that place rightfully belonged to him and he had taken it up publicly, neither bowing his head nor looking anyone in the eye. After all, the forest ranger currently in irons (or so Anonymous said) was actually standing right there alongside the master, 'which explained why they couldn't look at each other, even the ranger forsook all masks and challenged his rival openly. That woman was his; and he's as invisible now,' he added, 'as he was mute in life.'

The boy understood that the rivals had fought over the remains of that woman, which were now cold and lifeless. Who would win that struggle no longer mattered, because in his mind the lines between them could no longer blur, and they would never be smoothly interchangeable again.

The road to the cemetery was long and dusty. The boy would have wanted it to be longer still. In fact, he wished it would stretch out into the infinite: to a point from which there would be no return – because going back to the past was impossible. Instead, it grows cold and is buried forever. Even if his father had been released by the police and had come back, the threshold of the master's house would no longer be open to him, in fact it was barred forever. In fact, they would all have to leave their own house. And go where?

For the first time in his life, the boy felt that his father's mutism, which had hitherto been dear to him, as though they'd always been able to communicate without words, suddenly struck him as tragic. But maybe his father himself had once experienced a ceremony of the kind he was witnessing now: when you throw away what's left, the remains ('which are nothing but disconnected fragments by then,' Anonymous pedantically pointed out, who often weaves his own reflections into the boy's narrative), because the game is over.

Let us return now to the ceremony taking place in the cathedral, having been called back there by the sweet sound of the bells that melts in the air (*ein sanftes Glockenspiel tönt in Elis' Brust Am Abend,*[xci] as the poet said, or so Anonymous claims).

The unexpected apparition of that eminent man had shocked everyone. Why had he come? His sons were all grown up, they'd been confirmed ten years earlier. They had grown up to be rather different than him, they only resembled him physically in a vague, dull manner. They dressed meticulously well, as if attempting to balance out their father's unkempt appearance: there was a scruffiness to him that was the unintended fruit of his arrogance. 'And who do they resemble then?' a lady had once maliciously asked him. 'The future,' he had gloomily replied.

Was it really his intention to draw all that attention to himself? Had he decided to avenge himself?

The cathedral was bathed in light, as if it was an open space, and the white marble intensified the light as it bounced off it. It

---

[xci] The poet in question is Georg Trakl and the line translates to: 'A gentle chiming of bells rings in Elis's breast'. Alexander Stillmark, *Poems and Prose by Georg Trakl: A Bilingual Edition* (Northwestern University Press, 2005), p.45.

seems that this sacred rite also followed the seasons, and from the *gothic* winter of the North's cathedrals, where the ceilings vanish into darkness, it had now come down to the sun-drenched coasts of Africa for its prolonged summer.

While the man continued to walk ahead in his solemn gait, carrying with him his secret will, and the mass of faithful undulated, the Bishop remained perfectly still; he was a little pale, perhaps, but his white and azure vestments, which were sumptuously embroidered, hadn't lost any of the light they were reflecting. He had intuited that the man had not come to avenge himself. *But what had he come to do then?* Maybe it was the people's fault, since they had parted to make way for him, as though he'd been holding a gun, attributing so much importance to such a banal event, namely the arrival of that notorious and *wounded* man in his church at that late hour, on his own. But was this reason enough to interrupt that sacred ceremony?

The organ's notes were coming from behind him (having emerged from a modest mechanical organ), but they nevertheless climbed high towards the ceiling. Yes, it's true: while he had indeed stopped playing, the music had carried on performing its sacred function of its own accord, heeding the word of different priests.

There was nothing to fear. In fact, his taut expression betrayed what appeared to be light. The priest is meant to guide his flock, and when that beloved flock is confused, he alone should not quiver.

It was only at that point that all the assembled faithful noticed that the prisoner's son was among the semicircle of children waiting to be confirmed.

As though he'd just suddenly appeared at that very moment.

Given that the police couldn't be called on to intervene in a church, should the bishop therefore order the officers – who were present in their shiny uniforms, standing alongside the right side of the aisle, as though they too were performing a sacred ritual – to step in? Yet had those officers entered the church fully armed? To top everything off, there was the problem of how to keep public order – 'of course,' Anonymous said, 'that was only the tip of the iceberg' – there were other, more complex problems.

Somebody later said that the forest ranger's wife, who'd been living on the outer confines of this particular drama, had raised her hands to her face when she had seen that eminent man step inside the cathedral. The boy had remained mute ever since the drama had started, as if his voice had been kidnapped. Amidst tears that morning, the boy's mother had told the wounded man much the same. 'He's mute, mute… ever since that terrible day!' it was if someone had ravaged his soul.

Now, she had invoked the All-Mighty to give her boy his speech back; just like the priest had explained, those wanting to be confirmed needed to find their strength in faith…

'Yet how could he have expected,' or so Anonymous said (it should be noted that from hereon in, his narrative avoids many malicious or cynical little details) 'how could he have possibly expected that God would work his mysterious ways through the victim?' Because that eminent man, who was wealthy, yet nonetheless a cuckold (an aside which for once doesn't belong to Anonymous, but which is reported here to give a little flavour of what others said), crossed the length of the entire cathedral, as though he were officiating the ceremony himself, and before the assembled citizens of that colonial town and the devoted faithful, he placed his hand on his favourite nephew's shoulder, as dictated by liturgical law.

The corridor in the middle of the crowd had closed up again, and the music resumed its narrative, and the Bishop's face was serene once again: the friend he'd always esteemed had followed his orders, since one goes to church not only to be forgiven for one's own sins, but also to forgive those who have sinned against us, especially if an innocent soul is involved in the situation.

He made a wide, definitively sweeping gesture with his arm.

He had once seen a sculpture where Christ, looking modest, is sat down, wearing his threadbare tunic, and has placed his hand on John's shoulder, who is sheltering a small boy against his chest.

Imitation is the highest form of elevation, he thought.

Then, having thanked God for having illuminated another soul, he picked up the thread of the ceremony where it had been left off, aided by the exalting music which overwhelmed and erased, before the eyes of the assembled crowd of waiting little devils and little angels – all those miserable human vicissitudes from the air.

23

AT THE SCAEAN GATE

1940

The Teutonic dream seemed to be drawing nearer: 'The gates of Paris have been flung open,' Major Carli said when they were already back in their bedroom.

'And to think,' his wife said, 'that I've been dreaming the exact same thing for years now: it's true, we wanted to go there by train, but the Germans have gone there with their cannons: that said, they still got there before we ever did!' she angrily concluded.

She was wearing a pink nightgown.

'It's a matter of organization…' the Major said. An athletic man, even if only of slightly above average height – hairy as a monkey, as his wife put it – and with a baritone-like voice. 'Well, now you'll see how our Duce, the giant, carries us there himself: war is at our gates.'

He was wearing flannel pyjamas with blue stripes on a bed of white, and his feet were bare.

'Our heralded entrance into the war. But what are we at the gates of?'

The curtains had been parted to make way for the tranquil, African night.

'At the gates of what?' the Major replied, stretching his arms. Yet it wasn't a sign of resignation, in fact he looked like he was concentrating, gathering his strength, like a diver before his great leap.

'The abyss.' she said.

'So what will *the outcome of war* be?[xcii] Will we really WIN like all those gloomy graffiti on the walls are saying?'

'Maybe we'll end up winning by accident,' the Major replied, while scratching his back. 'The outcome of a war is sometimes as uncertain as an opera's opening night: maybe the soprano will hit all the wrong notes, or the crowd might be in a bad mood.'

His wife pointed her index finger straight ahead, even though there was nothing there, and the wall in front of her was bare, nothing except a few old cracks.

'Divine Providence seems to be in a bad mood, and it'll take this patch of Africa away from us, and we'll be tossed into the sea: back from whence we came,' he concluded, rotating his raised arms.

'If we lose the war,' the Major said, his voice made hoarse by tears – he was a fine actor – 'what will upset me the most is that I'll become a prey for the victors, possibly some English lord.'

'Oh, no, no: I don't like them one bit,' she retorted, with a touch of disdain.

'I can't for the life of me imagine who his successor will be…'

'You're such a fool,' Carolina said, tugging at her husband's hair, bending his head forward and planting a kiss on it: 'it'll be your own ghost.'

[xcii] Lines spoken by Amneris to Aida. Verdi.

'Of course… feelings are important – but so are our senses. Do ghosts have senses? Do you know if they do?'

The Major switched off the main light: the bedside lamp was already on.

'Ghosts inspire so many upsetting images that our minds experience an orgasm, or something like that – all explanations concerning ghosts are a little confused.'

'So,' the Major said, grabbing a hold of his pillow, 'does that mean we won't need beds anymore? Dear me! What I *don't* like about being dead is how little space there is inside a tomb – where people are placed on their own,' he added, disconcerted.

'You always complained of our little villa, which to be fair isn't much to look at – and here you are mourning its loss already…'

'The villa itself may not have been much, but look out of the window and see how vast the sea is, look up at the sky, even though it's gone dark already. What will I look at once I'm inside my tomb?'

'Are you afraid?' Carolina asked, clutching her husband tight to her.

'Dunno, *afraid*… When an actor belts out a speech, thundering about how he's ready to die for his homeland – for an ideal, for his faith, for his wife or his beloved, or for honour – I instead wink at him conspiratorially in the dark: maybe he's afraid, but he's reciting those verses – or bits of prose – with such conviction that I, well, I believe him, while he doesn't even believe himself. Together we make up a hero: but it takes two of us.'

'So I must have two men… to make a single one?'

'I see no homeland other than our conjugal bed, where you are, Carolina – and I'm ready to defend myself from my enemies right here instead of out there in the colonial desert!'

'Am I worth all of Paris, darling? Tell me.'

The coupled remained locked in their mute embrace.

'That said...'

'I like my private life,' the Major said, pointing his finger at himself, 'which I would manage any which way I pleased.'

'I'd like to hear you talk like this when we're out strolling along the shore,' Carolina replied, stroking her consort's hairy chest with the flat palm of her hand.

'If we win the war, Divine Providence will clear out path,' the Major said, making strange, mysterious gestures, like priests sometimes do, 'and we'll make this into our biggest and richest colony, even greater than Rome's Universal Empire.'

'Will we have to talk in Latin?' Carolina asked in an alarmed tone, laying her head against her husband's navel, or *the centre of the world* as she put it, whereas it was an obligatory pit stop in her explorations of her husband's rugged body.

'I like dreams with lots of sounds in them,' the Major explained, feeling a little ticklish.

'At the opera, all you need are a few feet on the stage in order to recreate a castle, a city, or even the entire universe: why can't we be happy with our little slice of Africa, why must we have it all?'

There was no answer.

Carolina insisted:

'Why do we have to enter the war? Let others take care of it. I would be happy to make do with this bed right here.'

'You don't mean to suggest you want to deny the Duce his triumphal entry into Paris!' the Major exclaimed at the top of his lungs, as though he was in the barracks at that moment, and was addressing a regiment.

'Oh, right, the Duce – all our destinies are in his hands. Oh my god, Ettore, he's your rival: are you going to kill him?'

'Shh! There are spies everywhere.'

'Under the bed?' Carolina leaned out and looked at the floor, where there was a cheap carpet, from Monza.

'I'm not willing to betray my oath,' the Major declared with bitter conviction.

Carolina squeezed herself against him, desperate.

'And what if *everyone* betrays him, darling, then what will you do? Will you betray him too?'

'Sure, but I'll laugh about it too.'

'Everyone will laugh!'

'Not at all! There are always heroes *of freedom, democracy, good, evil, dreams, mud…* but they always espouse something.'

'And what do you gain by laughing about it?'

The Major held his wife's dear, tiny face in his hands.

'Dignity, Carolina,' he said, with a firm tone, 'I like the heroes who leave for war a little later than the others, reticently, as though they were scared, whereas their brothers march off, ardent with enthusiasm – who then quickly fall back if things start to go wrong, and who do so slowly out of fear they'll get pinched and forced to foot the bill.'

'You mean: in order not to have any regrets.'

'If our bodies understand one another, it's because our minds paved the path.'

'Don't forget about the heart,' Carolina said, slapping her bejewelled hand on her husband's chest, just like in those paintings of manneristic nudes, all the jewels were fake though. The Major often said that he liked to clutch Carolina's thin wrists until he could almost feel them snap. 'A pure pleasure,' one of the ladies present during one of these confessions said. 'What do you mean 'pure', my dear lady, what do you mean by 'pure'?' the Major had replied, almost screaming, convulsing as though he were rowing.

'That said…' Carolina reflected, 'it seems truly miserable to be running after the Germans to get to Paris on time: I would have preferred to get there by train, which tend to go fast enough as it is, but not as fast as bombs, and I would have preferred it if we'd paid for the ticket.'

'Paying for your ticket in today's world means paying *in blood*! Do you mean to suggest that we are preparing to commit a shameful act? But this is exactly what goes on at the stock market: everyone chases after the most lucrative companies…' and the Major raised his arm in the air as though he were a stockbroker.

Carolina shrugged her shoulders.

'You don't seem all that sure to me, the comparison is a bit forced…'

'You know, there are stories, events, characters, nations, worlds…'

'All right: and then?'

'…that drop into our individual lives like novels. Now our lives have been thrown into a novel that is greater than anything Tolstoy ever wrote and is bombastically entitled *The World War*.'

The Major sniggered. He had a healthy set of teeth, all white and strong.

'So long as they leave us our conjugal bed, darling, even if our bed won't fit on a single page!' Carolina concluded, dejectedly.

'The World War will be like the wind in the desert, it will sweep away everything in its path, carrying clouds of sand that it'll deposit wherever it likes: and I am only one tiny grain of sand among many…'

'This metaphor's a little flat too.'

The Major shrugged.

'You're a demanding reader,' he muttered.

'Highly demanding, darling, just like in between the sheets, *chéri*. Where I'm never disappointed.'

'One must go to war the way one goes to the opera: you must imagine that it's a musical fable. Who goes looking for meaning and logic in operas? What meaning can one of Beethoven's symphonies truly have?'

'Do you think they've started to play symphonies at opera houses now?'

'How would I know? After all, you never took me to Paris.' Carolina complained, peevishly.

'Why don't you run off with the Duce? If you do, you'll be there by tomorrow, and the Führer will be the third wheel, as if Paris was a seedy hotel and the Führer its doorman. But our bed is worth a lot more than Paris, just like Balzac's city is infinitely richer than the modern city we see today.'

'Here we go! Again with Balzac…'

'All you need to do is think of yourself as a character in a book and you'll never be able to get out of it. *The World War* is a novel in which we've been trapped: our destinies are inside its pages.'

The Major switched on the radio on top of the bedside table. The sounds of a well-known, heart-wrenching song began to spill into the room: *One day you'll come back a …* – which was almost immediately interrupted so that an announcer could read out the following public announcement:

'At this great moment in our Homeland and Nation's history, it is necessary for foreigners and the unmindful alike to realise these simple and definitive facts:

'First, for the past eighteen years, Mussolini's Italy has conducted a peaceful political agenda – obviously, necessarily based on protecting its own interests – albeit one that was based on a far superior outlook on Europe's problems and interests.

'Second, Mussolini's agenda was either directly or subversively opposed by both France and Great Britain. Their opposition, which has been so petty and small-minded, lasted for the entirety of these eighteen years.

'Third, when the Italian people asked for lands to till, they were offered deserts instead. When Mussolini said that he wanted to resolve the Abyssinian question, they called it a bluff.

'Fourth, everything that is Italian has been ostentatiously devalued by both the French and the British, both in our internal politics as well as on the international stage. To hear the French and the British speak, the Italian people should have been dead and buried for the past eighteen years. Yet today, by God, the Italian people are more alive and vital than ever before!

'Fifth, the Italian people have reached the end of their patience. Things have gone too far: enough is enough. The Italian people destroyed the Habsburgs…[xciii]

[xciii] Author's Note: *Gli Annali dell'Africa Italiana,* Volume 3, Issue 3.

'However…' the Major said, and with a single motion, like slashing at something with his sword, he silenced the radio.

Silence re-emerged, like a shadow.

'I'll do my duty in the war – even the most stupid of men manage to do that, thereby at least reassuring themselves if no one else.'

'Don't stick your neck out too much, don't overdo it.'

'If I run away when the shots start firing, will you welcome me in your arms?'

'I would always prefer to see you running *forward*. I don't care for watching men's backs!' Carolina added, screaming this time. 'Darling, do you remember that time when we were ready to set off for the *ville lumière*, and then, because of your mother's pneumonia we had to settle for Ancona instead and were so gloomy about it?'

'Are you looking for gratitude?'

'Not in the slightest: but…' and she swayed her head as though following some tune, 'we're stuck in a circle, your every movement is matched by mine and the distance never varies.'

'By circle you mean our conjugal bed, right? You know, all the other officers think that victory is in our grasp – and it'll be lightning-quick too: *three months at the most*, the pessimists say.'

'You can't rule out the enemy committing suicide, for their own, enigmatic reasons. If they kill themselves, we'll take their place and rushing over we'll yell about how we've won. What is truly embarrassing, however…' and here Carolina lowered her voice, speaking in a hushed, confidential tone: 'is that at the same time that a Germanic tribe is invading Gaul, we the August Roman Empire, resurrected by the Duce, *are running after the barbarians instead of defending our transalpine province*. What atonement will be demanded of us as a result? How will the Roman Emperors welcome the fallen down in Hades?'

'The guilt will add to the frozen depths of the North, where we cannot take root, the sun makes us perpetually innocent, it washes our sins away like the confessional.' the Major remarked, stretching.

'You know… what I'll miss most when you're gone is having someone to talk to – with either my mind or my body,' Carolina added, stroking her slender foot against his misshapen one.

'But you'll hear of extraordinary tales.'

'You seem impatient to leave for the front. Are you getting bored here with me?'

Carolina distanced herself from her husband. The latter tentatively approached her and lay his head on her navel.

'Our libretto is our bed. All that's left is *obedience*, Carolina, the act of delegating one's destiny to others.'

'But that means you're a Fascist, you want the Duce's will to guide your destiny, you want him to take care of everything.'

'Except making love to you.' the Major said in a tender tone.

A pause.

'These pyjamas, your nightgown, they're screens and cloaks, they turn the entire scene into a labyrinth.'

'I get the feeling that even when it comes to music you listen to it as if you were winding your way through a maze.'

'Naturally.'

'You can't undermine everything I say by claiming that it's obvious,' Carolina said, spitefully switching the radio on the bedside table on again.

'*...the Italian people are the best judges of their own interests. All the Franco-English efforts, which to this day have tried to set themselves up as paladins against Italian aspirations by putting forward the various pros and cons of the situation in our new Europe, simply cannot be taken into consideration. The Axis of Rome-Berlin will dictate its own peace with the sharp blade of its victorious armies...*'

'That's right,' the officer commented, dismissing the voice and switching the radio off.

Then he scratched his knee – which, during one of her gatherings with her friends, Carolina had called *rock-like*.

'Talking helps to colour everything in: words trigger metamorphoses, like songs do.'

'Oh... the power of artists: they make the libretto unintelligible by overlaying with sumptuous, seductive sounds. Why is every libretto so wretchedly gloomy – including the Duce's speeches? Do you love me, Carolina?'

'Who would I talk to otherwise?'

'With my *mute ashes.*[xciv] Or rather, my deaf ashes,' and here the Major raised his voice, 'when I die I don't want to hear any speeches or chatter at all, not even the victory speech in Piazza Venezia.'[xcv]

'And what about me?'

'Oh, we'll let our bodies do the talking. As for our ashes, their intertwined shadows will talk to the darkness, and they'll dance for all eternity.'

[xciv] Author's Note: 'mute ashes' or 'cenere muto,' from 'In morte del fratello Giovanni'/'On The Death of His Brother Giovanni' a sonnet written by Ugo Foscolo in 1803.

[xcv] Square in front of Mussolini's headquarters in Rome.

'A fine thing to say, but just how do you produce shadows in the dark? The metaphor doesn't work on an *optical* level.'

The wind, which had been blowing harshly all afternoon, carrying clouds of dust with it, finally died down.

'How silent the night is, even the dogs are quiet. What could that mean? Are those dogs' oracles heralding extraordinary events to come? Caesar's death? Or is it that even dogs know when war draws near, that it will break out on the following day… and so they sit staring at the moon in silence, as though they wanted to run off to that distant satellite, and once there, start barking at the hubbub of war shaking the Earth down below?'

24

EVERYDAY LIFE

'And so, you'd like me to believe,' the journalist said in a mocking tone, slipping a finger through two buttons of his shirt, 'that there's a stylish sort of society here in the colony which celebrates the ritual of endlessly complex and varied conversation, that life for Europeans here in Africa is like being in a theatre, and that it has the same intensity, levity, rhythm and liberty…'

'I don't want to convince you of anything. I'm not a government spokesperson – I'm often my own worst spokesperson anyway: I pretend so as to conceal what would be useless to say, what others haven't understood, or in order to throw my interlocutor off his tracks and thus free myself from the situation. Occasionally, however, in order to honour my interlocutor, I engage in a conversation that isn't futile, where reality is condensed so as to make its true face perceptible.'

'Judging by the people I have spoken to, I've heard nothing but obvious truths, good sense seems to be firmly at the helm here; rather, it seems to me that you, as the narrator, are placing complex, difficult words directly in the mouths of whichever characters come to mind – which does not mean that it's not *good*.' the journalist added, bending his torso to one side.

'Shakespeare already tried that…' said the officer who was sat with his guest in the little garden of the villa on the leafy De Martino Avenue, which led one straight to the bridge before the Giuliana beach and its shandy shore: it hadn't rained in months, and even the plants had acquired the yellowish colour of sand. 'Why do you complain about all the banalities they utter, or about the fact that I try to avoid them; about all those who slyly simplify life while I try to search for truths, even if, it's true, I do so staking some claim to elegance, which really simply means modesty and reserve when you get down to it, so as to use it when – just to make an example – horror stumbled onto the scene?'

Paunchy but quick – like the servants in ancient comedies who were ubiquitous and yet incapable of perceiving the drama at hand, let alone respecting it – the journalist furtively snuck a glance at the officer, whose features were angular, his uniform spotless, his gestures thrifty and his voice cold and emotionless.

'Do you really think I could print such things in a newspaper? They'd laugh at me,' the journalist said, and in his crumpled white linen suit, he became the first to laugh.

'And I would laugh at them,' the officer replied.

A bricklayer, who was busily repairing a roof on the other side of the street, was singing. In actual fact, rather than singing, it seemed as though he was trying to recall some tune: he would ardently launch into a note only for it to flatten out a few moments later, as if the music had slipped away and had blended in with the stillness of everything under that implacable sun.

'What sets the colony apart is that it seems to have been subtracted from the passage of time itself,' the officer said as he watched the bricklayer balancing himself atop the roof while humming that song's fleeting notes. 'It's as if the entire colony was a waiting room, but waiting for what? For history's train to pass through? It's easy to answer such questions like that: but is it really true? Looking at the people here who are waiting: they spend all their time talking about nothing, and being so punctilious about it – look at them, they let themselves be led alternatively by banalities and ideas, and are always swinging back and forth on their mental seesaws.'

Given that the officer was speaking while looking directly at him, the bricklayer fell silent and stopped to return his gaze. He couldn't hear anything, but he was intrigued by that man who talked so much under such a brutal sun.

'At times… it was truly marvelous to lead a regiment into battle and plant the tricolour in the mysterious heart of Africa, even further than the ancient Romans had ever dreamed was possible, while the French and English empires waited to crumble. At times instead I wished that I would be chased out of this wretched colony so that the English and French could take our places here, as if those perishing empires weren't big enough as it is. I surprised myself thinking about running off in a miserable fashion, with the rolled-up tricolour under my arm. Regardless of the war's outcome, the Lombard peasant knows if he is going to survive the storm, like a plant he'll still be there, in the green, familiar plains of his fathers. But what about the colonist?'

'So, to put it briefly, you think of the colony as a game of roulette: it's certainly exciting,' at which the journalist emitted a sound, which seemed like a whistle, as though he were at a stadium.

'What do you mean, *exciting*?' the officer asked, disinterested in striking a familiar tone. 'Here in the colony, the government's speeches are even fierier than in Rome, as though we were in the front row. There's a collective passion at play here, among the people who came here from all parts of Italy. Yet conversations also carve their own paths, which can be arduous and solitary – we live in a situation of privilege and latent doom, so we sit and question ourselves, find the humour in everything, ironise, running away and chasing ourselves: it always seems like everyone's in a hurry and at the same time that nothing ever changes, because metamorphosis isn't accounted for in the rules of the game, whose only outcome is either complete control or utter ruin. This is what I was trying to explain to you last night.'

Alone in that deserted café, as midnight drew near, the officer had told the journalist a number of war stories, taking meticulous care with his details while the end lay always just out of sight. The hotel gave out on the public gardens, and tables and chairs had been arranged along the street separating the two, creating oases that were reclaimed from the light. Aided by his accomplice, wine, under the sway of the African night – which levels everything in its path – the journalist had listened to him attentively. Now what he had been told struck him as vacuous: *how could any of these stories be of possible use to me or my readers?* His good sense had taken its leave thanks to the fairy-tale-teller's efforts, just like in the plays of old. The morning's blinding light had made everything appear both improbable and ridiculous.

'Don't you like the metaphor of the waiting room?' the officer asked, after having poured himself a glass of orange soda; he was in his forties and tall, with a hint of authoritarianism to him. 'Think of all the preparation that goes on inside a dressing room, before stepping out onto the stage and giving shape to the invisible, the unacceptable. There are places where reality seems delirious, ironic, dramatic, and utterly spurious… choose whichever adjective you like. But it is within these nooks and crannies that reality, true reality, really lies. It's abundantly clear that this colony… is one of these places. Its very premises are unreal: we are treading a land that doesn't belong to us. Everything else necessarily flows from this flawed premise: the boorish *colonist*, who is disdainful and violent; *the functionary*, who has confused his control over such a vast space as license to build a new world; *the philanthropist* who wants to reshape Africa… I, on the other hand, feel entirely crushed by thought of all that space, by a history that monotonously dragged on through the millennia, by the absolute absence of any trace of the past over the entirety of certain regions… – Africa is a metaphor for the Temple, for a God who either takes everything away or destroys it.'

'But no!' the journalist exclaimed, rising to his feet and pacing back and forth; he was wearing brown shoes, which were caked in dust. His face had a reddish glow to it, the African sun left an imprint on all things. 'If I felt any pride here it was precisely because of the optimism espoused by the people here, which burns far brighter than in the homeland, no city on the peninsula can claim to be as ardently Fascist as this African town.'

'Which is an optimism I share,' his guest said, appeased. 'Reason tells me that we will *triumph*. But the heart follows its own path, telling me base, sorrowful stories.'

'Are you worried that I might be a spy, sent to report on your defeatism by the higher authorities? This is why you talk so prudently and *vaguely*, privileging metaphors over statements?' the journalist, whose name was Gigli, asked him irritatedly, laying his whitish hands on the cement table.

'If you want to fool yourself into thinking I'm afraid of you, then *soit!* I'm at your disposal. Everyone invents their own mythology, with their own angels and demons: life grinds to a halt without fictions. Perhaps you too have begun to succumb to the colonial aversion to reality. For those who love the arts, reality doesn't matter outside of how the imagination is able to recreate it: meaning that the arts are a science of the possible. The colony represents a possibility of an art of living: given certain artificial premises, we drive inevitable consequences in our favour, and all together we run to the end of the road, or rather to the end of many roads. Last night, when we were sat in that deserted café, I was trying to inform your vision of reality: rather I was trying to warp it under the pretext of trying to redeem you from it. Are you after *information*?'

The officer hesitated. But then he picked up his thread again:

'You've chosen the wrong interlocutor for this, I'm keen on… *deformation*. Do remember that the Greek theatre, which lies at the root of our civilization's wordsmithing arts made ample use of masks, which are a metaphor for deformation: only in such conditions can one lift the veil of reality, or of t*he possible*, the world granted to us mortals. Up on the plateaus lie the sublime ruins of the ancient theatres, you should make sure you visit them. When you sit on the bleachers of Cyrene's amphitheatre your gaze descends towards the valley below and a little further along lies the vague glimmer of the sea. All that awareness takes is a simple gaze across that valley: but you don't want to shed light on any real bonds and connections that would be too much, a lawyer could do that…'

'Yes, or a journalist,' the other ironically remarked, who after experiencing a moment of mimesis with his interlocutor, appeared to have regained possession of his former self, and had planted his feet firmly in reality again – and he had resumed his seat, crossing his large legs. Once he'd returned to the homeland, his friends would doubtlessly enviously ask him about his African adventure. He had experienced any adventure, he might as well have written his articles while comfortably ensconced in his house in Milan, situated on one of the side streets off the historic Corso Magenta. Yet he had met his doppelgänger in Africa: who wasn't his spitting image per se, but rather his speculative double, with whom he would inevitably fight a duel – not over control of the world, but instead over his imagination, meaning a different kind of narrative.

'What will you do when war is declared?' the journalist asked him, leaning his torso forward and aiming his large, sly, banal eyes towards the other: he appeared to be fighting against himself.

'At that moment, inside the psychological theatre which we all feed inside our heads, the uniform I wear will become the character that leads to the turning point in the drama: and the uniform will urge me to do my duty, *a soldier true and brave*,[xcvi] as the poet once said.'

[xcvi] Author's Note: from Goethe's *Faust*.

'So when it comes to the decisive moment you'll be on the side of the colonial optimists then.'

'That's exactly right: except that the colonist is out for victory, whereas I… in Russian novels, conflicts serve to expand our self-awareness. War has now become the immemorial archetype of those novels, and… it crushes everything in its path, just like dreams do. It too hurriedly and violently forces someone to know themselves; in this optic, the external events of a character's life, amidst the sinisterly all-encompassing fray, is nothing but the shadow of a process of growing self-awareness which nevertheless never leaves any traces on the scene. After all, in ancient times, heroism – at a time when individual physical prowess could prove decisive – was nothing more than a metaphor for this kind of inner journey.'

'Meaning that war has been downgraded to the category of passions!'

'Don't you think that's enough?'

There was a pause, as if the conversation, which was awkward and arduous, had momentarily faltered.

The journalist was the first to resume.

'Is there anything you would like me to say in my article?'

'I don't understand the question.'

'Look, at this point… it seems clear to me that you're not the dreamer, I am: maybe it's because I've drunk too much – or maybe I got a sunstroke, or I'm tired, or I'm under a spell… who knows – but maybe I fell asleep and in the middle of my dream, an officer from our present appeared to *translate* time for me in his own fashion. I don't know if this image is leading me towards temptation or salvation, or if that encounter means that I too have given myself over to defeatism, or whether his presence actually makes me flee from such a thought with horror: as if I'd conjured it all up simply to avoid it, as if my journey to Africa had planted some doubts even in my head, and all I did was give those doubts a face – meaning yours – in order to be able to chase him – or them – away definitely.'

'The uniform decides things for us in the way destiny does for others. We swore an oath.'

'There you go talking about *destiny*: I don't know whether you think of it as an anchor or a curse.'

'Why couldn't it be both?'

A pause.

'The mind is like the natural world: it retains everything, grinds everything up, and welcomes everything in. It is only our behaviours, our way of appearing before others in the world that seems to reveal the presence of choices, of characters, or of a unique way of being in the world.'

'You seem to be condemning form and conduct, whereas last night, when you described our dinner companions once they left after talking about such trite things, you seemed to be magnifying their importance.'

'When one's personality falls apart, form is a levee that holds back the floods: if a fire breaks out in the bleachers, you seek shelter on the stage.'

'Here we go again, back to the theatre: you're obsessed with theatres.'

'The stage is the traditional setting where irony flowers, sometimes into sublime shapes. Careful, though: I'm not talking about ironic conversations, which we celebrate with such pomp on the stage. It's that the mere, simple act of *making theatre* belongs to the world of irony: what could you possibly make up that could ever be more ironic than an opera theatre? Stories involving puppets and madmen: that said, how many wonderful things have been said thanks to those ridiculous premises, to all those fixed conventions that were both unacceptable and yet solid and well-defined. Well, by that logic, the colony, an unreal place, a land stolen from other people, where nothing at all justified our presence, where we've hatched sublime schemes that are possibly destined to vanish along with the rest of us tomorrow, is a stage, par excellence. Treading these boundless, deserted boards are the drama's lead protagonists, the soldiers: the colony's guardians, who are here to defend it, to increase its greatness, although tomorrow we will be the ones who will be pointed out as the ones responsible for out defeat – that is if the war is nothing but a trap. What about us, do you think we should sitting around talking with a Milanese shopkeeper's specious sense of calm? Who's been there forever? He was a shopkeeper yesterday and he'll be a shopkeeper tomorrow, right in the same square patch of earth, even if the homeland relinquishes all of its colonies in Africa, even if they end up cursing the day they ever set foot in Africa? The colonists here – and especially the officers, who are the supreme figures of authority – cannot afford to be frivolous with their banality because banality in Africa was not expendable.'

'That's what you say: I've spoken to colonists who were very pleased with themselves, in fact they were quite *arrogant*.'

'The imagination of the African colonist farmer has nothing of the avarice of their counterparts back in the homeland. The mere fact of living in the colony has allowed them to reinvent and rediscover themselves: there's something alluring about an illiterate colonist who says he's come here to bring civilisation to the natives. He's clearly a saint.'

'Or a buffoon!'

'Is there a difference? We abandoned all sense of measure back in the homeland, here a doppelgänger takes over for you: he's more active, aware, inventive – in short, he's freer – no, rid of all inhibitions – and his conversation is unpredictable and layered. Tell me: do you think an illiterate farmer in Lecco would really talk about civilising missions? Where? We are one step away from triumph – where all of Africa will be ours – or utter defeat – at which point we'll be denied even this patch of desert: we're hanging in the balance. This is the source of the unusual eloquence you've witnessed in the missionary colonists and in me, a captain in His Majesty's army. The colony is an artificial environment where *people do not gain any new and better faculties in this rarified, half-fantastic milieu. But the faculties they do have acquire much greater definition.*[xcvii]

'Is that a quote? I can see how artificial its diction is.'

'Of course… but don't ask me which book I got it from… I don't read all that much… a friend showed me the passage… and it is about a completely different place… – but a place, just like this colony, which is at an odd angle to everyday life. Perhaps our truly devilish dream was to try to convert such a fantastic place to a quiet normality. All of what the authorities have haughtily claimed – that this land used to be *Roman*, that it faces the *mare*

[xcvii] Author's Note: György Lukács, *Essays on Thomas Mann* (H. Fertig, 1965), p.36.

nostrum, etc. – are the same, mad aspirations shared by both the military and the colonists: we want to convert the authorities' speeches into a practical reality, into knowledge, into laws. Whereas Africa (and please forgive the humiliating banality here) is like a lover who one day loves you passionately, only to send you on your way tomorrow.'

'You're placing yourself on the same level as the illiterate colonist, given that you're both characters in a unique situation.' and the journalist illustrated his words with his fingers, 'but there comes a point where the differences between the two of you are *as deep as the abyss itself*: it is certainly true that we're treading a land that didn't belong to our ancestors, and it's equally true that Africa or the English might be waiting to play a nasty trick on us, the abyss – a lost war – but maybe… tomorrow everything will go the way it should. In the meanwhile, however, the colonist lives in horror of the abyss, you demonstrate an attraction to death, which is irresponsible. You seem to have given your blessing to our coming defeat, and I for one as a patriot hope that this attitude isn't shared by your fellow officers.'

The journalist's tone had grown stern and harsh.

The house where the bricklayer was repairing the roof had been rented by a single lady, who had just arrived in Africa. The Captain had candidly and obsequiously introduced himself to her as his neighbour, and that if he could ever be of any service to her, that he would not hesitate to do so.

They had lingered in conversation on the entrance steps, where there were vases of geraniums scatted around – reddish blots on a canvas where everything seemed bleached by the sun.

She hailed from the lands of lower Emilia, south of the Po River. She said she had sold everything she owned in order to relocate to the colony, where a friend of hers, who owned the Albergo Vienna, lived. She hoped to open a knitwear shop and had already spotted a few suitable locations in the city, but wanted one on the Corso – but there were no available spaces on that street, nothing except some ill-suited locales in various shady side-streets, which scared her a little.

It was the first time that she had taken up a profession.

She was in her forties, and still looked very attractive. Perhaps her voyage to Africa had brought out the ingénue in her, making her look like a debutante.

Even more pathetic was the unavoidable and predictable confession that followed: she had come there to *remake her life*.

'Yes, I was betrayed,' she added, with a touch of ironic sadness, 'by myself, naturally: because I'm still in love with him.'

'Do you think being in Africa will be of any help to you? Distance doesn't count for much in affairs of the heart.'

'Do you mean to say that I'll still love him from afar?' she replied, in the same questioning, melancholy tone as before. 'I've locked myself away in prison!'

'And who is that?' the journalist asked, his curiosity piqued, pointing out a woman who was leaning on her windowsill, right under the bricklayer's feet, and was looking down at the street.

'A woman willing to kill herself for love.' the officer said. 'She's here to bury the past.'

'What do you mean, 'bury the past'?'

'There's a haunting old belief that goes something like this: the souls of dead bodies that have been left unburied roam the earth looking for another body to inhabit, and this is why they're dangerous. Even passion is an unburied body. And that woman has fallen victim to passion.'

'This is all nonsense.'

'And yet it's also true.'

'Let's go back to the army's conduct, or rather its morale: is it riding high?'

'I'm not a spokesperson. Who gave you that idea?' the officer asked him, resentfully.

'I get it: you want to steer our conversation!' the wily journalist exclaimed, making a gesture with his hand, as though swatting away a fly or a bothersome shadow.

'Reflecting on our situation, which is certainly out of the ordinary – since *the fourth shore* is nothing but a metaphor – is what sets each and every one of us here in Africa apart from one another, and do please forgive me here for borrowing one of your earlier phrasings, creating a gulf *as deep as the abyss itself*: the ordinary erases all character from the archetype, while what is out of the ordinary redeems the archetype by turning him into a character, in other words a *unicum*.'

'Is this what the mal d'Afrique is?' the journalist asked, growing ever more curious, having finally found a *point de repère*.[xcviii]

'The expression can be more appropriately used to describe those who have returned to the motherland. But perhaps you're right: the *unreal* situation here in the colony brings characters to life, who can then no longer bear the constraints of the

[xcviii] French: 'point of reference'.

changeless *continuum* of life here. Everyone who lives here seems to be chased by a curse – as if those characters had suddenly swapped all their ancestors for different ones.'

'The colonists are here because of their ancestors' triumphs,' the journalist exclaimed, in a fit of passion. 'All the way back to our most distant ones: I haven't heard a single speech here in Africa that didn't reference the universal Empire of Rome in some manner or other.' his crossed leg slipped off and his foot hit the ground.

'All restorations are bound to end in failure, history teaches us that,' the officer observed, 'its an impervious impulse, that seeks to climb, whereas life loves the easy downward path – and yet the metamorphosis continues unabated – just as evidenced by nature, which is an inescapable example. The Romans, unearthed from their tombs where they slept silently and solemnly, are unpredictable ancestors – and having already been told of the future, they're probably laughing at us too along with the English and the rest of Africa.'

'You don't appear to have grasped that it is only through collective action that a man can both realise himself and cause his own destruction.'

'The situation for those who have ripped away from their homeland, their ancestors and their customs and are brought face to face with other ancestors and customs brings them to reflect on their own destiny, and it leads them to isolate themselves.'

'But answer me this: do you wish to escape that or do you instead yearn for it?'

'One oscillates between both answers. One performs one's duties because that is the easy oath to take, and so you eventually reach the end of that path, whichever end that may be, as is customary. A very learned friend of mine, who happens to be a businessman – whose quotes always have a veneer of irony to them whenever he cites them – once read out an essay that more or less said the following: *The new Faust is a Faust of the study. Nor does he seriously desire to leave it, that is, to translate his aims into deeds. Into this study crowds the whole complex of Faust problems, for the link that binds a quest for truth and life with social practice has been severed from the outset…*[xcix] It seems worthwhile to emphasise that the officer is a man ready for action, who safeguards society, stands for order, against the barbarians converging on his borders.'

From the little garden one could see the only palm tree in the street, which was an odd, alienating sight, given that North Africa was a land chock-full of palm trees, as the old adage went. It was as though that single tree had been stranded in that city of colonists, or perhaps, like the lone palm tree on the stage of Aida, it was making a courageous show of itself with its evocative power: it belonged to the realm of the significant but unreal, which of course differed from the obviously insignificant, if only because of its natural aspect. The journalist was observing the officer, who was nodding his head, as though answering someone's question. That *someone* was actually himself, given that for the necessity of sustaining that fictional dialogue, he was also playing the part of the other.

'Everything you've told me would be lost in translation in my newspaper column: meaning – and I don't need to excuse myself

[xcix] Author's Note: György Lukács, *Essays on Thomas Mann* (H. Fertig, 1965), p.61.

here since you are well aware of the situation – I am wasting my time talking to you.'

'And I am grateful to you for that. Not that I've wasted your time, but that you've understood that what I've told you won't be of any use to you at all.'

'Could you explain to me what attracted you to a life in the military, I still haven't quite understood whether you're proud of your service…' the journalist said, as though he were a judge trying to discern the facts in a roundabout manner.

'The authority decided it for me, and I swore an oath of allegiance: if the leader – the Duce, His Majesty… – makes a mistake, we follow them anyway: this is how we take measure of the hero in tragedies, where Fate is nothing but an authority. In other words, everything has already been predetermined. I can only express my own suffering: through harmonious verses, if they come to me. Being aware of the irrationality of everything and the need to do one's duty, has replaced the role of Fate in the old Greek plays, where destiny is no longer negotiable – a tragic situation which in some ways appeals to man in its own strange fashion…'

The bricklayer had stopped working and was now watching the two men, who sat in the garden scorched by the sun, talking around a cement table with a bottle on top of it. They looked like insects through a magnifying glass, intent on their mysterious rites. The bricklayer had a trowel in his hand. He looked as though he'd forgotten how to use it, perhaps even forgotten about himself. Only the occasional note still left his lips. To the journalist, who was looking at him from below, the bricklayer looked like one of the figures depicted in the pediments of the old Venetian villas. Yet the figure wasn't graceful, it was twisted in pain, like the images of saints in dark churches…

'You seem to nourish a cult of sterility within you.'

'Do you really think so? I hadn't thought about it. But woe onto anyone ready to take any way out of this: the dignity of a solitary man lies in his refusal to contemplate anything that might be deemed useful.'

In order to embarrass him, the journalist fell silent, depriving him of a pretext for further polemics. Nevertheless, the other carried on:

'We have spoken about a study, where Faust questions himself. Now the study could also be a living room. The stories I told you last night are derived from this very source: we don't want the artifice, it is actually an intrinsic part of colonial life, which is destined to disappear one day or the other: this is what history laughing guarantees us. Go visit the ruins of the Greek colonists on the highland plateaus: here are the *arches and the columns and the statues*[c] – and nothing else. At the date fate has fixed, we shall instead leave behind the interminable roads that lead to uninhabited places and the jetties of docks that shield from the tempests and currents ships that nevertheless never sail into the harbour anymore: but the progenies of the colonists will also die out one day. Just as with the ancient Greeks today, future peoples will discover tombs with white bones in them, where individual stories are no longer legible, and blood has been stolen away by the devil.'

'Captain!' the woman leaning on her windowsill on the first floor shouted, 'do come see me when your guest takes his leave, I have something to tell you.'

---

[c] Giacomo Leopardi, 'To Italy'. Tr. By Jonathan Galassi.

On the roof, the bricklayer tensed his arms, trying to suss out what she was saying. He looked as if he had just fallen out of the sky, an angel sent to that woman to help her *remake her life*; perhaps he'd even brought her a new life as a gift. He started singing again, in that enigmatic way of his, hinting at a tune, then falling silent, listening out, as if he'd just tossed a stone in a river and was waiting to hear its splash.

The woman was immobile, those notes had reached her and were working a spell on her.

Growing impatient, the journalist lit a cigarette. He felt as though he'd been dropped into a gigantic puppet theatre – like the Gerolamo theatre in Milan, a Sunday shrine for the city's children.

'The *theatrical* calculations of time here having nothing to do with subjective artifices,' the officer resumed, after a long pause, 'rather, they are an inescapable reality, because we don't have the patience to spell out everything that happened in history and thus stare nothingness in the face, just like we stare into the mirror. Everything is only appearance, at least for those who look on from the bleachers of history, which, I hope you'll allow the expression, I find a touch *mélo*[ci]. We soldiers don't do much at all: we're like animals in a zoo: we prepare for war, where death becomes part of our daily life. But the wait is long and thus we have more time on our hands than those devoted to industry, or teaching, or keeping the public order.'

'But what does any of this mean?'

The journalist was rapidly losing his patience.

[ci] French: 'melodramatic'.

'I meant to say that in Africa, which is the supreme *elsewhere*, reflections find fertile soil to prosper in: I don't mean that it's conducive to philosophical reflections given that most of us here are as ignorant as courtesans; I meant mundane reflections, exquisitely crafted outlooks on one's own life, like in the courts of old, yet another setting that was detached from the daily routines of others and whose life was unmistakably theatrical. We have more time on our hands and are a step away from the supreme apex of life, where everything ends. Isolation and artifices are a selection process. This is what frightens you – you're used to your newspaper, which instead endlessly multiplies reality every day.'

'You don't seem to think much of my profession.'

'What about you? What do you think of mine? Last night you said you were surprised that officers were capable of any depth or insights.'

The officer's thoughts had turned to what the woman in the house across the street had modestly told him earlier: that she'd been betrayed by a man, but that she had been equally betrayed by passion. The woman had explained that her lover wasn't free – meaning that he was married, since metaphors, like lies, are nothing but modesty and reserve used to distract one from one's suffering – and they hadn't managed to see one another except during brief, furtive meetings, with *agonizing* gaps in between each visit. Yet the figure of that man was present in her mind and the dialogues playing out in her mind were as long as time itself. 'What am I going to do now?' she had asked him with tears in her eyes, 'who am I going to talk to? With the African palm trees, which I'm seeing here for the first time? Who have I run away from? He was no longer there anyway…'

She had carried on in that manner for a while longer, in a kind of lullaby-esque way.

The man's wife had discovered the affair, and she had given him the age-old ultimatum: *either she goes or I will*. The man had told her that there was nothing to decide, that he was staying in their house. 'Only that there was a tiny *bureaucratic* detail to take care of,' the woman commented with teary irony: 'but out where?'

The man's most obvious promises – *I'll never see her again, I'll go tell her it's all over*, etc. – still didn't seem like enough, despite the fact he was shouting, to steel himself. Suddenly, Africa had appeared on the scene, to take her away from everything. '*Do you know what she told me*? he had told his wife, *that we could run away to the colony together*. He didn't need to finish his story. His wife gave him an express order: *then send her over there*. And that was the price she had exacted for their reconciliation. And I paid that price, because I was scared. Not for me, of course, after all, how would I matter? But what would have happened to him if I'd stayed? That man was dear to me, how could I let his reputation be soiled? You should have seen him, sir! – I mean, Captain! There he was, lying at my feet, in prey to his passions, for one last time, pleading with me to go: that only I could save him. Yes, he was a vile man, but he also nurtured a dream for a quiet normality within him, which isn't shameful at all. That is why he chose to stay with his wife and opted for the conjugal bond: he betrayed me, Captain, right during the final act, during the play's climax, but before all that he'd dreamed of running away with me to places even further than our colony, I'll tell you that!' – and as though overcome by emotion, she sighed.

'Please forgive me, but why did you accept to make such a sacrifice?'

'What would have happened otherwise? I knew Luigino well. It was the moment of truth and passion had given him wings. If instead I had refused to leave, he would have come back to his senses and would have only behaved in endlessly sordid ways. I simply had to take advantage of that magical moment, when the drama hadn't quite resolved itself yet, in order to run away. There was no alternative: on the other hand, Luigino appeared to be falling apart. In fact, he was *going up in smoke*. He wanted me to be a prisoner of misery, but I preferred… to die a heroic death: and here I am.'

'The solitude I bear – or rather carry within me, which this deserted Africa acts as a mirror for – is his legacy to me, do you understand? To love someone makes our souls noble, my friend, it restores that soul to movement and shelters it from all calculations. It's… a flight. Then we eventually plunge into the deep well of solitude and crash.'

The Captain shook all over. *Yes*, he thought, *she's performing a funerary rite: inside the tomb isn't the man she loved, but the demon of their love.*

'Didn't you notice that this woman talked only in clichés?' the journalist asked in an annoyed tone.

'That's what I told her too: we must shy away from clichés. 'Why?' she asked me in a fit of pride. 'They are lifeboats in the great night of life: woe onto anyone who dares open his eyes!' Once upon a time, people who fled their homes used to take cult objects with them that embodied the spirit of their dead ancestors who watched over their house. This woman keeps a photograph of Luigino in her sitting room, not to remind her of the vile man he was, but of the passion of which she'd been capable of. Even cults, like language, trade in what you so cheerfully called clichés.'

'Why don't you tell me your own story now? I mean the story of your life.' the journalist said, as though ordering the officer, astonished by the fact that it had taken him this long to ask a question that might force the officer out into the open.

The woman leaning on her windowsill was making strange gestures with her hands now, as though she was trying to send signals overseas, to her distant lover.

'My story is the summation (or an itinerary, or a landscape, whatever you like) of all the events that happened in other people's lives, many of which I have just told you about. My confession ended a long time ago, Mr Gigli.'